Bridle Path
Press

THE GOLDEN HOUR

A Nora Tierney English Mystery

M. K. Graff

Bridle Path Press, LLC
8419 Stevenson Road
Baltimore, MD 21208

www.bridlepathpress.com

Direct orders to the above address.

Printed in the United States of America.
First edition.
ISBN 978-0-9908287-8-5

Library of Congress Control Number: 2017944026

Illustrations and design by Giordana Segneri.

Cover photographs © Besjunior/istockphoto.com,
© mashabuba/istockphoto.com and
© Never_Odd_Or_Even/istockphoto.com.

Back cover photograph © Max2611/istockphoto.com and
"The Open Air Breakfast" by William Merritt Chase.

Bridle Path
Press

FOR BARBARA KATHRYN BOHNER JANCOVIC

Constant use had not worn ragged the fabric of their friendship.
Dorothy Parker

Great Britain

Bowness-on-
Windermere

Chipping
Norton

Castle
Combe

Oxford

Bath

Heathrow

Brighton

Cornwall

Cast of Characters

in order of appearance

"TOM BARNABY" — Nora's stalker

NORA TIERNEY — American writer living in England

SEAN TIERNEY — her young son

KATE TRAVERS — co-owner, Ramsey Lodge, where Nora lives

SIMON RAMSEY — Kate's brother; illustrator of Nora's children's books

DAISY — barmaid and owner, The Scarlet Wench Pub in Bowness

DECLAN BARNES — Detective Inspector, Thames Valley Criminal Investigation Department, St. Aldate's Station, Oxford; Nora's partner

EMMA JEVONS — painting conservator, Ashmolean Museum, Oxford

ELLY GRIFFITHS — award-winning mystery author; Nora's friend

VIKTOR GARANIN — wealthy Russian megalomaniac

VAL ROGAN — textile artist; Nora's best friend

DETECTIVE SERGEANT WATKINS — Declan's right-hand man

DR. IVOR CONLON — head of Infectious Diseases, Churchill Hospital, Oxford

NORMAN MARKS — head of Conservation, Ashmolean Museum, Oxford

NEIL WELCH — writer living next door to Haven Cottage

LUCY — Oxford estate agent; Val's friend

ED HARKER — paper conservator, Ashmolean Museum, Oxford

JANET WALLACE — friend and neighbor of Stanley Jevons

STANLEY JEVONS — Emma's father

DETECTIVE SUPERINTENDENT MORRIS — Declan's superior,
St. Aldate's Station

TAMSIN CHEN — MI-5 special agent

HARVEY PEMBROKE — Sean's paternal grandfather

MURIEL PEMBROKE — Harvey's wife; Sean's paternal
grandmother

NIGEL — Port Enys butler

HELEN SACKVILLE — Nora's friend from Oxford days

BETTY KAPLAN — retired pediatric nurse practitioner

JAMES FISHER — Director, Office of Special Exhibits,
Holburne Museum

CHARLES WRIGHT — Bath art gallery owner

ALEX THALMANN — Detective Sergeant, Avon and Somerset
Constabulary, Bath Station

NIC BOTTOMLEY — Owner, Mr. B's Emporium of Reading
Delights, Bath

PHILIPPA SACKVILLE — Helen's youngest daughter

CHRIS BURKE — MI-5 special agent

KIM — Emergency Services Dispatcher, Bath

CONSTABLE JANE MORROW — Avon and Somerset
Constabulary, Bath Station

PAUL PEMBROKE — scientist; Nora's former fiancé; Sean's father

MATTHEW SACKVILLE — Helen's husband

AMELIA TIERNEY SCOTT — Nora's mother

THE GOLDEN HOUR

"If from infancy you treat children as gods,
they are liable in adulthood to act as devils."
— P. D. James

"The life of every man is a diary in which he means
to write one story, and writes another."
— James M. Barry

Chapter One

The man watched Nora Tierney maneuver her son's buggy through the crowds milling along Bowness Bay quay, skillfully achieving headway past the tiny white and emerald green peaked huts near the ferry dock. The height of the tourist season meant the wooden quay stayed clotted with international visitors from sunrise until late evening. Cumbria's purple fells and glistening tarns drew hikers and backpackers with miles and miles of well-maintained walking routes crossing steep farms. Water enthusiasts reveled in England's largest lake, Windermere, in boats, on jet skis, or paddling kayaks. This was a nature and literary-filled haven, and he could see why Wordsworth, Beatrix Potter, Ruskin, Coleridge, and many others had been attracted to it. Few who'd been to the Lake District could forget the true blue skies and fleecy white clouds reflected in the lake's glossy surface. The area reminded him of Lake Geneva painted with a brighter brush, and he felt pleased for the moment to be surrounded by nature on such a glorious day. In his job, he didn't often get the chance to enjoy the countryside.

He knew the child Nora pushed was 10 months old. He paused in his forward progress as the mother stopped to re-do her ponytail. She was dressed comfortably for the warm weather in thin grey yoga pants and a green "Life is Good" tee shirt. After following her for weeks, he thought of her as Nora, someone he might like to know, even if she would never know him.

He knew more about her and her child than Nora Tierney could ever imagine.

Following someone was a learned practice. He'd grown used to quickly stepping into doorways or simply turning his back to avoid detection. There was an art to it, and he liked to think he'd mastered it, letting himself get lost in the crowds, blending in with small changes in his appearance, but always with one eye on Nora. Her auburn hair made her easy to spot, although her petite frame could be a hindrance.

Thankfully, his height allowed him to see over clumps of crowds to track her movements, and by now he had her schedule down: most days in Bowness she took walks in the afternoon with the child. Many mornings he'd see Nora work on her laptop in the garden of Ramsey Lodge, the brown stone and timbered inn where she'd lived since leaving Oxford. She wrote a series of children's books and worked on those and other freelance writing projects.

He'd noticed her first book for sale in the local bookshop, Corgi Books. Simon Ramsey, owner of the lodge with his sister, Kate Travers, was her illustrator. The landscape and portrait painter's cheery watercolours brought the Lake District to life with adventures of the band of fairies Tierney created. The child would play on a blanket at her feet, never far from Nora's watchful eye as she worked. On a few occasions near lunchtime, a young woman came out and scooped him up so Nora could keep working, but she was definitely a hands-on mum.

Her schedule left him with plenty of time on his hands, especially in the evenings. After exhausting all that Bowness and neighboring Windermere had to offer, he was working himself through a series of spy novels by Margaret Duffy about a husband and wife team, and thought the author had a good handle on the specifics. They helped him pass the lonely times.

Every other weekend, Nora loaded up her late-model Volvo for a Friday ride to Oxford, where she stayed with her boyfriend in his modern flat, saw friends, and looked at houses for sale in the town and surrounding area. She drove back to Bowness Monday morning. Checks on the boyfriend, Declan Barnes, revealed he was a detective inspector at St. Aldates with a reputation for closing tough cases. On alternate weekends, the boyfriend would drive to Ramsey Lodge in his classic MGB. Barnes had missed a few of those, down to a case most likely.

Nora's routine—and therefore, his—was becoming dreary in its predictability, but he didn't question his assignment. What he did long for was a good meal out, or a day at a museum of his choosing, instead of always following what Nora Tierney had on her agenda.

Nora stopped to let her child watch the swans. One of his chubby arms reached toward them, as if trying to grab one from the lake. His little fist opened and closed, while he kept the other arm wrapped protectively around a stuffed bunny. She sat on what the man knew by now to be her favorite bench, and pulled the buggy closer. She left a protective hand on what she, as an American, probably called a stroller, as she checked her mobile.

Two giggling boys walked past her bench, each holding a balloon. The shorter lad lost hold of his string, and the balloon floated away in the light breeze along the lakefront. The boy scowled, but Nora's son laughed, and leaned out of the buggy toward the brilliant red orb.

From where he stood, hidden by a rack of postcards at the kiosk nearest her bench, the man could hear the lad's expletive at his lost balloon. His friend chuckled.

He'd never gotten this close to Nora before, and fancied he could pick up her lemony perfume on the fresh breeze.

When he'd cloned her phone, Nora had been eating in The Scarlet Wench pub with Simon Ramsey. She'd left the large flowered bag she carried around on the bench when she went to the loo. A brush against their table upset Ramsey's pint, and his own stammered apologies and mopping up with a wad of paper napkins provided the needed distraction to drop a speaker bug into the bag. This allowed him to be privy to her conversations and plans. He drew the line at listening in when she had sex with her Oxford detective, finding it distasteful to hear their sighs and moans. Now once their lights were out in whatever town they were in, he headed to his own bed, moving amongst guest houses and inns each week under different names so he wouldn't be recognized.

He watched as she pointed out the rising balloon to her son, and while the older boys moved on, he, Nora and her son watched the red sphere ascend in the impossibly blue sky over Windermere, higher and higher toward the stark white clouds. The little boy whooped with glee and clapped his hands. Nora bent toward him and kissed his forehead, then smoothed his silky copper hair, shades lighter than her own.

He mused that life was quite like that red balloon. One minute you were sailing along, tethered to the earth, head down and buried in computers and paperwork in another country. The next you could be floating aimlessly without seeming to have much purpose, following the whims of someone else's schedule, trying to fill the hours while she was safely occupied. It was tough to explain to others what he did for a living. But it was what he'd signed on for, and what a lot of others he knew would gladly trade places to do, to be out and about in the glories of Cumbria and Oxford.

In the 10 weeks he'd been following her, it became obvious that Nora Tierney was a competent mother who loved and cared for her child. It seemed they had a fairy-tale life, bouncing back and forth between the storied city and the nature-filled village. From the overheard talks with Barnes, her friends, and phone conversations, plus the house viewings, he learned she planned

THE GOLDEN HOUR

to move back to Oxford. When would that happen? How long would she stay in Bowness this time?

How long could he keep following her?

As long as it took.

Wednesday, 21st September

7:10 PM

Nora Tierney sat across the table from Kate Travers in The Scarlet Wench pub. She sipped her shandy with a contented sigh, the combination of tart lemonade and beer quenching her thirst after a long afternoon: walking Sean on the quay to see his swans; proofing her new children's book, which would be debuting in two weeks; bathing Sean and getting him settled for the night.

"Tired, Nora?" Kate ruffled her curly hair, and took a hearty swallow from her half. "How did work go today?"

"Simon and I approved the proof, and it's off to the printers in plenty of time for the book signing in Bath next month." Nora moved her chair as Simon returned with a tray holding their meals. She didn't mention the leaf she'd found inside her bedroom by her locked French doors. That could easily be explained if she'd worked outside and tracked it in herself, only today she and Simon had worked around his large table in his rooms. She told herself it had been there from the day before and she'd missed it. Only part of her was convinced this was true.

"Three fish and chips specials all round." He deposited their plates and returned the tray to the bar.

Nora inhaled the scent of the crispy beer batter and fried potatoes. She automatically handed over the vinegar to the brother and sister she lived with for the moment. While she rarely went out in the evenings, this monthly date with the siblings had become a habit she liked. Nora left her son in the capable hands of her mother's helper, Callie, after she checked that those French doors of her room that opened onto the garden were firmly locked. "I still don't get the idea of vinegar on these."

"That's because you're a bloody Yank," Simon proclaimed good-naturedly.

"All I want is salt so I can taste the fish and potatoes." Nora made her point with the shaker. She grinned and the three tucked in to their food.

"What time is your book club meeting?" Simon sprinkled the vinegar liberally over his meal and handed the bottle to Kate.

"Not till 8 at the bookstore," Kate answered as she ate. "I brought the sketch I've made of how we could renovate the family quarters." She put her sketchpad in the middle of the table and flipped to a page, then laid the spiral book on the table for them to consult. "If we take out this one non-load-bearing wall, we get rid of that hall and add that space to what would be our main room and kitchen."

Nora perused the sketch with a jolt of mixed emotions. She was the one moving back to Oxford. Leaving the suite she'd been occupying would allow Kate and Ian, her detective husband, to swap sides of the family quarters of the lodge with Simon. It was time for them all to move on, and she felt like she was on the brink of a new chapter. They all were. It was as exhilarating as it was scary.

"What does Ian think of it?" Nora bit into a piece of flaky fish, enjoying the crunch of the batter as she looked at the sketch. "With you moving into my bedroom suite, you gain Sean's alcove as a nursery."

Simon looked up sharply. "Is there news you're holding back, Kate?"

Kate blushed and swatted him on the arm. "Don't be daft. You'll be among the first to know when it happens. We're enjoying our time together."

"Makes sense to me." Nora knew from firsthand experience with Declan Barnes the toll the uneven hours a homicide detective kept could take on a spouse or partner, especially when they were on a case, something Kate had quickly found out.

"I think it looks great." Simon polished off a handful of chips and pointed to the sketch.

Kate bit her lip. "You're certain Maeve won't object? You don't mind swapping studios?" She ate her meal with gusto.

"Maeve doesn't care a hoot, and I'll let you in on a secret: the light is better in your barn than in my current studio." Maeve Addams was the lodge's manager and Simon's girlfriend.

"Where is Maeve tonight?" Nora wiped her greasy fingers on a napkin. Her father used to tell her that the passage of time changed everything. As she matured, Nora grew to see how prophetic his words had been as her relationship with Simon had matured into a loving friendship.

"At her French course. Soon her accent will be better than mine." Simon drained his glass and pointed to hers. "Another shandy?"

"Nope, one's enough for me. I have to stay awake at Corgi Books or Dottie Halmstad will hasten to point out to everyone that I've fallen asleep," Nora said. She crumpled her paper napkin and threw it on her plate. Out of the corner of her eye, she saw the publican's wife, Daisy, wiping down the bar in a momentary lull.

"Nor for me," Kate said. "I'm done." She pushed her plate away.

"My shout this week." Nora jumped up and gathered their

plates before Simon could object. She hurried to the bar with their stacked plates and caught Daisy's attention. "I'll settle up, Daisy."

"Three specials, and three pints." The cheerful woman licked her pencil and tallied the check.

Nora put several notes on the bar. "This should cover it. Keep the change."

Daisy smiled at the generous tip. "Ta, Nora."

"How's the bed and breakfast business, Daisy? Rooms full?" Nora hoped she exuded the height of nonchalance. She needed information on a man she kept seeing in different places over the past weeks. The other day she'd pinpointed him from a distance and observed him entering The Scarlet Wench.

"Bursting at the seams. I could fill more rooms if I had them, but then Himself couldn't have me cooking in the kitchen."

"Glad you're busy." Nora kept her face straight as she asked her question. "Say, I've seen a tall chap going in and out I think I know from Oxford—wears a different baseball cap every day?"

Daisy concentrated, then her face cleared. "You must mean Grant Alan. He had a hat collection all right, but he checked out this morning. I asked him about them and he said he liked to keep his bald spot from getting sunburned when he was out walking. Funny, that."

Nora didn't know whether to feel relieved or deflated. "Oh. That wasn't whom I was thinking of. But what's so funny about wearing hats?"

Daisy leaned over the bar. "He took that cap off one evening in here and he had a nice full head of hair. No bald spot at all. Why lie about something like that?"

Why indeed?

CHAPTER TWO

She'd changed her scent.

The citrus perfume Nora Tierney always wore had been replaced in the two weeks since he'd seen her by something far more complex, and to his nose, intoxicating. Detective Inspector Declan Barnes liked it.

He noticed it immediately when Nora picked him up at his flat after a night with her best friend, Val Rogan. With Sean strapped securely in his car seat for the more than two-hour trip south to Brighton today, their hello kiss brought him the new aroma with its crisp scent of juniper, a reminder of cool gin and tonics.

"Have a good evening at Val's?" He buckled in and they set off, Nora navigating the traffic snarl that was Oxford on almost any morning. She'd spent Thursday night at Val's with a group of old friends, rehashing memories of when she'd lived in the town of golden stone spires, a place filled with centuries of history revolving around the many colleges that made up the university. He knew she loved Oxford, as did he, and now she was on the cusp of moving back. While they hadn't worked out all the particulars, he felt certain they had a future together. It was just a matter of deciding on the details.

"Great fun, even if Val's not used to all the gear a baby needs. Sean was the center of attention with her mates from Val's art world, but he's dribbling and I think he's cutting more teeth. She's found a great house she's taking me to see tomorrow."

"Poor lad." He took this news with a cheery grin, knowing that by Monday either the problem teeth would have come through, and the boy's sunny nature would return, or Nora would leave for Bowness, and he would have his peace and quiet restored for another week. The thought niggled at the back of his mind that if they lived together he wouldn't have that safety valve, or his own time alone. Since they'd been together, Declan had become more knowledgeable on baby habits and milestones than he'd thought possible. He still hadn't mastered dirty nappies, but wet ones were a breeze.

He glanced into the back seat and chucked the baby on his leg. Sean held out his stuffed bunny for inspection. The brown rabbit's ears and blue jacket looked shabby after close to a year of sticky hugs and drools. Sean gave Declan a wide smile of recognition and a shout of "Deca!"

"Hullo, Sean. You have Peter Rabbit in hand, I see." He turned back to Nora as they left Oxford's crowded streets behind. "Still talking in loud bursts."

Nora nodded. "And babbling at others. Auntie Val has now become Teeva with an emphasis on TEE-va." She checked her mirror and changed lanes. "Elly will be so surprised to see how he's grown. He was only a few months old when I saw her last, and now he'll be a year old in a few weeks. I can't believe it."

They were driving south to Brighton toward the beach for lunch with Nora's writer friend, Elly Griffiths. "I can see Val liking 'Teeva.' She'll embroider it on one of her tapestries soon, you watch." He leaned toward Nora, drew in a deep breath, and could swear he recognized the cardamom spice his mum used to put in coffee cakes.

"Why are you sniffing me?" Nora's throaty laugh was a balm to him after a long busy period at work.

Following months of investigative work, he and his team had

managed to arrest and charge the head of a cocaine ring who'd murdered an underling. It was a satisfying end to the case, but it wouldn't bring back the young man who lay dead in the mortuary at the John Radcliffe Hospital. Still, it was a good result for his CID squad and at least now the man's family could bury him.

"It's your new perfume. I quite like it." Declan squeezed her jeans-clad thigh and left his hand there. "It reminds me of a G&T, but richer."

"Good, because I like it, too. It's called 'Juniper Sling.'" She caught his eye. "Still off tomorrow?"

"You bet. We have today and all tomorrow to be together, until you leave for Cornwall Sunday." The driving they'd each been doing for months between Oxford and Nora's temporary home in Cumbria had become draining.

"And tonight. Heavenly." She ran her fingers lightly over his hand and put hers back on the steering wheel. "I fully intend to show you how much I've missed you." She slid him a wry glance. "Now behave yourself and put some music on. Sean falls asleep quicker if there's music."

"As long as it's not the Beatles." Sean had developed a decided fondness for the group after Nora played *Yellow Submarine* for him. Declan thought he'd go spare if he had to listen to *Eleanor Rigby* one more time. He reluctantly removed his hand and reached for a stack of CDs in the console, hovered over his own classic rock album, and chose instead one of Nora's favorites, Chet Baker. He settled back for the ride and watched the rolling hills fly past as Baker's version of *My Funny Valentine* with the Gerry Mulligan quartet filled the car, the trumpet mellow, Baker's high-pitched voice filled with angst. He'd never been much for music that wasn't rock, but Nora had educated him about jazz, the Great American Songbook, Ella Fitzgerald and more.

Nora hummed along with the song, and a sense of peace

stole over Declan. These were halcyon days and he soaked up the melody, her perfume, and his growing sense of rightness in their relationship as they skirted London on the M25 and headed south on the M23 that would take them to Brighton. Soon he would broach the subject of their long-term relationship, when the moment seemed right.

Declan rubbed his nose and the bump acquired playing rugby many years ago, and thought back to a time when he'd taken this same route with his team to play in Brighton. After the rough game, which his team lost, there had been the usual pub evening with the local team hosting, rounds of loud bawdy songs, and he and his friends had stayed over at different players' homes rather than risk driving back. Would that young man of his youth recognize the divorced copper he was now, solving serious crimes, partnered with an American woman, and helping her raise her child part time—soon to be full time? At least it seemed they were going that way.

Living together would certainly provide stability for Sean, but Americans did seem to still want that legal family unit. Did he really want to marry again? He watched Nora navigate the motorway with competence. It has taken her a while to become used to driving on the wrong side of the road in the wrong side of the car, but he sensed her new security behind the wheel. They'd spent their days this summer with her commuting from Bowness to Oxford to look at housing. So far nothing they'd viewed seemed right to Nora, who was buying the property. She always included him in these ventures, and he felt she valued his opinion, but they hadn't talked about the future of their relationship other than that she wanted to move back to Oxford with Sean, would buy her own house, and they would continue to see each other. The idea of them living together was one they both tiptoed around. It would soon have to be sorted out.

He thought they should be practical. He could sublet his modern one-bedroom flat while they tried living together and sharing expenses. That would be sensible.

But was he trying to hedge his bets in case it didn't work out? Women liked romance and commitment, didn't they? Wasn't that why he'd called Elly Griffiths and enlisted her aid for this afternoon?

The track changed to *Autumn in New York*. Declan remembered he had news for Nora. "My holiday at the end of the month's been approved."

Nora's face lit up. "Wonderful. My mom's so excited. She's been making plans for Sean's first birthday in Connecticut. I suspect there will be a Halloween costume for him somewhere, and trick-or-treating to visit every neighbor she knows so she can show him off. I can't wait for you to see where I grew up."

"I'm looking forward to it. First visit to the States." He glanced into the back seat and saw Sean had nodded off.

"Mom said she and Roger would keep Sean overnight when we're there. We can take the ferry across Long Island Sound and spend a night at Montauk Point. There are lovely vineyards out east, and we can eat lobster."

"On the beach, under a blanket?" He pumped his eyebrows in his best Groucho Marx imitation and waited for her reaction to his lewd expression.

She caught the look and laughed good-naturedly. "Maybe not at the same time."

As they discussed the trip, Nora kept her eyes on the road, and Declan remembered their first meeting in Oxford. She'd thrown herself into the middle of his murder investigation, trying to clear her friend Val of suspicion. There had been strong chemistry between them even then, despite her stubborn streak.

Then right after Sean was born, he'd visited her in Cumbria where she lived with Simon Ramsey and his sister, Kate. The spark between them flamed, and when he returned a few months later they became an official couple—enough for Nora to change her Facebook status, he'd noted.

He looked out as the rolling hills slid past, and thought that with the passage of time, Nora had also grown less sensitive about her unexpected inheritance last spring, as evidenced by the more expensive perfume, and buying her own house. A solicitor had brought her the news that her dead fiancé had provided for her in his will. As if she were reading his mind, Nora broke into his thoughts.

"I wanted to talk to you again about the money Paul left me, Declan."

"And I've told you each time you bring it up, I don't need the gritty details. That money's for you and Sean."

"Yes, but surely you must have questions, and with this house hunting—"

"You've said it's adequate to take the burden off you, and to buy a house alone." Was this her way of asking if he wanted to live with her? "That's all I need to know. It's tough to be jealous of a dead man, Nora." His thoughts tumbled over each other.

Did he really mean that? Was Nora really over Paul Pembroke? She'd told him it would never have worked with Paul, yet she'd recently developed a relationship with his parents. But then, they were her baby's family, too. "I'm just glad it's relieved your financial pressure," he ended. At least that was a true statement.

"True British reticence," she muttered, shaking her head.

He hoped he hadn't spoiled the day. They were still exploring their way around their cultural differences. American Nora would discuss everything in great detail and want his input when he felt it wasn't necessary. Declan functioned more on a "need to know" basis, heightened by his detective status. He tended to keep information to himself until it was necessary to share. An awkward silence fell over the car for a few miles until Nora broke it.

"Is Sean still asleep?"

He looked over his shoulder and nodded. The toddler dozed with his bunny clamped tightly under one arm.

"I need to talk to you about something." Nora took a deep breath. The sun came in the window and highlighted the freckles across her nose.

"What is it?" Was this it? Was she finally going to ask him to move in with her? This was one conversation he knew they needed to have. They would be in Brighton soon.

She kept her eyes on the road in front of her as she rooted around inside a pocket of the large bag she carried, and handed him what looked like a silver button. "Can you tell me what this is? Because I think I'm being followed."

CHAPTER THREE

Oxford

Emma Jevons sat back with a contented sigh. She stretched her sore back, taking a well-deserved break. She had arrived at work early this morning, signing in at the Ashmolean Museum's conservation room with only the security guard as company, after leaving early yesterday afternoon with a terrible headache and fever. She'd spent the rest of the day and evening in bed, swallowing paracetamol and drinking tea. Today she'd thrown on washed-out jeans with a soft shirt, then tied her brunette hair off her shoulders, ready to plunge back into work.

The cleaning of the painting was going faster than she'd dared hope. The colors her careful work revealed were vibrant, especially the Prussian blue that was the hallmark of most of Picasso's work from 1901-04 during his "Blue Period." This one, *Le Bock*, depicted a male figure nursing a glass of beer, and was on loan from the Pushkin Museum in Moscow in an exclusive transaction that allowed her to work on it. It would hang in a special exhibit as a companion piece to Picasso's *Blue Roof, Paris*, which the Ashmolean owned.

Emma stripped off her gloves, and rubbed eyes that itched with fatigue. The attention to detail blurred her vision today. The raised red patch she'd found this morning on her left hand seemed worse, and now she saw there were several similar areas, a few with angry pustules, on her right hand, too. They all itched. Must be a contact dermatitis from the paints she was unearthing, despite her gloves. Who knew what was in Picasso's version of Prussian blue? She'd run out on her lunch hour to Boots and buy some cortisone cream.

She took a sip from her Yeti cup, the water still icy cold. She'd pick up more paracetamol, too. She was practically eating them like sweets, to deal with the symptoms of this virus she'd picked up. It annoyed her to feel ill after just getting over flu. Her immune system must be down, so she added probiotics to her mental list.

Emma took another sip of water, and felt the crack at the side of her mouth with her tongue. She'd need to add to her list a second cream for this fever blister. Bloody pharmacy; she should own shares in the place. This wasn't like her at all. Her dad told her she was healthy as a horse, and he meant it in a kind way.

Usually she threw off any illness in a few days, but this was the fourth day she'd endured the annoying aches and raised temperature, just as her work was making real progress. She scratched an itch on her stomach, and stood up to do 10 toe touches to lengthen her spine. All her joints ached. She wondered if you could get the flu a second time, maybe on rebound like a bad romance?

Her frustration level rose. She wasn't one to give into poor health, and didn't have time to make an appointment with her doctor right now. Emma worked hard to have this position at the museum, first with dual undergraduate degrees in Fine Arts, and Conservation and Restoration. She shuddered when she thought of the student loans she still owed.

Then came the three-year MA program at the Courtauld Institute of Art. As one of only eight students chosen every three years, Emma had competed rigorously to get onto the course, and its reputation and her international experience led to this fantastic position. She liked living in Oxford, not too far from her father, and had a good relationship with her colleagues and friends in town. Even if there wasn't a special man in her life at this moment, she felt there was something momentous just waiting to happen to her.

Here she was, living in her favorite town, working at a job she adored. At lunch she'd purchase more effective medicines, maybe ask the chemist for something stronger, and continue her effort. It was exciting to see the vivid paint colors emerge from a century of accumulated dirt and grime. As she cleaned her brush, she imagined her name in headlines in the art journals, and her father's pride in her success.

Brighton, East Sussex

11:25 AM

Nora listened as Declan finished his call to Simon Ramsey, while she followed her GPS to the parking lot in The Lanes in Brighton.

He pocketed his mobile. "Simon said he'd ask the staff and get back to me. He hasn't noticed anyone hanging around, but then he's working in the lodge or in his studio much of the time. He did say the emergency exit alarm went off the other day when you were out walking Sean on the quay."

Nora's face fell. That door ended the hallway right behind her suite. Could someone have been in her room? Was it, too, bugged? She shuddered at the thought of someone listening into her conversations with her mother in Connecticut about their upcoming trip; with Val and her house-hunting assistance; with Declan, trying to be sexy. While the first two were decidedly banal, the last certainly wasn't. Declan sensed her discomfort and squeezed her hand.

"One more," he said, and called his sergeant, Watkins.

While Nora parked, Declan asked Watkins to research what

he termed a listening device. He read off the numbers and described the silver button and its markings. Nora winced at the thought of the huge invasion of her privacy if someone had been listening to her wherever she went. "They"—whoever they were—would have heard her singing lullabies to Sean. And when Declan visited and they made love? It was too awful to consider.

Declan unfolded Sean's buggy from the boot and put the nappy bag in the bottom, then quizzed her as they walked toward the seafront, asking questions while she described the sensation of seeing someone on the corner of her vision at times.

He tried to pin Nora down on details, but she didn't have any.

"I don't know what he looks like, because he doesn't show himself," she explained. "Maybe I'm imagining it."

"But you just said 'he,' so you feel your stalker is male," Declan pointed out. "If you really thought you were imagining it, you'd never have mentioned him to me, and tossed that button away as something that fell out of a toy you stuffed in there for Sean."

"You think you know me so well?"

"I'm learning. Tell me what made you notice him."

"For the past weeks I have a sense of being watched that makes the hair rise on the back of my neck—like there are eyes on me. Several times when I look back, I've seen someone tall in a baseball cap in the distance suddenly turn into a doorway. One time, I thought that person went into The Scarlet Wench, and Daisy said they'd had a boarder who wore baseball caps." She shrugged. "It's all speculation and guesswork."

"And this happens when you're out walking with Sean along the quay? Nothing at the lodge?"

She nodded. "I wanted you to know, but I don't see what you can do about it. Please don't mention it to Elly." They waited for the light to cross Marine Parade toward the waterside. Nora clasped Declan's hand as they pushed Sean's buggy over the uneven wooden boards of Brighton Pier that led toward its huge white Pavilion by the sea. Once a theatre, it now housed garish amusement games and videos.

"Fine, we'll keep this to ourselves, but you were right to tell me. Let's agree we won't have too many secrets from each other, all right?"

"But a few are fine?" she teased.

"Everyone is entitled to a few secrets."

"Thank you for taking me seriously." She glanced up into grey eyes that glinted aqua in the bright sunlight. "Does this mean someone's been listening to my conversations since it's been there—for who knows how long?"

He dropped her hand and pulled her to his side, wrapping one arm around her waist to pull her closer. "We'll figure it out, I promise. These devices have a finite amount of battery time. Best case scenario: It could have been dropped in as an accident, may already be dead, and you are only imagining being followed."

"And worst case?"

He shrugged, and Nora knew he was trying to keep her calm. "Someone wanted information about you and is following you. But until we have that confirmed, let's not jump the gun. There's no good reason I can think of why you need to be followed, or for someone to listen in to your conversations."

Nora arched an eyebrow. "You mean it's been a while since I've been involved in a murder case."

"Those that you were involved in are all solved, neatly tied with a bow, so until we know more, let's operate on the basis that there's nothing to worry about—"

"Until there is." Nora finished. She breathed in the sea air, watched the waves lap on the shingle below the pier and took a deep breath. "Agreed. Let's not let it spoil our day since we don't know anything concrete."

"A wise decision." He kissed the top of her head and she wrapped her arm around him for a quick hug.

"Mum!" Sean shrieked and pointed to the colorful carousel outside the Pavilion. Its horses and animals were painted in bright pastels accented with gold leaf, all festooned with flowered garlands.

"Right where we're headed, lovey." With schools in session, the number of people around in town surprised Nora. A few sat on blankets on the beach, faces turned to catch the autumn sun. Tourists mostly, she supposed, there to see the famous Royal Pavilion that King George IV had built for his seaside playground. The exotic palace, with its mix of Indian, Chinese and Regency design, was a huge draw for the area. Sean was too young to manage a tour, but perhaps when he was older she and Elly would take him through it. The kitchen with its fake palm trees and rows of shining copper pots would surely delight him.

She looked around while Declan bought a ticket. Many nationalities were represented, along with the ubiquitous college students. Yet there was one person who wasn't there: her follower. She could sense an absence, like a shadow that hadn't shown itself. Maybe it was Declan's presence, but she felt as if her stalker had disappeared. For despite her lover's attempt to reassure her, Nora was convinced the silver button would prove to be functional, and that someone *had* been following her.

They reached the carousel, and Nora took Sean out of his buggy. "You ride with him, Declan. I'll take photos." She passed the squirming toddler over and Declan scooped him up. "Wait, first one of the two of you in front of the carousel." She adjusted her iPhone.

The flamboyant merry-go-round with its blaring music captivated Sean's attention. She couldn't get him to smile for the camera; he kept turning his head to watch it whirl just as she touched her shutter. Both adults laughed, and Nora felt lighter than she had since finding the button. She would leave it for today in Declan's capable hands.

She took a few photos in succession as Declan settled Sean in front of him on a pink and aqua horse named "Victoria." The boy squealed when the music started and the roundabout jerked to life, spinning around slowly, gaining momentum. Nora prepared for Sean to be scared, even burst into tears, but he looked delighted, grabbing the horse's golden mane, babbling baby talk as they turned out of sight.

Nora glanced at the parents waiting for older children on the ride, but everyone's attention was focused on their own progeny; cameras and phones clicked away. Despite her best intentions, her thoughts lit on her nameless stalker. Maybe he lived in Bowness and would stay there when she moved. She could only hope so. Living in Oxford would change her relationship with Declan. She thought moving in together was what they should do. They needed to sort the living arrangements out, but she knew they would have time to talk tonight after Sean slept, and they could map out what each saw as their future.

"MUM!" got her attention and that of many others, who all laughed as Declan and the little boy whizzed past. Declan's smile was huge, hugging Sean to him, while the child crowed with delight. It melted her heart to see them together. She felt so fortunate that Declan accepted her as a package deal. He hadn't had children with his first wife, and she supposed Sean filled that void. She liked to think he saw Sean as an extension of her. She snapped more photos as they appeared again, firmly shutting her stalker away into another compartment of her mind for the day.

Oxford

11:48 AM

Emma couldn't wait for noon to get her medicines. Her fever seemed higher; her body aches intensified. Her eyes felt teary and heavy-lidded, like they wanted to close.

She hung up her smock, shoved her credit card in her jeans pocket, and threw on her denim jacket. She had worn a scarf over her shirt that morning, and pulled it up to cover her mouth as she walked past her colleagues, waving and averting her head, not in the mood for small talk. "Still germy," she said to a few in the staff room as she strode outside.

She hurried past The Randolph Hotel, her destination the Boots Chemist on Cornmarket Street outside the Covered Market. Students and dons, some in *sub fusc*, clusters of tourists, and local office workers on their lunch break all crowded the busy streets at this time of day. By the Martyr's Memorial, a wave of claustrophobia hit her when she inadvertently became swept up in a tour of chattering Germans. She had to cross the road to Balliol College to let them go by.

Finally the right building was in sight, but pungent exhaust belching from a bus in a dark cloud induced a swift wave of nausea. Emma stopped for a moment to lean against the pharmacy building.

Get a grip, Jevons. She lurched inside, hoping the floor wouldn't come up to meet her.

The bright artificial light of the interior hurt her eyes. Shielding them, she made her way past colorful racks of cosmetics and skin aids to the pharmacy counter. Ten minutes later, she left with a bulging bag of ointments and pills and entered the Covered Market. Her nausea had been replaced by a nagging emptiness in her stomach. The uneven cobblestoned floor, some parts centuries old, fought her progress, but she struggled to stay upright and made her way to Brown's Café, where she ordered a large tea and a bacon butty. Best to have something in her stomach for the pills, the pharmacist had advised. She washed down double the recommended dose with her tea. When her sandwich arrived, the scent of fried bacon set her juices going.

That's what's wrong with me, she reasoned. *I just need protein.*

She gobbled the sandwich down and finished her tea, people-watching the throngs who filled the market lanes, shopping or browsing the jumble of mixed goods on sale: butchers and greengrocers and florists all vied with leather and shoe shops, a hat shop, and a bakery where large glass windows let viewers watch decorators fashion the fondant figures that were their hallmark.

Much better, Emma decided, feeling her temperature start to abate. On surer footing now, she made her way back to the museum. She decided to give her father a call before plunging back into work. Maybe in a few days when she felt better, she'd make a point of going up to have fish and chips with him after work. She wouldn't want to risk giving him this ugly virus.

In their last call, he'd told her that over a game of snooker at the Kings Arms in Chipping Norton, he had bragged to all of his pals that his daughter, the art restorer, was working on a real Picasso. She did like to make her dad proud.

CHAPTER FOUR

Brighton

12:05 PM

Nora hugged Elly Griffiths with genuine warmth when they met as planned at the iconic 1899 steel arches of Brighton Pier. They'd been introduced years earlier when Nora interviewed the award-winning crime writer of two series for *People and Places* magazine, the job that had first brought her to England. The women felt an instant rapport. The popular crime writer had been generous to Nora in her efforts to get her children's books under way, and over time their friendship had grown.

"You must be Declan; so lovely to meet you." Elly shook hands with Declan but her gaze lit up when she saw Sean in his buggy. "Here's the little man. Look how he's grown! I still remember my two at this stage."

"Elly has twin teens just off to university," Nora explained. "Now where shall we have lunch?"

"Let's head toward The Lanes," Elly directed. "At night there are bright lights all along the promenade, from that huge Ferris wheel that really stands out to the mini golf and all the gaudy shops and restaurants along the way." She guided them across the street back the way they'd come. "There's a large LGBT community made welcome here, and a historic theatre. Of course, the lovely gardens draw visitors, too. We do get overrun with tourists at times." Elly laughed. "But it's all good for the economy."

She guided them toward the historic Lanes, where a restaurant stood on the corner of Prince Albert Street. Its window curved to follow the sharp corner. "It's called 'Food for Friends' and I thought it would be a good place as they're baby friendly."

Nora stifled a giggle as they were seated, anticipating Declan's face when he looked at the menu, and realized the restaurant was vegetarian. To her surprise, he didn't blink, and when the food arrived, he proclaimed it delicious, wolfing down a haloumi and portobello burger with crispy chips. Sean was at the stage where he liked to eat bits of food with his fingers, and Declan shared a few chips.

"He has a fondness for squash," Nora warned Elly, reaching into his changing bag for a plastic container filled with cooked carrots. She arranged several on his high chair tray as the child reached for Elly's dish when he heard her say *squash*.

"El-lee," he shrieked, pointing to Elly's squash ravioli. Everyone laughed.

While they lingered over coffee, Nora took Sean to the loo and changed his diaper, grateful for normalcy in her day. The adrenaline rushes she'd been experiencing were dulled, and she felt lighter than she had in days. When she came back, she listened to Declan and Elly talk about her teens' university choices while she helped Sean with a training cup of apple juice.

"You're seeing Sean's grandparents at the Cornwall estate, Nora?" Elly had a very good memory. "Are you going, Declan?"

He held up both hands. "Not me. I'm just a lowly policeman."

"I happen to know you're head of CID, Declan, so don't be so modest," Elly said.

"I'm going to the family estate on Sunday with Sean and staying the night. Quite daunting, my first glimpse. Then I go to Bath on Monday, to the reading my friend Helen fixed for me at the bookstore there. Oh, I have a signed copy of the new book for you in the car."

Declan made a noise somewhere between "humph" and a noisy clearing of his throat.

"You don't approve of Nora taking Sean to see them, Declan?" Elly asked.

"Whatever gave you that idea, El?" Nora rolled her eyes at Declan. They'd agreed not to mention the bug when with Elly, but was he worried about her traveling alone before the issue of her stalker was resolved? She was relieved when he kept his word and deflected the question.

"Nora met them halfway in Birmingham last May, and again over the summer. I think it's expecting a lot of her to travel to Cornwall alone with the baby when she's got this week on in Bath to follow."

"It's just an overnighter, Declan," Nora said. "They live right on the Devon edge of Cornwall. Harry and Muriel have been very sweet."

"Because now they know you have their grandchild," Declan said. "They weren't so keen on you before."

"The only time we met was at Paul's memorial service," Nora protested. "They blamed me for keeping Paul away, but the truth was, he never wanted to take me to meet his parents. Then when he died in the plane crash, it wasn't a good time for any of us."

"That's your nature, Nora. You're very forgiving. Better get used to it, Declan." Elly's blue eyes sparkled.

"I still think it's an imposition, but of course, it's your choice," Declan said.

"He says through gritted teeth," Elly proclaimed, which broke the tension and made them all laugh.

"Sean seems full up," Declan said.

Nora saw Sean's eyes had that heavy-lidded look that meant he was ready to fall asleep. She cleaned his face and strapped him in his buggy as Declan paid the bill, and they left the restaurant.

Once on the pavement, Elly took the buggy from Nora. "You two stroll The Lanes, have a little time together. I'll take Sean for a walk along the seafront. Sea air always knocks little ones out. We'll meet up to go to my house later."

"You don't have to do that, Elly," Nora protested. "I've come to see you."

"And you shall. We'll meet right back here in, say, 90 minutes, and you'll come to my house for tea before the drive back to Oxford. The twins are dying to see you all, especially Sean. Don't forget the game."

"What game?" Nora had no idea what Elly meant.

"When Andy and I window shop here, we always choose one thing from each display we'd buy if money were no object."

"That sounds like fun," Nora said.

"Let's go." Declan took Nora's arm.

"Only if you're certain." Nora let herself be pulled to Declan's side as Elly waved them off. "There's more nappies and a water bottle in his bag if you need anything."

Elly was already walking back toward the beachfront as Nora and Declan re-entered The Lanes. It felt comforting to have Sean with someone she trusted. Nora let Declan guide her along the twisted warren of narrow alleys running along both sides of North Street that made The Lanes famous.

She tried to let go of the defensive feeling she felt whenever she talked to Declan about the Pembrokes. The specter of Paul's ghost seemed to haunt them at times, and she worried that Declan wouldn't be able to accept that Sean's wealthy grandparents, for better or worse, were his family, and would be a part of their future.

They strolled the southern section and walked past a chocolate shop filled with delicacies, including a huge tower of ornate figures from *The Wizard of Oz*, all made of different kinds of chocolate. When Declan insisted they choose their pretend purchases, Nora decided on a huge tin of her favorite sweet, dark chocolate-covered orange peel. Declan chose a chocolate Darth Vader figure sprayed black and silver, complete with red candy light saber.

"I didn't know you were a Star Wars fan," Nora said.

"I have many depths you haven't plumbed, my dear." He smiled, and all of his charm hit Nora, his square jaw and light brown hair good company for the bump in his nose.

Nora felt her pulse quicken. "I plan to explore those depths this very evening." She turned her face up for a quick kiss.

Declan acquiesced. "How very modern of us—a public display of affection."

"Have I embarrassed you? Because you'll find I'm a thoroughly modern woman, Detective." And she pulled him into a dark corner and gave him a real kiss.

Heathrow Airport

1:57 PM

Viktor Garanin brought up the back of his first class seat as the British Airways flight from Moscow started its descent into London's Heathrow Airport. Despite the added width and comfortable leather of the pricey accommodation, the large man was ready to deplane after a nearly four-hour flight. He'd been well fed and offered drinks and wine, but at this time in the day, Viktor needed to keep his head about him. There was still border control to get through, and that was always a sticking point.

The flight attendants had been solicitous to his every need, although that one young man had looked Viktor fully in the eyes and hastily looked away when he saw the malice reflected there. They disgusted him equally, male or female, and he hadn't been able to hide how he really felt. They were *British*, and that was enough for Viktor to consider them no more than dirt beneath his bespoke leather shoes.

He glanced out the window at the azure sky and woolly clouds that surrounded them. Viktor remembered his mother had a robe in just that shade of blue. The plane suddenly plunged into the clouds; the window became white and foggy without a view, and the unbidden memory came rushing back before he could distract himself.

Viktor had been sent home from school early with a head cold. It was the housekeeper's day off, and when the nurse couldn't raise his mother on the telephone to pick him up, he'd played on her sympathies to walk the short distance home. All he'd wanted was to crawl into his own bed and pull the covers over his head. He would eventually do that when he arrived home, but not because of his cold.

The house was quiet, too quiet. He assumed his mother was picking his younger brother up from nursery school, which explained why the nurse couldn't reach her. Viktor went to the kitchen to sneak a bottle of juice to take with him to his room. He heard the sound of an engine, and when he looked out the kitchen door, he saw white clouds filling the garage, swirling around, at the same time he became aware of a noxious odor.

He remembered instinctively knowing he shouldn't open the kitchen door, and instead had run outside and around to the garage, pulling open the doors wide. The fumes spilled out, choking him. He recognized the sound of his mother's car engine, and saw the hose that ran from the exhaust pipe into the driver's window.

Viktor coughed deeply, the vapors making his chest hurt even as the cool air rushed in and they started to dissipate. He had to turn the motor off. The exhaust continued to leak out as he looked around wildly for something to cover his face and found a gas-soaked rag the gardener used on their lawn mower.

Covering his nose and mouth, ignoring the sharp smell of the gasoline on the rag, he opened the driver's door and reached across his mother to shut off the ignition. Blessed silence.

Then Viktor looked at his mother. She wore her blue and white robe. Her skin was bright pink, her lips cherry red, but not from lipstick. Her tongue protruded from between her clenched lips and he saw she'd grabbed the steering wheel tightly, both hands grasping it in a rictus of death to keep herself from turning the key off.

He felt warmth as his urine ran down his leg and into his shoe before his knees buckled. He collapsed on the floor of their garage, where a neighbor found him after noticing the dissipating cloud.

Viktor shook the memory off and roused himself. He rarely allowed his thoughts to stray to that day, and refused to wallow in the feelings it brought back. The bitch had made him feel weak, transferring her own weakness in the face of his father's repeated abuse over to him. He hated her then for abandoning him, a rage that grew over the years. It became cemented in his feelings toward her native country, and now he was going to do something about it.

He would need to keep his wits about him and project calm as he carried out the next step in his plan. It had taken him years of planning, and a considerable amount of money, to bring his scheme to this point. He was so close he could taste his victory. V for Viktor, and V for Victory. He closed his eyes and spent a moment becoming just a businessman on his way to the lovely Oxford hotel his assistant had booked for him, nothing more.

When the plane touched down, a round of applause from the cheap seats let the pilot know they appreciated his smooth landing. Death cheated once more, Viktor thought. If they only knew he had it within his power to kill each and every one of them, and that he couldn't wait to make that happen.

Viktor grabbed his carry-on and made his way to customs. The tall, outsized man in the quality suit carried himself erect to his full height, earning a modicum of personal space around him. He pulled out his boarding card and passport, checked to be certain the one he carried was the same name he'd used to book the ticket, and moved up the line, pretending to check for messages on the phone, while scouting the perimeter and noting the placement of police and border agents on security.

The customs agent was an older man, bored with his job, who stifled a yawn as Viktor stepped up for his turn. Still, he scrutinized Viktor's passport photo carefully.

"What is your reason for travel to England today, Mr. Kokut, and how long do you plan to stay with us?"

"I have a business meeting in Oxford over the next several days. My secretary has assured me I will enjoy the Old Bank Hotel. Perhaps you've heard of it?"

"I'm sure it will be fine." The clerk stamped the passport and handed it back to Viktor. "Enjoy your stay." He waved Viktor on and motioned to the young woman next in line to step up.

Viktor blew out a breath and headed for the exit. He would need to find a train to take him into London, and stop for a late lunch, perhaps Claridge's. He'd read in a magazine that Gordon Ramsey had taken over their kitchen. Then he would catch a second train for the 90-minute ride to Oxford, where he would put his plan into action.

The crowds mulled around him, the international airport a cauldron of mixed races, languages, and skin colors. Viktor missed Russia and his garden already, but his heart beat with the anticipation of a long-held dream ready to become reality.

2:20 PM

The day was going better than Declan had expected. Nora accepted that Elly wanted Sean to herself. When their plans to visit had first been made, he'd called Elly earlier in the week and made his request. Although they'd yet to meet in person at that point, they'd each heard enough about one another from Nora that Elly readily warmed to his idea.

"Leave it with me," she'd promised, and the crime writer had been true to her word.

Now as they played "Elly's Game," their arms wrapped around each other's waists, he inhaled this new scent of hers, and thought life was amazingly good. The game was designed to show him Nora's likes and dislikes in what kind of ring she liked, just in case they were headed that way. He'd already noticed when they passed a contemporary goldsmith's window she had difficulty choosing something she'd want to own.

"Lovely work, but not my style," she explained, finally pointing out a gold bangle bracelet with etching.

He pretended to choose a signet ring and they walked on. He wasn't surprised the modern designs left her cold. Nora had a collection of vintage jewelry she often wore, and he knew she favored antique items over new when it came to most furniture, too.

There was an armoury store with breastplates, swords, and knives of all types, and they each chose ornate swords. "Can you imagine kids playing pirates with those? We could defend ourselves if we had them," Nora said, entering into the spirit of the game. "Hide them under our coats and brandish them at just the right time against our enemy."

"We'd have to have a code word to coordinate our attack," Declan said.

"To attack at the same time? Or be warned something bad

was happening? What about 'en garde,' or what the Crusaders said, 'Deus vult?'"

"Dues what?" Declan laughed.

Nora smiled. "It means 'God wills it.'"

"Hmm, I was thinking something more subtle, like King Arthur in *Monty Python and the Holy Grail*: 'RUN AWAY!' And you would know to either drop down or bolt!"

They laughed so hard tears came down their faces.

"Run away!" Nora chortled. Several people walked around them as they laughed uncontrollably.

"I didn't think it was that funny." Declan wiped his face and offered Nora his handkerchief.

"I didn't know you liked Monty Python so much!" And they were off again. When they finally composed themselves, they shared the good cheer mutual laughter brought while they carried on over the cobbled stones.

They turned into Meeting House Lane, passing cafes emitting delectable scents. A pricey clothing boutique stood next to a row of gaudy stores, one with **JEWELLERY** in large gold letters.

"That's another thing you spell funny," Nora said.

They stopped by the large window of the Little Gem Jewellers shop. Row upon row of estate jewels under strip lighting dazzled their eyes: bracelets, rings, watches, garish necklaces worn to balls in another era, all studded with diamonds, sapphires, emeralds, rubies and pearls.

"The Americans dropped the extra 'L' just to be snarky to us Brits." Declan gave her a squeeze. "Let's look inside this one."

The owner was helping another customer and nodded to them as Declan guided Nora to a display case of antique rings.

"Which one here?" He pretended to scan a row of men's rings, and watched Nora's eyes roam the rows.

"Too many to choose," she protested.

The browser left and the shopkeeper moved to them. "A woman of discretion," he said. "You appreciate vintage, I see." He pointed to the Edwardian bar pin on her jacket, a carved gold bar with an opal in its center.

Nora extended her arm and showed him her watch. Declan had never taken much note of the classic small-faced watch she wore daily, but the jeweler was clearly interested.

"A fine Tiffany specimen. I'd guess 1950s?"

Nora removed the watch and held it out for his inspection. The jeweler turned it over and read the inscription aloud: "'Judy, 10-8-1951.' Happy birthday to Judy, wherever she is. You're far too young for you to be Judy."

Nora smiled. "I'm Nora. My father gave it to me for my 16th birthday. I've worn it ever since."

The jeweler gave a little bow. "Charming. Now which of these rings catches your attention?"

Nora gave an embarrassed laugh. "Oh, no. We're playing a game, I'm afraid, at your expense." She explained about the routine they'd been using to window shop.

"People do that all the time. A purchase such as this should not be taken lightly." He took off his glasses and cleaned them with a cloth. "Humor me. Which one catches your fancy?" The man smiled benignly.

"All right, then." She refastened her watch and leaned over the counter.

Declan watched Nora's eyes roam over the case and suddenly widen.

"That one," she said without hesitation.

"As I said, a woman of discretion." The jeweler reached inside and brought out the ring she pointed to and handed it to the couple for their inspection.

To Declan's inexpert eye it looked like a flower in gemstones set on a pinky gold band that had swirls cut into it.

"Edwardian?" Nora asked, and the jeweler nodded. She showed the ring to Declan. "The center oval is a diamond, of course, and those four blue marquise stones angled on the side corners are sapphires. The two tapered pear shapes in green are emeralds. That etching is called chasing and all done by hand." She looked up at the jeweler. "Rose gold?"

The man nodded. "A rare specimen. Probably made for a member of lower royalty."

Declan tilted his head. "I forgot royalty had classes."

The jeweler smiled. "To be sure. This isn't important enough in terms of the size of the jewels for a princess or duchess, for instance, but it might have been commissioned for a baroness."

"Try it on, Nora." To his surprise, Nora blushed deeply and quickly handed the ring back to the jeweler.

"Bad luck. But thank you very much for letting us see it up close. It's the prettiest ring I've ever seen."

"Yes, thanks." Declan followed Nora out of the shop. "Shall I call you My Baroness for the rest of the day?"

Nora smiled but the day had suddenly lost its levity. What happened? Was it something he said?

Nora's mobile rang and she answered it. "Hello? Elly, I'm so sorry. We'll meet you at the car park right away." She started to hurry away, Declan at her heels. "Elly can't get Sean to stop crying. She's meeting us at the car to head to her house for tea. Maybe the ride will calm him down."

Declan sighed as he followed Nora. Interrupted again. One moment everything was going along fine. The next they were under the stress of a crying baby and Nora's unpredictable behavior. Two things were certain: his experiment had been a complete flop—and he'd never understand what made a woman's mind tick.

CHAPTER FIVE

Oxford

4:15 PM

"Grant Alan" had followed Nora Tierney to Oxford yet again yesterday. When he'd seen her packing multiple bags into her station wagon in Bowness, he'd known this trip was going to be longer than the usual weekend. Her parting conversation with Simon Ramsey confirmed her plans to be gone for a week, and as she'd gone over her entire itinerary, Grant had noted it down. Then the speaker had suddenly stopped working, and he'd have to see if the powers that be wanted him to try to get close enough to her again to fix another.

Of course, there was always the slight chance he'd been rumbled, but it was more likely the damn thing had broken or run out of power. These newer models were supposed to be top of the line with a longer battery life, and he'd already had months out of the one he'd dropped into Tierney's bag.

Last night she'd pulled up in front of the Somerville building where she used to live. He recognized the address where she parked from her dossier. She'd taken in an overnighter and her son's diaper bag, juggling one on each shoulder and carrying the boy. Two women came down a few minutes later, and retrieved a travel cot and a chair that strapped to a table for feeding the child. A one-night stay, he'd decided. He'd taken himself off to a lovely hotel under yet another assumed name, enjoyed a fine Indian meal nearby, then had a good night's sleep tucked up under a feathery duvet.

This morning he rose early, and by 7:00 AM parked half a block away from the Somerville address in his rental car, a takeaway of milky builder's tea in the cup holder and the morning paper in his lap. He arrived in plenty of time to see Nora leave the building at 8:10 AM, carrying Sean. Her friend Val Rogan trailed behind. Wrapped in a fuzzy dressing gown, she rubbed sleep from her eyes. A wide-awake Sean waved to Rogan over Nora's shoulder. Rogan carried their bags and feeding chair. He watched Nora buckle the child into his seat as Rogan made a second trip for the cot. The two embraced and talked a moment longer before Nora left.

A few minutes later she pulled up in front of the detective's flat. When Barnes entered her car without any luggage, this confirmed they were off to Brighton just for the day he knew she'd planned. Frustrating without the audio linking her conversations, but her next week's schedule had been discussed enough that he had it down. He'd have to play it by ear while he waited for further instructions.

Not necessary to follow her when she had a detective in tow, so he gave himself the day off to explore Oxford on his own. First he returned to his hotel to leave his car and made certain he could retain his room for a second night. The young woman behind the counter was too young to have watched too many *Midsommer Murders.*

"Of course, Mr. Barnaby. We can let you have that room for another night."

"Tom Barnaby," as he was here in Oxford, smiled until his dimples showed. "Wonderful! So much to see here in town. How's your breakfast?"

"We have a full English, sir, one of the best in town."

He ate a proper English breakfast, right down to the beans and fried bread, and added an extra rasher of bacon for good measure. After eating, he returned to his room for a light jacket and set off for a walk of his own choosing, instead of where Nora Tierney led him.

Oxford hadn't changed much since he'd last spent time there. The chances of him coming across anyone who might recognize him were slim, especially with his looks changed. His own mother wouldn't recognize him. That was the whole point.

He tried to see the medieval town through a visitor's eyes: the multiple colleges sprinkled throughout the town's buildings; the golden Cotswold stone that changed color with the time of day and weather; the sense of preserved history wherever one looked. Autumn still had color, toned down and bronzed from the blowsy pastels of summer. The leaves he crunched under his feet released the scent of woody mushrooms.

He attached himself to a tour, and spent a long time in Duke Humfrey's Library in the Old Bodleian, its oldest reading room with marvelous architecture as intriguing as its contents. It was a place he'd ignored before, and he enjoyed the carvings of the medieval building and the docent's spiel about hidden messages and meanings in them, as much as he did the priceless manuscripts and music scores.

As the tour ended at the gift shop, Tom ruminated on what else he had missed with his interests so focused on his career. He didn't have anyone to buy anything for, no real home to bring a memento back to. He thought of his sterile bolt-hole and its minimal furnishings. His job had been the driving force of his adult life, eventually crowding out any real socialization or meaningful relationships. You couldn't maintain those when you never knew where you'd be posted, or for how long.

While he prided himself on his abilities, at what cost had they been derived? How did he begin to quantify if it had been worth it?

Following Nora Tierney these last months had reminded him there could be joy in simple pleasures: a lakeside walk in lovely weather, holding hands with someone you loved; planting a window box full of showy yellow daffodils and bright purple tulips; watching a red balloon float toward the clouds until it was lost to sight.

He resolved there and then that this would his last assignment. If his unit couldn't find him a desk job, Tom would look for employment elsewhere. He'd made good contacts, and surely there would be something for him in the corporate world. He turned to follow his tour out into the sunlight, his eyes blinking to adjust to the brightness after the dim interior. It was an apt metaphor for how he felt.

Oxford

9:15 PM

As they neared Declan's flat, Nora thought she'd never endured a longer two-hour drive.

Sean whimpered the entire way, out of sorts after a lovely afternoon and evening, rescued by Elly and her family, who fussed over him, and in part by the gel Nora had rubbed on his gums soon after meeting up with Elly at the car park. At the Griffiths' home he'd entranced them with his stumbling walk, holding hands with Elly's daughter as he lurched around the yard. She knew she was blessed that he took to strangers so well. He'd been run off his feet by their dog, Jethro, who licked the remains of tea-time cupcakes off his shirt, making the little boy giggle as he squealed his attempts at the dog's name: "Jed-o!"

They'd gotten on the road right after barbequing hot dogs and veggie burgers, hoping Sean would fall asleep in the car. Nora changed him into his pajamas and a fresh diaper just before they left, picturing Declan scooping up the sleeping boy and carrying him to his cot for the night and their time alone. It soon became clear that wasn't the way the evening was going to turn out.

"Apparently he's left his good mood in Brighton," Declan said as he drove them home.

Nora tried to defuse the mounting tension in the car. Declan was usually very patient, but they were all tired, and Sean's grizzling wore on them. With his vocabulary limited to bursts of parroted words, she spent the ride half-turned toward the boy in the back seat, trying everything in her bag of tricks to soothe him. Knowing the cramped situation they were heading to in Declan's bachelor flat added to the edginess they both felt. This clearly didn't promise to be the evening they'd hoped for, where Sean would fall asleep and stay asleep until early morning.

"He's over-stimulated and teething, a wicked combo." Nora pushed her hair behind her ears.

"When we get upstairs you can rub more of that gunk you have on his gums."

"I'd already planned to, Declan." Nora bit her lip as she heard her strident tone. She turned toward the front of the car after the baby quieted for a few blessed minutes, watching the headlights of oncoming traffic and noting the chill outside had reached the inside of the car.

She wasn't in a great mood herself. Somehow talking to the jeweler about her father, and then immediately after that looking at what could clearly be engagement rings, pointed out his absence to her. It hit her hard.

She'd experienced this before: when Sean was born, and again when he was christened, the knowledge that her dad was missing the highlights of her life. Grief could be compartmentalized, sometimes for years, but would rear its head on a wave of emotion.

Then, too, there was the issue of looking at rings together. Was Declan gearing up to ask her to marry him? Did she want to be married, after the mistake she almost made with Paul Pembroke?

Declan's ringing mobile startled them both, and as he hit the button to answer on Bluetooth, Nora looked around to see if it had disturbed Sean. The baby gnawed on his bunny's leg and whimpered.

"Barnes."

"Declan, it's Simon."

"You're on speaker, Si. Any news?"

"Hi, Nora. Actually, there is. Callie thought she'd been followed when walking Sean last week for Nora. She thought it was this lad she knows who's too shy to ask her out, but on reflection, she can't be certain it was him."

"That's a surprise." Nora squirmed in her seat. Callie hadn't mentioned anything to her about being followed.

"Callie has Nora's reddish hair. Looking at her from the back, pushing Sean's buggy, it would be easy to mistake her for Nora," Simon pointed out.

Declan's face took on a dark look. "Did Callie get a look at this guy?"

"Only a sense of someone tall—should I ask her to call the shy friend and see if it was him?"

"He might not be honest with her if he's been too reluctant to approach her," Nora said.

"Nora's right, Simon. Just ask her to keep her eyes open. Of course, if he does summon up the courage to ask her out, she can find out then. With Nora going to Cornwall Sunday and then on to Bath for a week, let's all hope this is a huge mistake."

"Right. Stay safe, Nora."

Simon ended the call. Nora blew out a breath she didn't realize she'd been holding. It was one thing to hope her stalker might be in her imagination; another to hear someone else thought he was real. "I'm glad I'll be away from Bowness for a while." Why would someone stalk her? Could her inheritance have made her a target? And how did she know her stalker wouldn't follow her to Cornwall? It all set her on edge.

"So am I." Declan's mouth set in a grim line as they drew up outside his building. "We're here."

Nora noticed he hadn't mentioned the silver button to Simon. She could only hope that meant Declan thought it would turn out to be something innocuous. How long would it be before she found out what it was?

They turned as one to the back seat to see Sean, in angelic innocence, head to one side with a bit of drool making his lips shiny, fast asleep.

Chapter Six

Declan's goodbye kiss to Nora ended with him stifling a yawn. Sean and his teething had kept them awake all night, cancelling any sleep, much less romantic plans.

"I'm sorry about last night," Nora said. None of her usual ploys had soothed the fretful child.

He noticed the circles under her eyes. Nora had paced the bedroom with Sean slung over her shoulder, her bare feet slapping on his wooden floor. Declan had taken a turn at one point so she could use the loo and slug down a drink of cool water, but the inconsolable boy only wanted his mum.

"Are you certain that shouldn't be gin or vodka?" he'd asked her. "Maybe a sip for him?"

"I may have to put it in his bottle soon." She'd insisted at one point that Declan try to sleep and took Sean out to the sitting room, where the boy's crying and her footfalls persisted.

Finally a second dose of baby paracetamol, Calpol, let them all grab a few hours of sleep just after dawn. Then Declan's sergeant, Watkins, woke them a few hours later with his call. After a terse discussion with his partner, Declan showered and dressed for work. She'd thought Watkins had news about the silver button, but it was the weekend, and the news was a suspicious death for the department.

"Sorry I have to go in." He headed for the door, stepping around Sean's travel cot and tripping over a stack of toys. He felt a tad guilty about leaving. Declan looked at the clean, contemporary lines of his flat, with its large picture window and slim blinds, and then at the glass coffee table that now sported rubber bumpers for its four sharp corners. Life with a child was cumbersome at times, difficult at others. Ultimately, he knew there were moments of pure joy. This was life, warts and all, and he tried to embrace it wholly for the first time in a very long time. "I hope your time today with Val goes well."

"Don't think I'm missing that spring in your step, mister, heading into work where there are no teething babies." Nora tried on a weary smile.

Declan sensed her unease. He turned around and came back to give her a hug, hoping to reassure her. Sean lolled against her shoulder, momentarily spent, and he reached out to stroke the baby's soft cheek. "He'll be his old cheery self soon enough. And I'm not escaping you. A woman from the Ashmolean Museum has died and something's off there. Watkins needs me on this one."

"I'm sorry for her." She blew him a kiss. "We'll see you tonight."

"Don't forget Mrs. Tink comes this morning." Mrs. Tink had cleaned for Declan for years.

"I won't have to leave until after she's here. We're supposed to meet Val at The Old Parsonage for tea this afternoon, and then see that house she's found near there."

"Great area. Why not let Mrs. Tink watch Sean so you can get a shower? She'll be delighted."

Nora brightened. "I may do that. Want me to cook tonight?"

"No, let's go out for pizza. Sean can chew the crusts and we'll get those teeth to pop through." He needed the time at work, and dinner out would be nice for Nora. They could all escape the clutter. And maybe after a bottle of wine to recapture their mood, coupled with a baby who quieted down, they could salvage the last of their time together before she left for a week.

Nora's eyes shone. "Go on, detective. Get to work and do the tough stuff, Declan."

Sean raised his head. "Deca," he blurted out.

Nora gave him a jiggle. "You little traitor. You've got that one down pat."

Declan chucked the baby under his chin. Sean hid his face in Nora's neck, suddenly shy. A last kiss for Nora, this time longer, without the yawn and with more promise.

Then he was out the door and headed to St. Aldates' Station to see what Watkins had sourced about Nora's silver button—and what his sergeant found about the death of a young art restorer that required the attention of the Criminal Investigation Department.

10:30 AM

After reading Sean two storybooks, Nora settled him in his cot with a musical toy and tried to tidy Declan's flat. She didn't understand the impulse to clean for the cleaning lady, but reasoned it was one thing to dust and vacuum, and another to deal with people's personal belongings.

Nora filled the kitchen sink with soapy water and discarded the used liners from Sean's bottles they'd used yesterday and overnight. She threw the bottles, nipples, and caps into the soapy water to soak, and wondered who cleaned Port Enys, her destination in Cornwall tomorrow for her visit to Muriel and Harry Pembroke. Did they have staff? She pictured the liveried butlers of *Downton Abbey* or a competent Jeeves and shuddered.

Paul had grown up at the Grade-I-listed house that Sean would presumably inherit as his only heir, unless she was very wrong or things went off kilter, and the Pembrokes left it all to a pet society. Nora's head spun when she thought of the huge responsibility the future presented her son, but that was years and years away. With her usual skill at coping by boxing up difficult ideas, Nora tucked the thought into the recesses of her mind. She concentrated instead on searching through her luggage for the least-wrinkled clothing to wear. Ironing wasn't on her list of things to do today, and she reached for her comfortable jeans and a patterned jumper that brought out the green in her eyes. She rumbled through her travel jewelry case, chose an oval silver pin with intricate chasing, and affixed it to the jumper.

When Mrs. Tink arrived, the spry woman promised to keep a watchful eye on the exhausted baby who'd dozed off, and recommended Nelson's Granules for the teething issue, then shooed Nora off to shower while he slept.

Hot water revived Nora's spirits. She wondered if Mrs. Tink would be amenable to coming in to help her in her new house. If she could trade cleaning Declan's flat for the house, it might work. Now all she had to do was convince Declan that he should give up this flat, and his independence, and move in with her and Sean. She had planned to bring their relationship up last night in the afterglow of time alone, but her teething baby had put a stop to that.

It couldn't be helped, but there was still time to sort things out. Neither of them was going anywhere soon after her week in Bath, but she still worried about Declan's reluctance to hear about her finances. How would he feel living in a house she owned? That could easily be changed, of course, if they were to marry. Did she want to marry Declan? She knew she wanted to be with him, but she also knew she wanted to provide a stable environment for her child. Was it enough to live together or was the idea of marriage, with its permanent commitment, what she really wanted? It was a lot to toss around and decide.

As she scrubbed her body, inhaling the soothing scent of the

lavender soap gel, Nora acknowled
nancial status and its rapid change stu.
level, with all she had gained through Pau.
surance with its double indemnity clause thr
her situation significantly. After many meetings w
financial advisor, she had provided for the people si.
with her largesse, then placed a portion in investments and .
nuities for herself. The bulk of the funds were held in trust for
Sean's future.

Ramsey Lodge's home equity loan had been paid off, allowing
Simon and Kate to plan those renovations needed in the family
wing to accommodate Kate's married status. Nora had instituted
a few other gifts, and had her own generous house fund. With
the monthly income from the investments relieving her previous financial pressure, Nora could breathe easily when it came to
money matters for the first time since moving to England.

Not that she would be on anything near equal footing with
the Pembrokes. As she dried off, Nora admitted she was equally
curious and apprehensive about Port Enys. In Paul's reluctance
to bring her to meet his parents, Nora had formed the impression the Pembrokes were country farmers. As if.

Nora dressed and sprayed herself with her new perfume. She
liked light scents, but realized her lemony scent was one she'd
worn for years. It had been time for an upgrade. She gathered
a load of towels and clothes from suitcases for the wash, and
speculated on whether Sean's initial good impressions would
last when she arrived on the Pembroke's doorstep with a cranky,
teething baby.

CHAPTER SEVEN

Oxford

11:18 AM

Viktor Garanin sipped his coffee. It was very good coffee and he was drinking it in a quaint Oxford café, but the experience was lost to him as his annoyance grew and raged. The timbered beams and charming uneven floor did nothing to improve his mood. The chatter was noisy, though, and that worked for his purposes, as the espresso machine roared and the scents of scones and toasted crumpets added to the fragrance in the shop.

The large man consulted his watch for the third time. He loathed tardiness of any kind, and his contact was now 18 minutes late. If he were back in Russia this would not be tolerated. But he had to be careful whom he used here in England. Bloody England.

When the young private detective slid into the seat opposite Viktor, the newcomer didn't apologize for his delay.

"What have you found?" Viktor saw the waitress approach just then, and cautioned his companion with a raised eyebrow before he could answer. "What will you have?" he asked pleasantly, slickly hiding all traces of his annoyance.

"A mocha, please." The detective waited for the woman to leave and leaned forward, lowering his voice. "The art gal died in the middle of the night at the John Radcliffe."

"And who else?"

The man shrugged. "No one else yet."

Viktor had to swallow a shout. This was incomprehensible. The mutated strain was supposed to be virulent, to spread and kill most of the English he hated. He barely kept his anger under control and forced himself to take a sip of the coffee. He took a breath, and made himself inhale the roasted scent and taste the richness. He took a second swallow, pushing his rage back down to simmer level. Better. "What else?"

"A houseman wised up on symptoms figured out it was almost certainly smallpox. All hell's broken loose up there, moving patients from her ward out and —"

The waitress returned with the mocha and placed the steaming cup in front of the young man. "Will there be anything else?"

Viktor took in her creamy complexion and pleasant figure, but the ring in her eyebrow put him off. "Just the check, please." He wanted her out of earshot. She tore the bill off her pad and left it on the table. Viktor leaned toward his companion and inhaled the chocolate in his coffee. "And?"

"They're deciding if the staff need to be quarantined. Public Health and local police already involved. It will be all over the news by tonight."

Viktor slapped the table in front of him. Only one death? How could this be? "This is what happens when incompetents are allowed to—never mind. Drink up. I have work to do."

2:32 PM

Nora left Boots with two boxes of Nelson's Teetha teething granules, the chamomile packets Mrs. Tink suggested, sold in dose sachets she could simply pour into Sean's mouth. The woman behind the counter assured her many women afforded them high praise and they were a consistent seller to mothers and nannies. Nora certainly hoped so.

She headed past the Martyr's Memorial toward The Old Parsonage on St. Giles. Leaves crunched under her feet, releasing the musty odor she associated with the piles raked by her father in Connecticut days of her youth. The autumn sun took the chill off the day, and Sean seemed comfortable for the moment.

He'd gnawed on the teething biscuit Mrs. Tink had given him when he woke and tolerated applesauce later through his drooling. Nora had packed extra bibs and a dry shirt in his bag, and given him a dose of Calpol before leaving the flat. She threw in a portable phone charger that would revive her mobile phone if she were out longer than planned.

Nora bumped Sean's buggy over the uneven pavement, and reached the iron gate in the stone wall surrounding the 17th century lodge. The Old Parsonage had a thick gnarled wisteria vine at its front entrance that crawled up the building and sent its tendrils across the stonework. Currently green and wispy after the scented lilac blooms of spring, it was kept carefully pruned back from the hotel-restaurant's mullioned windows. This quintessentially English spot was one of Nora's favorite places in Oxford.

Out of recent habit, as she cleared the doorway Nora leaned back quickly, checking to see if anyone lurked behind her. A clump of tourists walked up St. Giles, and she searched for anyone who looked remotely familiar. A glance in the other direction showed too many people to single someone out. Directly opposite her, a woman walked a Scottie dog sporting a tartan collar and leash. Nora shook off the idea and refused to let her day be spoiled with the threat of menace.

"There's Auntie Val."

Val Rogan had scored a table in the shade of the wall and perused the lunch menu. She waved when she saw Nora. The textile artist with the golden eyes made Nora think of an Audrey Hepburn lioness. Yet with her cropped hair and slender frame,

Val was an exotic animal all her own.

"Yankee, there you are." Val sprang up, reinforcing her cat-like image, and gathered Nora in a hug. "I know it's only hours since I've seen you, but I'm so happy you're coming back to Oxford."

Nora returned the hug. If she'd wavered at all about returning to Oxford, Val's presence, and now Declan's, cemented her move back.

Val knelt down to Sean. "How's my godson?"

The baby gave Val a toothy grin and yelled, "TEE-va!"

Nora laughed. "Declan said you'd be embroidering Teeva on something soon."

"I have the perfect denim jacket, now that you mention it." She sat back down. "I wonder what he'll call Sophie?"

"O-fi!" Sean obliged, grinning wider when both women laughed.

"You little parrot," Val grinned, and pulled his buggy closer to her.

"Don't encourage him." Nora sat opposite her. "He's an incorrigible ham." Sophie worked as an archivist in the Rylands Library at the University of Manchester. "How is Sophie? Still enjoying work?"

"Actually, I have news." Val blushed. "She called right after you left this morning. She's up for a position in the OUP archives. If she gets it, she'll be moving here, too." Val's eyes shone.

"Oxford University Press—she must have wonderful credentials and experience." Nora reached across to grab Val's hand. The murder of Val's former partner had been the vehicle for Nora to meet Declan, while it had devastated Val. Bryn Wallace had been a lovely model turned photographer whose death was a tragedy. Val had approached a new relationship slowly, and with trepidation. "It's wonderful, Val, and Bryn would be happy for you."

Val smiled. "I agree. Janet has met her and they got on really well." Val stayed close to Bryn's mother, Janet. "Now are you going to tell me what you avoided talking about the other night?"

Nora busied herself setting up a set of plastic stacking blocks on the tray of Sean's buggy. How much to tell Val? They'd never had secrets from each other. She met her friend's searching gaze, and directed a nod to Sean.

"You won't believe what I found in that bag I carry around."

"Dirty nappy?"

"Silver button, probably a bug."

Val frowned. "To quote Gershwin, 'How long has this been going on?'"

"All summer? Unknown at this point. Thought it might be my overactive imagination but then I found that. Made a mistake and told Declan yesterday."

"Confiding in your detective boyfriend isn't a mistake, even if you are totally bonkers, as my old Army uncle used to say."

"Yes, but the first thing he did was call Simon. Turns out Callie thought someone followed her when she had Sean out in his buggy."

"Bu-bu-bu." Sean made his presence known, clapping two blocks against each other, then shoving the end of the smaller into his mouth to furiously bite down on it.

"Thank you for that contribution." Val leaned over to tickle Sean's neck and was rewarded with a string of dribble. "And for that, too." She wiped her hand and the baby's chin with a napkin. "Callie's a bit taller, but looks a lot like you from the back."

Nora nodded. "Simon pointed out the same thing. It was a relief to be in Brighton yesterday and I felt we were alone. But I can't shake the feeling—"

"You think he might be here? Is it a man?"

"I don't know, but I think so. That's if he really exists, and isn't a figment of my imagination."

"That button thing isn't your imagination."

Nora looked down. "I know."

Val grimaced. "Anyone you can think of who would do this?"

Nora shook her head. "No. He's a tall male. Switches baseball caps. I haven't gotten a decent look. He'll disappear into a shop, never close by, and I can't just leave Sean to run and investigate. I surely don't want to get close to him when Sean's with me, anyway."

"Absolutely not." Val covered Nora's hand with her own. "Look, you've told Declan. Let him work his wonders and do his job. You keep your eyes open for details that can help him, all right? Maybe it will be a huge misunderstanding, and it's not a listening device. This man could be a huge fan of your books, if he even exists." Val smoothed her frown. "Let's order. Share high tea and the chicken sandwiches?"

While Val ordered, Nora thought back to her conversation with Daisy. Grant Alan, who wore baseball caps to protect a bald spot he didn't have. Something about the name was familiar. Then it dawned on her: Golden Age crime writer Josephine Tey's detective was Alan Grant.

A coincidence of her overactive imagination? Or a savvy stalker? Either way, she hadn't imagined the tracker device. Part of her wished she'd never found it. Her stomach clenched in anxiety. She still couldn't fathom what there was about her that would make her of interest to a stalker.

Nora placed a few apple slices she'd brought on the tray of Sean's buggy. He grabbed one and chewed. She fastened a bib around his neck and distracted her thoughts by describing the previous night and their lack of sleep. "Just in time for his visit to Muriel and Harry tomorrow."

Val waved her fears away. "They're besotted with my godson. And Declan is, too, you know. People understand babies aren't easy. But how are things progressing with Declan? Have you settled on him living with you? Any thoughts of putting a ring on that finger?"

Nora flashed back to the pretty Edwardian ring in Brighton yesterday. "I'd planned to have a talk about our future last night, but it never happened."

"It will, Yankee. You're perfect for each other and he's crazy about you."

"I hope so." Nora hoped her friend was right about so many things: Declan, the Pembrokes, and most of all, her stalker. "Just—am I ready to be married? Remember that time I sat in the Italian restaurant on my birthday for two hours waiting for Paul, and he showed up as I left? He would get caught up in work, and no one else mattered. I always felt second place to his work. I really had to ask myself if I wanted to marry and raise children with a man who would be so distant I'd be basically a single mom. Yet now I really am." She bit her lip. "And here I am in love with a blasted detective who works all kinds of crazy hours. Am I repeating history?"

"First of all, these two men are worlds apart." Val counted off on her fingers. "Paul was self-absorbed, nothing like Declan. All right, he was brainy, but so is Declan, in a different way. Secondly, I've seen the way Declan looks at you, Nora. He's smitten. And third, Declan's out solving crimes, and his busy cases are balanced with time off. It won't be all work and no time for you and Sean."

Nora saw the truth in Val's words and brightened. "Besides, if I really have a stalker, what better boyfriend to have than a detective in my pocket?"

Feeling reassured, Nora caught up on news the two friends hadn't talked about when they were at Val's.

"Claire's settled in at Exeter. She's made friends already and said she loves the school and the town." Claire Scott was Roger's daughter. Nora's stepsister was at Oxford, working on a Masters in English Literature.

"She stopped in to see me at the co-op earlier this week, brought a lovely young woman with her, a fellow student. She also bought a waistcoat of mine." Val beamed. She had started and managed the Artists Cooperative in Oxford, which showcased the wares of local potters, painters, quilters, jewelry-makers and other artisans. "She's another one who'll be happy to have you here in town."

"A bit of Connecticut for her," Nora agreed, and thanked the waiter who delivered their food on a triple-tiered silver stand, along with individual pots of tea. She was suddenly very hungry. "This looks great." She pointed to the triangular-cut sandwiches with their crusts off on the first level. The second tier held fresh scones, and on top were an assortment of small pastries and tarts.

"I wish I didn't have to cover the co-op or I'd drive down with you tomorrow to see Port Enys. Take photos, please." Val helped herself to a sandwich. "Are you excited or nervous about seeing Sean's pile?"

"A bit of both," Nora admitted. "I still have mixed feelings about Paul and the Pembrokes. It feels shoddy to be comfortable with his money when we were breaking up when he died." She bit into one of the sandwiches. "Delicious; love this version of chicken salad." She forced her stomach to relax as she ate.

Val took another. "It's the curry powder mixed in. Coronation Chicken was originally made for the Queen's coronation meal." She chewed and added, "But you never asked Paul to put you in his will. That was his idea."

"It's still weird at times." Nora realized Sean had paused in playing to watch the food being ferried to her mouth. She broke off a corner of bread for him. He busied himself examining it with great curiosity before he put a piece in his mouth. His immense curiosity and joy in small things hit her, and suddenly all thoughts of being tired left her. "I just hope the Pembrokes have wisdom when it comes to babies."

Val helped herself to a scone, split it, lathered on raspberry jam, adding a dollop of thick cream on top. "But speaking of money, here's something else interesting that's happened at the co-op."

"How do you think the Queen takes her scone?" Nora split one. "You do it the Cornish way I do, jam then cream. I never understood the controversy with Devon and their insistence of putting cream and then jam on top."

"Yankee, don't avoid the topic."

Nora added cream on top of her jam. "What?" She maintained eye contact with Val and an air of supreme innocence.

"*Someone* has paid outright for us to have a long-term lease on the co-operative building. You wouldn't know anything about that, would you?" Val arched her eyebrows and those golden eyes bored into Nora's.

"I have no idea what you're talking about. Jam tart?"

CHAPTER EIGHT

Oxford

3:05 PM

Three miles east of the center of Oxford in Headington, Declan and his sergeant sat at one end of a long, sleek table in the cool conference room of the John Radcliffe Hospital, Oxfordshire's main accident and emergency teaching hospital. Declan wondered if the same antiseptic smell of hospitals ran throughout the world, a fake flowery scent that was designed to cover up the astringent hit of antibacterial cleansers.

He and Watkins had been to the Ashmolean Museum earlier and secured the dead woman's workspace. On their way there, Watkins told Declan he'd dropped off Nora's silver button to their IT department to be further researched on Monday, but it looked at first glance like a standard listening bug.

At the museum, they'd left a message with the dead woman's supervisor after he sent her co-workers home, and promised to return after this meeting with Dr. Ivor Conlon, the head of the Infectious Disease Department of Churchill Hospital. The doctor's call that morning and his initial report had formed the basis for Watkins' decision to ask Declan to come to work on his day off.

After a morning spent dealing with a wing shutdown and all of its patients being transferred out, the specialist with the slight build and receding hairline told them he was ready to answer their questions about the death the previous night of the young female art restorer. Declan nodded to Watkins to start the questioning.

"Miss Jevons was transported by ambulance from the Ashmolean directly here after she collapsed at work?" Watkins consulted his notes. "She was admitted from your Accident and Emergency Department in the early evening, but her condition continued to deteriorate."

"She refused to allow anyone from work to accompany her, but her supervisor phoned in to alert us she was on her way. He said she'd been unwell for several days, with body aches and a fever she'd treated with over-the-counter medicine. Miss Jevons recently had a severe case of flu with a bronchial infection, and had only returned to work a few days earlier. On examination she had pustules inside her mouth and on her hands. One of my brighter registrars put her symptoms together and called me in to consult. We immediately isolated her." Conlon brushed back his missing hair in an absent-minded familiar gesture. "I agreed with his diagnosis of smallpox."

Hearing the specialist pronounce the dreaded disease had a chilling effect on Declan. He shifted in his seat, aware his trousers stuck to the chair with nervous sweat, despite the chilly air in the room.

Dark circles under the doctor's eyes spoke to the long night he'd had, and even longer day. "By rights Miss Jevons would have been transferred to Churchill, but before we could stabilize her, she suffered cardiac arrest and died around 2 AM this morning. I've already called in Public Health England."

Declan took up the thread. The idea of an outbreak of smallpox, a disease he'd thought wiped out, was as puzzling as it was upsetting. "Watkins said you had any staff who worked on the woman isolated immediately. I understand from her supervisor that her colleagues at work were sent home, and will be seen by a health care provider today."

The specialist nodded. "They'll be on house quarantine and have their temperatures taken regularly. The museum director indicated this group is small, and have limited contact with outsiders at work." Worry creased the doctor's brow. "You have to realize the last known case of smallpox in the US happened in 1949 and endemically in Somalia in 1977. Several labs kept the virus on hand after that for vaccine testing. But here in the UK, Birmingham's lab had a containment breach of sample strains with two cases in the late '70s. After that, our stockpiles were all sent to the Centers for Disease Control in Atlanta. You'll be hearing about the CDC a lot in the next few days, I imagine. The only other stockpile is in Russia."

"What about a vaccine for it?" Declan asked.

"We can vaccinate the workers here and at the museum if we decide to use it within three days of exposure. I've consulted with the CDC on that, and believe their recommendation will be that anyone in direct contact with this patient, such as the staff who treated her before she was on isolation, be vaccinated. That being said, 90 percent of normal smallpox virus lives outside its host for only about 24 hours."

Declan didn't miss the undercurrent of the doctor's words. "You said 'normal,' as if this isn't?"

Dr. Conlon took a swallow from the water bottle in front of him. "Let me give you a crash course in smallpox. The virus is spread by direct contact, face-to-face, or from contact with soiled bedding or clothing before the virus dies. After exposure, there's usually an incubation period of anywhere from seven to 14 days, followed by a phase when the initial symptoms appear over the next two to four days. Then the high fever, malaise and body aches appear, followed by an early rash and eventually the pustules that we saw on Miss Jevons."

Declan became aware he and Watkins were both leaning forward in their seats. "But in this case?"

"All her symptoms were exacerbated—sped up—significantly. We're having her cultures analyzed to compare to the stockpile. This could be a superbug—a genetically modified strain."

"A superbug!" Watkins voiced Declan's thoughts. "The press will go crazy, not to think of the implications for the country if there's an epidemic."

"We're looking at mass hysteria if it spreads to other countries," Declan said.

"Let's not get ahead of ourselves, gentlemen." Dr. Conlon screwed the top back on his water bottle. "Most residents have had vaccinations when young, although there are some younger people whose parents are against inoculations of any kind, and they'd be at first risk. But even if you were an adult vaccinated as a child, the older you are, the less effective that resistance becomes. In this case, if we're dealing with a super-mutated bug, a previous vaccination may turn out to be worthless. We just don't know what we're dealing with yet."

The doctor unscrewed the cap he'd just reseated and took another swig of water. "The health department is already checking Miss Jevons' neighbors and family to see if she'd been in contact with anyone who was ill or recently out of the country. We've checked other hospitals, and there are no other cases or bodies with even a hint of this illness. This woman worked in her own office space, and since she hadn't been feeling well, avoided close contact with her co-workers this week, eating at her desk. That act of courtesy on her part may be our saving grace."

"A small kindness that has huge implications," Declan conceded. "But how would this happen, even an isolated case like this? How could she contract it?" Declan tried to wrap his mind around the idea of an eradicated disease rearing its potentially fatal head.

"I have no idea," Conlon admitted. "Smallpox can't just appear in a vacuum. If Miss Jevons had received this from someone else, they would be just as ill, or dead, and we haven't identified anyone—yet. It would be almost impossible to hide a death if we are talking about someone in Miss Jevons' circle. There has to be a chain of infection, or something used as a fomite."

At Declan's puzzled expression, the doctor elaborated. "A fomite is an object, say a utensil or a towel, that harbors the disease agent, and becomes the vehicle capable of transmitting it before it dies. We need to urgently identify the fomite that carried the virus which infected Miss Jevons." He shook his head. "My team will be examining her culture sample to see if there's a genetically engineered mutation. Finding the locus, this fomite, should be the priority of your team, in conjunction with the Health Department. A superbug would be deliberately mutated to live longer outside the body. We must find the origin and isolate it from anyone else."

Watkins said what was on everyone's mind. "This is a bloody nightmare."

3:43 PM

Val thought her stomach would burst from the last raspberry tart she hadn't been able to resist. She noticed that Nora had overlooked admitting she was behind the co-op's new lease, but that was the only explanation. Val would continue to be the best kind of friend she could to Nora, and accept her largesse, while acknowledging her inheritance still made Nora uncomfortable.

She changed Sean under Nora's watchful eye, folding down the back of the buggy to lay him flat, and followed that with spooning a pot of yogurt into his bird-like mouth. His bib was a mess of apple, scone, and yogurt, yet she reveled in the contact with the toddler. "Never thought I'd get the hang of changing a nappy or feeding a baby."

"You're a natural." Nora leaned back with a contented sigh. "That was wonderful."

Val scraped up the last spoonful from the pot and wiped Sean's mouth, then took off his bib, folded it in half, and stuck it in the plastic bag Nora handed her. "Good as new."

She lifted the boy out and dandled him on her knee. "What's your mum mean, calling you a fractious mess? You look pretty happy to me. Must be my brilliant influence."

Before Nora could snap back a retort, her mobile rang. She pulled it from her pocket, and a wide smile spread over her face when she saw the caller. Val knew it must be Declan.

"Hello. Sean and I have just had a lovely tea with Val. How's your day going?"

Val watched Nora's face cloud over. Couldn't be good news.

"Of course. I understand—can't be helped. Talk later then." Nora stuffed her phone back in her pocket. "Declan's new case will keep him out late. We're not to wait up for him." She frowned. "I've never heard him sound so distracted."

"Murder will do that for you. It is a murder?"

"It's a suspicious death, for now."

"Sorry, Yankee. You know how he is when he's involved in a case—even I know that." Despite once being the object of Declan's investigation, Val had made her peace with the detective, and the two respected their places in Nora's life. "We just had this discussion, remember? Don't make the mistake of thinking he's avoiding you because Sean is teething. Give him more credit than that."

"I know. It's just after last night, and with me leaving in the morning for a week—" She sighed. "Missed connections. This is what life's like with a policeman."

"And a baby," Val said. "More reason to move in together; more to look forward to when you get back. You're in it for the long haul, after all."

Sean started squirming and his drooling increased. "Might be time for some of those granules you bought." Val checked her mobile while Nora ripped open a sachet and tipped the contents into the baby's mouth. "He looks surprised at the taste but didn't spit them out, so that's good. Time for us to get a move on to see this house I've scouted out for you. We have to meet the estate agent, Lucy. She's one of my best customers."

"Not the one who had you embroider a coat for her Yorkie?"

"The very same."

3:50 PM

Declan and Watkins parked and made their way in subdued quiet to the office of Norman Marks, the Head of Conservation for the Ashmolean Museum. They delivered their update on Emma Jevons' death from a probable virulent strain of smallpox while standing just inside his office door. The stocky director stood behind his desk.

Declan saw the color drain from the man's face. He seemed to shrink even smaller as their news sunk in.

Marks finally cleared his throat, and invited Declan and Watkins to take seats. "I promise I haven't touched those chairs in ages, nor has Emma—had Emma."

The three men sat. Marks templed his fingers. "This is unbelievable. Emma was a valued employee as well as a talented art restorer. She was cleaning a painting on loan from the Pushkin Museum, something of an unusual situation. They would normally have the work done by their own conservator." He shook his head in disbelief. "Her death is a difficult blow. Has her father been notified?"

Watkins nodded. "He was informed last evening by the local force of her death. We'll visit him and explain the circumstances when we have more lab tests back."

"I wish you could explain them to me. I've stayed in here since you called this morning as asked, but when you said a communicable disease, I had no idea you were talking smallpox—how can that be?"

"We're hoping to find people Miss Jevons had been near and are tracing her movements the past few days for the source. We're working in conjunction with the Health Department, and their infectious disease team is examining her office and workspace now. They'll take care not to damage anything as they take sample cultures in different areas," Declan said. "They've devised a grid overlay system to take samples from each square to see if they can zero in on the source. A similar team has been sent to her flat."

"Obviously this is a huge priority," Watkins said. "We'll get the results to you as soon as we have them."

Marks sighed. "That poor young woman. She wouldn't let me take her when she collapsed, so we called the ambulance. I could see she was gravely ill, but I believed her when she said her flu must have returned. Now I'm sorry I didn't insist. She was all alone there—she must have been terrified."

"You wouldn't have been able to help her, and she ended up protecting you." Declan pulled out his notebook. "Have you heard from her colleagues?"

"After you called this morning I sent them all home without out a clear explanation, other than that Emma had died from a communicable disease. They're waiting for me to update them.

Several called in for news, and I'm afraid I blamed you for not knowing more at that point." The ghost of a smile flicked across the man's strained face.

"Her colleagues are in different departments under Conservation?" Declan asked.

"Besides Emma in Paintings, we have three conservators in Objects, two in Paper, and one each in Textiles and Projects. I have an assistant Deputy Head, too."

"So 10 people, including Miss Jevons, in your department." Watkins jotted notes.

"Yes. I told the A&E staff last night that Emma thought she had a virus, and kept from close contact with any of her usual friends here." Marks tapped his fingers on the desktop. "What will happen to them—to all of us, medically speaking?"

Declan answered. "Dr. Conlon of the Churchill is having each worker interviewed and examined in their homes, along with a baseline temperature. They'll explain the supervised surveillance you'll have to all stay under for the next 10 days. The health care consultant will ask them not to kiss or hug any family member, and to sleep in a different room from spouses. They should use separate plates and utensils, or paper to be discarded separately in red bags for now."

"You mean we're all under house arrest." The department head grimaced. "I suppose that includes me."

"This wing of the museum will be closed until we know more," Watkins said. "At least it's not a public area."

"You'd best pack your briefcase and prepare to work from home." Declan stood. "As soon as I have any progress or results, I'll call you." He added the man's contact details to his mobile while Watkins noted them in his notebook. "It might be late tonight before I have any reports."

"I'm sure I'll be awake. Call at any hour." Marks stood as

well, put out his hand, then jerked it back. "You'll understand if I don't shake hands just now."

CHAPTER NINE

Oxford

3:58 PM

"Where are we headed?" Nora pushed Sean's buggy as she followed Val past St. Giles Church, just next to The Old Parsonage. The trio rounded the corner from the Banbury Road to the Woodstock Road. Nora looked behind her for shadowy figures, hating the way her stalker had compromised what should have been an enjoyable outing in a safe place.

A few people gazed at the old headstones in the graveyard as they cut through the church grounds. One woman bent over a lichen-covered headstone, jotting down its specifics.

"Around the corner. Lovely church, isn't it?" Val asked. "Most of it's from the 12th and 13th centuries."

"Charming, but why the history lesson?"

"I really researched this one for you. I want you to like it." Val turned right and led them up Woodstock Road. "Next year Sean will be old enough to enjoy the lights and rides of the St. Giles Fair right on this corner, when the road is closed for two days."

Val stopped at a driveway on the right, next to the church grounds. A tall hedge hid whatever stood behind it. "This way." She turned up the drive and waited for Nora to follow her.

Nora started up the drive, pushing Sean's buggy through the gravel. "This is the house? Where is it?"

"Trust me, Yankee." Val turned back to Nora and walked backwards up the drive. She motioned her friend on with her hands. "Come on."

Nora dutifully followed Val up the drive past the hedge, then slowed as a lush front garden, filled with perennials, came into view. When she saw the house beyond, it took her breath away.

With a thatched roof and three eyebrow windows on the upper floor, the V-shaped cottage was painted a pale peach color that glowed in the afternoon light. It looked terribly British to Nora, like something she would see on the cover of *English Home* magazine. A sign hung from a light pole: *Haven Cottage*.

Val approached the front door at the center of the V where a young woman with glossy blonde hair, wearing a chic business suit, waited for them. "This is my friend, Nora Tierney—" Val was cut off by Lucy's ringing mobile.

"Sorry, I have to take this." Lucy answered the phone as she unlocked the door and motioned them to look inside. "Go ahead," she whispered. "I'll be with you shortly."

Nora unbuckled Sean and took him out of his buggy to join Val. The gothic-arched front door had iron strap work over its aged wood planks, and was topped with a small mullioned window. Beds of roses flanked the doorway, and a vine past its flowering grew up one side of the door and was trained around it.

Val threw the door open with a flourish. "Welcome to Haven Cottage!" She ushered Nora and Sean inside.

The ceiling's exposed timber beams immediately caught Nora's attention. Thick window ledges showed the building's sturdy construction. At the far end of the main area stood a fireplace with a huge mantel. "Perfect for Christmas stockings," Val said.

Light flooded in from tall French doors that stretched across the back wall of the kitchen and dining area. They opened onto a back garden, and the lack of interior walls in these rooms made the area feel much larger than if the rooms had been walled off.

"Someone renovated this nicely," Nora said. "Maybe a fresh coat of paint here and there, but it's basically move-in ready, at least down here."

"Check this out." Val opened a door on the left into a shelf-lined library that overlooked the garden through a large bow window, complete with a window seat. "Your desk could go right in front of that window. Once he's older, you could see Sean play outside while you work."

"I have to admit your excitement is contagious. This modernization was done without losing any of the charm of the cottage." Nora moved back through the spacious front room into the kitchen area, where a large pine Welsh dresser stood near a forest green Aga. The other appliances were modern, and the large soapstone sink, nestled into the head of the V, looked out onto a yard with flower borders on each side. Hedges ran across the back and behind the flowerbeds. "The name suits it well."

"Isn't it gorgeous?" Val enthused. "Let's look upstairs." She pointed out a small loo under the stairs as they passed.

Nora followed Val up stairs set on one side of the drawing room over the library, and found three bedrooms on the first floor with a small study tucked under the eaves at the end of the corridor.

"Good home office for Declan," Val murmured, and led the way to the bedrooms.

"These need a new coat of paint, but that's about it," Nora mused. She could picture a soft blue in one, maybe a pale green in another. The main bathroom had been the most recent project and still held the pungent scent of fresh grout and tile work. The master bedroom was large and had its own modern en-suite bath, newly outfitted in white marble, with a modern soaker tub. Nora liked the pale heathery tone on the walls, a hint of lavender.

"The middle room could be Sean's, and that far bedroom would be a comfortable guest room when my mom and Roger visit."

Except for the massive dresser downstairs, there was no other furniture in the house. Nora mentioned this as Val led the way back downstairs.

"That's half the fun, Nora. You get your lovely possessions out of storage to start, and then we'll have fun finding things to fill in once Declan moves in and you see what you need. We can hit estate sales, and do a bit of refinishing on weekends. It's close to the co-op, too, we'd see each other all the time."

Nora shifted Sean on her hip and thought with longing of her favorite wing-backed reading chair, and the table, trunks, and cartons of books that currently languished in a storage unit outside town. "It certainly is charming," she allowed, wondering what the price tag would be.

Val put her hands on her hips. "That's an understatement if I ever heard one. This place looks so like you." She stood in the kitchen, the outside light making her golden eyes glow. "Here's the best part. You can rent it with an option to buy, nothing lost, but your rent goes toward your down payment if you do decide to buy."

"I admit that's a practical idea." If she settled here and things didn't work out with Declan, it would be easier to leave a rental than to sell a house.

Nora's thought dismayed her. Was she in this relationship to hedge her bets it would fail, or did she believe in a future for her and Declan? She felt like a cautious old lady, especially when Val named a rental figure she could easily afford, and a sale price within what she'd budgeted. Situated where it was, close to Declan's work, near shops, and right in the center of Oxford, it was a very fair asking price.

"Why so reasonable?" she asked. She'd never been a home-owner before. Maybe there was damp to contend with, or mould, or wiring needing to be replaced.

"Lucy said the niece who inherited lives in Scotland and wants a quick sale. She had the bathrooms done, the plumbing and wiring all updated—there's even central air, unheard of here. She's hoping for a quick sale."

That allayed some of Nora's fears. Of course, she could have an inspection. Was she seriously considering this house?

Yes, she was—it was the first one that felt like home to her.

Nora put Sean down while she looked more closely around the kitchen. A door led to a butler's pantry with tall storage cupboards and shelves for dry goods. She helped Sean walk through the French doors into the compact back garden. "Those two trees fronting the hedges could hold a hammock." A scene rose in her imagination. She pictured reading out here on a lazy afternoon, watching Sean play on the grass from the sway of the hammock. There were camellias and lilacs past their flowering, but a few fall roses and straggly blue hydrangeas remained in bloom. Clumps of asters and Michaelmas daises added late color. The entire space felt private and secure. Nora felt the threat of the shadowy figure receding.

She could picture herself living here with Sean and Declan in this leafy oasis. It felt right.

"Can't you see yourself bringing out a table? We could have dinners outside, and you could work out here in nice weather?" Val urged.

Nora laughed. "Editing for typos."

"TY-PO!" Sean yelled, tuned in to their conversation. He struggled to be let down.

"You little mimic." Nora hugged him and sat him on the grass.

Suddenly through a gap in the hedge, a beagle puppy bounded toward them.

"Typo!" Sean screeched. The little dog made a beeline for him, followed quickly by the crashing sounds of a man trying to push through the hedge in pursuit.

"Come back here!" the man shouted. He ran into the yard and slid to a stop when he saw the two women.

"Typo!" Sean bellowed, reaching his arms out. The dog leapt at the baby and licked his face, making the child laugh with delight.

Nora grabbed the puppy's collar and separated dog from child. "Sit," she said with authority, and scooped the puppy's rear to match the action to her command. The puppy sat, wagging its tail expectantly. Sean crowed with delight, his pudgy fingers reaching for the little dog.

"I'm so sorry," the man panted as he reached them.

"It's fine," Nora assured him. Taking Sean's hand, she showed him how to stroke the dog's silky pelt. "Don't grab," she instructed, making him use a flat, open hand. The puppy preened and sat patiently for his petting.

"You definitely have a way with dogs. All he wants is a bit of attention, sorely lacking at our house at the moment." He stuck out a bony hand. "Neil Welch."

Nora introduced herself and Val to the lanky, ginger-haired man. "And this is Sean."

"Who, it would seem, has named this rascal." Neil pointed to the dog, which had rolled on its back to present his soft underbelly for petting.

Sean stroked the puppy's belly under Nora's watchful eye. "Typo," he crooned.

"He's in the stage where he echoes bits of what he hears," Nora said.

"It's a great name, actually, and he needs one. My wife will love it. I'm something of a writer," Neil explained.

Val laughed. "You haven't decided yet?"

Neil blushed. "I've been trying to write a novel for the past year, but little things like a toddler, a busy wife, and now this puppy get in the way."

"Nora's a writer, too." Val turned to her friend. "See, I told you this was the perfect house. A colleague right next door."

"My wife Sally's the vicar at St. Giles," Neil said. "I stay at home with our son, Sam, who's napping." He checked his watch. "I'm supposed to be writing, but somehow life more frequently gets in the way."

"And this is your pup?" Nora shaded her eyes and looked up at Neil. She didn't think she'd ever met someone whose hair was quite that shade of carrot orange. It almost looked artificial but his skin was heavily freckled to match, and the hair on his arms was the same color.

"No, we have an older shepherd, Angus, but my wife's a rescuer and she's fostering Typo until we find him a home." He brightened. "I don't suppose if you're going to live here you'd be interested in adopting him?"

Val touched Nora's arm. "Look—"

Typo's antics had tired him and he slept in the sun. Sean had laid his head on the puppy's side, his eyes fluttering as he dozed.

"Instant babysitter," Val whispered.

❖

4:30 PM

The man who today was Tom Barnaby had been parked for hours outside Declan Barnes' flat when Nora Tierney finally appeared after noon. He'd had time to file his updated report but was bored. His rented car was turning into a rubbish dump, its back seat littered with magazines, empty coffee and teacups, and takeaway containers that were beginning to smell like a compost heap.

He'd have to have it valeted before returning it or lose his deposit. It wasn't the money that mattered. It was the scrutiny it would attract, and make him stand out if he returned a stinking car. One more job to add to his list. This was getting tiresome.

With Oxford parking such an issue, he'd decided to leave the car, and followed Nora on foot as she pushed her son in his buggy. She made a beeline for the Boots Chemist near The Covered Market. A few minutes later she continued up the road until she reached The Old Parsonage.

It had been a close shave when she looked back at the entry gate. Thank goodness for the anonymity of tourists. He'd quickly merged into a large group being herded toward The Oxford University Press on Walton Street. Tom fancied he could feel Nora's eyes boring into his back. At the next corner when he hazarded a look back, she'd disappeared inside the grounds.

He'd retraced his steps, and as he passed the open gate, he risked a glance inside the gate, and there she was, her back to him, sitting at one of the outside tables with the Rogan woman. For a moment he hesitated by the stone wall, almost convinced if he went into the grounds and took a table, she wouldn't notice him.

Something told him not to chance it, and he continued to the corner to wait in the grounds of St. Giles Church. She should pass that way on her way back to the detective's flat. He wandered amongst the ancient headstones, not the only person out on this fine day to do so. Some lichen-crusted stones leaned with age, looking ready to topple; others were set into the ground. One young woman had a piece of tracing paper, and was using a pencil rubbing to try to get the intricate carving to come through. At one point he sat on a bench with his face turned toward the sun, a casual visitor at rest. Tom kept his eyes peeled through his lashes to the street where Nora Tierney would pass.

Instead, she'd surprised him yet again by turning into the graveyard with Rogan and walking through it. He pretended absorption in a headstone, and when he looked up, he could see her back disappearing up the Woodstock Road. A few steps took him to the edge of the graveyard, where an older tomb-stone supposedly caught his attention. With his head down, his eyes darted to the right in time to see Nora turn up an almost-hidden drive.

That did it for him. With Rogan in attendance, knowing Nora's plan was to drive tomorrow to Cornwall, he loped back to retrieve his car, and headed back to his bed and breakfast. Next door there was a rubbish bin at the kerb, and he added the contents of his back seat before heading inside. A solid meal awaited him, and then an early night with his book before checking out. Tomorrow was a long journey to Cornwall, and with the loss of his audio bug, he wanted to be in place early to follow Nora Tierney.

4:33 PM

Nora stood in the garden at Haven Cottage and watched Neil Welch, Typo slung over his shoulder and duly named, hurry down the drive to check on his sleeping son next door. "He seemed nice. At least he didn't have to go through the hedges again."

"Yankee, you have to get that puppy for Sean. Did you see how they bonded?" Val urged. "You know what they say about a boy and his dog."

"Moving to a new house and training a puppy at the same time might be a big bite right now."

"Don't be silly. You have this lovely space. You can always fence in the back if you want to. Typo will keep Sean distracted."

Nora laughed at Val's infectious enthusiasm. "You mean keep me sidetracked from what I should be—"

"There you are!"

Both women turned as Lucy appeared around the corner of the house from the drive as fast as her high heels would allow, her shiny blonde bob swinging with her haste. Her shoes sank into the lawn, abruptly stopping her progress. She kicked them off, and swooped down to retrieve them, dangling the slingbacks from one hand as she made her way over to them.

"Lucy!" Val said. "We've toured and even met the neighbors." She introduced Nora to the estate agent.

"Pleased to meet you properly." Lucy shook Nora's hand. "But I'm rattled because I had an urgent message to call back the man who looked at this house last week. He dithered over the price but it seems he wants to make an offer to rent. I told him I had someone else interested, and would have to call him back. If you really want it, Nora, I always carry a rental contract with me, and I'll tell him he's too late. I know you want her near you, Val."

Val's eye blazed. "What do you think, Yankee? Is he too late?"

Nora looked at the two women. She hadn't expected to be rushed into making a decision about this house. "Give me a minute." She walked deeper into the garden in the cool shadow of the hedge where she'd pictured a hammock.

"This is my godson." Val stood talking quietly with Lucy while Sean slept on.

Nora looked back at the house. The soft peach color pleased her. She already knew the rooms inside were more than adequate, and the site was perfectly placed in Oxford for her needs.

Could she really do this? Could she make up her mind to rent a house she'd just seen, and expect that Declan would move in with her sight unseen, all on the basis of a half-hour visit?

She looked at Sean napping on the grass, and thought of what her father would advise if he were around. He'd tell her to list the pros and cons. All right, the rent was affordable. There was the playmate next door, and another writer for her to bring a sense of community nearby. Val was close, Declan could walk to work on a sunny day, and she could walk to shops. It checked all her boxes, and she could see them living here. She thought another moment. What was the con?

There was no con. *Be spontaneous.*

She walked back to Lucy. "Tell him he's too late. The house is rented."

CHAPTER TEN

Declan rubbed eyes that felt grainy from lack of sleep. That was life with a child, and with this case, he wouldn't be getting rest any time soon.

Watkins drove them toward a Somerville neighborhood for their last interview of the day with one of Emma Jevons' colleagues. When Declan's mobile rang, he answered Ian Travers' call. He had known the Cumbrian detective who had married Simon Ramsey's sister, Kate, would call once Simon mentioned Nora felt she had a stalker.

"Hi, Ian. Simon told you about Nora's feeling?"

"That's why I'm calling. I wanted you to know we've talked with Agnes and all of the day staff. No one noticed anyone hanging around the lodge, but we're all on high alert now. Any description?"

Declan told Ian of Nora's sensation of a tall male who favored baseball caps.

"The entire thing is peculiar, Declan. Why would Nora be followed, particularly by someone who's a pro?"

"I don't know, and that's worrying, but I'm trying to keep it light for Nora's sake. I keep hoping he's a figment of her imagination or it's a gross misunderstanding, but until we know more I'm letting everyone know to keep an eye out."

"Understood. We'll keep an eye on things here, and definitely on her when she comes back next week."

He rang off. Declan felt that the more people keeping their eyes on Nora, the better. "Bloody odd, Watkins."

"You're telling me. Almost as odd as having to deal with a potential smallpox outbreak."

"McAfee did a decent job setting up the incident room." Declan thought of the young detective constable, McAfee, whom he and Watkins had been keeping an eye on.

"Not much on our board pinned up yet—Emma Jevons' photo and a listing of numbers from the Health Department of her colleagues."

"We're running out of where to look next for the fomite locus." The idea of a mutated smallpox virus made all of their thoughts immediately stray to bioterrorism, which Conlon's theory seemed to support. Declan shuddered to contemplate it.

"I never thought we'd have a case that used words like bioterror and fomite."

"All we can hope, Watkins, is that some small-town chemist somehow obtained a sample of the virus, and then somehow figured out how to mutate it, and then somehow Emma came into contact with it—"

"Lots of 'somehow's' in that theory, guv."

Declan's chief had notified his own higher-ups along the chain of command, who were talking with Public Health England and other government officials on a confidential basis, hoping to prevent a public frenzy. "The international level of concern is far above either of our pay grades, Watkins, yet we're still responsible at the local level for working out who's accountable for the death of Emma Jevons."

"You mean her murder, guv." Watkins turned onto the correct block. "Her father called in, refused the family liaison officer. Said his neighbor was there, and she was all the company he needed or wanted." He searched for a parking spot near the house they wanted. "Poor chap. Victim was his only child; mum died of cancer when Emma was a teenager. He sounded stunned."

Declan nodded. "That was some surreal scene at the museum, too." He'd watched the suited and hooded forensic investigators

take samples from Emma's workroom, including from her laptop. Emma Jevons might not have been known in the art world
before her death, but her name would be on everyone's tongue
before the end of the week.

Watkins grunted as a car by the kerb put on its blinker. "Move
your blooming arse—" He honked and motioned to the Audi
vacating the space he wanted.

"Whoa!" Declan's voice bounced off the interior of the CID
car. His own restored MGB stood parked in the station car
park. It had felt insensitive to arrive at the houses of Emma's
colleagues for their interviews today in his vintage vehicle, especially with the seriousness of smallpox hanging over everyone.

The address they sought was near the building where Val
Rogan lived, the same house split into flats where Nora had
rented when Declan first met her, newly pregnant, defensive for
her friend, and stubbornly attractive.

He'd hated to call her earlier and cancel their evening plans,
but it soon became evident he wouldn't be able to leave for home
at any reasonable hour. She'd been her usual trouper self, understanding when his work interfered with their plans, but he
felt her disappointment down the line. It mirrored his. Tonight
was their last night together before she left in the morning for a
week, and they'd had no time alone for two weeks before due to
his case.

On second thought he probably shouldn't go home tonight at
all, to protect her and Sean, just in case there was the slightest
chance of contaminant from him. He'd never forgive himself if
he brought harm to either one of them due to one of his cases.
Conlon hadn't seemed to worry about them, but it was better to
be safe.

Plus, if he only had a few hours to rest, with Sean's teething
he would get better sleep on the couch in his office for a few
hours, and then head home.

He wanted to believe Dr. Conlon's theory that only those in close contact with Emma could have been contaminated. But if this were an unknown genetically modified superbug, who could say with all certainty it would behave as expected? He shivered, thinking of the havoc that would happen if a mutated virus were let loose on the island that was Great Britain.

No, he would wait until Nora left in the morning before heading home for a few hours' kip and a shower. She'd be off to Port Enys tomorrow, their time together this week over before it even began. He yawned loudly as Watkins switched the engine off, parking accomplished.

Watkins locked the vehicle as Declan came round the car to meet him. "Why are you so tired, and who's the last of the co-workers we're seeing here? By the way, I didn't give her details, but I told Julie we had a big case on, and this might be a good time for her to get in a few days' visit to her mum, do some baby clothes shopping."

"Good thinking. His name is Ed Harker." Declan explained about Sean's teething as they walked to the front door of a red brick semi.

Watkins groaned. His wife was due with their first child in two months. "That's what Julie and I can look forward to?"

Declan slapped him reassuringly on the back and rang the bell. "Just the start, old man. I missed most of Sean's first few months, when he rarely slept at all."

The door was opened by a man in his thirties whose brown hair fell over his brow, skating close to his dark-rimmed glasses. Declan produced his warrant card and introduced himself and Watkins. "Sorry to arrive so late. We just have a few questions, Mr. Harker."

"Sorry I'm not allowed to invite you in. I've had the health officer around. He explained Emma died from smallpox." Ed Harker's thoughts tumbled out in an anxiety-riddled spew. "I still don't understand how she could get that. I've sent my wife and baby to her sister's for a while. Have you any news? Are we in danger? It's just awful about Emma. I'm the Paper guy, by the way."

Watkins took out his notebook. "Your workroom is closest to Miss Jevons?"

"Next door," Harker said. "We each have our own work areas. Emma kept away from all of us this week as she'd had flu recently, then couldn't seem to throw it off. Plus she knows—knew—I have a baby at home. She even ate lunch at her desk." He paused to catch his breath. "I hate talking about her in the past tense. She was a lovely young woman."

"We do understand. We're sorry for the loss of your friend," Watkins said.

"You didn't notice any visitors to her office this week?" Declan asked. "We know she hadn't been out of the country recently."

"No, no visitors at all." Harker brushed the hair off his forehead. It promptly fell back into place. "They'd have to pass my office, and I'd have seen someone or heard her talking. I only heard her talk to her father on the phone once when she took a break."

Watkins made a note. "We're hoping Miss Jevons kept you all from being exposed by her actions."

"How could this happen?" Harker lost his composure. "This is the 21st century, for God's sake. Smallpox has been eradicated. Who would dream of conjuring up a lethal strain? Probably the bloody Russians—but why?"

That, thought Declan, was the crux of the entire question.

9:49 PM

Nora checked on Sean, asleep in his travel cot in Declan's sitting room, his small fists bunched up on either side of his head, his bunny snuggled next to him. Thanks to Mrs. Tink's recommendation, at the first sign of him fretting, Nora iced his gums and sprinkled the contents of another packet in his mouth. He gave her a look of surprise as the chamomile granules melted, and half an hour later dozed off.

She doubted they would last all night, but while he slept, she headed back to the bedroom to sort their luggage, and finish packing her suitcase with clean clothes. Mrs. Tink had emptied the dryer, and left everything neatly folded on Declan's bed. Next time she saw the woman she would have to tell her that in two weeks she'd be moving to Oxford.

She still had trouble believing she'd handed Lucy a deposit check. All evening as she fed Sean and played with him, it had been on her mind. She resolved to get a paint sample book when in Bath and make some decisions on the colors for the walls that needed freshening. She felt very adult, making decisions so swiftly, and with such certainty. It was only now that she was alone she was second-guessing herself.

She closed her larger case after laying out what she and Sean would wear tomorrow. Her mobile ringtone startled her. She knew when Adele started singing it was Declan.

"I'm afraid I won't get home tonight at all. Just wanted to say goodnight. Sorry to miss seeing you off in the morning." He hesitated. "There's an unusual component to this case I can't discuss over the phone."

Nora hoped she kept the acute disappointment from her voice. "Duty calls. I have no doubt you'll get to the bottom of it. I will miss that goodbye kiss, though, and your warm body next to me tonight."

"Thanks for understanding. I'll call tomorrow when I can. Travel safely." Declan sounded distracted. "Need to go."

That didn't go quite as planned, Nora thought as she packed up Sean's changing bag. She didn't have time to explain she worried constantly that her stalker had followed her to Oxford, nor about the house she'd found. Once she'd arrived home, she started to wonder how he would react when she told him she'd rented a house he hadn't even seen.

Not my fault he wasn't there, she argued with her conscience. She remembered the summer weeks she'd dragged him around to look at houses. He would have taken the first one just to have that decision crossed off their list, so perhaps his first feeling would be one of relief. She could always tell herself that.

Nora made certain she put the second box of Nelson's granules in Sean's bag and the open box in her carry sack. She crossed things off the list she had made. Clothing all set. Toys and snacks readied for the car ride. Suitcases packed, one awaiting her toiletry bag.

She left her list on the nightstand and plugged her mobile in to charge. Her thoughts turned to seeing Harvey and Muriel and Port Enys, the place where Paul had grown up. How would she react upon seeing it? How would they handle Sean? So many unknowns, but at least she'd found a place to live. She tried to feel good about that.

Knowing she had a long drive ahead of her tomorrow, Nora crawled into Declan's bed, alone in the darkened room. She closed her eyes to drift off, inhaling Declan's woody scent from his pillow. She pictured her storage unit and where she would put the items it held in Haven Cottage.

In the sitting room, Sean woke and started to cry.

9:51 PM

Viktor Garanin barked orders into his mobile. He could not believe the stupidity of these people he'd thought were experts, geniuses even. If he could reach down the line he'd strangle the underling he pictured cowering on the other end so many miles away. You could use money to make things happen, even to have people do unspeakable things you asked of them, but you couldn't guarantee they would have the brain cells of a newt.

This plan had taken him years to put into effect, with large handouts to make it happen—not that money was an issue. He knew that his was a master plan of thoroughness unheard of in history, cultivating first the scientist, then the museum security operative. He simply refused to believe all his work and coordination would be for nothing.

"How could that happen?" he shouted to his museum contact in Russia. "Not one, but two sent out from the museum? They were NOT to be released before I'd given the order that everything was in place here. You fools—you idiots! The release was premature. The entire scheme will be ruined!" Suddenly aware he yelled out of control, Viktor reined in his anger and lowered his voice. "The first one did not go as planned at all. Exactly where was the second one sent?"

He listened and scribbled on a notepad the Old Bank Hotel thoughtfully provided. "How far is that from Oxford? By train, you idiot! Ninety minutes, good. I will check out of here tomorrow and head to Bath and this Holburne Museum. Book me a place there. The best place but not the most expensive room. Text all the details to this number."

He took a deep breath. "We must not allow this kind of thing to happen again, you understand? Years of planning are at stake. We must rectify the situation, or heads will roll." His voice took on a harder quality. Pure steel poured down the line, thick and menacing. "I do not say this lightly."

Viktor disconnected and threw the phone on the bed. He poured himself a large vodka and took it over to the window seat that looked out over High Street. Across the road stood All Soul's College. Behind its ancient buildings, he could see the spire of the Radcliffe Camera lit at night, the top of its rounded dome visible. There was no denying Oxford, in its way a charming city steeped in history, was a jewel in the crown of this kingdom.

But it had become Viktor's deeply held personal mission to overturn that history, to see Russia re-emerge supreme, with himself a key player. When the Soviet Union fell, he'd been at university. Everything changed. His father's power had rapidly declined, and soon after, his health, although he'd been canny with his money, and there was plenty for Viktor when his father died. Years later when he'd left the museum and landed in the Belgian lab's security, he kept his eyes and ears open, watching and listening, and made extensive notes on projects in progress. He'd cultivated connections, then maintained them for years as he formulated his plan. He *needed* England to fall as much as he needed air to breathe. It was the legacy his father had left after his British mother had taken the easy way out. In his mind, his father's fall from grace was connected to Russia's, and the fact that his mother had abandoned them all made England his focus.

This mission had become his driving force, and he'd finally figured out the way to make it happen: release a genetically modified smallpox virus that would cause a national epidemic. Reduce the English nation with its warped belief it deserved to be superior over all others to a vast wasteland of weakened, quivering, pocked citizens, mass graves, a ruined economy, and international ridicule. These were the images that filled Viktor's dreams.

It was unthinkable that only *one* person had died, which meant the mutation must not have been strong enough. He would need to retrieve the second painting, and have its mutated virus reworked and strengthened.

He already knew the one scientist who could make that happen, and had spent today researching how to bring the man into the open. After an overheard argument between a particular scientist and his handler, Viktor had ferreted away that information for potential future use. This wasn't a man to be bought, but he could be coerced. That moment had arrived, and his pathway to enhance the mutation would be easier than he could have hoped. Viktor allowed himself a brief hard smile. Knowledge was power, he'd read somewhere.

His research surprised him with delight. Finally something going his way. It was fascinating how easily the Internet supplied information with a few clicks. Soon the one object he needed to make everything fall into place would be in Bath. Perfect for his needs, killing two big birds with one hefty stone. The painting and the scientist would both be within his grasp.

He'd worked too hard and too long, not to mention incurring vast expense, for it to all be lost when he was so close to his triumph. The paintings were the method to get the virus into the country. Then he would have at his disposal the means to spread it.

He had spent considerable time deciding which places would give him the best coverage. Trains and underground stations were high on his list, of course, plus the larger tourist destinations, and several stadiums. In one slightly drunken, heady moment, he'd even added Buckingham Palace to his list.

No, this new plan had to be put into action. It would happen soon enough.

He poured himself another vodka. At this moment it was

within his grasp to be remembered as the man who changed the face of a nation.

Declan bellowed orders into the phone for the forensic team as Watkins drove them toward the Ashmolean Museum.

"Are you sure about this, Dec?" Watkins asked when Declan rang off.

"Not sure at all, but when Ed Harker said bloody Russians, it reminded me Emma was working on a painting on loan from a Russian museum."

"It'll wreck the overtime budget if you're wrong."

"Yes, but it's an idea I can't dismiss. Conlon says time is what matters here." He consulted his contacts and punched in another number. "Mr. Marks, DI Barnes. It's important that I have the forensic team back in Emma Jevon's workroom immediately. How do we get into the Conservator wing at this time of night?" He listened as the man agreed to call security to have the rooms opened.

Watkins smoothly navigated a curve. "He'll do it?"

"He's calling security to override the alarms and let us in." Next, Declan called Dr. Conlon. "Sorry to bother you so late, sir, but I have an important question: could paint be used as the fomite you mentioned to transport the virus?"

Half an hour later, Declan stood with Watkins at the door to Emma Jevons' space, watching two forensic investigators, fully garbed in respirator suits. The specialists threw around words like electron microscope and negative stains as they assembled their equipment for specimen collection, and the containers the samples would be stored in for transport back to the lab. The techs carefully took minute scrapings and swabs from the area of the painting that Emma had been cleaning—the Picasso on loan from the Pushkin Museum in Moscow.

CHAPTER ELEVEN

Cornwall

Sunday, 10th October

11:33 AM

Nora pulled onto the verge on the B3249 and stopped the Volvo before she would turn into the drive for Port Enys, also the entrance for the Tideford Cricket Ground, according to the sign at the entry. Apparently the Pembrokes allowed a cricket team to use part of the vast grounds. Sean was still napping. She knew better than to disturb a sleeping baby. He'd be cranky if she woke him on her arrival, which she wanted to avoid, and so she delayed to allow him to wake naturally. If she were being honest, she needed a few minutes to herself before the upcoming visit.

All during the more than four-hour drive to southeast Cornwall—through the stop to change Sean's nappy and give the fussy child a break from his car seat; as she sang songs to distract him and played *Yellow Submarine* loudly; as she'd handed him a teething biscuit to soothe his sore gums, and resorted to more Nelson's granules—she'd noted the cars around her, and checked her rearview mirror repeatedly for signs of a car following her. Nothing.

She should have felt relieved.

Instead, when the granules worked and Sean dozed off, Nora worried how she would react when faced with the home that would one day be her son's responsibility. That was assuming he didn't do something between now and then to upset the Pembrokes and merit disinheritance. One thing she had firmly decided: she was determined not to be overwhelmed.

Her resolve to remain casual deserted her at the mere look of the tall iron gates. Neither the stately home nor its outbuildings could be seen from the road. She gathered her thoughts, tapping her fingers on the steering wheel.

When she'd met with Muriel and Harry this summer, their focus had been on their grandson, and they'd dismissed many of her questions about the house.

"Plenty of time for that," Harvey Pembroke had said, watching his wife bounce Sean on her knee. "It's full of local history. We'll show you around when you come down, dear." He explained the house and grounds were open to the public from March through June to help fund the upkeep. There was a tea room, too. "The roof, you know—always a bit leaking somewhere. If you visit after the end of September after cricket season, we'll have the place all to ourselves except for our pup, Juno."

This summer Nora had done research on the former priory, and learned the house and grounds remained a popular rental site for weddings. Each had been used in film shoots and magazine spreads. There was a church on site, although according to Harvey, St. Germans Priory church was on its own trust now.

The Port Enys website could do with an update, Nora decided, for the pictures of the house nestled in stands of trees were shot from an aerial view, and didn't give a clear perspective of the house. She couldn't judge its size other than to note it wasn't too many storeys tall, maybe three, and there was only one small turret she confirmed on Google Earth. Small mercies.

The website described a thatched-roof boathouse; there was a train line with a Romanesque viaduct designed by Brunel. The extensive gardens contained several summerhouses, fountains, and even a maze. The highlight of the house was its Round Room, whose walls contained a hand-painted mural that was not to be missed. A conservatory annex let in natural light, and had a door that still retained bits of its original 18th century glass.

She was bringing a teething baby to a house chock full of antiques of the kind usually seen in museums. The only saving grace for this first visit was that Sean wasn't careening around independently—yet. He walked holding on to things and didn't have his sea legs enough to take off on his own.

Nora pictured subsequent visits, running down long hallways after a squealing toddler, trying to keep him from touching priceless artifacts and objects. Not for the first time did she question her decision to let the Pembrokes know they had a grandchild. What had she gotten herself into? And how would Declan react in the future when they came here together?

Nora glanced in her rearview mirror. A silver car headed up the road behind her, and she waited to see if it would turn into the drive. The Volkswagen Polo passed her without stopping, and it was only as it sped by that she realized she'd noticed one like it at the rest stop on her way here. She couldn't see the driver clearly, but had a vague impression of a tall man wearing a cap. *Was* she followed to Cornwall?

Her mobile rang. She felt relieved at Declan's call for its distraction.

"Just awake from a nap. Going to shower and head back in. Watkins and I need to drive up to Chipping Norton this afternoon to meet with Emma Jevons' father. He's been interviewed by the locals, but I need to meet with him, too. I wanted to see how your drive is going—you must be near."

The familiarity of his voice grounded her. "Janet Wallace lives there," she reminded him. "We stopped once for a rest, nappy change, and a toddle around after a snack. Now Sean's asleep. I'm actually sitting at the turnoff to the house, letting him doze a bit longer. I thought a car from the rest stop just passed me, but I'm trying to put that down to my imagination."

"Without that bug, let's hope you're in the clear and your

imagination is in overdrive. Not getting cold feet?" His chuckle annoyed her.

"And what if I am? This is a big deal, you know." She stopped herself abruptly from saying more.

"Sorry. Of course it's a big deal. Just trying to help you find your gumption. The Nora Tierney I know has tons of it."

"My gumption's picked up and left today. I'm more like a bowl of jelly."

Declan's voice softened. "Sweetheart, they already love you and Sean. It's only a pile of stone and mortar."

"Sorry I snapped."

"You're tired, and it didn't help I couldn't get home to see you off. I miss you already, both of you."

"Nice try. You're not missing a teething baby and his gear all over the place." It hardly seemed the time to tell him about Haven Cottage. "How's the case?"

"The murder room is up and running, and we have teams out on several areas of investigation. There might be a small break in the case but we won't know more until later."

"Practice that often? You sound like a press release."

Declan sighed. "It's a strange case. I'll talk to you about it when you're back. By then I should have more answers, maybe even a bloody solution."

Sean stirred. Nora turned to watch him wake. "Time to go. Sean's waking and we're expected for lunch."

"What do you Yanks say? 'Give 'em hell, Harry?'"

"All right, you made me smile. Job well done. Love you."

"Love you, too."

Nora promised to call him that evening, and hung up feeling better. She reached back to tickle Sean's leg until he giggled. "All right, lovey, here we go. A dry nappy awaits you."

She turned into the drive, passing through the ornate iron

gates, and wound her way along, entering park-like grounds. Suddenly a majestic view unfurled in front of them, and the house stood at the center of her gaze.

"Oh, my, Sean—we're definitely not in Kansas anymore."

Chipping Norton

1:53 PM

The sunny fall day was perfect for the MGB, and with most of the station cars out, Declan decided it was reasonable to drive. With Watkins beside him, he navigated their route northwest on the A44, past Woodstock and Blenheim Castle, to the bustling market town that exemplified the Oxfordshire Cotswolds. Known locally as "Chippy," its elevation as the highest town in the area gave it lofty views across the countryside.

"You can see Bliss Mill from here," Watkins pointed out as they entered the town 40 minutes after they left Oxford. The Victorian landmark was a highlight of the area. "Julie wants to move here. Says we'd have more of a garden for the baby to play in when he's older."

"Julie, but not you?"

"Too far from work. He won't need a garden for a while, either, so I say just postpone that decision, can't we? Anyway, the little bugger won't be walking for at least a year after he arrives."

"Decided it's a boy then, or did you bribe the ultrasound tech to tell just you?" Declan took great delight in getting a rise out of Watkins. It was a bone of contention between Watkins and Julie that she'd insisted they be surprised by the baby's gender.

"It had better be a boy. Don't get me started. What the hell do I know about little girls?"

Declan laughed. "I'd say that die has been cast, my friend, and you'll have to deal with whatever Fate sends your way. You'll look very sweet when your daughter paints your nails."

"Gah. None of that girly stuff for me. Here's your turning."

They drew up in front of a row of terraced Cotswold stone almshouses as Declan's GPS announced: *You have arrived at your destination.*

Declan parked on the road and the two men pushed open the stone and metal gate to the fenced-off property. "Amazing that these were built in the 17th century for widows and are still in good nick."

"Third from left, guv." Watkins directed them. "That case where you met Nora, Bryn Wallace? The dead woman's mum lived in one of these."

"Janet Wallace. And it's lives—she still does. Val brought her to Cumbria last year for Sean's christening." Declan wondered if Janet Wallace could be the neighbor keeping watch on Emma Jevons' father. With only eight homes in such close quarters, the residents must know each other and share news, happy or devastating.

The door opened before he could knock. A slim woman with white hair at her temples greeted them. "Declan, I hoped it would be you. And Sergeant Watkins, too."

Janet Wallace turned to the interior of the cottage and announced, "You've drawn lucky, Stanley. Declan and Watkins will get to the bottom of this." She gestured for them to enter, and escorted the two men into the dim interior of the low-ceilinged room, then excused herself. "I've got the kettle on already."

Thick beams and a rustic fireplace defined the space where a man stood waiting for them by the mantel. The scent of cherry blend pipe tobacco lingered in the air.

Declan wished he shared Janet Wallace's assurance as he

introduced himself and his sergeant. Awash with quiet grief, Stanley Jevons' face was devoid of color. He shook hands and gestured for them to take seats, then took up his post by the unlit fireplace, his long nose in shadow. A trimmed salt-and-pepper beard matched his thinning wavy hair. The man looked as if he hadn't slept in a week, although the news of his daughter's death had only been delivered yesterday.

"Here we go. A nice hot cuppa, Stan. Do you good." Janet returned with a tray she placed on a low table, and gestured to her neighbor. "Sit down. You've been holding up that fireplace for hours."

Janet's mild rebuke worked. Stanley Jevons took a seat on the couch next to her. As she poured tea into mugs for them, Watkins withdrew his notebook, and Declan spoke.

"Mr. Jevons, please accept our condolences on the loss of your daughter. We've been talking to her supervisor and colleagues, and everyone thought very highly of Emma." He made certain he used the dead woman's name. To her father, she was not "the victim." She was his daughter, a real, breathing person he'd raised and loved.

"My wife was very bright. Emma takes—took—after her. She was a star." The father's eyes shone and met Declan's in appeal. "They wouldn't let me go down to see her."

Poor sod. "I know, Mr. Jevons, but the Health Department people didn't want to put you at risk until we know exactly what we're dealing with." Declan took a breath. "You were told Emma died of a communicable disease?" He'd go spare if the notifying officers hadn't made that clear.

Jevons nodded. "Possible smallpox, they said. But we shouldn't worry about getting it as I hadn't seen her in a few weeks. Smallpox! How can that be?"

"Indeed, that's our biggest question. Emma wasn't out of the country recently, correct?"

He nodded. "She was so pleased with her position at the Ashmolean she barely had time to get up here to see me." This was not said with petulance, but with regret. "I was happy for her, working at what she loved in such a prestigious place. Proud of her, too."

Janet pointed to his tea. "Drink that while it's hot, Stan."

He took a meager sip, then put the mug back on the tray.

"And she'd not had any visitors from abroad that you know of?" Declan had to tell the Health Department these questions had been asked and answered in the negative.

"No one. When she had that flu several weeks back she came home then for a long weekend. Janet here coddled her with soup and such, and between us we got her back on her feet."

Janet patted his hand and took up the thread. "Emma insisted on going back to this new painting that had arrived while she was here. We told her to take more time off, but she couldn't wait to get back to work."

"Maybe she went back too soon?" Stan Jevons asked. "You know, made her susceptible?"

Declan felt like a heel but he had to make these gentle people understand the situation. "Nothing either of you did or could have done caused this, please believe me. We're trying to find the exact site where Emma came in contact with the virus that caused her death." He couldn't decide if it would be better or worse if the work that Emma loved had led to her death.

"Wouldn't that be at the museum, then?" Janet asked, just as Declan's mobile rang.

He glanced at his phone and saw his office calling. "Excuse me. I have to take this."

DS McAfee's voice rang out loud enough for everyone in the room to hear. "Guv! You were right—it's in the bloody painting! The smallpox is in the Russian Picasso!"

CHAPTER TWELVE

Declan roared back to Oxford with Watkins holding onto the door strap for leverage, as the low-slung car swept over the roadway. He waited for the phone to connect on Bluetooth with Dr. Conlon. He'd already had a call from his chief, and was on his way to see him.

"I hear it's confirmed, doctor, that the painting is the smallpox fomite?"

"A minute area painted over with Prussian blue is the infected area. Everything else in that room is negative." The doctor's voice boomed heavily in the small car. "We have a team on the way back to the museum who will wrap the painting. They'll bring it to our lab for safekeeping under lock and key in a quarantined area as discussions take place between our government and the Russians. This is not for public consumption, please stress with your team. We're trying to keep the press out of it."

"I've instructed my team that any leaks traced back to them would result in immediate dismissal. We've also emphasized the need for discretion in our interviews with Emma's colleagues. But please remember that painting is evidence in a murder," Declan said. "We'll need a way to contain that until Emma Jevons' killer is brought to justice."

The doctor sighed. "I know, but it's also the locus for a virulent strain of smallpox, detective. This is new ground for all of us. We'll have to figure out how to satisfy any trial requirements down the road. At the moment, the safest thing to do is contain the painting and any tools Miss Jevons used on it."

"I agree. I imagine powers above both of us are discussing how to ultimately handle that painting."

"Thank you, Barnes, for thinking of the painting itself as the locus. You probably saved many lives with your quick thinking."

The doctor rang off and Watkins gave a dramatic sigh. "Great. I suppose now I'll have to listen to how you saved all of mankind."

"As if." Declan pushed a button. "Call Mr. Marks, Ashmolean." The mobile dialed and shortly afterwards the connection completed.

"Marks here. I heard the news from Dr. Conlon. The painting—I can't believe it."

Declan explained that Conlon's forensic team was on its way to handle collecting the painting, and all of Emma Jevons' tools. "The rest of the samples from Emma's office were negative."

"Does that mean we can have a cleaning crew in there tomorrow to deep clean and decontaminate the area?"

Declan recited Dr. Conlon's number. "You'd better coordinate that with him."

"Thank you for the swift resolution, Barnes." The conservator disconnected.

Watkins sighed again with a flourish. "That's two for two. Next thing you'll have the Queen herself thanking you for saving the monarchy."

"I'd punch you if I wasn't driving."

"You just keep both hands on that wheel, Oh Savior of Our Nation."

Oxford

4:20 PM

Declan took the stairs to the CID floor and the chief's office.

The chief in question was Detective Superintendent Morris. Declan's immediate superior, a Detective Chief Inspector, was out on sick leave after a heart attack, poor guy.

It was unclear yet if the DCI would return to duty or take early retirement. If he left, there would be an opening that Declan, with his experience and success rate, would be expected to apply for—but Declan wasn't certain he wanted the promotion. It would mean more time doing evaluations, schedules, and administrative stuff; he liked to be out on the streets doing interviews, and what he was good at: detecting.

On the other hand, if he and Nora were to marry and then add to their family, it would mean more chance of regular hours, plus a DI to hand things off to at times, not to mention a useful jump in pay grade. He was old-fashioned enough to want to be able to support his family, even with the knowledge that financial security was always there on Nora's side.

When he knocked on the super's door and entered, Declan was surprised to see a petite woman in a suit and heels standing near the window. She turned at his entrance, her shiny dark hair swinging as she moved, and scrutinized him with almond-shaped eyes.

Morris made the introductions. "Declan, this is Tamsin Chen, assigned to assist you with the Jevons case."

They shook hands. The woman had a quick, definitive grip. Declan noted Morris hadn't specified who had assigned Chen. MI-5 then. The Secret Intelligence Service would obviously be alert to the bioterrorism aspects of this case.

"How would you like us to proceed?" Declan was not pleased to have someone looking over his shoulder at every step of the investigation. He narrowed his eyes as he tried not to glare at his superior, but to send a message. The subtext of his look was: *Thanks all bloody hell and what do I do with her now?*

Morris returned his look with spread hands that communicated: *Not my idea; out of my hands.* "Bring Ms. Chen up to speed on all aspects of the case at it stands now, Declan. I've assured her she'll have our utmost cooperation."

"You'll have my assistance however you need it, DI Barnes. Surely you understand the international nature of this case?" Chen brooked no argument but had sensed the undertone and his misgivings. "I'm not here to take over your case or watch your every move. I'm here to make certain you have access to any information or resources you may need."

"Of course." *Be a gentleman.* "Welcome aboard." Declan opened the office door and ushered Chen out, but not before shooting Morris a backward glance and rolling his eyes. "Last door down the corridor," he directed Chen.

Behind him, his superior whispered: "Just remember you want your evaluation to read 'plays well with others,' Declan."

Cornwall

4:25 PM

Nora followed Harvey as he led the way to the glazed observatory and the garden where she could see a fountain beckoning in the distance. Juno, the Pembroke's Corgi, padded alongside her master at every step.

Nora had already visited the round drawing room with its renowned mural, and seen the family's collection of Reynolds portraits. They walked through a series of interlinked rooms Harvey termed "enfilade" that led to the glass-walled room. Nora knew she might easily get lost in the maze of 11 staircases, 15 back

doors, and 82 chimneys at Port Enys. It felt like visiting a museum, but one that showed signs of human occupation, from the
magazines piled on a side table to the row of wellies lined up in
a metal tray by one of the many doors.

After a relaxed lunch, and time spent just chatting at the
table, Muriel had insisted the two go ahead. Both grandparents
had taken Sean's teething in stride. Nelson's granules had done
the trick once he became restless and started to grizzle as they
sat around the table talking after lunch. Thank you, Mrs. Tink.

Muriel decided she would wait for Sean to wake from his
afternoon nap, and parked herself in the upholstered rocking
chair in the well-appointed nursery, reading while the baby
slept. When Harvey pointed out that Muriel had the newest
baby monitor available at the ready, and so hardly needed to stay
in the room, the sturdy woman shot him a look that silenced
him on the spot and made Nora laugh.

"I had such fun decorating this," Muriel confided to Nora
when she showed her to the nursery. A sleepy Sean hung over
Nora's shoulder. "We would normally have used Paul's cot but
we gave all of that furniture to my sister when it became obvious
he was going to be an only child."

Sean slept in an elaborate hand-carved cot with a padded headboard on one side, which someone had painstakingly embroidered
with the Pembroke crest in silky royal blue threads. Nora pictured
a nun in a convent somewhere assigned to labor over it. There was
a day bed, too, in case Nora ever hired a nanny. *Unlikely.*

"That becomes the headboard to a big boy bed when he gets
older," Muriel said with pride, pointing to the crib. An oversized
wardrobe complemented the cot, and a dresser with a changing
pad on top featured hand-painted Beatrix Potter figures. "Harvey says it's very 'new' money of me but I quite enjoyed picking
the things out. Then I remembered he liked the Potter char-

acters, so I had those done for him," Muriel explained. "Local artist, quite talented. There are several changes of clothes in the drawers in case he needs them, and a few toys around."

Nora glanced at the filled toy chest and the shelf full of storybooks, her own included. Then she looked at the woman's glowing face and felt her resistance weaken. These people meant well, even if their lavish actions overwhelmed. "It's lovely, Muriel. All of it is very special."

"He's special to us, Nora, as are you." She reached out to touch Nora's shoulder lightly. "I know we had a rocky start, and there's no denying this huge house must seem a bit much at times. But I hope someday you'll come to see it as a second home for you and Sean." Her cheeks pinked, highlighting her faded blonde hair.

It was true that despite its outrageous size, the Pembrokes made the areas they lived in daily feel homey. Lunch had been served in a small dining room off the enormous kitchen. Painted French blue, the high-windowed kitchen was strung with a huge battery of copper pots, and boasted a Regency patisserie oven. Muriel insisted Nora meet their cook, who proudly showed off the bunny-shaped teething biscuits she'd made for Sean. "Organic, too," the woman pronounced.

Sean behaved at lunch, his natural exuberance conquering his teething discomfort while he was the center of attention. Perched regally in a sleigh highchair that had been Paul's, padded with extra pillows, he held court as Muriel tried to coach him to call her "Nain," which to Nora's ear sounded like "nine." Sean managed a string of "Ni-ni'" which pleased her.

"Nain is Welsh; we have Welsh blood going back on both sides of the family." Muriel laughed at the child's babble. "He does chatter quite a bit."

"My relations were from South Wales and Muriel's from North Wales," Harvey threw in. "Sean's vocal because he's around adults, and besides, he's quite bright," he pronounced, pride evident on his long face.

Nora explained about her search for more permanent lodgings in Oxford and described Haven Cottage. "Once we've moved in, I'll look for a play group so he's around other children to socialize with his own age. There's another toddler living right next door, too." She turned to Harvey. "What would you like Sean to call you, Harvey?"

He looked pleased to be asked. "Old-fashioned 'Grandpa' sounds good to me."

They spoke of Nora's trip home to Connecticut for Sean's first birthday in two weeks. The Pembrokes knew of Declan's presence in Nora's life. When she mentioned Declan would be accompanying her to the States, it didn't appear to bother either of the grandparents. A hurdle passed.

"On your next visit, we'll celebrate his birthday here," Muriel said. "We didn't think you'd want a big dinner tonight, dear, but perhaps we could invite a few locals next time for you to meet? We'd love if you brought Declan and a few of your Oxford friends with you—make a weekend of it."

Nora acquiesced. She could see how these events excited Muriel. Shopping for the nursery provided distraction from what must be a settled country life with all the routine duties pressed on her that came with owning such an estate.

"Of course. We'll look at the calendar before I leave, and set it up for when we get back." Val would be all over her when they spoke about Port Enys, and knowing she and Sophie were invited for a weekend would be the icing on the cake. She'd like to see it through her friend's eyes, too, and Declan's, and gauge their reactions to what they both called "the pile."

"If you need help packing up or moving, Harvey and I are prepared to help. We're good packers, aren't we, dear? The estate has a large van used to ferry tables and chairs around the grounds for rentals that we can press into service."

"Grand idea, Muriel. Yes, let us help, Nora."

"I want to have several of the rooms painted first, but I'll be sure to keep that in mind. I only have the one suite at Ramsey Lodge to pack up and Sean's alcove. Most of my things are in storage in Oxford and already nearby." She saw Harvey's face fall. "But maybe you could help me retrieve those things and bring them to the new house? That van would be very useful." She was rewarded with huge smiles from the grandparents, and felt she'd struck the right chord.

Now with Sean settled, and Muriel as watchdog, Nora and Harvey took their abbreviated tour of the house. Once outside, she admired the fountain. They walked away from the huge Norman church that sat next to the house and headed toward the woods.

"That's St. German's Priory I mentioned, once owned by us, but thankfully, now under a trust by the C of E," Harvey said. "Our house and its buildings were the original monastery attached to the church."

Nora felt safe walking with Harvey on the grounds. Company took the stalker worry away. If he hadn't approached her when she was alone, she felt he surely wouldn't when she had company. "Why thankfully, Harvey?"

"Port Enys is one of the oldest residences to be continually inhabited in the United Kingdom. That makes it well over 1,000 years old, Nora. The upkeep is enormous; dry rot is our constant enemy. The roofing alone covers almost half an acre, and I can't recall a time when all of it was watertight. We're always having repairs somewhere."

They approached a thick copse of trees, and as Harvey led Nora on a path inside a clearing, she saw the ring of tall hedges they'd walked through enclosed an oval depression lined in granite. Four stone steps led down to a small open area where the bottom step ran around in a horseshoe shape, forming a seating ledge that surrounded the flat end wall. Juno danced down the stairs, then laid down gracefully in what must have been a practiced routine in front of a large bronze plaque with ornate script set into the far stone wall.

"I wanted to show you this so you wouldn't think we've forgotten Paul." Harvey stroked the plaque, and sat on the stone ledge near it. "This hollow was his favorite place to play when he was a little boy. One day it was a fort or a castle, the next a spaceship or a cave. He had a vivid imagination. He'd bring a sleeping bag and wheedle snacks from the cook, then sit here for hours with a science book." Harvey shook his head. "With no body to bury, we came up with this." His sadness touched Nora.

Tears pricked her eyes. She couldn't bear to think of losing her son after she'd only had him such a short time. What grief must it cause to watch that son grow and prosper into an intelligent man, only to lose him in a plane crash with no body to decently bury?

The sun began to lower in the sky and cast a golden glow about the space. Nora leaned in and read the inscription:

> *Farewell to thee! But not farewell*
> *To all my fondest thoughts of thee:*
> *Within my heart they still shall dwell;*
> *And they shall cheer and comfort me.*
> *~ Anne Bronte*

> *Paul Taliesin Pembroke*
> *1975 - 2012*
> *Lost now but loved forever*

Nora's tears ran down her face and she wiped her cheeks with her shirtsleeve. "It's lovely, Harvey. I never knew his middle name was Taliesin." She sniffed. So many things Paul had kept from her. "I know that name from the Frank Lloyd Wright house, but isn't there another in literature?"

Harvey ran his fingers over the lettering, burnishing it. "It's an old Welsh name. Means 'shining brow' literally. You're thinking of the 6th century bard. In some Welsh legends, Taliesin is the companion prophet of King Arthur."

"A very regal name."

Juno suddenly stood. The dog looked around, on high alert.

"Must have heard a deer—we have a herd here on the grounds, and Juno's instinct is to round them up." Harvey looked at his watch. "Think I'll head back now, see if the little lad is awake."

Nora looked at the plaque in the peaceful nook. "Would it be all right if I stayed a few minutes longer?" She thought Sean would still be sleeping, but if he awoke, Muriel seemed capable of handling a teething baby.

"Of course. When you come out of the trees, head in a straight line for the church tower and you'll see the house. We'll have a glass of sherry in the little drawing room next to where we ate lunch."

Nora nodded. She wouldn't call any of the rooms she'd seen at Port Enys "little." "I'll find you." She didn't tell Harvey that in her jeans pocket she'd secreted one of the tour maps she'd found in the entrance hall.

Juno leapt to the top of the stairs and stood looking around. "She'll run if she sees something to herd," Harvey said. The dog tensed, her muscles rippling, head cocked, then shot off, hurtling through the trees on her sturdy short legs, soon lost to sight. "That's her gone. I'll see you back at the house, Nora."

Nora watched Harvey leave and turned back to the plaque.

She sat on the ledge, thinking about Paul and their time together. The highs after the initial attraction, and first blush of dating; the lows when it turned poorly, and they tiptoed around each other when they were together, times which grew sparser as Paul worked more and more, neither of them having the courage to end the relationship as it fell apart on its own.

It was peaceful in this hollow, surrounded by the thick stand of hedges and woods, where a light wind rustled dried leaves. She thought of Harvey and Muriel, trying so hard to make up for their first meeting, after having just lost their only child. *Time changed everything*, her father's voice echoed. She re-read the plaque.

Paul Taliesin Pembroke. This man whose middle name she'd just learned was her child's father, and now he would never know he had a son. She knew it was common to change the nature of relationships when considered in hindsight, but Nora felt she'd had the time and perception to have an accurate view of what went wrong for her and Paul. His sudden death had left too many things unsaid. She could almost feel Paul's presence in this space where he'd experienced childish joy.

"You have a son." The sound of her voice echoed in the small grove. "He has your eyebrows. He's a happy child—at least, when he isn't teething. I wish you could know him."

The wind answered her, a sigh carried on a breeze. "But that would be complicated, wouldn't it? I have Declan in my life now, and he's good to me and to Sean. We'd grown apart, Paul. There wasn't time in your life for *us* any longer. You were so caught up in work, it became your driving force." She sighed. "Of course, I knew your work was important to you. Maybe I'm trying to justify hurt feelings because you weren't around much those last months. But that wasn't the kind of relationship or marriage I wanted." Nora found she was crying again and fumbled to brush tears from her face with her already sodden sleeve.

"I'm sorry. If you hadn't died, I was getting ready to call off the engagement, if you could call it that without a ring or any kind of fuss."

Even to her own ears, Nora knew she sounded petulant. She scrubbed her face with both hands. Withheld anger at their situation flared. "What was that about not introducing me to your parents? They're hardly the farmers I'd pictured, and have been very kind to Sean, and to me. They can't understand why we never met. *I* don't understand. And now I'll never have any answers."

Nora shoved her hands in her jacket pockets, and gave in to the wave of emotion that made her tears flow, sobbing and heaving as she leaned against the cold, hard stone. Resentment and disappointment mingled with her grief.

Finally, she felt spent, wrung out like a wet dishcloth. Nora took a few shuddering breaths. Gradually her breathing evened. The light breeze dried her tears.

"I'll need to wash when I get back, if I can find the damn place. Maybe you didn't want this responsibility, or thought I wouldn't want it, either. It's a shame we didn't get to make that decision together. It's a beautiful estate, and the history is amazing."

Nora stood and placed her hands on the plaque. "Thank you for thinking of me in your will." She pulled her long hair off her damp face. "I promise your son will know you. I'll tell him stories of when we first met; how you swept me off my feet because you knew the authors I read and loved. I'll tell him how you could be charming, and loved to punt and picnic on the Cherwell, and how terribly smart you were. I'll let him know you could make a pasta dish out of whatever you found in the fridge." She steadied her voice. "I'll tell him the good bits, and leave out the hurt, because he doesn't need to know that."

She took a deep breath and let it out slowly. "There *were* good bits, Paul. Just not enough over time to sustain me. I'm sorry for that. I did love you, but I've let you go. I have to move on."

She turned to go. A gasp reached her.

Nora stiffened. The noise sounded human. The trees in the woods seemed to have arms reaching out for her. She scanned the circle of tall hedges, stiff and formal. She felt claustrophobic in the enclosed space, yet at the same time, exposed, and on view.

The sun dropped lower, long fingers of shadow reaching through the trees around her. Nora scrabbled up the stone steps, searching the thick foliage with her eyes.

No more sounds.

Perhaps a woodland creature, nothing more. Even as she tried to convince herself of that, Nora felt the hair rise on her arms, and prickle the back of her neck as the wind picked up. She strained to hear beyond the rustling wind and the creaking trees. The pathway loomed darkly in front of her.

She had the urgent feeling she was not alone.

Without pausing, Nora hurried along the path through the trees, refusing to look right or left, afraid of what she might see. She felt like a child; if she couldn't see the threat, it wasn't really there.

When she reached the open meadow, Nora galloped across the fields like the low-slung corgi had, heading for the church steeple, and then the house and the safety of a closed door.

CHAPTER THIRTEEN

Bath

8:33 PM

Viktor Garanin's deluxe room at The Royal Crescent Hotel was the third level down in price. No sense calling attention to oneself. It was well-appointed, with an en-suite bath. The large king-sized bed, decorated with a tall scalloped headboard, padded for propping up to read, was upholstered in a hideous green and black tartan to coordinate with the repulsive woodland scene wallpaper.

The trip to Bath today by train was brief and uneventful. He'd rented a car and checked in to the outlandish room for an hour of local research. Then he'd taken the car out, carefully navigating the roads, for a scouting trip that would lay the groundwork to set his plan into action in the next days.

The older woman, Betty Kaplan, had been easily fooled with a flash of his fake credentials. Amazing how his photo ID on a lanyard, hanging around his neck, worked as identification and reassurance in so many places. He pretended to inspect the house on the pretense of an unannounced drop-in visit, which the hospital website proudly announced was part of their program. Whilst making a snap judgment, he asked questions and verified her routine. Yes, Kaplan would do very nicely when he needed her, and now that his face was familiar, she wouldn't question him when he showed up on her doorstep in an urgent hurry in two days' time. Things were falling into place, and his visit to Bath would not only accomplish regaining the second painting, it would bring him closer to his second goal of refining the mutated virus.

He'd returned to the hotel and had the car garaged, intending to complete the rest of his tour on foot. The hotel gave out local maps, which Viktor used to make his way to Great Pulteney Street, and then the Holburne Museum, stopping to grab a free city guide that included escort ads in the back.

The sun shone, the autumn sky dotted with a few wisps of clouds. He'd noted the forecast to remain seasonably clear for the rest of this week with only a chance of an occasional shower. Perfect. Even the weather gods were smiling on him. He drew in a deep breath of fresh air and took in his surroundings as he walked.

The Georgian heritage was on display everywhere in the Bath-stone architecture used on so many buildings, hiding the city's Roman underpinnings, and the famous hot springs. It felt distinctly foreign and worse, incomparably British.

He couldn't stand England or the English, with their twittering cheeriness hiding an inability to talk about their feelings. His British mother had been a simpering blonde his father at one time had found pretty. They'd married after she'd fallen for his accent and the idea of living somewhere foreign. At least that was the story she told him when he was small.

His father had used her as a punching bag. The old *bychit*—bull—had attitude in spades. He'd taught his oldest son to always fight as if he crawled on concrete through a jungle, every day. *Use your brain first, think through your options; then control your body, and hit hard until the blood runs into your eyes.* That was power and toughness. That was a real man.

But Viktor had been bright enough to see that bull-headed toughness was not all that would give him power. He used his intelligence to obtain a high-quality education, worked hard in the areas he needed, and now he was on the cusp of greatness.

Greatness was bestowed on only a few. Stalin, Hitler—these

were names that inspired Viktor. He considered Putin a brag-gart, always ready to display his naked torso—*bah*!

Despite his careful and thorough vetting, if only the few peo-ple he'd employed in his master scheme had the same drive and total dedication to their task as he did, things might never have gone off track.

The grave error in the mutation and release had been Yuri's first in a long and costly relationship, but also his last. The sci-entist had brought Viktor far forward in his plan, to be sure, but Yuri's new abode at the bottom of the Moskva River ensured he would never make such an egregious mistake again.

The Holburne Museum had been a surprise. There was its odd collection of porcelains, paintings, silver and other objects d'art collected by its founder, Sir William Holburne. These min-gled with bequeathed and donated paintings by Gainsborough, Turner, Stubbs, and Ramsey. Then there were the porcelain col-lections—Meissen, Chelsea, Derby, and Worcester—as well as workshops and talks for adults and children. A modern glazed addition held a café. Viktor had looked carefully through the top gallery of special exhibits, eyes searching for several hours, and while he had to admit several items were indeed exceptional, where was Chagall's *Nocturne* on loan from the Pushkin?

He found several seemingly knowledgeable docents, but no one had information about the Chagall. Then one pointed out that the offices, where he could find his information and ask questions, were closed. He'd forgotten it was Sunday. *Soak blade.* Motherfucker.

He'd have to come back tomorrow. He walked back to his ho-tel and requested a massage, which went some way toward cool-ing off his temper. The masseuse was brisk and efficient, but he had to keep telling her to push harder. Not strong enough hands, to his mind, but sufficient to let the negative tension release. He needed that release. Ordering Yuri's death from a distance had not carried the same satisfaction as if he'd done it himself.

Freshly showered and wrapped in a plush robe, he took out the city guide and examined the escort ads. He chose the one executed with the most care and expense: "Discreet, professional, high class companions." He called the number, and yes, Kate could be with him for an hour at 11 PM.

He checked restaurant listings while he looked out of his window onto the small but elegant gardens behind the Royal Crescent. The thought of getting redressed and mingling with the wandering humanity below put him off, and he decided to order room service. He would eat by his window while he waited for the terribly British Kate. She would probably be rail thin and without tits, but she would be enough. Seeing this garden made him think of his pride and joy at home. He made a mental note to call his gardener tomorrow. He would have Josef send him a picture of the asters in bloom, and remind him it was time to prune the roses and fruit trees, and cut back the gooseberry bushes for winter.

Oxford

10:30 PM

Declan called Nora as he loosened his tie. He wanted to check with her about her day before he fell asleep. He felt drained, and contrary to Watkins' teasing, not at all triumphant, despite finding the locus of the smallpox. Now he was saddled with Tamsin Chen. To be fair, she had remained unobtrusive throughout his team meeting after being introduced, and read through the case files with little comment. Whether this proved to be a good or bad thing remained to be seen.

"Is this a good time?" he asked when Nora answered.

"Very good. Sean is asleep. I need to thank Mrs. Tink for the idea of chamomile granules. If he gets too fussy, there's a day bed in his room. I'm installed thoughtfully next door to the nursery in a sumptuous bedroom about the size of your entire flat."

"Four poster?"

"What else?"

"So how's the pile? And the almost-inlaws?"

"The more time I spend with them, the more I like them. I can't believe we each had such different impressions at Paul's funeral. The pile is huge. Really impressive and terribly ancient. As is some of the plumbing, but that's all being retrofitted as we speak. Picture if Christ Church College and its cathedral had the Tate and the National Portrait Gallery collections hanging on its walls. I'll need my map to find the breakfast room."

Declan laughed. "How are the grounds? I imagine they're equally impressive."

Nora paused. The quiet stretched so long Declan thought the connection was lost. "Still there?"

"Um, let's see. Multiple gardens plus a maze, summerhouses, a thatched boathouse, ornamental ponds, all wrapped up in a mere 6,000 acres, give or take a few on loan to a rugby team. You can rent bits for a wedding, and be married in the church on the property."

Declan whistled. "Unbelievable."

"But the thing is, Muriel and Harvey are really down-to-earth in a tweedy way, and very, very impressed with Sean."

"Of course they are. He's his mother's lad. Did he behave himself?"

Nora gave him chapter and verse on the nursery, and described the candlelit dinner, served by Nigel. "We need to do candles at dinner more. It makes everyone look rosy and happy."

"Nigel? White tie and tails?"

"Hmph. Today's modern butler wears chinos, and a navy polo shirt embroidered with a gold "P" and "E" above the Port Enys crest. Discreet. Oh, and Sean fell asleep at the table."

"Well done."

"Tired out after playing with their corgi. I fed him first, and he had one of their cook's organic teething biscuits as we ate. He got along famously with the dog. He says her name, Juno, like a mantra, and didn't pull the dog's tail once. I think he's a dog person."

"I can see where this is heading already. They don't allow animals at my flat, I'm afraid."

"But they will at my house. We'll talk. There's a lot more to my visit, and the weekend, but we can discuss that when I see you. How did your day turn out?"

Declan felt the abrupt change in direction. What was Nora hiding? He'd learned not to push her, or the stubborn streak she strongly disavowed would rear its ugly head. She'd tell him when she was ready.

"This case is strange and rather frightening." In rapid detail he told her about the genetically modified smallpox virus loaded into the paint of a Picasso on loan from the Russian museum. He stressed the need for her to keep this information to herself. "We're preventing mass hysteria here, and so far Public Health England has assured me there's no cause for concern."

"Declan, that's horrid. That poor woman."

"Watkins and I saw her father today. A widower, and Emma was his only child. He's Janet Wallace's neighbor. She sends her regards."

"He must be devastated. But Declan, do we have to worry about you becoming infected?"

"I think not. I've had a crash course in the virus from the Head of Infectious Diseases at Churchill, and he feels it's contained within the paint. Still, Emma's colleagues are on house arrest until that shakes out."

"Until you find who's behind it, as I know you will. There must be a Russian connection if the painting came from one of their museums."

"We're investigating, and so are international levels far above me. Please, don't say anything about this. I've told you more than I should have. It's a matter of national security." He lowered his voice. Who knew if Tamsin Chen could be listening in even now? "If word gets out that there's been a case of smallpox, the country will go spare. It's why I've been saddled with someone from MI-5."

He heard Nora take in a huge breath. "Oh, my. That's a first. I'm not making light of the situation, but is he at all like James Bond?"

Declan smiled. Leave it to Nora to calm him down. "Not at all. And he's a she."

"A female spook? You're working with a woman partner now? Watkins' nose must be out of joint."

"First off, she's not my partner. Second, he's happy to collate information at the office. He's acting as information officer from today on, easiest slot to fill if Julie goes into early labor."

"That's right, she's due soon." Nora yawned. "I miss you. But I'm glad Sean isn't around Oxford right now, until you catch the people behind this and make sure the smallpox is contained again."

"That's my feeling, too. Now get some rest. Sean will be up soon enough."

After they said their goodnights, Declan changed into a T-shirt and an old pair of rugby shorts, faded from many washings. He padded to the kitchen to pull down the bottle of Balvenie that Watkins had given him last Christmas, and poured himself a good measure of the scotch.

He walked back to his bedroom and took a sip of the smooth single malt, enjoying the taste of heather and honey. Declan looked at the big, empty bed. He sighed, and after placing his drink on the night table, sat up against the headboard, and opened his briefcase on his lap, taking out files and reports to comb through. There might be nothing concrete he could do tonight, but he kept seeing Stanley Jevons' pinched face, and his eyes hollowed with grief. At least he owed the man, and his dead daughter, a try.

Chapter Fourteen

Cornwall

Monday, 11th October

7:40 AM

Nora woke with a start. She had a muggy feeling of disorientation and lay in a cloud. Her vision cleared, and she distinguished the gauzy hangings on the sides of the Jacobean four-poster carved bed. Port Enys.

She slumped back against the pile of feather pillows. She hadn't slept so well in months. The down duvet had enveloped her, and she'd fallen into a heavy sleep after she'd checked Sean near midnight. She felt badly she hadn't told Declan about Haven Cottage, but that wasn't a conversation to have on the phone, although she didn't closely inspect her reasons for avoiding the subject. She picked up her mobile, smothered a yawn, and looked at the time: 7:40 AM.

What? She threw on her robe and ran next door. Sean was always up around 6:30, and what about his teething in the middle of the night? Had she not heard him?

She flung open the door and stopped short. Sean sat on the carpet playing patty-cake with a robe-clad Muriel, both surrounded by a pile of stuffed animals and blocks. The day bed was mussed.

"Hello, Mummy. Have a good rest?" Muriel's face glowed with happiness.

"Mum-mum!" Sean shrieked and held out his arms.

Nora sat down with them. The baby crawled into her lap and snuggled. Clean and dry. "Muriel, you should have woken me. I don't know why I didn't hear the baby monitor."

"I turned it off when I peeked in an hour ago. You were sleeping so soundly. When I checked Sean, he was awake but playing quietly in his crib."

"Ni-ni," Sean said, pointing to Muriel.

"We have a surprise, Mummy." Muriel leaned over and tapped Sean on his lips. "Show Mummy."

Sean opened his bird-like mouth. Nora felt along the ridge of his gums. The two teeth had broken through the gum. "Success!" She kissed the back of his neck, inhaling his sweet scent. "Thank you for letting me sleep, Muriel. That was very kind."

"I enjoyed this time alone with him. We read books in bed, and then we built towers." She looked at Sean with serious intent. "He's very good at knocking them down."

"Tell me about it." Nora grinned. Perhaps having a grandmother closer than across an ocean wasn't such a bad idea.

There was a discreet knock at the door, and Harvey came in, carrying a tea tray, already dressed for the day. "Where shall I put this?"

Over the next hour, the three adults and one child sat on the carpet and shared tea and toast soldiers. Sean drained his bottle, and laughed at Harvey's attempts to get him to say "grandpa." The played silly games, and sang him nursery rhymes.

"Muriel, you and Nora take showers. I'll stay here with my grandson and get him dressed. We men have a few things to chat about."

"Harvey, you don't have to do that," Nora protested. She saw the man's disappointment. There was a learning curve here for her. "Unless you really want to," she amended.

"Don't come back too soon." Harvey carried Sean to the changing table. "Now young man, let's figure out these nappies and see what clothes your Nain has for you to wear."

Under the hot shower, Nora relaxed. The visit had gone far

better than she could have imagined. A good night's sleep gave her the perspective to understand why she'd hesitated to thoroughly discuss Haven Cottage with Declan last night. The sadness of the conversation at Paul's memorial with Harvey had influenced her, along with the shadows and the setting sun and her stalker worry. Her emotions seemed so jumbled recently, and Declan was understandably caught up in this important case. There was time for everything.

In the bright daylight, well rested, she felt assured and refreshed. Somehow even the idea she had a stalker, despite that silver button, seemed almost ludicrous.

Two hours later, party date chosen, Nigel brought the wagon around and loaded up her gear.

"Checked your oil and tyre pressures. All set."

Nora wondered if she was supposed to tip him, and decided not to, settling for shaking hands and thanking the man. This must have been the right thing to do, for Nigel saluted her, and with a wave, disappeared into the house.

Harvey came out carrying Sean, dressed in a jaunty sailor suit. At least he left the hat off, Nora thought as she stowed her bag and readied her phone in the car's charger. She'd bet anything there was a little tam with a bobble and ribbons on it that Harvey left behind, deciding it either too feminine or too babyish.

She had her water bottle freshly filled, and a bottle and snack for Sean on the passenger seat next to her for the drive to Bath up the M5. She planned one stop unless Sean dozed off.

She was looking forward to seeing Helen again. Their time in Oxford together seemed like another lifetime. Their visits had been constrained by Nora's move to Cumbria, but Helen had driven up and stayed for Sean's christening. With a start, Nora realized that had been last December, when Sean was still an infant. Helen would be surprised by his growth, his prodigious speech, and his efforts to toddle around.

When she stood up, she watched the Pembrokes with their heads together, kissing their grandson goodbye. The two had wide smiles and similar salt-and-pepper hair, Muriel's fairer. Nora realized they weren't as old as she'd thought when they first met. Harvey must be in his late 60s; Muriel seemed a few years younger. Grief could age a person. Being with Sean seemed to have revitalized them both.

"All right, young man, let's see if Grandpa can strap you properly into this car seat."

Sean reached his hand out to graze Harvey's cheek. "Pop-pa."

The beam of delight on Harvey's face spoke volumes.

"We'll see you when you get back from the States for his party weekend." Muriel hugged Nora. "Have fun in Bath at your signing. I'll have such fun planning his party."

"No clowns," Nora warned Muriel, and the two women shared a laugh. Nora pictured a bouncy castle decorating the ancient lawn, and the celebration was bound to entail a pony ride. After checking the straps on Sean's car seat, Nora gave Harvey a hug and slid behind the wheel.

She honked the horn. The grandparents waved madly as she drove off down the long drive, retracing her steps. Nora took a deep breath and felt a sense of new freedom. She would have her own relationship with Sean's British grandparents. The specter of Paul and unfinished business had finally been left behind.

Oxford

11:22 AM

Declan waited for Tamsin Chen to enter his office before he closed the door. At the morning briefing he'd given his team multiple chores. One important item to be covered saw DS McAfee and a constable assigned to interview the air courier service for the delivery of the Picasso. They would gather and take into evidence any documentation from that order. Another pair had been dispatched to London's Heathrow Airport to obtain copies of the customs forms filled out at the Pushkin Museum.

The team accepted Chen's presence without question today, and Declan stressed the international perspective of the case. A few raised their eyebrows when she spoke up and instructed them to call her "Tamsin."

"We'll be working together, and I want to feel integrated to your team," she told them, casting an inclusive look at Declan.

"We're fortunate to have Tamsin as an advisor," Declan pointed out, acquiescing to her wish. Most of the senior members of his team understood this translated to: *It doesn't matter what we call her. If we can't solve this in a reasonable time frame, the case will be taken away from us.*

Watkins had cornered Declan before he left with Tamsin. "IT says that's a bog-standard listening device, guv. Voice-activated, nothing special. You can buy them online. No way to find where it came from."

Declan had nodded his thanks, still perplexed about why someone would drop a listening device into Nora's bag. Could this have something to do with the money she'd inherited? Could her stalker be someone she'd spurned who was infatuated with her? He was pretty certain after Paul she'd been alone for a while, but then he didn't know her every move in that period. When they first met, he thought Nora and Simon were an item, but that seemed to have been more of a loving friendship. He guessed she could simply have pissed someone off, and they were taking it too far.

Before Tamsin could sit, her mobile rang. She walked to the window to keep her indoor connection strong, and answered.

Declan couldn't glean much from her side of the conversation, which consisted of a few "um-hmmms" and one "I see." He checked his watch. Nora would be on the road from Cornwall to Bath. She was due at the bookstore to meet the owner at 3 PM to see her reading space for the event the following day. Last night she'd mentioned she wanted to arrive at her friend's house first. She would feed Sean and change him before Helen took her to meet the bookshop owner.

Tamsin ended the call and took a seat across from him. "A body's been pulled from the Moskva River this morning, shot in the head execution style. The victim is Yuri Novikov, a virologist."

"Our madman scientist?"

"Even if he's responsible for obtaining and manipulating the virus, someone else hired him, and then decided he'd served his purpose. This could be the person who gained access to the virus to affect the mutation. Someone with access to the Pushkin would have added it to the painting."

"So a huge step forward, but not the main man?"

"The thinking is this: Yuri was a hired gun, or in our case, a hired bug man to mutate the virus. But we need the mastermind who came up with this entire plan, and had connections to get near the painting to implant it. We still don't know his main objective, either, but it can't be anything good."

"And does your outfit have any ideas on that?"

Tamsin's smile transformed her face. "I'll have to tell them you called them that—'the outfit.' I like it."

Declan returned her smile. He realized the woman had her

own superiors who must be exerting pressure for her to avert a national crisis. "This is an unusual case for all of us."

"My 'outfit' is researching megalomaniacs who would be likely to come up with this kind of scheme, with or without access to the painting."

"Profiling the idea man, then."

"Unfortunately, several candidates fit the bill at the moment. We have people ascertaining their whereabouts, while others will investigate if there are ties between any of them to this Novikov or the Pushkin Museum. You should know that the head of the Museum who worked on the loan with the Ashmolean has already been cleared."

"Good to have that aspect covered." Declan realized there were benefits and outcomes to having this assistance from Chen's outfit that his Oxford detectives would never be able to access.

"My outfit excels at that kind of thing."

They smiled in mutual understanding.

"So can I ask—how did you become involved with your outfit?"

"Are you asking to be interviewed?"

Declan held up both hands and shook his head. "Hell, no. I'm a local boy, happy to lead a team here. Just intrigued." Her face, with its mix of British and Asian features, appeared exotic to him.

"I was approached my last year at Cambridge, finishing a degree in geo-politics. I've been with them in one capacity or another since graduation."

"You must have been very bright to capture their attention."

This time she looked down modestly. Declan knew it was time to leave the closed environment of his office and get back to work before Tamsin Chen thought he was flirting with her.

Bath

1:46 PM

As she drew closer to Helen's house, Nora smiled in anticipation. It had turned into a lovely fall day, the shining sun making thoughts of her stalker seem unreal. She opened her window a crack, and could hear the flock of starlings that peppered the sky overhead as they passed. Sean had napped and been in such a good mood, she'd only stopped once en route for a quick nappy change a few minutes ago.

Helen Sackville had been a good friend and mentor, she saw now, acting like an older sister to the college-aged Nora, who wrestled with the loss of her beloved father. She'd been convinced at that stage if she'd turned down a date to go sailing with him, he might have survived the squall that came out of nowhere and took his life. It was Helen who had echoed her mother's feelings: "You might both have been lost, which he would have hated—and how would your mother have coped?"

Helen had been right. Amelia had been alone for years, but eventually Roger crossed her path, and while Nora knew her mother had never stopped loving her father, she'd been able to open her heart to a new love, one that allowed Nora to live outside the States without worrying about her mother being lonely.

Helen had two lovely teenage girls, Bella, studying art and jewelry design in Edinburgh, and Phillipa, ready to go to university next year. Helen's own art degrees led to her work in different fields. She'd been an interior designer, and worked at the Holburne Museum before opening her own gallery in a new wing of their house.

Nora turned into the drive for Hill House, and as she pulled up the drive, she saw Helen had opened the gate for her. She drove to the parking area by a tree, where the rise at the top of the hill fell away to an undulating view. She found Helen's dogs gamboling on the lawn that fronted a cleared field once used for the girls' horses.

The Sackvilles' house in Somerset outside Bath looked out on an expanse of rolling valley dotted with mature trees, their patchwork fields dressed in fall colors of gold and muted green. A recent addition to their stone home on its east side was the green oak annex Helen had dreamt of for years, finally built, up and running as a contemporary art and sculpture gallery. Helen worked mostly by appointment with private clients and decorators, and held art evenings in the airy space for exhibitions by new artists.

Hester, the Sackville's wire-haired dachshund, ran over and barked at Nora as she leaned in to retrieve Sean from his car seat. Their other dog, Violet, stood aloof in the sunny forecourt with all the insouciance a whippet could muster. Nora was surrounded by dogs these days.

"Hello, Hester. Remember me?" Nora greeted the dog, and held out her hand for Hester to sniff. She saw her hand trembled. That man who'd passed her at Port Enys upset her more than she'd realized. Her usual efforts at compartmentalizing were failing her. *Get a grip, Nora.*

"Typo!" Sean yelled from the back seat.

"That's Hester, lovey. Not every puppy is Typo." Nora waved as Helen came out to greet them.

"You're in time for a cup of tea before we go into town." The slender brunette gave Nora a hug and held out her arms for Sean. "Come to me, little man? Hasn't he grown?"

"Typo!" Sean yelled again.

"Hester," Nora coached, speaking slowly.

Sean gave her a quizzical look.

"That name seems beyond his skills yet," Helen said as they

entered her large homey kitchen. A huge center island anchored the space, with a black Aga on one wall and apron-front sink facing the garden. A long elm table ran at right angles to the island, serving as dining and worktable.

Both dogs followed them inside, to Sean's delight.

"Etta!" Sean shrieked and both women laughed.

"Close enough." Helen gave him a hug. "Babies smell so good. Wait till Philly sees him. She has crew practice after school today, but she'll be all over him tonight. Matthew's in Plymouth on one of his projects, but he'll be back by the end of the week. Philly's offered to babysit so we can eat out."

"That will be fun." Nora dropped Sean's changing bag on the table.

"Maybe Declan can drive out and meet us?"

"Maybe. He's involved in a big case, a death at the Ashmolean."

Helen's ears pricked up at the name of the famous museum. "I'll want to hear about that." She sat Sean in the high chair her daughters had used, kept for visiting babies. "Hard biscuit all right?"

Nora nodded, and explained about Sean's new teeth.

"I read online about a woman at the Ashmolean dying under suspicious circumstances." Helen handed Sean a biscuit. "It said her colleagues are on house arrest. That sounds like a communicable disease to me."

"It's all very mysterious," Nora admitted, thinking of Declan's admonition to avoid discussing his case. When she thought about it, she didn't have that much information to share.

Helen busied herself with the tea while Nora used the loo and then sat down, determined to relax.

Her friend caught her out. "Here's your Earl Grey." Helen put two mugs on the table with a plate of homemade cookies. "So why are your hands trembling?"

Nora stirred sugar into her tea. "I'm afraid if I talk about it, it becomes real." She found herself pouring out the entire tale, ending with finding the audio bug in her bag.

"There must be something Declan can do."

"He's working on it. It's almost like this creep knows my every move." The minute the words left her mouth, Nora knew them to be true.

Helen stirred sugar into her tea. "If you're being followed by someone who knows your every move, he has to have a means to know your routine besides that bug."

The two women looked at each other. "Your car!" Helen exclaimed.

Nora ran out to the drive. Where would a bug be?

She crouched down and looked under the wheel wells. Nothing.

She ran her hand under the frame of the car, starting at the driver's door, and worked her way around the front of the vehicle. She managed to get a hand full of dirt, grease, and a few dried leaves for her trouble.

When she hit the back bumper, she felt a raised area and got down on her knees to peer up. Too dark.

Nora opened her glove box and grabbed the torch she kept there for emergencies. Not only would this prove she wasn't going crazy, it would stop her stalker from knowing her every move, at least by car. Since the other bug was gone from her bag, she might feel safe again.

With the light from the torch, it was easy to spot the small box clamped to the inner side of her rear chassis. The magnet was powerful, and she had to use two hands to pull it off. The device rested in the palm of her hand. "GPS TracKing" was stamped across it in yellow letters. On one end, a red light pulsed.

Nora dusted off her knees and sprinted back inside the kitchen, holding up her find in triumph. "What now?"

Helen ran into her boot room to fetch a screwdriver. Nora held the box while Helen pried the lid off and removed the small battery. The red light went off.

Helen put one hand on her heart, then pushed her house phone toward Nora. "Call Declan—now!"

Bath

2:10 PM

It never ceased to amaze Betty Kaplan how much a service engineer was prepared to charge for fixing an appliance she was perfectly capable of figuring out. Google and YouTube did have their good side.

Her dishwasher's lower filter had a habit of clogging, she'd discerned. It didn't take an engineer to figure out how to remove the bottom rack, and undo the bolts that held the sprayer arm to take that off to find what was causing the clog.

Ah, yes, the culprit this time was a small label from the new thermal drink container she'd bought. She'd been certain she'd removed them all, but here was one more, probably from the bottom, small enough to miss but large enough to stick over the filter. Her machine wouldn't clean properly when that happened.

Betty deftly replaced the parts she'd removed in their proper order. "Great. That's all fixed," she told the cat, who watched from the windowsill over the sink. Toby's grey tail twitched; his green eyes glowed in the sunny spot.

She washed her hands and looked out at her garden. Time to get out there and start the autumn pruning. That last emergency child had distracted her. His new sibling made her appearance two weeks before she was due. With the mother needing an emergency Caesarean section, and no family living nearby to help the harried father, the social worker had recommended their Caring Angels program.

The boy spent three days and two nights with Betty, who lavished attention on him. She even brought him to see his new sister and parents in the hospital. Both mum and dad were profuse with their thanks. It was Betty's delight to care for the child until his mother was discharged, and the parents could handle both children on their own.

It was just what Betty needed, on-call temporary foster care for short periods. One of the first nurse practitioners in pediatrics, Betty's work with public health made her a natural candidate for this kind of volunteer work in her retirement. Run in conjunction with the local authority through the social work office of the hospital, Betty had professional supervision and support, and aced all of the training courses she attended. The bonus was that all of her visits with children were in short bursts, a welcome change to her usual daily routine with only her cat for company after her husband died. After raising two boys and two girls, all out on their own, coupled with her work, she missed the company of the young.

Betty fluffed a grey curl, and took the sheets for the toddler bed from the dryer and folded them. She never knew when she'd get a call, and liked to be prepared. Once her youngest daughter, Lisa, had moved to Scotland, these visits kept her mind alert and her heart full.

She'd made over the formal sitting room of her cottage into a bed-play room for her visitors, then scoured charity shops for used toys and books in good condition to fill baskets that brimmed over with different age-appropriate delights. The council gave her funds for the cot, daybed, and changing table, and regularly sent her coupons for food and nappies. It was a win-win situation for everyone, and since there was a roster of volunteers, if Betty were unavailable or wanted to travel to Scotland, she didn't feel guilty passing on to the next Angel.

"All set for the next child, Toby. Let's tackle that garden."

Oxford

2:15 PM

Declan and Tamsin Chen returned from a hasty, late lunch and bent over a report that had come through on the possible suspects. Her profiler indicated a male would head this plot, and her unit had identified three men, all with a history of wanting power and control, all with rampant egos to match such aspirations.

"The profiler says we're looking for someone with at least a rudimentary amount of scientific knowledge, but the most important thing is if they have the funds to carry this off. It takes money to hire the people to support this kind of scheme, plus buy their silence." Tamsin tucked her hair behind one ear.

Declan nodded. "He'd have to be connected in some way to the other people he needed." He ticked them off on his fingers. "There would be the scientist who did the actual work on the virus, but that person would first have to procure it. Then there's the person working at the Pushkin who would have applied the fomited paint to the original painting." His cell phone rang and he saw it was Nora. He almost didn't answer, then reconsidered. Nora rarely called him at work unless it was important. She would text a casual question or a message if it was just to say she'd arrived at Helen's. "Excuse me a moment."

He stood near the window as Tamsin had this morning and spoke into the phone. "Arrived at Helen's in good form?"

Nora's voice sounded tense. "Fine. But when I got to Helen's, I looked under my car and found another device."

Declan turned to Tamsin and motioned for her to note what he wrote on a pad. "Describe it, Nora." He wrote down: "GPS TracKing - 3" x 2" - magnet." Under that he added, "Black - battery - red blinker." Tamsin took the pad and read his notations.

"I'm very glad I thought to look for it." Nora didn't sound relieved. Her worry came down the line. "What should I do now?"

"What's your schedule?" he asked.

"I'm supposed to be in Bath at the bookstore at 3 to meet the owner and see the room for tomorrow. We have to get a move on."

"Can you take Helen's car to the bookstore?"

"I suppose so."

"Then do that. You've both touched this tracker?"

"Unfortunately, yes."

"Put it in a plastic bag until I can get it. Go about your business today but try to stay inside tonight at Helen's and lock yourselves in. Is Matthew home?"

"No, he's in Plymouth until Friday. But the house has an alarm."

"Use it. Let me call a contact I know in Bath. He'll get the locals to keep an eye on the house." It took all of Declan's resolve not to bolt to Nora immediately.

"There's no chance you can come here, I suppose, with this case?"

Nora's wistful tone made Declan close his eyes. "I'm sorry, darling. There's a lot going on here. I'd be there if I could, you know that. I'll come as soon as it's possible."

"I understand. I shouldn't have asked."

He lowered his voice. "You have every right to ask. Just know how much I want to be with you. I love you." He cleared his throat and raised his voice. "Let me ask about this around here. I'll get back to you tonight, promise. You do your site visit, act naturally, but keep your eyes open and try not to be alone."

"Don't worry. We'll be fine."

Her voice tried for braveness, but Declan heard the quaver at the end. He ended the call, feeling frustrated at not heading directly to Bath. He sat down and gave Tamsin an abbreviated version of Nora's stalker and the button she'd found. Then he tapped his pad. "She just found this on her car."

Tamsin nodded. "The TracKing is a standard GPS tracking device. Her stalker can follow her car on his laptop, and know where she is and how long she's stopped anywhere."

Declan felt chilled to the bone. This couldn't be passed off as any kind of accident now. Nora was being deliberately followed. But by whom—and more importantly—why? "Doesn't it need to be in the open to get the satellite signal?"

"No, these work pretty well in glove boxes or under bumpers. The button kind you described is a voice-activated recorder. Those work well with other noises within about 30 feet of the device, but also pick up things like television and radio noises, so they're less useful. But say your partner—"

"Nora."

"Say Nora is talking on her Bluetooth while driving, and the radio isn't on. If her bag is on the seat next to her, the conversation would come through very well."

Declan nodded. He felt he was letting Nora down by not rushing to Bath, but there wasn't a clear path for him to get there right now. His worry increased. "I should be there," he blurted out. "Does she need police protection?"

"Call your contact and have the house watched. Any idea who it might be?" Tamsin tapped the pad with her pen as she thought.

"None." His voice rose. "She's an American who's lived here for a few years. She writes children's books. I can't think why either thing would cause someone to follow her or want to know her every move."

"Could be a nutter." A frown crossed Tamsin's face. "Did Nora do anything to put her in the news recently?"

Declan explained last spring's case, when a theater troupe's stay at Ramsey Lodge led to murder. "I was there on vacation. There was press coverage and her photo in the papers when she helped stop the murderer."

"That's her?" She pointed to the photo of Nora and Sean that stood in a wood frame on one corner of his desk.

They'd taken Sean punting on the Cherwell, picnic and changing bag in tow, and on the way back, Nora looked down at the baby as he slept in her arms. Declan called it her "Madonna" shot and loved the adoring way she looked at her son. "Yes, that's Nora and her son, Sean. He'll be a year in two weeks. We're going to the States to her family, a first for me."

"Your only child?" Tamsin tilted her head.

"I'm not his father. But we've been together as a couple since he's 5 months old." He plopped down in his chair. "At least we don't have to worry about his biological father being behind this. Paul Pembroke was killed in a plane accident before Nora even knew she was pregnant."

As he uttered this, Tamsin's face blanched. She glanced down but not before he saw her startled look.

"Wait a minute." He stood up. "What do you know about this?" He thought about what he'd just said. "Or was it the mention of Paul Pembroke that made you go pale?"

Tamsin fiddled with her mobile. "What's Nora's last name?"

"Tierney. Tamsin, you need to tell me what's out there that you know about. Be honest. My partner's in danger and you know something I don't."

Tamsin met his worried look. "Paul Pembroke worked at Porton Down for the Ministry of Defence."

"That sounds right. A good 90-minute drive from Oxford, and he would frequently stay overnight at his lab." As he spoke his mind whirled ahead. He supposed Paul's crash would have been on the radar of Tamsin's outfit. Was his plane sabotaged?

Tamsin nodded. "DSTL is there, the Defence Science and Technology Lab."

"Nora said he was very good at what he did, but he wasn't allowed to discuss it. She talks like he was a genius."

Tamsin stood and walked to the window. With her back to him, he heard her mutter, "You could say that."

Defence Science; bioterror; a genius scientist. The penny dropped. Declan whirled to the window. "Are you telling me Paul Pembroke is involved in this? How can that be when he's dead?" Was Tamsin trying to tell him Paul was the architect of the genetically altered smallpox?

CHAPTER FIFTEEN

Bath

2:35 PM

Viktor Garanin strode into the Holburne Museum, a man on a mission to recover the second tainted painting.

It had been a frustrating morning. He arrived promptly as the museum opened, only to be told that the man he needed to speak with, Mr. James Fisher, would be out of the building all morning for a talk at an historical society. He wasn't expected in his office until 2:30 that afternoon.

Viktor did a good job of hiding his contempt for the secretary who imparted this information. With her public school accent and haughty manner, all that creamy pale skin and soft blonde hair, she was so condescendingly polite she reminded him of his mother. So terribly British. She represented everything he loathed about the English.

He couldn't face wasting more hours examining the art or objects that filled the museum's rooms. After yesterday, he could quote from their brochure: Sir Thomas William Holburne inherited family treasure of Chinese armorial porcelain, silver, and portraits, adding his own collections of 17th and 18th century *objects d'art*, from old master paintings and furniture to Roman glass, coins, and enamels. Holburne's sister eventually bequeathed the enormous collection, over 4,000 items, to the people of Bath.

What a ridiculous family and an obscene assemblage of useless items. Wastrels, all of them. He could believe the British were keen on this stuff, but waves of tourists from other countries seemed to eat it up, too.

He'd left the museum in a tense state, fists clenched, wanting to strike out at something or someone. If he knew the town better, he would have looked for a boxing gym to get a bloody nose, or to give a few.

Instead, he attached himself to a tour headed behind Bath Abbey to the Roman baths, where the green, glowing water, laden with over 40 minerals you could taste—*bah!*—steamed up into the colonnaded terrace. This was topped with a collection of statues the Victorians had erected of Roman emperors mixed with British governors. Who else would they put up there but themselves? More than just hating British architecture, he hated the people, their looks, their customs and their bloody-minded assurance that they were superior beings. He hated his mother.

He'd followed the tour to Pulteney Bridge, the Palladian edifice executed in pale Bath stone often compared to Florence's Ponte Vecchio as two of the world's prettiest bridges. This one had a road running through its center. Along either side, shops sold tat of all kinds, strung out across its span. Hideous.

His contempt for the whole British nation surged, cementing his resolve to see his plan for their ruination through to its culmination, whatever the cost. What was one pitiful life of a dead art restorer compared to the greatness he would achieve with a national outbreak of smallpox that destroyed the entire British population? Then there would be no more weaklings, like his mother, who couldn't take what his father had dished out.

At the back of his mind, a small voice whispered that if he succeeded in what he'd hoped, there was no guarantee the epidemic wouldn't spread to his beloved Russia. Being an island had its advantages for quarantine and control. Viktor thought the world would rise up and make certain that no one from anywhere in the British Isles would be able to leave or travel anywhere. The thought of the resulting international upheaval satisfied him almost as much as the ensuing deaths. If he were extremely lucky, Ireland might be included in the ban, but he wouldn't dwell on that. Only Vanya would have notice and time to get himself to Russia and join Viktor, back to his homeland.

Viktor lingered by the weir. The guide informed them that this had been built as part of a flood prevention scheme in the late 1960s. Viktor recognized the site from the most recent film version of *Les Miserables*, where Russell Crowe as Javert committed suicide. Viktor stared at the thundering water, and pictured himself holding James Fisher of the fancy Holburne Museum over the weir by his ankles, as the man screamed and bucked and pleaded for mercy. The daydream blossomed, and he felt satisfaction flood him when he let go and watched the idiot's body falling, falling, falling into the rushing water.

That had been the highlight in an otherwise tedious day. He'd lunched at the Pump Room, and had to admit while the pheasant terrine on top of a warm bacon and lentil salad was tasty, the duck confit and white bean cassoulet that followed had been missing caraway seeds to make it a stunning dish. Sufficiently sated, he returned to the office of the Special Exhibits at precisely 2:30 PM to find the one punctual person in all of England had actually returned 10 minutes earlier.

Viktor projected an aura of bonhomie James Fisher responded to, after glancing at his credentials, once he saw **PUSHKIN MUSEUM** on the heading of Viktor's ID card. He smiled and shifted in his seat when Viktor explained the museum had sent him to examine the Chagall to be certain it had arrived safely.

"I'm afraid the Chagall isn't on the premises at the moment," Fisher stammered, his previously pallid face turning a shade of crimson that made his nose, framed against his window's view of the green of Sydney Gardens, look like a bulb on a Christmas tree.

Viktor raised an eyebrow and waited. This was outside the usual procedure.

"When we unpacked it, there was a small defect in the frame. A minor crack, to be sure, but we wouldn't hang it in that condition." He assured Viktor the repair was being done at the gallery of a man with an excellent reputation with whom the museum had a contract for such repairs. "I promise Mr. Wright does excellent work. We entrust our minor repairs to him frequently; he's bonded and quite reliable. The painting was brought over by a special courier, and Charles signed for it." Fisher started to perspire under Viktor's glare. "Here, let me give you the address. You can call by, it's such a fine day, and see for yourself that the painting is totally unharmed."

Viktor acquiesced and stood, his black mood covered by his public persona once again. Fisher chatted amiably as he wrote down the address. "The thing with driving in Bath is that it's full of one-way systems, wasn't designed for cars. Damn those Georgians for not thinking ahead." He looked up with a smile and handed Viktor the note. "It's a brisk 10-minute walk. Give Charles my regards."

Viktor's veneer of charm returned as he accepted the slip of paper and shook hands with Fisher. He left the museum, walked down Great Pulteney Street and Laura Place over the bridge, where he stopped to look again at the roaring weir. Now that he had a face to add to his image, Fisher's red nose glowed in his mind's eye as Viktor held him over the rushing water and let go. It brought a small sense of satisfaction to work out these things in his imagination. All that was missing from the scene was the metallic scent of blood.

He passed the public Victoria Art Gallery, turned into Milsom Street, then left into Quiet Street, which was anything but. The narrow streets were a mix of cobble and larger paving stones, filled with shoppers and tourists, chatting in a multitude of languages. A right into John Street, and he approached his destination. He crumpled the directions and threw them into a bin. The gallery had painted woodwork and a large sign overhead: CHARLES WRIGHT, FINE ART AND CUSTOM FRAMING.

Viktor composed his features in a smile as he opened the door, where a bell jangled to alert the owner he had a customer. He certainly intended to convey Fisher's best regards. Soon Viktor would be with his Chagall, the one with the image of a bride in her white dress and veil, lying on a red horse and floating with a lit menorah over a tiny village below. One of the houses sported a bright blue door.

Bath

2:38 PM

Nora appreciated Helen's competent driving through Bath's complicated maze of one-ways, and bus gates not used for cars, while she tried to tamp down her feelings of unease.

Helen drove the family's Audi A6. Sean's buggy folded easily in the boot of the dark green estate car. She'd readily agreed it made sense to leave Nora's car parked at the house after their find. Stowing both dogs inside, Helen set the house alarm, and texted Philly she'd done so, in case the young woman arrived home before they were back from town.

Nora's stomach soured after finding the tracker. There was no pretending she didn't have a stalker. "For the life of me, I just can't understand why someone would want to follow me. I suppose it could be a criminal Declan's had dealings with, looking to exact revenge." She rubbed her temples, where a headache was starting. "But that's a far reach. We're not married. How many people know about our relationship?"

"Maybe it's a fan of your amateur sleuthing skills," Helen teased. She squeezed Nora's hand. "Look, we're taking precautions and will keep our eyes open. No one will approach you if you're not alone, and I'm glued to your side."

Nora bit her lip. "Thanks, Helen. I don't want to put you in any danger."

"Nonsense. Declan will sort this out as soon as—and you'll see it's some nutter who's in love with you."

"As if." Nora smiled in spite of her fears. "If only it were that simple."

"We'll leave the car near Victoria Park and walk back. It's only a few minutes."

Nora scanned the edge of the vast park as Helen slowed down, searching for one of the coveted spaces near the park's entrance. "There's someone pulling out."

"Mission accomplished." Helen parked and retrieved Sean's buggy, while Nora unbuckled him from his car seat. "After you talk with Nic, we can take Sean for a walk here. The park is lovely, lots of mature trees and different paths." It was cool but sunny, and the leaves crunched underfoot as they walked toward the bookstore.

Nora started to agree, then remembered Declan's admonition. "Let's think about that. Declan said we were to keep a low profile."

The air smelled of damp earth and dying leaves. Sean pointed to things as they walked and Nora responded with their names. "Tree." She bent down and picked up an orange leaf, twisted and dry. "Leaf." She handed it to him after reminding him not to put it in his mouth.

"Lee," he repeated. He sniffed it, then crumpled it in his hand

and chortled. Bits fell over the front of his jumper. "Lee, Mum."

Nora stopped to brush off his jumper and tousled his hair. "Yes, leaffff." She stressed the "F" and laughed as the child bit his bottom lip in imitation.

Nora admired the Bath stone buildings and sense of history as they walked, while Helen wove the buggy in and out of the people they passed. Soon they reached John Street, and approached the bookstore that would host Nora tomorrow for her reading and signing.

Despite her stress, Nora's spirits rose. This was something she'd wanted for a long time. It had been one thing to hold her first book in her hand from the printer. It would be another milestone to stand before a group of people, no matter how small, and talk about writing this second book, and the stories she'd developed for the band of fairies, gnomes, and sprites who lived on the Lake District's Belle Isle in the middle of Windermere.

"Here we are." Helen stopped before the shop spread over two storefronts. Crisp cream paint picked out thick molding around the doors and large windows. **Books** headed each display window, along with numbers over each of the two entrance doors, painted purple. A sign hung overhead sideways from an ornate iron arm matched a larger version set on the wall between the two windows, also in purple:

Mr B's Emporium of Reading Delights

Nora checked her watch. 2:56. Perfect.

"Look." Helen pointed to a poster set in the corner of each window, advertising tomorrow's appearance. She read aloud: "'Nora Tierney, author of The Belle Island Fairy series, will delight us with a reading and signing. Tuesday, 2 PM.' We'll ask Nic to save one of those for your scrapbook."

Nora's heart lifted. She opened the door and they pushed their way inside, Helen carefully navigating the buggy. The rooms were small, filled floor to ceiling with a maze of shelved books, exuding the scents of ink and paper. There was a rack of stationery and fine art cards. Nora could see the original stairway down to a basement, and up to the first floor. A studious-looking young woman with her hair in a bun sat at the till, reading a dog-eared copy of *Breakfast at Tiffany's*.

"Hi, Lucinda." Helen introduced Nora. "This is Nora Tierney, your author for tomorrow."

"Sorry to interrupt your reading." Nora held out her hand. "I'm here to meet Nic Bottomley."

"No worries." Lucinda shook her hand and put her book down. "It's the sixth time I've read it." She hit an intercom button on their phone and listened after announcing Nora's arrival. "Yes, I'll smooth the waters."

"Is there a problem?" Nora could see her day being cancelled. Suddenly it seemed to matter to her very much.

"Nope. Nic just asked if you could find something to do for half an hour. He's tied up with a buyer's spring catalogue—they ran over time."

Nora breathed in relief. "No, that's fine, but we're in the way here."

Helen shifted the buggy to allow a group of teenagers to enter the crowded space. "We'll come back closer to 3:30." Helen was already backing the buggy out.

"Brilliant!" Lucinda picked up her book. "See you then."

Out on the sidewalk, Nora felt a sense of anticlimax. "It's a lovely bookshop, Helen."

"It is, jam-packed with goodies. Wait till you see the Reading Booth upstairs." She jostled the buggy onto the sidewalk and looked around. "Just half an hour, not enough time for tea."

Nora didn't want to go far. Clouds made the sky decidedly darker. She spied a gallery next door and looked into the window, where a tall, broad-shouldered man wrapped a package with bubble wrap.

"Let's wait in here." Nora pushed the door open and a bell jingled. The man looked up sharply as Nora glanced around. The room was airy, with freshly scrubbed wooden floors and simple white walls covered with clusters of framed art pieces in a pleasing jumble. Contemporary art hung next to vintage etchings and Impressionist paintings, which all hung near something that reminded Nora of Sean's scribbles. Several standing racks held lithographs, signed posters, and engravings. The wall behind the counter was laden with row upon row of moulding samples for frames, thick and thin, ornate and plain, painted or stained woods and metals. Best of all, there was a large open space in front of the desk, ample for the buggy.

"Park Sean right here." Nora helped Helen lift the buggy over the sill. Sean looked sleepy and she lowered the backrest and handed him his bunny so he could nap. The man frowned as he watched them.

"Can I help you?" His voice was husky, with the trace of an accent Nora couldn't place. He was dressed in an impeccably tailored suit and tie, and while Nora thought of gallery owners as being more eclectic, even casual, in their appearance and dress, she was comparing them to Val and Helen, apparently worlds apart.

"Just browsing," Nora said, choosing to ignore the man's dark expression.

"Closing early today," the man grunted, snapping thick tape around the packing material. The tape dispenser screeched with each turn of the roll.

Sean didn't seem to notice, his eyes at half-mast. He clutched Peter Rabbit and chewed one ear absently.

The owner came out from behind the counter and turned the door sign over to CLOSED, then disappeared with his package into a back office.

"We can try to park at the same gate by the Botanical Gardens tomorrow," Helen said, examining a bust that stood on a plinth in one corner. "I'll take Sean for a walk and we'll meet up afterwards. You don't need the distraction while you're trying to talk."

Nora wandered the large room, taking in the art. "If you say so. I don't want to take advantage." A small painting caught her eye, and she walked over to inspect it.

"Don't worry on that score. I'd like my own private time with Sean."

The Impressionist garden scene startled Nora. A woman in a white dress rested in a hammock in an enclosed garden bordered by shrubs and climbing roses. A young girl stood to the right of a table set for breakfast. At the table sat another woman with a young child in a high chair. A dog dozed on the grass at their feet.

Nora could have been looking at the scene Val painted in her imagination of the back garden at Haven Cottage, even though the clothing and furniture seemed late Victorian or early Edwardian.

"Helen, look at this." Nora whispered. Sean had dozed off; Helen crossed the room to join her.

"This could be the garden at Haven Cottage I've just rented." She explained about the house Val showed her that she'd inexplicably rented with an option to buy, adding that not only hadn't Declan seen it, she'd neglected to work into their Sunday conversations that she'd signed the contract.

Helen waved her off. "Declan won't care as long as there's room for him and you like it."

"I hope so. But look here." Nora pointed to the card mounted next to the painting:

Study for THE OPEN AIR BREAKFAST

William Merritt Chase, c1887 18" x 24"

"Chase is one of my favorite American painters. I had posters of the series he did of Long Island beaches and dunes in my room at home." Nora leaned closer. The painting called to her with its idyllic setting. She'd been drawn to that garden at Haven Cottage as much as the house.

The price of the picture was hefty but not astronomical, and Nora thought of her last conversation with her mother. Amelia Scott insisted her daughter spend a bit of her inheritance on something beautiful to take to her new home.

"My mom told me Paul left me that money as a gift. She said I should find a token to take into my new life with Declan as a remembrance of the good times we shared." With a jolt, Nora remembered there had been good times, at least early on in their relationship. She'd been so remorseful after his death about wanting to break their engagement that she'd forgotten she'd once loved the man.

"This certainly fits the bill," Helen pointed out. "Chase is good value if you like Impressionists."

"They've always been my favorite. This would be a little piece of the East Coast in my English home." Still, Nora hesitated, feeling at that moment like Val's stepmother, a consummate shopper whose favorite expression was "wrap it up!" Should she spend money on herself just because she could? She felt Helen's hand on her shoulder.

"Nora, it's not wrong to surround yourself with things you love. Remember what William Morris said: 'Have nothing in your house that you do not know to be useful, or believe to be beautiful.'"

Helen's words pushed Nora over the edge of indecision. "I've always been a Morris fan." She felt like a schoolgirl at Christmas as she lifted the painting off the wall, and together she and Helen inspected it critically. The frame was gilt, thick and ornate, the perfect foil for the simple pastoral image it contained.

Nora carried it over to the desk and looked around. Charles Wright was the owner, according to the cards in a holder by the cash register, but Mr. Wright seemed to have disappeared.

"Ring the bell," Helen suggested, pointing to a call bell like those most hotels used for a porter. "It's a good thing this is the study. The full-size is one of his largest paintings. I think it's in the Toledo Museum of Art."

The sharp ding did the trick. Mr. Wright didn't appear happy to have a potential sale, but took his place behind the counter. "I'd like this painting, please." Nora handed him the price card, and laid the painting carefully on the desk. She fumbled in her purse for her credit card.

Mr. Wright's eyebrows rose. "No credit," he pronounced, and tore off a large piece from the roll of bubble wrap for the piece.

Nora was taken aback. "Excuse me?"

"The machine—is not functioning today. Cash, maybe?" His sudden animation at the thought of a healthy wad of cash disturbed Nora.

The man was a monster. Nora rooted around inside her bag and found her checkbook. "Will a check do? I do have ID. I don't carry that kind of cash around."

"Fine." The man's curt manner reappeared, and he taped the bubble wrap in place. He handed Nora the painting after she wrote out her check and displayed her driver's license.

"Don't I get some kind of receipt?" Nora was nonplussed. This was the strangest transaction she'd ever had.

"What about the provenance?" Helen said. "There should be documentation that this really is a Chase, after all. She's entitled to a copy of that."

"Of course, sorry. Silly of me. You've caught me on a bad day. One moment."

Mr. Wright ducked into a back room and they heard file drawers opening and closing.

Nora checked her mobile. "3:25. We should get back next door."

Helen laughed. "Relax, Nora. Nic will wait for us. He's not going to cancel your signing. You were there on time, after all."

Wright returned and handed Nora a folder with the heading "Chase-Breakfast," which Helen took from her and inspected.

"This seems fine," Helen said. "These appear to be the originals." Art dealer Helen was in full force, and Nora let her do her work.

"Um, there's a copy in the files." He jerked his head, indicating the back room. "Is fine."

"Thank you." Helen stuffed the folder in Nora's bag and hefted the painting. "I'll carry this—you get Sean's buggy for a change."

3:27 PM

Viktor watched Nora Tierney and her friend leave the art gallery and enter the bookshop next door.

When he'd arrived at the gallery earlier he'd been delighted to see that he walked right past the site of the bookstore where Tierney would be speaking tomorrow. Easier to find again. Then the woman had walked right into the gallery. It was kismet.

Perhaps his luck was about to change. It would make his plan that much easier to carry out, and with any luck, by the end of this week he'd have everything—and everyone—he needed *nailed up* and hard at work.

Viktor laughed at the image brought to mind by his thoughts: *nailed up*, as in a crucifixion. What would be nailed down, like the top of a coffin, would be the future of Great Britain, and he himself would be the man responsible for it all.

CHAPTER SIXTEEN

Oxford

3:28 PM

Declan left Tamsin Chen in his office working on her laptop while he sought out Watkins, his sounding board. He needed to check on the information coming into the murder room. The room had been set up with extra computers and two large whiteboards, but this was hardly their usual kind of murder case. On the way, he dialed Simon and reiterated for everyone to keep their eyes open at Ramsey Lodge. While he never mentioned the two bugs, he told him Nora was concerned her stalker had followed her and might circle back to Cumbria.

His thoughts strayed to Stanley Jevons, and the defeated look on his face when Declan had seen him. It upset the natural order of things for a child to die before her parents. He was glad Janet Wallace had been there to support the man, especially after the medical examiner had isolated the poor woman's body, so the father hadn't been able to see her. He had learned in this morning's update it would be recommended that Emma be cremated.

"Anything new?" Declan asked Watkins, who monitored the input of new information.

"Some good news, if you can call it that. None of Emma's co-workers are showing any symptoms. No blisters, no fevers. Dr. Conlon told me none of the staff who treated Emma are, either, but the CDC is recommending those who worked with her before she was put on isolation be vaccinated." Watkins shifted a pile of papers and slid them into a folder. "Still waiting on McAfee, taking his bloody time at the shipping agents. Let's hope this case is settled soon. Julie will never forgive me if I miss her having the baby."

Declan slapped him on the back. "I won't tell her you'd rather sit in the waiting room and be handed a clean squirming bundle."

Watkins winced. "I hate when you use words like 'squirming.' Gives me visions of a slippery eel I'm liable to drop."

"I can even show you how to put on a nappy correctly."

"We did that in our prenatal class and I was brilliant." The expectant father gave Declan a wide smile.

"See? You'll be a winner."

A civilian analyst dumped a stack of fresh reports on Watkins' desk. "More for you. Witness statements from the drug case pretrial hearings."

Despite Emma Jevons' murder, this wasn't the only situation the team juggled. "Take a walk with me," he told his sergeant, and the two stepped into the rear car park for a breath of air.

"What's up, guv? Chafing at the Tamsin bit?"

Nora's safety was the thought at the forefront of his mind. Declan brought Watkins up to date on the GPS tracker Nora found on her car. "I have to get to Bath, make sure she's protected. But between this smallpox, the chief, and Chen, I don't see how that's possible."

Watkins lowered his voice. "With this second one, maybe go around Chen? You need to check on Nora, I'll cover. Say you went back to the John Radcliffe or the Ashmolean, and you can zip there and back if you must see her."

Declan paced, thinking out loud. "Thanks. Nora's meeting with the bookshop owner this afternoon so she's out already. Helen is with her, and then they'll go straight to her house overnight." He appreciated his sergeant being willing to cover for him, but he examined the situation from all angles. "If I suddenly show up, Nora will know I'm worried and I don't want her to know how much this has me bothered. I certainly don't need her panicking. Maybe taking a three-hour round trip to reassure myself for no reason isn't wise."

"Nora's not the panicky type, but I hear you, Dec. No need to raise the alarm bells if she seems safe. Speaking of alarms—does the house she's staying in have one?"

Declan brightened. "Yes, Nora said Helen set it before they left for town."

"Our experience with stalkers is that they stay distant until some inciting incident makes them escalate their approach, right?"

Declan nodded.

"So if you don't feel you can leave right this moment, let's use Chen and her contacts to get this wrapped up so we can get you to Bath as soon as possible."

"In the meantime, I'll make certain there are extra patrols on Helen's house." He clapped Watkins on the shoulder. "Thanks for talking me off the ledge."

"We aim to please." Watkins held the door open. "Just remember you owe me one when I'm in the teething phase."

The sergeant headed back to the murder room. Declan called the Bath and North East Somerset District Headquarters, a division of Avon and Somerset Constabulary. He hadn't heard back from his morning voicemail to his contact in Bath, and now he called the headquarters directly, only to find the DI he knew was on vacation.

"Off sunning himself in Tenerife, lucky bastard, while the rest of us hold down the fort." Alex Thalmann was the detective who spoke with Declan.

Declan explained the situation succinctly about Nora and the two tracking devices that had been found.

"We can send a Wiltshire patrol car on regular rounds to Hill House. I'll alert uniform to keep an eye out for lurkers. Any idea of the home's normal inhabitants?"

Declan breathed a sigh of relief that Thalmann took him seriously. He described Nora's car and remembered what Nora had said about Helen's. He didn't know what Matthew currently drove, but mentioned he was out of the house until the end of the week. "There's a sixth-form daughter due to arrive home later, Philippa. That should be who's at the house overnight with Nora's son, a toddler."

"I'll have them keep me apprised of any suspicious loiterers, but it will be difficult for anyone to get to that house. If it's the place I'm thinking of, the driveway is narrow and gated, and the house literally sits on top of a hill."

"Thank you, sergeant. I owe you a pint when you come to Oxford."

As he hung up, Declan reckoned that was two favors already outstanding he owed people.

Bath

3:29 PM

Nic Bottomley met Nora and Helen at the bookshop door on their return from the gallery. He apologized profusely for being tied up earlier, and his charming smile made it easy for Nora to see why his shop was so popular. Nic had a way of tuning out the chaos around him, and concentrating completely on the person who was with him.

"Happens all the time, I'm afraid. As the day goes on I fall further behind in my schedule."

Helen held up Nora's package. "Nora's not sorry. It gave us time to shop next door."

"Charlie Wright's place? Lovely, isn't he? So friendly and down-to-earth."

Nora and Helen exchanged looks. Helen's eyebrows rose. "I don't think Helen and I had quite that experience," Nora explained. "He actually seemed quite odd."

"Really? Must be an off day." Nic pointed to the painting. "Do you want to stow that behind the counter? Lucinda will keep an eye on it."

"Perfect." Helen handed him the painting. "I have to pick up some paint samples at Davies on Monmouth Street." She motioned toward Sean, who slept peacefully on. "I'll just take Mr. Sleepyhead with me, and Nic can show you around, Nora."

"Redecorating, Helen? More work for Matthew?" Nic teased.

"Always." She commandeered the buggy from Nora and waved them off. "I'll be back in half an hour or so."

Nic helped her out with the buggy, then he and Nora walked past a claw foot tub filled with books and up the restored staircase to the first floor.

"Neat idea for a display, that bath tub," Nora said.

"My wife, Juliette, is the chief decorator." Nic led the way through several book-filled rooms with stripped flooring, one with walls decorated with pages from Tintin books, into a far one with a fireplace whose walls sported deep pink polished plaster that complimented its olive green bookshelves.

A thrill ran through Nora as she took in the space that would hold her first event as an author. It was a day she'd hoped for since her debut book was published last year. That one had made decent sales, and with the second launched, her publisher was prepared to reimburse her travel to signings if she could find bookstores or libraries willing to host her. Gone were the days of publishers having large budgets to spend on marketing their writers. She'd learned it was up to the majority of today's authors except the top two or three percent to find their own outlets.

"You'll stand in front of the fireplace to speak," Nic pointed, "and we'll move that green Queen Anne chair and the leather club chair to the back, and add folding chairs up front. Then you'll be signing in Professor Dupont's Reading Room, here." He led the way to a second small room behind the one they stood in. "This used to be an office."

"Professor Dupont from the Quentin Blake book, *Cockatoos*? I love that book." Nora explained she had been given a copy but Sean was far too young for it.

"Yes, it was my idea for the name, but Juliette got carried away with the decorating. We use this for our book spas, too, where you can have cakes and rummage through a stack of books specially chosen for you—great gift."

He pointed inside a small space that, with its dark green walls and harlequin floor, reminded Nora of Henry Higgins' mum's garden room. "She and Helen love to compare decorating ideas," he said. "Don't get them started on how many shades of white there are."

Nora took in the space. The feel was pure Edwardian, from the wicker chair, vintage lace curtains and faux butterfly collection, to the stand holding a wooden gold and white cockatoo. She hoped the oak claw-foot table would be the one she sat at to sign her books. A frisson of excitement that drowned out all thoughts of stalkers and danger ran through her.

Nora ducked back into the larger room and tried to picture herself standing in front of the fireplace.

Nic's phone beeped with a text. "Sorry, minor issue downstairs with a customer."

"Go ahead. I'll stay here a minute and soak up the atmosphere."

"Take as long as you like."

Nora heard his footsteps on the rickety stairs and noted a sign describing the book spa:

With a Mr B's Reading Spa you are invited to our gorgeous shop in

Bath for some bookish pampering in one of our sumptuous bibliotherapy rooms. One of our team of booksellers will learn all about your favourite reads by having an informal chat with you over coffee or tea and some delicious cake, before introducing you to a tower of books especially selected to suit your tastes.

Gift certificates available.

That might be a perfect thank you to Helen for having her to stay this week and setting up the reading at Mr B's.

While there were browsers on the other side of the fireplace wall in the children's room, for a moment Nora had this room to herself. She stood in front of the fireplace and pictured a handful of people, largely women. She hoped they would ask questions after she gave her prepared talk, one she'd agonized over back at Ramsey Lodge. She'd decided to write down bullet points on an index card and segue from one topic to another in terms of her ideas and process, instead of a formal talk she read.

Thinking of Ramsey Lodge led to her thinking of Simon and Kate, and she knew she owed them a call to tell them about Port Enys. She should call Val for the same reason, and let her know there was strong evidence of a stalker. She'd make those calls tonight from Helen's after Sean was asleep.

Nora took several pictures of the room, the fireplace, and the Reading Booth, and sent them with a group text to Declan, Simon and Val. *This is where the magic happens tomorrow!* Then she moved to the tall window to get a clearer signal, and looked out at the back entrances to Jolly's, the department store and tearoom across the street.

A man lounged against the inner corner of a set of double doors, out of the way, but obviously wasting time. He wasn't having a smoke nor checking his mobile. Something about his stance seemed eerily familiar.

The man moved forward into the sunlight and looked up and

down the road. Maybe waiting for a ride? He turned to the side, checked his watch, and Nora scrutinised his profile from her downward angle. He wore jeans and a dark jacket with a baseball cap that kept his features in shadow, except for a thatch of hair curling on the nape of his neck. Nora's mouth went dry when she realized why he seemed familiar. She could swear he was the man who'd passed her on the road while she waited to turn into Port Enys, and his gait was that of her stalker from Bowness.

What was he doing in Bath? Could this be her pursuer? Had he learned enough of her plans before she'd found those trackers to follow her here? Her stomach knotted with anxiety again, and she tried to cement his appearance to describe him to Declan, but from this height and angle, she couldn't see facial details.

Then she remembered her phone. She turned the camera back on just as a police car pulled up in front of the Wright gallery next door, lights flashing, and blocked her view of the man as he hurried away.

CHAPTER SEVENTEEN

Oxford

5:50 PM

Declan thanked Watkins and the rest of the team after their meeting with the Public Health England supervisor. Everyone known to have been in contact with Emma Jevons remained without symptoms. Her movements had been traced on her last day to the Oxford branch of Boots Chemists, and the sales assistant who'd served her was fine, too. There was nothing in the PHE report that couldn't have been sent over in an email, but the official had insisted on coming down to the station and speaking to them in person.

She must need to dot her i's and cross her t's, Declan decided. Her own bosses would be looking over her shoulder at this case with its severe international implications. The very real task of preventing an epidemic was her responsibility, and Declan didn't envy her the job.

His team had worked flat out since Emma Jevons' death. The initial rush was over, interviews concluded, systems set in place. Now would come the more tedious job of watching and monitoring new information obtained by either Tamsin Chen's team or what they'd ferret out themselves as they inched forward to find the person responsible.

"Best get some rest while we can," Declan told them, sending everyone home at a reasonable hour for a change. There were no new developments to warrant extensive overtime at this point. A three-hour round-trip to Bath might be out of the question yet, but knowing patrols were alerted to Hill House comforted him. He rubbed eyes itchy with fatigue.

"You, too, Watkins," he told his sergeant, who hovered nearby, waiting for instructions as the room cleared. "Get an early night with Julie before that baby arrives."

"I was waiting for McAfee to come back in." Watkins blew out his cheeks. "This baby—it changes everything, doesn't it?"

Declan nodded. "But for the best, I promise. You'll be smitten with her."

"Him," Watkins growled, and turned to go. "Say, guv, you and Nora ever talk about having one together?"

Declan tilted his head to one side in consideration. "Not yet, but it's something to think about, isn't it?" *Was it, with the specter of Paul Pembroke rearing his ugly head just now?* Declan felt disconcerted as he walked back to his office. Would he ever be certain Nora was over Paul?

Tamsin Chen disappeared when the meeting was announced, mumbling she would talk to her office for any updates. He had the distinct feeling the woman knew more than she was telling him. He could hear the chief in his ear when they'd been introduced and remembered the tenor of that initial conversation: "I've assured Ms. Chen you will be amenable to making her part of your team, and including her in information as it comes in so she's fully apprised of the situation."

What his super hadn't mentioned was that the lovely Ms. Chen was under the same obligation to share her information with Declan. Information should flow both ways. He felt on edge and slightly righteous when he returned to the second floor and approached his office, only to see Chen coming down the hall toward him.

"I have an update and it's not good news." She twisted the slim gold ring set with an opal she wore on her right hand.

"Do I need to call the team back? I just let them go home on time for a change."

"No, we need to discuss this first." She re-entered his office and sat down by her laptop, stationed on the corner of his desk. "I'm waiting for an email to download."

Declan leaned over her shoulder as she opened an attachment. A photo of a painting in the style of Chagall filled her screen. A bride leaned on a horse in the sky over a small village, where one of the few houses had a blue door.

"What am I looking at?" He caught Tamsin's scent fully for the first time, a hint of jasmine and patchouli. It suited her, exotic and mysterious.

"That's a Chagall the Pushkin owns, *Nocturne*, painted in 1947. It was the second painting sent over in that shipment." She looked up at him, her dark eyes narrowed.

Declan's mind went into overdrive. How had McAfee missed this when he spoke with the shipping agents? Was it possible they were sent separately? The young sergeant might be due for a stiff talk when Declan got his hands on him if he'd not ferreted this out. But hadn't Watkins said McAfee was still on his way back in? Still, he should have called in with information this important, instead of waiting to make a formal report. How did Tamsin get the information? Of course: her outfit. Why didn't they just take over now?

He tamped down his irritation to get more details. "You're thinking that bit of blue door or wall or whatever it is might be infected, too? Where is the painting now?"

"It was sent to the Holburne Museum in Bath for an exhibit." Chen clicked the image off.

Declan raised his eyebrows. A second painting on the loose? Hopefully this one had not needed cleaning. "We have to call them and have the painting taken into quarantined evidence immediately."

"Already done. My outfit went over this afternoon to take it into custody. I'm waiting to hear from them." She snapped her laptop closed. "This thing is bigger than we originally thought."

What was on her laptop she didn't want Declan to see? With any luck, this new development might provide the reason he needed to travel to Bath. But Declan realized he needed to finesse the situation to gain the agent's confidence. After all, his chief had practically ordered him to cooperate with her.

"How about a quick bite before we wrap up?"

Ten minutes later they sat at a corner table down the street at St. Aldates Tavern. The pub was noisy enough that their conversation wouldn't be overhead.

After ordering, Declan brought Tamsin up to speed on the lack of symptoms in Emma Jevons' colleagues and acquaintances, as well as the staff at the hospital. She, in turn, assured him she'd been coming to find him when she'd received the news about the second painting. Détente.

Then he asked what he really wanted to know. "Any luck with information on Paul Pembroke?"

"It's as you said. Died in a plane accident on his way to give a lecture to a group of biologists in Switzerland. No bodies recovered, but wreckage in the Alps pretty definitive. They decided it was some kind of mechanical catastrophe."

Declan sipped his beer. "Any idea what he was working on?"

She shrugged elaborately, a trivial gesture that didn't sit well on such a decisive person. "Microbiologist, could be anything. Brilliant guy, all those degrees."

Declan shrugged back. Two could play this game. "If you say so."

She counted off on her fingers. "BSc (Hons) in Biochemistry from Magdalen here at Oxford; Masters in Microbiology from Harvard; then a PhD in Biochemistry and Cell Biology from the University of Nottingham. Plus assorted research papers and awards."

Declan felt an uncharacteristic surge of jealousy. "Of course."

Their food arrived and as they started eating, Declan realized he'd never given Paul Pembroke this much thought, beyond the obvious fact that he was Sean's biological father. He hadn't bothered to think of him alive, as a breathing, thinking person who must have had some redeeming qualities, or Nora wouldn't have been attracted to him. He'd deliberately shied away from picturing Paul and Nora making love.

Now that he thought of it, he realized he'd never seen a photo of Paul, and resisted an urge to Google Image him as he ate his shepherd's pie. To hear Paul called "brilliant" by Tamsin Chen shouldn't come as a surprise, given his position at the Ministry of Defence, but it still had.

The fact that it bothered him so much was the second surprise.

Bath

7:25 PM

Nora listened to the giggles and splashes floating down the Sackvilles' stairs from Sean's bath. Helen's daughter had taken possession of the child the minute they'd returned from town. Philly scooped him up after protesting she didn't have any homework but a few chapters of reading she could do once Sean was in bed, and took him outside to play. After his dinner, she'd insisted she could handle his bath while Nora helped Helen make their meal.

"It must be nice to have someone at home who's a real help," Nora commented as she washed lettuce for a salad.

Helen arched an eyebrow. "You, my friend, have a lot to learn.

Wait until Sean is an adolescent, and there are endless arguments about lifts he needs, then about borrowing the car, or whining about gadgets he simply must have. You'll think back and miss this stage, time-consuming as it is."

"You're probably right." Nora tore the lettuce into a wooden trug. "It helps that this is such a peaceful spot." After Declan's text that the house would be patrolled, she and Helen had both relaxed. With everyone in for the night, the gate was locked and she felt safe in Hill House.

"The cottage you told me about sounds equally peaceful." Helen put her dish of chicken into the Aga baking oven and set a timer.

Nora explained about the puppy that seemed entailed to the property. "I don't think we can live there without that little beagle Sean's named Typo. Sean would be on a therapist's couch years later."

"Every child needs an animal to love. It teaches them responsibility, gives them a friend who's always there."

"You mean when they hate their mum?" They shared a laugh. "How does Bella like Scotland?"

"She loves it and wants you to bring the fairies to Edinburgh."

Nora brightened and dried her hands, then took out the notebook she carried in her bag. "Great idea! I've been wondering where to take them next. Tell her it's a go." She scribbled a few lines and snapped the book shut.

"Don't tell me you have a storyline already." Helen took tomatoes from a hanging wire basket and gave them to Nora to slice.

"Just noting the setting. Edinburgh Castle, the fairies slipping into someone's backpack for an adventure. I'll work on it as I try to fall asleep. I do my best plotting then, a surefire sleeping pill."

Helen laughed. "I do enjoy hearing about a writer's process."

They settled in the sitting room with cups of tea, waiting for

Philly and Sean. Nora took a deep breath, and looked around the pleasant room. She'd called Val and Simon, updated them on Port Enys, and reassured them that Declan had arranged for police patrols at Helen's.

There wasn't more that could be done at the moment. She could hardly call pubs and hotels around Bath to ask if they had any tall guests who wore baseball caps. The lack of opportunity to investigate on her own was a source of frustration for Nora. Even the alias the follower used—the Grant Alan that Daisy had mentioned who'd stayed at The Scarlet Wench—showed he was playing with her. Nora tried not to focus on what it would take for the police to become more actively involved at this point.

Instead, she admired the Sackvilles' antiques mixed with Bella's art on the walls. Thick drapes pulled across the locked glass doors that usually allowed views of the patchwork-quilted Somerset hills in daylight gave Nora a sense of closeted security. She felt herself start to unwind.

Helen held up a paint chip. "What do you think of painting this room navy blue?"

Nora's mobile rang. Declan. "Sorry—let me get this. I think it would be stunning with the white woodwork." She walked into the room used as an office to talk to Declan.

"I've already found my next storyline, thanks to Bella." She updated him on Helen and her family, whom he'd met on several occasions in Oxford. "Right now Philly's giving Sean his bath, and he's loving the attention. How's your case?"

"Coming along, but there's a new connection to Bath. I'll know more tomorrow, but fingers crossed I'll be there in the next day or so to liaise with them."

"Great! I really miss you. I feel like so much has happened and we haven't had time for a decent conversation." Nora launched into a description of her visit to Mr B's and the space where she would be reading tomorrow. It was now or never, telephone be damned.

"Do me a favor, Declan, and close your eyes. Are they closed?"

"Sure."

"Now pretend I'm sitting right next to you and we're having this conversation in person."

"What are you wearing, if anything? Just so I can make this real."

She laughed. "This is not phone sex, you pervert." She took a deep breath. "I bought a painting today at a gallery next to Mr B's because it reminded me of Haven Cottage, which I've decided to rent." She skipped over saying aloud that she'd made this decision without him; that was patently obvious. "I didn't want to lose it, and the place just felt like home to me. When I get back to Oxford, we'll tour it together and talk about paint colors and the garden—and maybe that puppy."

She held her breath, waiting for a firestorm that never came.

"Sounds wonderful. I'm anxious to see it, and you. If you liked it, I'm certain I will. We need the space, and the garden will be great for all of us. That's if you intend on my moving in with you."

"Of course I do! It's the main reason I'm moving back to Oxford."

"Well, glad we've got that sorted."

His gentle laughter made her smile. "Sorry we're not having this conversation in person. We seem to be pulled apart by circumstances."

"Your travel and my case. We'll sort out the details, don't worry. But the house sounds great, and I'm happy to have that settled. It means you'll really be coming back to Oxford. I miss you both, but I really miss you in my bed."

"Soon to be our bed."

"King size?"

"What else? Perfect for babies and puppies in the morning."

"And the middle of the night, alone together." They let their minds play with that thought for a while. "We'd better get off before this call gets X-rated. Anything else at your end? No suspicious people loitering?"

"Not here at the house. But the weirdest thing happened at the bookstore." Nora described the man she'd seen who highly resembled the one she'd noted near Port Enys, and how his gait reminded her of the man in Bowness. "You told me once it's really difficult for someone to change their gait if they don't know they're being observed."

"You remember that?"

"I remember all of your pearls of wisdom."

"I'll have to watch my back. Next you'll be looking for my job."

"Really though, my mind is in overdrive with the second bug we found." She noticed the prolonged silence on Declan's end of the phone and heard him scribbling.

"What did this person look like?" he finally asked.

"I couldn't see much. I was upstairs and he was across the street." Could they really be having this discussion in such a cool manner? "He wore a baseball cap. The usual: tall and lanky, but I could see dark hair curling over his collar."

"Just writing this down."

"I was feeling so safe here, Declan."

"Nora, you are safe. If I didn't think you were, I'd be there already. We have the patrols, and you're in an alarmed house behind a locked gate. This person hasn't approached you, ever, so he may just be a far-away admirer of some sort. I'll have Tamsin Chen look into it more thoroughly, too."

Nora thought Declan didn't believe for a moment in a simple devotee, but knew he was trying to reassure her. "I'll stay on high alert, just the same."

"Nora, this man—does he remind you of anyone—anyone at all?"

"No. Should he?"

"Just checking. Try to get some rest. And enjoy tomorrow, I know you're looking forward to it."

They rang off and Nora bit her lip. Declan had taken the house news so well, she should have felt relieved. But his question if her stalker reminded her of anyone she knew caught her off guard. She thought back to the shadowy presence that had haunted her for the past months. She combed her memory banks for the image of the man who'd been at Port Enys, and then perhaps, if it even was the same man, across the street from the bookstore today.

She could swear he didn't remind her of anyone she knew. So why had Declan asked the question?

Oxford

7:50 PM

Declan hesitated only a minute after Nora hung up, then pulled his laptop toward him and Googled "Dr. Paul Pembroke, MoD."

His search page quickly filled with multiple articles starting with the tragic plane crash that had taken the scientist's life. Research articles appeared further down the page.

Declan skimmed the first news reports that repeated what Nora and then Tamsin Chen had told him. The celebrated scientist died in a plane crash on his way to deliver an important paper in Switzerland.

He paged back up and hit "Images" and was surprised there

were so few, mostly repeats of the man in his white lab coat standing in front of a huge microscope that accompanied several of the articles he'd written. Paul Pembroke was slender, but of average height with sandy hair.

Declan wasn't clear why he felt such a sense of relief, but Paul Pembroke didn't resemble Nora's stalker at all.

Bath

7:55 PM

Tom Barnaby enjoyed his meal at The Eastern Eye, a northern Indian restaurant on Quiet Street located above a bank. He admired the lavish, giant murals of Indian life painted in vibrant colors on the walls under its triple domes, while he ate a subtly flavored lamb tikka nowabdar, its sauce flavored with cashews and fennel seeds.

Although he'd lost the two bugs on the Tierney woman, he'd gleaned enough of her itinerary from the voice bug for him to know she was scheduled to be at the bookstore today. He'd watched her enter, leave, visit the art gallery next door, then re-enter the store. He'd loitered across the street until the panda car had materialized at the gallery next door. That was one thing he didn't need—for his presence to come under police scrutiny. As it stood now, he was ending this assignment on a high note without incident. Mission accomplished.

He'd hightailed it out of the area and gone back to his pub, only to be contacted by his handler less than an hour later. The assignment to follow Nora Tierney was over. He could relax. No reason was given why the urgency had suddenly been deemed diminished, but then, he was on a need-to-know basis on these assignments, and he'd learned he would only be given the information deemed necessary to operate.

Still, it was the perfect ending to this assignment without real issues, capped by a fine meal now, a good bed tonight, and home to his bolt-hole tomorrow. "Tom" knew following Nora Tierney had taught him what his life was lacking. He'd been given holiday time for two weeks, and thought he would head back to Cumbria under his own name and visage this time, and explore the area. After that, he'd be talking to his superiors about a different kind of assignment, one that let him have a private life. He'd been at the whim of others far too long.

Chapter Eighteen

Bath

Tuesday, 12th October

6:45 AM

For the second morning in a row, Nora slept in, this time in the large and comfortable Sackville guest room. She opened her eyes as Sean stirred, and admired the wall color in the morning light. The pale blue-grey color would look wonderful in the guest bedroom in Haven Cottage, and she thought more of a periwinkle, one of her favorite colors, in the master bedroom, if Declan didn't mind. After his easy reaction last night to her rental, she hoped he'd leave most of the decorating to her. This soothing color looked more blue at times, more soft grey at others, depending on the light. Changeable, rather like the thoughts that whirled around her mind.

She heard Philly tiptoe in when Sean woke fully after a solid sleep, his teething behind him for the moment. All the play outside with two dogs had tired him out, and after his bath, despite new surroundings yet again, he'd fallen asleep quickly in his travel cot next to Nora's bed in Helen's peaceful room.

"I'll just take him downstairs, Nora," Philly whispered. "Mum says you're to sleep in today."

Nora turned over and fell back to sleep for another delicious hour. When she woke this time, she felt rested. Her sleep last night hadn't come easily. She'd tried her trick of working on the next book plot, picturing her troupe at Edinburgh Castle, but she kept returning to the menace of her pursuer. Why was she being followed? Who had she upset to the point that someone would track her, with not one but two devices?

It made her brain ache to think these thoughts. Declan had tried to reassure her last night. He said Tamsin Chen was looking into it, too, and wasn't that a chummy relationship in such a brief time? But then she realized for all she knew, Tamsin could be dumpy and mean, headed toward retirement.

She couldn't live her life like this, wondering every place she went if someone was watching her, or if Sean was at risk. The whole experience had given her an unsettled feeling in her stomach that accounted for her small appetite these days. One moment she felt peaceful, and the next her stomach lurched into knots, and her heart raced with anxiety. She wasn't a dithering person, but this situation had made her skittery. Look how she'd resisted telling Declan about the house, and about clarifying their living situation. That wasn't how she usually behaved at all.

She hated this. She was done with being an ostrich, with not taking action. After today and her signing, she resolved to do her best to flush this person out, make him show his face, and come out into the open. She would make him tell her what he wanted, and then she could deal with it in a safe, rational manner. She was proactive, not someone who sat home and quivered in fright.

In the shower, Nora simmered with anger. Today was supposed to be a special day for her, one she'd wanted for a very long time. It seemed that the highlights she'd always thought as a child she would remember most, one's most important days, she'd been denied. No wedding to the father of her child, for one. Then a murderess robbed her of being aware of Sean's birth, when she'd been pushed into Windermere, and been unconscious before an emergency Caesarean section. These milestones evaded her.

Her determination grew as did her ire, and she scrubbed her scalp till it tingled. This day might seem like a small accomplishment to someone else, but its importance grew in proportion to her resentment as she threw on a robe and wrapped a towel around her wet hair.

One of her strengths was her ability to compartmentalize. That had helped Nora when her father died, and when she'd dealt with three different murderers since moving to England. She sorted things into mental boxes, and addressed them when she had to, or when an outcome appeared to her. Otherwise, she had become an ace at not dwelling on stressful issues. She was determined to enjoy this afternoon. Mentally, she pictured boxing up the tall man in the baseball cap where he couldn't harm her and taping the box shut. After that, all bets were off.

Nora glanced out the large window, which overlooked the side yard at the back of the stables. A few hens pecked at the earth. The grounds and trees stretched down the hill, but she fancied she could see a patrol car passing the road at the hill's bottom through the leafless trees. It was comforting to know they were keeping an eye on Hill House. She mustered up her good mood, and tried on a smile for good measure.

She dressed casually for now, and used her new perfume. The soft blue-grey walls glowed in the morning light as she slipped on the watch her father had given her, her good luck talisman, and sent him a silent prayer to watch over her and her son. Time to relieve Helen.

Helen was scrolling on her iPad when Nora entered the kitchen. "Here's Mummy." She tapped on the tray of Sean's highchair to bring his attention away from watching Hester.

"Mum-mum." Sean reached out fingers coated with cereal and banana.

"And I love you, too." Nora dropped a kiss on his head and wet a paper towel to wipe his fingers. "You wear your breakfast well."

"Water's hot on the hob. Help yourself to porridge or toast, or I'll scramble you a few eggs after I check the local news from the *Somerset Press*."

Nora made herself a cup of tea and cut bread from a loaf standing on a cutting board. "Did you make this?"

Helen nodded as she read. "Wholemeal. Philly loves it as toast. She's off to school, but had great fun with Sean this morning."

"I need to thank her for letting me sleep in. To get showered and dressed in quiet was a luxury." The homey scent of toasted bread filled the kitchen. "Is there a better smell than toast?" She broke off a crust for Sean, who grabbed at it with a toothy smile. "Toast."

"Toes," he agreed, swiping the crust from her.

"Nora, come look at this." Helen scowled as she read aloud: 'Authorities say the body of Charles Wright, owner of an art gallery and framing store on John Street, was found in the back of his shop late yesterday afternoon. No details are forthcoming at this time. The 68-year old Wright had been in business for over 30 years and was a John Street fixture."

"Wait—" Nora looked over Helen's shoulder. "The man who waited on us couldn't have been that old."

Helen scrolled down to a photo captioned "Charles Wright last year at Bath's Chamber of Commerce Dinner." Both women froze.

The kindly balding man who seemed embarrassed to be given an award looked nothing like the man who'd sold them Nora's painting.

Oxford

8:12 AM

Declan received Tamsin's alert at 7:30 in the morning. After a round of texts to notify his chief, and make certain his team were in the murder room by 8:30, he showered and rushed into work. The second floor was buzzing with motion and noise as phones rang, and once he'd looked over the reports that landed on his desk overnight, he assembled his team meeting. It rankled him that he'd been kept out of the loop when Tamsin admitted this morning that the body of the Bath art dealer had been found by her team late yesterday afternoon. Even as they were eating dinner, her unit had known of the death and the theft of the Chagall. He couldn't imagine someone hadn't notified Chen last evening, since she'd known about there being a second painting, yet she'd waited until this morning to notify him. He decided her outfit was good at keeping things close to their chests until they wanted them known.

"Here's what we know." His team looked at him expectantly. "A second painting, this one a Chagall, was sent out of Russia from the Pushkin Museum along with the Picasso. It was delivered to the Holburne Museum in Bath. A crack in its frame during shipping resulted in the museum sending it out to a local dealer for repair. This was a reputable man they'd used on numerous occasions and trusted highly."

He caught Tamsin's eye. "When members of Tamsin's unit went to this shop to retrieve the painting for quarantine, they found the body of the gallery owner, Charles Wright, in the back room." Low whistles and hum of conversation filled the room. "Pipe down. I'll let Tamsin take over." Let her explain why they were only receiving this news now, when they could have stayed at home another half an hour and caught it on the radio.

He gestured for the woman to step up and speak to his team. The gathering of men and women sat up straighter as Tamsin cleared her throat. It was immediately apparent she had no intention of apologizing for any delays in getting information to them. So much for cooperation.

"It appears Mr. Wright suffered a broken neck. There are signs of a skirmish in the back workroom where his body was found. The attending medical examiner estimated the time of death between 2 and 4 PM yesterday afternoon."

Declan had been leaning against the wall but stood up at this news. Wasn't that when Nora and Helen were in a gallery buying the Chase study she told him about? Could it be the same place?

"What about the painting?" a female constable sitting up front asked.

"There was no sign of the painting. Coming from the same museum as the Picasso probably means the retrieval of the Chagall was the motive for the killing. We're pulling out all the stops in concert with Bath's department—" Tamsin's mobile rang, off-putting in the midst of the discussion. She glanced at it, then put it up to her ear and turned away. "I must take this." She muttered into the phone.

Declan met Watkins' eye. His sergeant spread his hands up. *What's going on?*

He shrugged his shoulders eloquently. *Wish I bloody well knew.*

Finally Tamsin slid her phone into her pocket. She returned her attention back to the gathering. "It appears there may be several witnesses who were in the art gallery yesterday afternoon who've come forward. I'll be heading to Bath immediately, and will keep you posted. That's all for now."

She strode quickly from the room. Declan hurried to catch up with her. He heard Watkins handing out assignments as the door swung shut behind them.

"Just a minute, Tamsin." He had to stop himself from grabbing her arm.

She had the grace to stop, but turned to him with a warning glance. "Don't ask, Declan. You're Oxford, not Bath."

"Yes, but this is obviously connected to my case, and it's a good likelihood the murderer in Bath is also responsible for Emma Jevons' death on my patch. These witnesses—they wouldn't by any chance happen to be named Helen Sackville and Nora Tierney?" He watched her shoulders slump.

"I told them I wouldn't be able to keep you away from this." She shook her head.

"Why should I be kept away? This involves me now more than ever, Tamsin."

"Which is precisely why my unit doesn't want you there, Declan." A civilian pretended not to hear them argue as they passed. "Let's talk about this in your office."

"Instead of squabbling here like schoolchildren?" He contained his annoyance and opened the door for her. Once inside, he launched his attack again. "I'm right, aren't I? Nora told me she and Helen were in an art gallery yesterday. She bought a bloody painting from this murderer."

Tamsin put her hands up to stop his tirade. "It does appear that way, but I won't know until I get there. Let me handle this. I promise I'll keep you informed."

Declan had been looking down at the pattern in the rug to control his temper and lifted his head at this. "Like you've been keeping me informed on what's going on with Paul Pembroke?"

"It's so much more complicated than I thought." Tamsin blew out a breath that ruffled her thick fringe and seemed to make a decision. "Let's sit down."

Bath

8:55 AM

Once Helen called Bath police to report that Mr. Wright hadn't been in the gallery, Nora was relieved they sent a detective around without question. Detective Inspector Alex Thalmann knocked on the kitchen door within 20 minutes of Helen's call. He was accompanied by a second detective with a shaved head wearing a snazzy suit, whom DI Thalmann introduced as "consultant detective" Chris Burke, whatever that meant.

"We called because we were in that gallery yesterday where my friend bought a painting," Helen said. "I didn't know Mr. Wright personally, but when we saw his photo today, we knew it wasn't the man who'd served us, pretending to be him."

"We're not surprised something's hinky because we thought the man's behavior was odd if he really ran the shop." Nora saw the men's befuddled expression. "Hinky, you know, peculiar, odd."

The men nodded.

"In what way?" Thalmann asked.

"He seemed annoyed Nora actually wanted to buy something," Helen said.

"Plus, he didn't know how to use the credit card machine," Nora added. "He told me it was broken, and wanted cash, but finally took my check." Her hand flew to her mouth. "Now he has my address in Cumbria."

"I need to see that painting," Burke said.

Helen gestured to the painting, still in its bubble wrap, lying at one end of the long table.

Nora watched Burke draw on plastic gloves he took from his pocket and carefully peel back a corner of the bubble wrap. He shook his head and rewrapped it as Helen recounted the timing of their visit.

"Nic Bottomley at Mr B's Emporium of Reading Delights can confirm those times," Nora said. Burke gave Thalmann an inquiring look when she said the name of the shop. Did he think she was making it up?

"Well-known establishment," Thalmann assured him.

"Did you see anyone else on the gallery premises?" Burke asked.

"No one. And no one else came in when we were there," Helen said.

Nora added that the man turned the door sign to CLOSED after they came in. "He told me he was closing early."

Burke asked, "Could you see the size of this package the man was wrapping when you arrived?"

"Quite large, wouldn't you say, Nora?" Helen held her hands up, sketching the size.

Nora agreed. "Fairly flat, like a painting wrapped in bubble wrap and then brown paper. Too big to carry under one arm when he took it into the back room. Do you think that painting is the reason for the murder?" She wanted to tell them she'd been involved in murder investigations before, but somehow didn't think they'd appreciate her expertise at just this moment.

Thalmann ignored her question. "Now, a description of this man."

Nora and Helen agreed the man was tall and heavyset, spoke with an accent, had a pale complexion, medium brown hair, and was expensively dressed.

"What kind of accent?" Burke asked.

"Definitely European—something Slavic?" Helen suggested.

"He took pains not to talk to us," Nora said. "His suit was tailored, very pricey, and he wore cufflinks. I remember thinking he dressed more like a banker than a gallery owner." She resisted a glance at Burke as she said this.

Thalmann deferred to Burke. "Anything else?"

"Just where you can both be reached today."

Nora explained about her book signing later in the day, and gave them her mobile number, and threw in that of the bookshop. Helen added her mobile number. The men prepared to leave.

Thalmann turned back at the door. "One moment." He flipped back through his notebook. "Nora Tierney. And this is Hill House." He flipped more pages. "You know DI Declan Barnes from Oxford?"

Nora beamed. "He's my partner."

"He called in yesterday. We've had extra Wilts patrols on this house all night."

They sat down again while Nora explained about the bugs and her stalker.

"Surely the two things aren't related?" Helen asked.

"I can't see how." He glanced at Burke. "One has been going on for months and yesterday's event sounds more—spontaneous." Thalmann closed his notebook. "Patrols didn't report any suspicious activity around the house."

"Good to know." Nora noticed Burke keep silent through this exchange.

Helen saw the men out. Nora let her thoughts drift over the turn of events as she took Sean out of his highchair. She sat on the floor with him, playing with his blocks.

The baby blew bubbles with his lips and made sounds like a motorboat. Sunlight streamed in through the large window and glinted off his copper hair, making it glow. Warmth filled her when she looked at him in his innocence and wonder at small things.

She thought of her joy in finding the painting that hinted at her life in Oxford with Sean and Declan. She could conclude, as she was certain the detectives had, that the man who'd sold her that painting had murdered Charles Wright. Was she a suitable mother, taking her son into a shop where a murderer stood behind the counter? But how could she have known that at the time? She hoped her enjoyment of the painting wouldn't be tainted by the burly man who might have killed Charles Wright.

Helen returned holding out a pair of wellies. "Let's go tramping through the woods a bit, get some of this anxiety out. We don't want your afternoon spoiled."

Nora hesitated.

"Come on," Helen insisted. "Sean needs the fresh air. No prying eyes on these hills, we'll stay up here."

She looked at Sean, chewing on a block, and knew Helen was right. They needed a few hours of normalcy. Maybe she could recapture her excitement about her signing. Maybe those detectives would find the man who'd killed the art dealer and find an explanation for his murder. Maybe her stalker would suddenly disappear.

Maybe.

Bath

12:10 PM

Viktor Garanin waited for hot water to fill the jetted tub in his room. His headache had finally cleared. This was what happened when he lost control of his drinking. He didn't often imbibe to excess—if he were being honest, not *too* often. Last night seemed like the right moment for that bottle of Chateau Lafite, and the champagne that followed with an excellent meal. Then back in his room, the vodka. There had to be vodka to end a day like he'd had.

Mercifully, something had finally gone right. He'd retrieved the canvas, and the art dealer hadn't touched the painting itself, and only started to gather his tools to fix the frame when Viktor entered the gallery. Yes, there had been that awkward moment when Wright refused to part with the damn thing—*idiot*! If he'd just let Viktor take it away without argument, he might still be alive.

On consideration, perhaps not left alive, as he'd seen Viktor's face. The man's scrawny English neck snapped like a green bean, reminding Viktor of his grandmother in Lake Lagoda. She used to pinch the ends off beans to cook with fish his grandfather caught in the lake. She'd fry the boned fish in butter, the flesh turning white, almost sweet in his mouth. Such sturdy stock, good people, strong and filled with a love of nature. Hard at times to see where the force and anger in his father had come from, but that was family for you.

But all was not lost. In fact, things were looking up for Viktor as he put his plan back on track. The Chagall was carefully hidden in his room. He had time to decide how to handle its disposition, and the special present it carried for British people, once the new scientist pumped up the mutation. Then the cowardly nation, the home of his mother and all she'd represented, would never be the same.

Viktor dropped bath salts in the swirling water. "Quietude," the bottle read, and he nodded to the empty chamber. He needed a relaxing hour to himself, soaking in the hot water, letting the jets chase away the tension from his broad neck to erase the vestiges of his hangover headache. He lowered himself into the warm bath, surrounded by the scents of thyme, lavender, eucalyptus, grapefruit. He inhaled deeply, turned on the jets, and as the water surged over him, fondled his penis. Maybe he should have that Kate woman return, but he couldn't chance a repeat with the same person, and didn't feel like making the effort to find another bitch right now. Later, when he'd settled down. Maybe tomorrow.

Instead, he thought of his afternoon and how he'd decided to achieve his goal. Before he could get away with the Chagall, the American and her friend, the English woman, had come to the gallery with the child. He'd seen the bookstore posters, and knew this was whom he hunted when she signed the check. He couldn't believe his luck. Nora Tierney right at his disposal. He wouldn't have to search for her after all. Even better, the women had talked about their plans for the next day as he listened from the back room. Forget the bookstore. A new plan formed, and once he consulted maps of the area, he was certain it would work perfectly.

He could have dispensed with them right there, but it was the baby who stopped him. That was the irony, that this young mother invading his space at just the wrong time was the very one he sought to fulfill his plan.

Her child reminded him of his brother, Vanya, born as a surprise to his vapid mother when Viktor was starting school. Even at his young age he'd recognized the resignation in her eyes when she'd found out she was pregnant, making an escape to her native England too difficult. Weakling.

He watched over the little boy, and when his mother died, Viktor protected him from his father's abuse as best he could, even as Viktor adopted his father's attitudes. Too bad Vanya abandoned his family the minute he could. They had no contact now, and when he thought of his brother, he always thought back to those days when he'd been his little brother's protector. They would soon be reunited. He would see to it.

He recognized he'd let his annoyance show in his desire to leave the gallery once the Chagall was in his possession, but it couldn't be helped. When he'd seen the red-headed *malysh* dozing in his stroller, he'd hoped the women would leave quickly so he wouldn't have to use force on them.

But then killing Nora Tierney would prevent the next important step in his plan, and so he'd settled himself down to play the role of gallery owner. She and her child were key if he was to flush out the scientist who could help him correctly put his plan into action. By the end of this afternoon, he would have made contact with the man, who would run back to Bath to see Nora Tierney and her son.

And so would Viktor.

Chapter Nineteen

Oxford

1:48 PM

Declan glanced out of his office window. Other than the newish carpeting he loathed, the opening was the one luxury his small office contained, even if it looked out at the car park and the clanking gates that opened to admit staff cars and patrol pandas, with or without suspects for the cells downstairs. No rest for suspects with that noise.

He'd been rocked to his core after his talk with Tamsin Chen and needed to assimilate what she'd told him. He closed his eyes and replayed the scene in his office.

"I've decided to take you into my confidence." Tamsin frowned as she used Declan's computer to print out several pages. "This is not for dissemination to your team until we see how things fall out. Even then, there are certain aspects of this that you'll never be able to discuss with anyone else unless they've been involved. That includes your sergeant."

She printed out several pages, and when he saw the heading, he swallowed hard. The Official Secrets Act. She pointed to one section and said: "Read it carefully if you want to know, but only sign if you can abide by it." He read:

A person who is or has been a Crown servant or government contractor is guilty of an offence if without lawful authority he discloses any information, document or other article to which this section applies and which is or has been in his possession by virtue of his position as such.

Declan scrawled his signature. "What's so secret that I must sign this?" He had a sinking feeling he knew what Tamsin Chen was about to reveal.

"Paul Pembroke is alive, known under another name. That fact must be kept secret. It's a political and national situation."

As he listened to her revelation, Declan felt shock setting in.

"Paul Pembroke alive? I must get to Bath—Nora could be in danger. Her safety and Sean's are paramount."

"There's nothing concrete you can actually do," she insisted, counting off on her fingers. "You don't have jurisdiction, and it would be unprofessional to abandon your post here. Plus, you'd just confuse the situation for Nora, don't you see that? I can't take the chance of you reacting emotionally until I see what's happening there."

"I know how to remain professional," he urged. He hated the desperation he heard in his voice that validated her argument.

She reached over and took his hand. "I understand these people are important to you. You have my promise on this. If I think there's any way you can be of help, or if the situation deteriorates, I'll tell you to come to Bath immediately. Then your chief will have to allow it."

"But I *want* to go, under any circumstance."

She shook her head. "It's much better if you've permission to be there in an official capacity, than barging in and ruining an operation where you'd have no status or clout." She squeezed his hand before dropping it. "You have my word."

He wanted to tell her what he really thought of her "operation" and her entire unit, but he held his counsel, and nodded instead.

The next hours were unmemorable. He signed forms and initialed reports until his in-tray was uncharacteristically empty. He let Watkins bring him a sandwich he didn't eat, and tried to act naturally around his team as they went about their work. He spoke with McAfee, and dressed down the man for not contacting him or Watkins immediately when he'd found out there was a second painting shipped from the Pushkin.

All the while he thought of the ramifications of what Tamsin told him, and how that would affect his future with Nora. If he still had a future with Nora after the revelations of today.

Paul alive. How would that affect her feelings toward him when she found out the father of her beloved child had entered a scheme for political purposes that had everyone thinking he had died? She would be angry at first, but would she feel any kind of residual pull to be with the man who'd fathered her child? What if she thought they should become their own little family and went off with him to wherever he now lived?

Declan scrubbed his face and consulted his watch. He needed to call Nora and wish her luck at her signing. He hoped he hadn't left it too late as he sat mulling over their future. He was afraid he wouldn't be able to hide his new knowledge in his voice. What an infernal mess.

Bath

1:49 PM

After their tramp through the woods, then a brief lunch and change of clothes, Helen found a parking spot near the same gate as the other day. She offered to keep Sean occupied with a walk in Victoria Park while Nora spoke.

"You look nice, Nora." Helen pointed to Nora's dress jeans, tucked into brown leather boots she wore with a green tweed blazer that complemented her auburn hair. She'd pinned a vintage oval pin, hand-painted with tiny forget-me-nots, at the throat of her crisp white blouse.

"I was aiming for casual but composed." She put the full

changing bag, packed with snacks, in the bottom of Sean's buggy, and kissed him on his forehead, each eye, his nose, and his chin. He giggled. It was their little game and she would trace each part of his face with one finger and say the name aloud when she was trying to get him to sleep. Kisses were for fun.

"Well done. Think you can find your way back to Nic's?" Helen buckled Sean in the seat and pulled on a bright yellow fleece. "Say goodbye to Mummy and let's find ourselves some squirrels."

"Bye-bye Mum-mum." Sean clenched and opened his fist in his version of a wave.

So much for separation anxiety. Nora snapped a photo of him and tapped on her phone. "Google search all set to guide me."

"Where would we be without our technology?" Helen waved and the two set off. They agreed she would text Helen when she was through at the bookstore, and meet up at the first bench along the path.

Nora found her way back to the bookstore, reveling in the bright autumn afternoon. She nodded to Lucinda, manning the desk, and went right upstairs to find Nic talking to a group, already gathered to hear her speak.

Her phone rang and Nora declined Declan's call and put her mobile on vibrate. She knew he was checking in to wish her luck, and would leave a voicemail. She looked at the spectators assembled to hear her speak, waiting for the rustles to die down as people found seats and took their jackets off.

The turnout was better than she expected. About 35 individuals sat in chairs or stood in corners. She felt surprised at the number of men who formed part of her audience. Several mothers held copies of her first book to sign while clutching copies of the new one.

It felt daunting and thrilling in equal measure. Her experience as a journalist allowed her to be comfortable with public speaking, but this was her work she would be talking about, not politics or someone's divorce; not a celebrity wedding or a royal birth. Just Nora and her books, and the work and process it took to produce them.

She practiced three deep breaths to clear her mind. At breath one, she thought of Helen and her goodness in setting this up, and helping her with Sean.

Nora took in her second breath and hoped Sean was enjoying the park. This is what was important, she thought, taking her third breath: her son, Declan, good friends, good health. All the rest, like these books, was icing on her cake.

But that didn't mean she shouldn't enjoy dessert when it came around.

Nic Bottomley introduced her, and Nora faced her crowd. She thought of each person peering at her expectantly as frosted cupcakes, and plunged right in.

"Thank you for that gracious introduction, Nic. I'm very happy to be here today to talk to you about the inspiration for my band of fairies living on Belle Isle in Cumbria's beautiful Windermere, England's largest lake. The natural setting provides the perfect backdrop for Simon Ramsey's wonderful illustrations ..."

Nora spoke for half an hour, describing her ideas for story-lines, and how she and Simon decided on the illustrations. After she finished her prepared talk, the questions flew at her about her process, and where she found her ideas. One young woman wanted to know how tough it had been to get published. A man asked how she designed her stories for young children so they learned a life lesson without frightening them. Most of the questions she had ready answers for, but a few made her pause to think before she spoke. She realized she put more hard work into these books than she often acknowledged.

"One last question." This from a mother in the front row.

Nora checked her watch. Nic had told her to run about an hour before signing and she was just over that. "You seem to have a feel for how to keep a young one's attention. Do you have children of your own?"

Nora beamed. "I have a son who'll celebrate his first birthday in two weeks."

To a chorus of "ahs" and "oohs," Nic came forward. "Nora will sign books in Professor Dupont's Reading Room." He guided Nora to the office, accompanied by a hearty round of applause that made her cheeks burn. She took her seat at the claw-foot table, surrounded by stacks of her books, and talked with parents while she autographed copies. Some went to parents to bring home as gifts for their children; others were to be sent to grandparents to read when little ones visited.

When the last person left, Nora stood and stretched, looking at her watch. 3:50 PM. Goodness. She hoped Sean had behaved for Helen. She thanked Nic as they walked downstairs, and left with the promise she could come back next year with book three in her series. As she stepped outside, Nora saw the autumn sun was already starting to wane, and she hurried back to Victoria Park before it closed its gates, glancing at Charles Wright's shop, where crime scene tape still fluttered by the door. A hand-lettered sign in the window said: CLOSED UNTIL FURTHER NOTICE.

Nora shivered. She walked away without looking back, shoving Charles Wright and the burly man from yesterday into a rear compartment of her mind. A large weight fell off her shoulders. First signing, first time talking about her books, done and dusted. Nic had been happy with the sales, and she'd been invited back. It couldn't have gone better. She felt lighter than a leaf that chased the mild breeze down the ancient street.

She listened to Declan's voicemail from before the event,

congratulating her on the occasion, as she walked. He sounded tense, almost harried, despite his warm support, and she sent him a text to let him know it had gone very well. She would talk to him tonight. Maybe there had been a break in his case.

Nora walked through the narrow roads, glancing in shop windows she passed. She'd come back tomorrow with Helen, maybe indulge in a bit of retail therapy for the new house. She lingered for a moment in front of a lovely shop with children's clothing she wanted to poke about, and another with house-wares. She'd stop in Helen's paint shop tomorrow, too, and bring color cards with her to the house this weekend. Haven Cottage was starting to feel real to her. The future stretched out before her, full of promise, filled with delight.

When she reached the park, Nora stopped by Helen's car. Empty. The parking meter was good for another 15 minutes. She texted Helen that she was walking to the bench where they'd agreed to meet, and entered the park.

Nora admired the glossy black paint of the tall gates at this entrance, their leafy detail picked out in shiny gold. She started down the path, past a charming little house with green trim, and surveyed the multiple plantings along the way. Nora knew the park had been opened by the future Queen Victoria at the age of 11, and it spanned so many acres, the children's playground had a zip line in addition to the usual climbing frames and swings.

She drew in a deep breath, inhaling the autumnal scents of evergreens and dried leaves amongst trees full of brassy gold and red colors. Many of the shrubs and foliage had discreet plaques that imparted their names, and some perennials had the occasional late bloomer hanging on, a spot of vivid pink or bright yellow. The path led to a small bridge over a pond whose water level was low, and she reached the metal bench where she was to meet Helen.

She checked her mobile. No text from Helen.

Nora didn't know how far away the children's area would be. She should just stay put at their agreed spot. This was where Helen expected her to be.

She looked around, admiring a stand of weeping silver limes. Nora blew out a sigh. She checked her mobile again. Unlike Helen not to reply. The car would get a ticket if they didn't hurry.

A young couple walked past, arm-in-arm, and smiled at Nora. She tried to quell her rising anxiety. Why did she feel something was wrong? *Don't jump to conclusions.* An older set of grandparents passed with a young girl in tow. She watched the child navigate the path and run ahead, then stop to see that her slower grandparents followed.

Nora checked her mobile again. Directly across from her, a set of stone steps cut into a berm, flanked by lush greenery. She looked around. Surely she was in the right spot. She stood up, and looked down the path for any sign of Helen with Sean.

Nothing.

She walked from the bench to the steps and back, her pacing increasing her alarm. On her second loop to the steps she heard a moan.

Her breath quickened and she climbed up.

A spot of yellow in the bushes to her left caught her eye. She pushed aside the foliage to find Helen lying there, hidden by the greenery and piles of dead leaves and brush.

"Helen!" Nora knelt and brushed leaves off her friend's face. The tips of her fingers came away bloody from a gash on Helen's scalp. "I'll get help. Steady now." She wiped her fingers on the grass and squeezed Helen's hand, but there was no returned pressure or sign Helen heard her.

Nora fumbled for her mobile, hands suddenly slippery with anxious sweat. *Where was her baby?*

She wiped her hands on her jeans and dialed 999 while her eyes darted further up the slope and searched the greenery for signs of Sean and his buggy. *Where was her baby?*

She mounted more steps, pushing bushes and grasses aside frantically, looking for Sean, or any sign he'd been there. Two more steps and the path leveled out and stretched before her. Nothing.

Mounting terror squeezed her heart.

"This is 999, what is your emergency?"

"My friend's been hit over the head in Victoria Park. She's unconscious. And my baby—" Nora's voice caught in her throat. She couldn't form the words she needed to get out. To say them would make them true.

Fear gripped her heart with fingers of ice.

"Take a breath, dear." Her calm voice strove to be reassuring. "Where are you in the park?"

"I don't know!" Nora shouted. "I came in the gate near the house with green trim, and then over a small bridge." The words tumbled out and over each other. "Just after that—up stone steps—please hurry."

"That's the Botanical Garden entrance. Ambulance is on its way. Don't move the victim until help arrives. Stay with her and keep her warm." The woman's voice took on a softer tone as she tried to calm Nora. "Help will be with you soon. What's your name, luv?"

Nora took off her blazer and laid it over Helen. She searched the woods for signs of Sean, then gulped and tried to force herself to speak slower, but her voice rose. "Nora Tierney. It's just— my baby—Helen was watching my baby, and he's—he's gone!"

A fist of fear took hold of Nora's chest and crushed it tighter and tighter. Hot tears fell on her shirt. She felt if she gave way to crying she'd shatter in a million pieces.

Nora gulped air and sat by Helen. She put her mobile on speaker and laid it next to her. She grabbed Helen's hand and warmed it.

"Nora, my name's Kim. We're going to send help for your friend, and help you find your baby. Stay calm and give me the information I need to make that happen. Now tell me about your baby."

"His name's Sean. He's almost a year and he can say words and tries most others." At the thought of Sean yelling *Typo!* in glee, Nora's heart twisted.

"Nora, how is Helen?"

"She's pale and breathing, but hasn't moaned again." Nora slid her fingers around Helen's slender wrist. "Her pulse is strong and steady."

"Good, that's all good, Nora," Kim soothed. "Now give me a description of Sean and what he's wearing."

God, please let me wake from this horrible nightmare. Nora felt the tears drying on her face. Concentrating was good, useful, anything to get her baby back.

She gulped and tried to form words, her mouth dry. "Strawberry blonde hair, blue eyes, about 24 pounds. He's wearing a blue jacket—with a teddy bear on it. Under that—a blue and white striped onesie. Jeans. Navy sneakers."

"That's very helpful, Nora. I'm already putting that description out."

Nora cocked her head. "I hear a siren." Helen stirred. "I think Helen's coming around." She leaned over and whispered. "It's all right, Helen. Help will be here soon."

"What about Sean's pushchair?" Kim asked. "No sign of it?"

Nora's heart thudded. The tight fist in her chest wouldn't let go. "I've looked around here but I don't want to leave my friend."

"Quite right. Can you describe it?"

"It's a MINI, royal blue, with parts of a Union Jack on the lid and footrest. There's a changing bag stowed in its bottom caddy, green stripes with Beatrix Potter characters." She pictured Sean's feet tapping a staccato beat on the footrest and thought she would throw up.

"Wonderful, Nora. That's all helpful. The ambulance is at the entrance, they'll be there very shortly."

"Kim—can you get in touch with Detective Alex Thalmann? He was at Helen's house this morning." Nora briefly described being a witness at the art gallery. "I'm afraid that might be connected with what's happening here." Nora's teeth started to chatter. Shock. It didn't help to know what was happening.

"Hold on, Nora—" Kim blocked the line. Nora rubbed Helen's wrist. Less than a minute later the dispatcher was back on. "Detective Thalmann will be with you in 10 minutes, Nora."

Nora let out a breath as she heard voices and moved down the walkway to see two paramedics. "They're here." One pushed while the other pulled a stretcher over the bridge. "Thank you, Kim, very much."

"Nora, we're going to find your baby. Stay strong. Let me speak to one of the ambulance crew, please."

"Up here." Nora pointed to where Helen lay. The first medic grabbed a medical kit off the stretcher, and ran up the steps. She handed her phone to the second, who gave his badge number to Kim, and ended the call.

He returned Nora's phone, and pulled out a pen. "Need me, Harry?"

The medic with Helen took her blood pressure. "Stable here."

Helen was lying on her back. The second medic pulled out a form and asked Nora questions about Helen. Some she knew: name, address, age, height. Others she didn't, like Helen's weight and medical history.

"I'm sorry. She doesn't appear ill but I don't really know her medical history." Nora was frustrated. Now that these medics were here to care for Helen, she needed to be looking for Sean, to call Declan, to call Val. "Look, my child is missing. Can I leave to search the park for him—please?" Her voice quivered. She bit her lip to keep from screaming at the man as her teeth chattered.

"Sorry, miss." He saw her distress and whipped out a foil blanket. "Sit here and wrap up in this. Kim said a detective is on his way to see you; he wants you to wait here." He stowed the form. "Coming up, Harry." He unstrapped the backboard from the top of the stretcher and carried it up the steps.

Nora watched them logroll Helen onto the board and strap her in place. Her head was held with padded chin and forehead straps, and she had a bandage on her scalp. There wasn't room for Nora to join them on the narrow steps. She felt helpless.

She should be doing something, anything, to find Sean. She pulled out her phone and tried to stop her fingers from shaking long enough to call Declan. A cluster of people ran over the bridge toward her, led by Detective Thalmann and an Asian woman, accompanied by several uniformed police. A few others at the rear appeared to be onlookers from the park who'd seen the ambulance.

Gawkers, that's all she needed right now. Or worse, the press. Could they have gotten wind of the happening already? "Mugging in Royal Victoria Park," the headline would say. Only it wasn't a simple mugging, was it? Her child was gone.

She stowed her phone as Thalmann reached her and introduced Tamsin Chen. The constables held the onlookers back before the bridge. One went ahead to stop foot traffic from the other direction.

Chen? "I thought you were in Oxford with Declan," Nora blurted out.

Chen met her question with a steely gaze. "I was. Now I'm here."

"Tell me the sequence of events," Thalmann said.

Nora started, but they were interrupted when the medics brought Helen down and strapped her onto the stretcher. Nora ran over as they covered her with a blanket.

Helen was awake but groggy. "Nora—so sorry. Sean?"

"No sign. What happened to you? What happened to Sean? Who attacked you?"

Nora blamed herself for not taking her stalker more seriously. This was all her fault. She had put her son, and her friend, in danger while selfishly signing her books.

Helen shook her head. "I didn't see him. I was hit from behind."

Nora blinked back tears. "We'll find him."

Helen's eyes closed for a second. "Oh, God. Call Matthew. And Philly—she'll be home from school, trying to reach me. Mobile's in my jacket pocket."

Harry reached under the blankets and straps, and handed Nora the phone. "We're taking her to Royal United."

"I'll take care of it," Nora promised Helen. "Let them patch you up. I'll come up later when I can."

Helen started to cry as they wheeled her away. Nora called Matthew and was happy to reach voicemail. She left a brief message and her mobile number. Then she called Philly and assured the young woman her mum was fine, but had had an accident and was being taken to the hospital for tests. Philly said she would get to Royal United with a friend after feeding the dogs, and Nora left it at that. She didn't mention on either call that Sean was missing. They would both find out the details when they reached Helen. Nora's tears gushed in full flow as soon as Philly hung up.

Thalmann guided Nora to the bench and tried to take a statement from her about finding Helen. Nora blubbered until Chen handed her a pack of tissues.

Nora helped herself liberally and mopped her tears. She tried to compose herself. Why was Chen here?

"I need to call Declan," Nora said, sobbing jag over. She blew her nose noisily. She was lightheaded from crying and stress, and needed to be doing more than sitting here talking.

Chen said, "I already did."

Thalmann had been talking on his phone and gave her his attention. "Ever heard the term 'the golden hour?'" He sat next to Nora on the bench and faced her.

"I know artists and photographers call the hour before sunset that, when everything's lit with a golden glow—oh, and in medicine they say after someone's had a heart attack or a stroke, the golden hour is the first hour if they are to get the best result." What did that have to do with anything?

Thalmann dipped his head in acknowledgment. "In a police investigation, it's our best time to get the most accurate information from eyewitnesses and forensics. I have a team on the way to canvass the park and speak to any witnesses. A forensic team, too, in case there's been anything left behind where your friend was found. We have this under control, Nora. Experienced people are looking for your son. You can help most by telling us what happened."

A few people lingered in the wake of the medics leaving with Helen. Nora couldn't bear to look at them. She hoped no one was taking her photograph. She concentrated on describing how she'd found Helen after she'd failed to arrive at their meeting place, and how she'd called for help.

" … Sean is gone, no sign of him or his buggy, and I don't know why he would be taken." Her mind refused to utter the words that fell like bricks into her mind: *kidnapped; murdered.*

Oxford

4:42 PM

When the call came from Chen, she was so brief and precise, Declan thought he'd misheard her: "Come to Bath, now."

"I don't understand." He rose anyway, closing his laptop, reacting to the urgency in her voice.

"It's been run by your chief. Call in at home and pack a bag for a few days. Come straight to Bath Headquarters. I'll be there with Nora."

"Nora? Why is she with you?" For a brief moment he felt annoyed. "Please don't tell me Nora's become involved in this investigation beyond being a witness. She has a habit of doing that."

There was a pause. He pulled on his jacket. Chen spoke up again.

"That item we discussed before I left to come here? Nora's to be included." Tamsin's circumspection must be how she conducted herself most days. It was obvious she didn't consider St. Aldate's to have a secure line.

"I see." But Declan didn't see at all. He had no idea how Nora would react when she found out Paul Pembroke was alive. He knew it had shaken him to his core, and he'd never met the man or had a child by him. Could Paul have been the architect of the mutated smallpox? Was he to blame for this mess? "Does she know?"

"Not yet." Tamsin's shortness surprised him. "Look, there's more. You'll have to be here in an unofficial capacity, for Nora."

Declan roared. "This is my case! The first painting and first murder came from here, and I'm involved from the outset. I should be able to liaise with them."

"It's not that. It's that you're *too* involved. It's become ... very tricky."

He could feel there was more and waited.

"Sean's missing."

Chapter Twenty

Bath

5:12 PM

Betty Kaplan smoothed the hair of the sleeping child's head. Like a shiny copper penny, she thought, and wondered from which parent he'd inherited that gorgeous color. He might not like it later in life if it stayed so bright. A ginger, they'd call him at school. But it might darken as many babies' hair did, turn more auburn, and then he'd be all right.

That was the thing with young babies. They had a different face every month the first year, it seemed. This little lad, Sean MacBride, fitted his Irish name. Poor mother traveling alone with him had been in a car accident and broken her leg, requiring an emergency operation. It was a miracle the child was unharmed, thanks to the newest car seats.

The social worker who'd dropped the baby off this afternoon was the same large man from the other day, and had the nappy bag and buggy from the mother's car, but not much else. The bulky man in the nice business suit was quite dapper for a social worker, but then Betty wasn't one to judge. Nice to see a respectable suit on a man. Pavel Perminov was probably one of those teddy bears with a big heart.

But no paperwork! Pavel told Betty someone from the office at Royal United would drop the paperwork off tomorrow morning.

"There was a rush to get the mother to theatre, and pin that leg," he'd said. He had a noticeable accent she couldn't place. "Didn't like to keep the baby in hospital too long, expose him to too many germs."

"No father?" Betty asked, taking the child from Perminov.

The boy had obviously been crying, eyes reddened, and now mewed like a kitten and rubbed his eyes.

"In service on a nuclear sub," the social worker explained.

Betty had never had a case like this. No notice and no paperwork, but Perminov seemed well versed in the Caring Angels program. She could hardly have turned the poppet away, poor thing. The baby was grizzling, and tired after being handed around to a bunch of strangers. When she cuddled him and sang to him in the rocker, he fell asleep clutching a raggedy stuffed Peter Rabbit.

She found some clues in his nappy bag. Finished nursing, on whole milk. That was easy enough. Betty looked in her fridge. No known allergies, Perminov had said. She always had cheese and eggs on hand, of course, and what child didn't like to munch toast soldiers? There were bananas to mash, and she could always make custard. Without paperwork she would stay away from meat for now, but when they arrived, she'd have a better idea of what he was used to eating. The Caring Angels worker stationed at Royal United would have taken a good briefing from the mother if possible, unless she was unconscious before being sedated.

Until then, since she didn't have a change of clothes, she looked at the tag on his jacket for his size and riffled through the basket of clean, used clothing she picked up at jumble sales for just this kind of purpose. She found a pair of footed pajamas that should do the trick for overnight, and the bag had plenty of the nappies he used, too.

"Mum-mum."

Betty turned. Sean had pulled himself up and stood, holding onto the cot's edge, tears forming in his eyes. Enough nap, then.

"Muuummmm," he moaned, collapsing back into a sit.

Betty picked him up to soothe him. "You miss your mummy? Of course you do. I'll tell you what." She walked into the kitchen. "Let's sit and have something to eat. After I'll read you a story. Would you like that, Sean?"

She installed him in the highchair, and he allowed her to tie a bib on him. When she poured milk into a sippy cup, he drank greedily. "You have a drink and I'll rustle us up some dinner."

Toby chose that moment to make his appearance. He jumped up on the counter and stared at the new foundling.

"Kit-tee!" Sean pointed.

Betty picked up the cat and brought him over to the child, who reached his hand out to slide his hand along Toby's soft fur. "Kit-tee." He smiled shyly at Betty.

"Your mummy has taught you to be kind to animals. She must be a very special mummy."

5:13 PM

Nora stared out of the back seat of the patrol car. A bandstand, tennis courts, Georgian buildings flashed by, but she wasn't focused on them. All she could see was Sean's face as he slept or fussed or cried, and she would do anything—*anything*—to have him keep her up all night with his teething.

"Why can't I help search the park?" she asked Thalmann. He'd tried his best to calm her down before they left the scene, and appeared to have the search for Sean in control.

He met her eyes in the rear view mirror. "We need you to be available in case a ransom demand comes in. The park staff is organizing a volunteer search to kick off. We're setting up large lights at different points and our staff will hand out maps and separate the park into sections so not a leaf is missed."

Beside her, Tamsin Chen spoke up. "We may need you to make a press appeal, too, Nora. Think you're up for that?"

"Anything you need me to do." Nora liked their assurances, but nothing would make her feel better until she could hold her son in her arms.

When they arrived at the station, she was ushered through to a squad room, the smell of burnt coffee filling her nostrils and turning her stomach. She used the rest room to wash her tear-stained face. The floor tiles were worn from use, although an attempt had been made to keep the space clean. Someone from the staff had left a large container of hand cream on one side of the sink; an equally large pump of antibacterial gel stood on the other.

There were no tears left. She was dry, an empty shell, carved out from the inside. If only she could be sleepwalking. This couldn't really be happening. Cool water felt good on her puffy eyes. She let it run down her face and over her chin before drying her face with a few scratchy paper towels. The disinfectant scent brought her back to the Oxford police station when Val had been arrested.

Nora texted Val: *"Need you to come to Bath Police Station. Sean kidnapped."* She had to believe he was kidnapped, taken on purpose, because she would not entertain the thought that he might be dead.

She looked at her phone, considered, and hit delete. If Val came here, they might not let her into the room where Nora waited. She could picture Val pacing an exterior room for hours, annoying the desk sergeant, or worse, giving in to that volatile temper of hers. That would increase Nora's own anxiety, and it wasn't fair to Val. She might need Val later. She decided she would call Val when she had more news. Good news, she told herself—news that Sean had been found.

At least Declan was on his way. She'd read his text three times for the lifeline it provided. She needed him, not just because she loved him, but because she had a complete and utter lack of control over what was happening, and right now she needed someone around her she trusted.

Declan slapped the steering wheel of the MGB in frustration. He'd taken off at a run for his garage after Watkins ran him home, and he tossed a few things into a hold-all. He could smell Nora's perfume, and the sight of one of Sean's toys next to her side of the bed filled him with foreboding, as did Watkins' look of pity when he took him aside to leave him in charge, after explaining where he was going and why.

Over an hour later, he sat immobile in traffic outside Oxford on his way to Bath. The timing couldn't have been worse. He'd tried to call Nora to let her know he was on his way. Her mobile had gone straight to voicemail, which made sense if she was inside a police station, where the connectivity would be awful. He didn't trust his voice to a message, and sent her a text, which just might get through. "On my way. Hold tight. We'll get him back. Love you both. D xx"

That seemed to go through, and he drummed his fingers on the wheel, beating out an exasperated tattoo. The sign for the next exit was Swindon, and he mentally cast his eyes over side roads that would bring him to Bath, but no, this was the most direct route. Nothing for it then but to coast along the hard shoulder with lights and siren, and hope some local plod didn't pull him over. Tamsin would back him up if it came to that, but he couldn't waste time with explanations. He set off on the shoulder, driving close to the speed limit to avoid attracting the ire of the other drivers.

Paul Pembroke was alive. Declan had been incredulous when he'd had to sign that document for Tamsin. The scientist has been in a protection program, living in another country she wouldn't name under a different name she wouldn't give him. What would make a man do that? He must have been a threat to people very high up. Declan hoped his fear that Paul had developed this mutated smallpox was unfounded.

Poor Nora. Bad enough to learn the man who'd fathered her child was alive, he'd chosen to leave her in such a horrendous way. Sure, Paul had made arrangements to leave her money, but really—as if that would make it all right? Where did that leave Sean? Who would kidnap him and why? Could Nora's stalker have been waiting for just this moment?

It seemed to Declan that Sean's kidnapping was the direct result of Paul Pembroke's actions. That man had a lot to answer for, to a lot of people. It was a nightmare. The whole thing was a bloody nightmare.

He prayed to a God he wasn't certain existed that Sean would be found safe and sound. The alternative didn't bear thinking about. His police experience told him that if Sean wasn't found quickly, it was likely his kidnappers would find it difficult to care for a toddler, to keep him under wraps for long … no, he couldn't go there.

He didn't want to picture the little boy he'd grown to love— yes, he would admit he loved the child—as a pathetic body hastily buried, or tossed aside like garbage in a skip. It made his blood boil to think of the motive that lay behind all of this. A man who was so egotistical that he would conceive of a scheme to spread a potentially fatal disease surely was mentally ill, and yet had some connection to Paul. This must be all interconnected; it didn't make sense otherwise.

Declan drove carefully, no one stopping him despite his decidedly un-police vehicle. Nora must be beside herself. How would she handle hearing about Paul? Would that have happened before he could get there?

Nora had told him time and again that her relationship with Paul had been over when he died; she'd found out she was pregnant several weeks after. If he were Nora, right now, the emotion he'd most be feeling toward the man would be—Declan searched to picture how Nora would be feeling. Bewilderment, confusion, yes she would be feeling all of those. But then he hit on the emotion that felt right: pure rage.

Bath

6:32 PM

Viktor sat at the hotel bar and consulted the restaurant listings, looking for one that specialized in fish. He felt like having grilled sea bass tonight, accompanied by a bottle of a peppery Hess Small Block Syrah to balance it. He enjoyed the nouveau way of pairing a red wine with fish. It seemed so decadent. With the next part of his plan set, he had to fill up the hours while things fell into place. He could relax in the meantime, before he went into work mode again.

He thanked his father mentally for his business savvy in the petroleum corporation that had funded Viktor's expansive education in sciences and history, as well as art, wines, cuisine, and attire. There had been friends from high places in their home as he grew up, even a bishop from the Orthodox Church. On those nights, his mother would dress in light, flowing clothes, and bring in help to cook good Russian food, but there were nights they were treated to food from other cultures, depending on their guests: French, Italian, Greek.

His father's friends and colleagues came to expect special treatment at their house, and always found it, whether in drink or food. His father knew where to hit his mother, too, so the bruises never showed, and if she drank too much wine on these occasions in order to be bright and sparkling company, no one commented except to note how pretty she was, and how fortunate Viktor and his brother were to have her for their mother.

He knew better, of course. The cowering, simpering woman would literally crawl away from his father's wrath at times, hoping to defend her broken body. She had tried to protect him when he was little, before his brother was born, he would admit that. There were long buried memories of tenderness from his mother that he didn't dwell on often. Once it became clear at an early age that he had his own strength, and favored his father in personality, she grew afraid of him, too. *Bah!* The only good things he'd gotten from her, now that he paused to realize it, were his brother, long gone, and his love of his garden.

After she'd taken her life, a series of housekeepers and servants filled her various functions. There were women, too, but no one who stayed, and as Russia fell, the fancy evenings grew less frequent. By the time death came from pancreatic cancer eating away at him only a few months after being diagnosed, Viktor's father hadn't hosted a dinner party for two years.

Eating and drinking well were important to Viktor in homage to his father's memory, and tonight he would have a good dinner, yes, even if early for his usual tastes. A different escort service had promised to find him a woman with a bit of meat on her. They would have dessert in the room, he decided, champagne and raspberries with dark chocolate sauce. You could do inventive things with that sauce. And then a nice whirling bath to wash it all away later. A simple plan for a simple man, which at the heart of it all, he considered himself to be. When the woman left, the next stage of his master plan would go into production, and Paul Pembroke would help him bring England to its knees.

"Another vodka martini, sir?" The barman broke into his thoughts and pointed to Viktor's empty glass.

Viktor nodded. "More ice this time, please, and a double twist." He needed to keep his head clear. It had already been such a rewarding day. He wished there were more like this, when a well-planned, thought-out scheme worked without a slip.

He'd stationed himself at the corner of the Botanical Gardens entrance, and ostensibly read a guidebook on the delights of Bath. The one negative was that he didn't know what car the women would arrive in, but when he saw the Audi drive in slowly, searching for parking, he recognized the women right away. Back in Oxford he'd originally tossed around the idea of taking the Tierney woman, but the child—well, that was infinitely more interesting. Once he'd worked out how to use Betty Kaplan to keep the boy in his care for less than an hour, he knew it was the way to go. With all of the CCTV around, he didn't need to be picked up on camera with the missing child. Who could resist saving the life of a child when it was dangled in front of them, especially of their own son? It was the perfect way to flush out Pembroke.

"Here you are, sir." The barman deposited Viktor's fresh drink, made according to his directions.

Viktor felt a moment of giddiness. It was even within his power to save this barman's life or to take it.

It had been ridiculously simple to follow the brunette pushing the buggy into the park. He waited until the foot traffic around cleared, then closed the gap between them. Before she became aware of him, he'd coshed her soundly. The woman had fallen at his feet. He'd scooped her up, then unceremoniously dumped her in the shrubbery next to a set of stone steps where she wouldn't be immediately found. He hadn't even stopped to remove her yellow jacket, but shoved her as best he could under the greenery and grabbed handfuls of leaves to cover her.

The child frowned at him warily as he dusted his hands and stepped behind the buggy. Best to make friends so he didn't cry. He knew his name, too, from the women yesterday at the gallery. "Hello, Sean." Before the child could break into a howl, Viktor put on his most disarming smile. "Let's go see the flowers and find Mummy."

Viktor commenced a brisk walk through the park, just another grandparent out for a stroll with a favored child. He'd remembered to bring a lollipop, which fascinated the child as they walked through the lovely grounds and out through a different gate, one where Viktor's rented car was parked.

He laughed as he sipped his cocktail, the icy vodka sliding down his throat. It had been an inspiration to call himself Pavel Perminov to the retired nurse. It fit his accent and was his idea of a private joke, as close to Paul Pembroke as he dared come.

When Betty Kaplan became suspicious by tomorrow afternoon that no one dropped off those papers she needed for the boy, her first call would be to the hospital, where she'd ask for information on Mrs. MacBride and her son. There would be no mother recuperating at the Royal United with that last name. The ensuing confusion would give him more hours, at least until tomorrow night, maybe even into the next morning, before the kidnapped child was connected to the social worker with the accent, and the child he'd dropped off.

Eventually someone would figure out who the child really was, but by then Viktor would have flushed out Paul Pembroke, and returned to Russia with the mutation formula.

The barman wiped the counter near Viktor, who checked his watch, and noticed the man's mobile clipped to his belt. "Could I borrow your phone?"

"Of course, sir." He handed it to Viktor, and stepped away discreetly in anticipation of the large tip Viktor had primed him with on his first drink. Viktor consulted his throwaway for the number. He knew the call would be taped, and he had to speak quickly. He dialed Nora Tierney's phone.

Chapter Twenty-One

Bath

6:34 PM

The lights at the Bath police station hurt Nora's puffy eyes. She closed them against the glare. This waiting had become endless, the few hours feeling like days. Each time someone opened the door of the interview room to check on her, or ask if she wanted yet another cup of insipid tea, she'd risen, hoping to see Sean in someone's arm, recovered unharmed, healthy and whole.

She'd received Declan's text earlier but he hadn't arrived. She knew the traffic snarl he would hit at the time he left Oxford, and paced the small room, glancing outside it through the reinforced glass window. The other detective who'd come to Helen's yesterday, Chris Burke, hovered around Chen, and Nora surmised he must be part of her team.

Pacing distracted her from the waiting. Her phone had been taken briefly, and its number set up to a tracing program. It sat on the window ledge to get the best signal, mocking her with its silence.

Her baby, her child she loved so deeply, had been taken for a reason. She could only hope it was something she could fulfill. Could her money be at the root of it all? She would give away every penny if it meant she could have Sean with her, safe and unharmed. She'd seen doubt cross the detectives' faces when she'd mentioned that she had inherited a large sum, but it made sense to her.

Anxiety swirled in her gut, giving Nora a physical pain she welcomed. The golden hour, as Det. Thalmann had called it, had come and gone, and she could only hope it had given his team useful, concrete information. She waited for him to return with news. He checked in with her every so often, each visit bringing hope, followed by disappointment.

Nora stopped pacing and watched him approach her room, this time holding a bottle of cold water. He was accompanied by a female constable in uniform who carried a book. She could tell by Thalmann's face he hadn't found Sean.

"All right, Nora?" He put the water bottle on the table. "This is Constable Morrow. She'll stay with you in case you need anything." The young woman took a seat in the corner of the room, out of the way.

"There was an appeal during the dinner hour news," he continued, "and we've established a hotline for witnesses who'd left the park. We enlarged the photo you gave us from your phone, and we're already fielding calls. Would you appear on the late news if we decide that's necessary?"

"Of course." Finally, the chance to do something proactive and useful. "I'll do anything you think will make a difference— anything to help find my son."

The young man smiled. "Good. I want you to see something." He motioned her to the door, and pointed out the window into the large general room they'd walked through. "See those people?"

Nora took in the civilians and uniformed force manning desks, sitting at computers, answering phones.

"Every one of them is helping us find Sean. I've had staff volunteer to stay over their shifts without paid overtime to answer the tip line." Thalmann patted her back. "We're doing all we can."

Nora bit back a fresh flood of tears as Thalmann left the room. She had to stay strong.

She smiled at the young constable, who raised the manual she carried. "I'm studying for my sergeant's exam, so don't feel you have to talk to me, but I'm here if you need anything at all. I'm Jane."

Casual conversation did seem beside the point. Nora thanked her and sat back down, the seat's hardness a penance for any perceived harmful thing she might have done in her life to make her deserve what she was going through. She welcomed how it bit into her backside.

Nora rested her head in her hands. It had become heavy, too heavy for her neck to hold up. She had to hope whoever had Sean was caring for him adequately. Nora refused to let her mind stray to picturing his little body abused or broken. She would not lose hope. She could *feel* he was alive. It seemed like a betrayal to her child if she let her thoughts stray to negative images. She tried instead to fill her mind with memories of Sean playing in the yard at Haven Cottage.

She closed her eyes and could see him lying against Typo's belly in the sunlight once again. She would hold onto that picture. Her head pounded behind her eyes, the ache so severe it made her feel they were being forced out of her head. She sat up and rummaged in her bag for paracetamol, then downed two tablets with sips of the cool water, hoping they would stay down. She'd refused all offers of food, and that might have accounted for some of her headache, too, and the light-headed feeling that made her feel spaced out. She didn't care.

"Headache?" Morrow asked, and Nora nodded. "Not surprising. All I can tell you is that I've never seen Alex Thalmann so determined. If anyone can find your boy, it will be Alex."

"I'm grateful for that."

At that moment the door opened, and Thalmann strode back in, face glowing. "Some good news. A witness at home called in from our appeal. She remembers seeing Sean's buggy, and gave us a good description of the man pushing it. It matches that from two other witnesses we found in the park."

Nora's heart leapt. This was real progress. She noticed he hadn't mentioned the two park witnesses before, but now that they had confirmation of a sighting from someone else, surely this was hopeful.

Thalmann read from his notebook: "Tall, hefty, well dressed, brown hair, pale—"

Nora interrupted him. "That's the man from the gallery yesterday."

"We thought the descriptions matched, and hoped you'd recognize him. We have people looking over CCTV from the park entrance where all of these witnesses were located. Now we know the death of the gallery owner is definitely related to your son's kidnapping."

"But why—"

Nora's phone rang, the shrill noise startling them. Everyone froze.

She looked to Thalmann as instructed before answering as it rang again. He'd told her the longer she could keep the line open, the better chance they had of triangulating the kidnapper's position.

Her heart hammered. He glanced out the door window at a colleague, and then back to her, and nodded as it rang a third time to answer it.

"Nora Tierney."

"Tell Paul Pembroke to come to Bath if he wants to see his son again."

6:59 PM

Declan put his official card on his dashboard and sprinted into the Bath Station. His only point of reference to the area was Peter Lovesey's fictional Detective Superintendent Peter Diamond mysteries. He'd met his detective contact at a joint task force conference, and had not been to this station before, although he'd read they'd had a recent move. The paint on the walls smelled new.

He pulled out his warrant card, and introduced himself to the desk sergeant, trying not to dance with impatience. "DI Declan Barnes, St. Aldates, for DIs Thalmann and Chen—the Tierney case."

The sergeant spoke into a phone, then pushed a buzzer under the counter and ushered Declan through a closed door.

"Straight back to the detectives office. DI Thalmann will meet you. Good luck."

Declan thanked the man. The large room buzzed with activity, civilians and uniformed working side-by-side like worker bees. The familiar cacophony of noise and activity reassured him.

A door opened at the end of the corridor, and a dark-haired, clean-shaven young man appeared and held out his hand.

"Alex Thalmann. Good to put a face to your voice. Thanks for coming." They walked toward an interview room at the back, passing a similar one on Declan's left. When Declan glanced inside, he saw Tamsin Chen in earnest conversation with someone he couldn't see.

"Let me catch you up on where we're at." Thalmann took his elbow. He stopped him just outside the end interview room to explain about the call from the kidnapper.

"We had an appeal on the evening news, and sightings of Sean with a man whose description matches from three different witnesses. The search at the park is still in progress, but we're probably looking more for evidence than any real hope the boy is still there. CCTV is being combed. We feel certain this man left the park with the boy. Miss Tierney agrees his description matches the man from the art gallery she saw the previous day." He repeated the caller's message.

"Nora knows Paul's alive?"

Thalmann shook his head. "She was confused by the kidnapper's statement, but Chen isn't ready to tell her yet. We put her off for now, but she's obviously in a state, and I don't blame her. Chen's group already helicoptered Pembroke here once they knew his son had been taken. Remember not everyone here understands exactly who he is, just that he's a key player, the boy's natural father." Thalmann opened the door.

"Declan!" Nora leapt up from the table and into his arms.

Her body shook as she cried into his neck, holding onto him tightly, shuddering with the force of wails that made his own eyes tear up. Thalmann and a female constable tactfully withdrew. Declan saw Thalmann stop at the door to hold up his fingers. *Five minutes of privacy.* He nodded.

Declan rubbed Nora's back, his nose in her hair, her scent reaching him as they held onto each other for a long minute, until she started to wind down. He lifted her chin and kissed her forehead. "They'll find him, Nora. I'm so sorry this happened."

She reached for a tissue from the box on the table and wiped her face, then buried it back into his shoulder. He felt sorry for himself, too, because what good could come of Paul Pembroke showing up? He'd never met the man, and already loathed him for playing with Nora's emotions and deserting her, only to still be alive. He bloody well hoped Pembroke didn't intend to show up and play the hero.

Declan dragged a chair around to her side and sat next to her, brushing damp waves of hair off her face. Her green eyes were huge in her face, the reddened lids swollen from crying. His heart filled with love and pain in equal measure. "We'll sort this out, Nora." To his ears, his promise sounded hollow.

She repeated the call she'd received. "I don't understand about him asking for Paul. Chen said they're looking into it, but why would that even come up?"

Declan hesitated. What a spot to be in, with knowledge Nora didn't have yet. He felt guilty withholding information from her. What was Tamsin thinking? "Let's let them do their work."

Nora cleared her throat. "They found two witnesses who gave a good description, and now a third has called in. They think it's that horrid man from yesterday. Threes are lucky, right?"

He held her hand, so much smaller than his own. It had been hours since the abduction. What was this kidnapper thinking? His only experience with kidnappers had been for ransom demands, and in those cases, the abducted children were rarely returned home alive. Could it already be too late for Sean? He fought the tremor that ran through his body. "Threes are very lucky, Nora."

7:03 PM

Nora held Declan's hand. She'd stopped crying, and took stock. She needed to get hold of her emotions. Repeated crying jags weren't helping Sean, and they certainly weren't helping her headache. She felt bewildered and anxious, unable to focus on anything but Sean.

"Stuffy in here." She stood and walked to the only window and tried to open it. It slid up five inches to a stop, and Nora put her face near the opening and sucked in the cool night air. She felt Declan rise and stand behind her. He rubbed the back of her neck. "My mind is all over the place. Is Sean warm? Is he somewhere he can easily breathe? Has he been fed and changed?"

Declan turned her to face him. "Don't torture yourself with the unknown, Nora."

The word "torture" stayed with her. "How can I not, Declan? Playing with a child's security and trust, his very life. Who knows what Sean's feeling? I know it can't be good. Christ, I'm so *angry* at the maniac who took Sean." She pointed to her stomach. "It's a burning, right here, affecting my mind, too. I picture that big man in front of me, strapped to a chair, and I'm applying every kind of evil device ever designed until he screams out where Sean is hidden and then I—" She broke off as the door opened.

Tamsin Chen, Alex Thalmann, and Chris Burke entered. Burke carried a chair in each hand and brought them around the table.

"Declan, good, you've arrived," Chen greeted him. "Let's all take a seat. We have fresh coffees on the way." She fussed with papers as they sat down.

Nora sat with Declan on one side of the table. Chen and Burke took the opposite side. Thalmann sat at one end near Declan. Her stomach clenched. Their serious expressions let her know something was up. Nora shifted toward Declan, who put his arm around the back of her chair.

Chen found what she was looking for, and thrust a paper at Nora. "I need you to sign this before we can proceed, but first you must recognize what it means. You can never tell anyone outside this room what we discuss in here today."

Nora read the heading. The Official Secrets Act. She turned to Declan to gauge his reaction, but he was studying the names scratched into the plastic tabletop.

Nora reached for the pen Chen offered her and signed it. She wouldn't have answers if she didn't, and she needed answers. She deserved answers. She pushed the paper toward Chen. "Doesn't Declan have to sign this?"

"He already has." Chen added the sheet to a file and shuffled them. Constable Morrow knocked on the door, then entered, carrying a tray laden with coffees and fixings, and a paper plate piled with biscuits. She put it in the center of the table and left.

Everyone busied themselves adding milk or sugars, or taking a biscuit, as Nora digested what Chen had said. Declan already signed this? On his way in to see her, or before?

Declan put a coffee with milk and sugars in front of her. She turned to him in confusion. "You already signed this?"

"Tamsin had me sign before she came to Bath, a matter of hours."

"Yet you didn't see fit to tell me when you got here?" Nora heard her voice rising.

Chen rapped on the table. "Miss Tierney, he couldn't tell you until you signed, which you have, so let's move on now."

Nora sat back, exhaling loudly, surrounded by people she didn't recognize. She might be irrational, but she didn't care. Her child was missing. Secrets should not be kept from her. She sipped her coffee, almost choking on it, but she needed sugar and caffeine. She needed to stay alert and awake, because right now she didn't know what was going on, and she desperately needed to find out.

"There are a few ground rules," Chen started. "You—" She gestured to Nora and Declan. "—will be given such information as you need for us to find the child, and return him to his mother. Anyone making claims to the contrary of what will be decided is for public consumption, now or in the future, will be held in direct violation of the Official Secrets Act you've signed. There will be no whistleblowers without dire consequences. Do I make myself clear?" She looked across the table, her eyes boring into Nora's.

Nora nodded at the scrutiny, as intimidated by the thought

of going to prison as much as she was by Chen's professional demeanor and clipped instructions.

"A scientist has been fished out of a Russian river. We believe he was working for the person behind this to achieve a smallpox mutation strong enough to cause an epidemic here in the United Kingdom." She tucked her hair behind one ear and continued.

"Detective Barnes has established that the mutated smallpox was implanted within the Picasso painting loaned to the Ashmolean Museum, which led to the death of the art conservator who was in the process of cleaning that painting. We believe a second infected painting, a Chagall, was sent to the Holburne Museum, and subsequently to the gallery, leading to the death of its owner."

Nora was confused. Was Chen saying Sean's kidnapping was tied to the smallpox virus? This must be why she had to sign the paper. But why did the caller ask for Paul?

Chen flipped a paper and threw Declan a little smile. "Now my outfit has come up with three suspects for consideration who would be likely candidates for this kind of maniacal scheme."

Nora bristled. This didn't make sense. What did a smallpox mutation have to do with Sean? And what was with Declan and Chen? Only a few days working together and he was taken into Chen's confidence before Nora, the missing child's mother? She shook her head and directed her attention to the agent.

Chen droned on. "One suspect has been ruled out, as we've verified he's been in Tokyo for the past six months. We're still tracking down the whereabouts of the remaining two, Pyotr Rustovich and Viktor Garanin, and are leaning towards Viktor Garanin because—"

Nora broke in. "Wait—I don't understand why you think Sean's kidnapping is tied to this smallpox mutation."

Silence fell around the table. Nora turned to Declan, who

raised an eyebrow and gave Chen a pointed look. Something passed between them. Nora felt sick.

Chen scraped back her chair and stood. "There's someone here who can answer that for you." She left the room and silence descended again. Burke drank his coffee; Thalmann fiddled with his pen.

Nora's sense of anxiety rose when Declan stroked her back. "Declan, what's happening?"

The door opened and Chen walked back in followed by a mustachioed man with fair hair. He wore chinos and a blue Oxford shirt with the sleeves rolled up, exposing the fair hair on his arms. The slight stoop in his shoulders looked so familiar.

Nora frowned. She rubbed her eyes as the man stood before her, and shifted his weight from one foot to another in an uncomfortable manner as she absorbed who she was seeing. All at once the caller's message made horrible sense.

Paul!

7:07 PM

Nora couldn't believe her eyes. How was this possible? Paul alive, when she'd sat through his memorial service and cried her eyes out? When his parents thought he was dead and mourned him? She sat back in shock. Declan gripped her shoulder.

She realized her mouth hung open, and snapped it shut. Nora's feeling of disbelief only grew as Paul took the open chair at the head of the table next to her. He avoided her gaze while she inspected him. His chin had softened with a few additional pounds, and the mustache was new, but otherwise it was Paul Pembroke, alive and in the flesh. He had the same sandy hair, and his eyebrow shape and blue eyes were the ones their son displayed. His rounded shoulders spoke of someone who spent hours every day hunched over a microscope. There was no question it was Paul.

"I realize this must come as a shock," Chen said, retaking her own seat. "As far as the British government is concerned, Dr. Paul Pembroke is deceased. A death certificate has been issued to that effect. End of story. I will remind you all of the Official Secrets Act you've signed."

Nora felt herself tremble. "How is this possible?" she asked Chen. "How?" she turned to Paul, her disbelief giving way to bewilderment. "What happened to you? Where have you been? I thought you were dead. We all did. We mourned you. Don't you realize what you put your parents and me through, Paul?"

As she absorbed the fact that he sat beside her, alive, her confusion gave way to a growing sense of anger. "You have a son now, Paul, did you know that? It wasn't just me you abandoned, it was your child." She leaned toward the man she'd thought dead, anxious to hear what he had to say for himself.

Chen sighed. "This is unhelpful, Miss Tierney. We will not be answering your questions."

"Call me Nora." She rounded on Chen, with her sleek hair and firm manner. "After all, we're in this together, aren't we? All signed members of the Official Secrets Act community, a regular club. Does that make me an honorary spook?" She was being obnoxious but couldn't help it. Declan squeezed her shoulder, whether in sympathy or to shut her up, she couldn't tell.

"Nora, just stop. I know what you're doing." It was the first sentence Paul uttered since entering the room.

Nora rounded on him. "Of course you do! You're the super-duper scientist, the brainiac whose scheme got us into this mess in the first place, right?" She looked across the table at the others. "Aren't I right? That's why he's here, isn't it?" Her anger surged, hot and frothy. It was all becoming clear. Paul was behind this smallpox mess. Somehow he was the reason Sean had been taken.

Declan put a restraining hand on her shoulder. He whispered, "Calm down or they won't let you stay."

"*Let* me stay!" she roared. "*My* child is missing. My baby was kidnapped because of some scheme he cooked up in his lab to make a superbug—" Nora gasped for breath. She turned to Paul. "It was you, wasn't it? Your superbug was stolen so you're the one responsible for that young woman's death in Oxford, that poor gallery owner killed, too, and for my friend being hurt, and my son *kidnapped*!" She rounded on Declan. "Don't talk to me, Declan Barnes, about being allowed to stay." She stood up and pointed a finger at Paul. "You should be in a cell for treason for what you did, instead of swanning around wherever you live, fancy-free, while the child you didn't even care to know about was brutally taken. *I hate you!*" She reached across and slapped Paul so hard his head snapped back.

Declan grabbed her and made her sit. Nora's hand stung. Her anger seeped out, her rage spent. To her horror, one side of Paul's face reddened. She looked across at Chen, who pointedly had her head down, and at Thalmann, who picked at a hangnail. Only Burke reached for another cookie as if she hadn't just had an enormous outburst.

Finally she looked at Declan.

He hugged her around her shoulders and spoke softly. "We understand how distressed you are, Nora. We're all upset, but it must be hellish for you."

Chen spoke up. "Nora, blaming Paul won't help, and it isn't even true. I told you the scientist most likely to be responsible for the mutation was fished out of a river in Russia. Dr. Pembroke feels your son's kidnapping is a direct attempt to flush him out of protection."

Paul cleared his throat. "I could never commit treason." He looked right at Nora. "It's true I left you, Nora. And I—" he hesitated, "therefore left the child, too. But we both know it wasn't working for us. I didn't even know you were pregnant when—" His voice took on a pleading tone, begging her to understand. "I had an opportunity to do good in the world. My country called and I responded. They needed me to work at a top-secret scientific facility on viral genetics, but I had to disappear. They told me there was no other way. I've worked on that virus since a small amount went missing two years ago. But it was to learn how to alter it so I could figure out how to *stop* the gene's dangerous mutation." He turned to Chen. "I'm convinced we're looking for Viktor Garanin. It makes sense. He handled security at the lab where I am now, and witnessed the argument I had with my handler about protecting Nora. Viktor's scientist didn't make the mutation strong enough. I'm the only one in the world who knows that virus well enough to mutate it—for good or evil. Garanin needs me. He wants my formula to strengthen it to make it effective."

Paul brushed his hair off his forehead in a familiar gesture. Nora inhaled the clean scent of his shaving soap, the sage and suede notes of the aftershave he'd used that morning, the coffee he'd been drinking. She still couldn't believe the man she'd thought dead sat next to her, breathing, talking, and very much alive.

"This is why I agreed to go into the secret program in the first place." He turned to Nora again. "I wanted to keep my parents and you safe from any crazies connected to my work. I was recruited for my research on mutated viruses for just such an eventuality. Only now Garanin has his hands on the boy."

Nora sat back in horror. The imprint of her fingers stood out in stark relief on Paul's face. What had she done? "I thought—"

"We understand what you thought." Chen stood and smoothed down the front of her skirt. "Gentlemen, I suggest a five minute break to allow Nora to regroup. Do you want ice for that?" She pointed to Paul's face. When he shook his head, she strode out of the room.

Burke grabbed the last cookie and filed out with Thalmann. Declan stood up and went to the window. Nora leaned back in her chair and felt the flush burn her face. "What a mess I've made of things."

CHAPTER TWENTY-TWO

Declan looked out of the window. The room faced the car park behind the Bath station. A light rain had started since he arrived, coating vehicles with a silvery sheen. He knew if he went outside he'd smell the pungent odor of oil rising from the pavement.

He couldn't blame Nora for her outburst. She'd leapt to the same conclusion he originally had until Chen sorted him out. With Sean kidnapped, Nora was wounded, her normal strength turned inside out. It worried him they were waiting for the demands of a maniac. Garanin was a zealot with his own agenda.

Then there was that annoying voice all day in the back of his mind that told him things had radically changed. The father of Nora's child was alive. Who was to say once she calmed down she wouldn't feel they should be together, and want to go with him, wherever he lived now? Would Declan stand in her way? He had to hope what they had between them held them together, tighter than the biology of parenthood.

Paul had a side to him that revealed more than a touch of narcissism. Declan noticed when Nora slapped Paul in the heat of the moment, the scientist's eyes had glowed, and he'd raised his noble chin a fraction. Jesus wept.

Just when he and Nora were on the brink of consolidating their lives, raising Sean together, becoming their own family, it could all fall apart. No matter how angry Nora felt toward Paul today, he was still the father of her child. Declan wondered if she would soften her stance if Paul were to stick around. He didn't trust Paul Pembroke one bit, and felt like he might be fighting for his future once they had Sean safely back.

What a mess. He opened his mouth to speak, but Nora put her hand up.

"No, Declan. This is between me and Paul."

Nora tried to assimilate her feelings. She scrutinized the man who sat next to her, someone she had once loved, the father of her child. Her emotions tumbled around in disarray, but the pure outrage she felt overrode any glimmer of residual nicety toward Paul. She strove to explain what she was feeling.

"I can see it was a difficult decision to give up your known life and all of your loved ones. It has a very altruistic ring to it. I suppose others have managed it. It sounds like the secrecy and protection applied mainly to your parents. I feel like I was an afterthought, someone you felt you should protect, rather than someone you had to."

"Of course you weren't an afterthought." Paul strove for outrage. "Remember, I didn't know there was a child when I made you my beneficiary."

"Yes, the infamous inheritance. How convenient and how conscience absolving." Nora put her head on one side. "You've had someone following me," Nora stated as fact. "He was in my rooms, pawing through my private things."

"I receive updates from the government on my parents in case anyone tries to harm them. When I learned about the child, I argued with my handler, and made them promise to watch you. We get British newspapers where I live, you know, and your exploits were all over them last spring. Your room may have been checked, but only to see if there were bugs or cameras watching you. It was just a matter of time until Garanin stole the virus and made a move."

"One listening device is better than another? Do you know how it felt to find them in my purse and on my car?" She didn't wait for an answer. "Of course you don't. You're in your secure place, all wrapped up neatly. Your handler went along with following me to find this creep?"

"We had to track Garanin down so I could stop him." Paul raised his chin.

"You didn't know at the time it would be Garanin. You never considered how this might impact us at all." She pursed her lips, her thoughts starting to coalesce. "How do you live knowing you won't see your parents any longer? Did you think of them when you decided to disappear? Wasn't there any other way to protect them?"

"This *was* to protect them. How can I make you understand that? We all have to make sacrifices at times. It's a dangerous world. I needed to do my part."

"Really? That's what you're going with?" Nora was less than satisfied with his altruistic answer. "I can't conceive of letting my mother think I was dead. Isn't there a way to let them know you're alive without compromising your current situation? This maniac found out about you anyway. I visit your parents with Sean now, Paul. They have this memorial to you, and they're still grieving—"

Paul smacked the tabletop. "I *said* it was to protect them. You have to cut ties to everyone."

Nora saw Declan flinch. "Yes, but—"

"There is no *but* about it. This is why things were rocky between us, Nora. Your inability to let anything drop."

Nora bit her lip, deep in thought. What about *me*? How could you walk away from me so easily? But she knew she'd been considering breaking the engagement herself and didn't voice her hurt. All this time she thought he'd still truly loved her, but now she saw he'd moved on before she had. The knowledge stung.

At the window, Declan tilted his head and gave her a look that said *I'm sorry.* He'd figured out Paul had left Nora emotionally before he ever pretended to be dead.

"Thank you for putting me in your will." Nora's voice was faint. "It's made a huge difference. I didn't know I was pregnant when you—disappeared." She was finding it hard to buy into his excuses, government backing or not.

Paul nodded once, a sharp jut of his head. "Least I could do. I did care for you once, and the powers that be—" He cut himself off.

Nora's hackles rose at the perfunctory statement. Now she was a duty plus a way to salve his conscience?

"They thought it would make your 'death' more believable if you left your grieving fiancée taken care of in your will?" Nora's voice was tight. Absolute silence reigned for a few beats. "Tell me how you spend your days, wherever you live."

Nora observed the sudden animation in Paul's voice, with the glow that came to his face. "I have a magnificent lab, fully outfitted. Latest up-to-date equipment. Tons of staff and research in conjunction with the government of—where I am. Really glorious."

"Guess I should be happy for you, Paul." Nora was quiet. Paul saw himself as a soldier in a war, trying to fulfill his duty to his country. She had to respect that. There must have been times this had been hard on him, whether he would admit it or not.

Her head ached and she felt ready to explode, but needed to keep her emotions in check. All that mattered was getting Sean back. If Paul was responsible for her son's kidnapping, he could damn well help her.

"But it's difficult for me to be happy for someone who hasn't asked once about the son he's fathered. The son who was kidnapped, despite you having me followed for months and driving me crazy, all to ferret out this maniac so you could get on with your work. Great plan, wasn't it?"

"I did it to protect you!"

Paul's repeated protest sounded false to Nora.

"No, I think not." Nora spoke with thoughtful consideration. "Look, I appreciate you have a brilliant mind, and maybe you are the genius who can save humanity from evil people like this man. But I also think you were protecting your precious research with your name on it. It's always been about the work with you, Paul. That's how you allow poor Harvey and Muriel to think you're dead. You don't want to take your place at Port Enys. You don't care about your heritage, or the legacy in that beautiful house and land. It's why you didn't take me to meet them."

Nora pushed back her chair and stood up. Declan's back stiffened. Paul watched her with an enigmatic expression, his mouth set in a firm line.

"Forget me," she continued. "Even if you truly have no idea of the guilt I carried after you supposedly died because we weren't working out, or of the pain you've caused to your parents."

Paul sat still, his head high, staring past Nora.

His impassive pose annoyed her, but she had to get out what she needed to say. "You say you did this to protect us and to serve your country, but you also did it to get what you always wanted: your own lab, everything at your fingertips, people running around under your thumb."

Paul flinched as Nora leaned toward him. She saw Declan move closer to her, ready to grab her if her rage got the best of her and her hands flew.

"Don't worry. I won't slap you again, not that you don't deserve it. Forgive me for losing my cool, when it's only our child's life at stake." Her voice was steady and menacing. "You have one purpose here today, the way I see it. Help me get *my* child back, and then I never want to see you again." She started to leave the room, then turned back to add, "You're an absolute shit!"

8:12 PM

Nora leaned against the wall in the main room, trying to cool off, working to shove back the anger she felt toward Paul. She needed a few minutes of space from him. Leaving him sitting alone to consider his actions seemed like the best idea.

How had she ever thought she could be happy married to a man who could throw her and his own parents away? She acknowledged his dedication to his work—in some people she admired that, like Declan. Paul might be a genius in biochemistry, but brilliant people often had skills with things, and not with people; with concepts and formulas, but couldn't deal with relationships and emotions. This fit Paul to a T. The lab was his comfort zone. Maybe it wasn't that she hadn't been enough for him. Maybe no one ever would have been, and on some level he'd recognized that. It felt true.

She watched the police and civilians working hard to help find Sean, and felt Declan sidle behind her. He stood close to her, and she leaned back into him, inhaling his familiar woody scent, an oasis of sanity and reassurance.

"They're working hard for us." Declan's breath warmed her ear as he directed her attention to the far side of the room, where Chen leant over the shoulder of Burke, seated before her, intent on a computer terminal, picking away with his index fingers at her direction.

Nora sighed. "I should feel embarrassed for slapping Paul, yet I don't. I've never had the kind of temper some people do—Val springs to mind. I promise I've never hit someone in anger before."

"Are you assuring me I shouldn't be worried about us?"

"A small part of me admits it felt very good, a kind of release. Best not to get in the habit of losing control. I don't condone it, and it isn't who I am—or at least who I used to be." Who she'd once been seemed very far away.

No one told her love could be agony. Her heart had been ripped out and replaced with a cement block she lugged around with each breath. Where was Sean? Why hadn't this maniac called with further instructions? Paul seemed convinced it was this Viktor because he knew what Paul worked on. She should see a photo and she could tell them herself.

As she watched the two agents from MI-5, Chen's hand rested briefly on Burke's shoulder as she pointed to the screen with the other. She stood up straighter, then walked to the printer. "They've found something."

"Let's hope they have good news about Sean."

"I could use a bit of hope." Nora clenched her fists, and turned to Declan. "I'm frustrated. Not allowed to search the gardens, stuck in here—I feel like I'm being punished, and letting Sean down at the same time by not doing something useful."

Before Declan could answer, Chen looked up at that moment and saw them. She spoke to Burke, then came over wearing a hint of a smile.

"We've had a big break. Pyotr Rustovich has been tracked to a hospital for the criminally insane in Belarus. He's definitely out of the picture."

Nora drew in a breath. "So Paul was right?"

Chen nodded. "Interpol has a sighting on CCTV of Viktor Garanin, traveling under a Polish passport, entering the UK last week through Birmingham. We're trying to track his movements now, but it appears he's our man." She showed Nora the printout. "This is Garanin."

Nora drew in a breath. "That's him. That's the man at the gallery." The hairs rose on her arms. The photo wasn't crisp, but there was no mistaking the large man.

"Who is Viktor Garanin when he's at home?" Declan asked.

"The son of a Russian oligarch who rose to prominence with his petroleum company. The father was a bit of a canny mobster, extreme violence all around him. Businessmen who crossed him would disappear, but nothing could be laid at his door." She blew her fringe off her face. "Flashy dresser, bit of an epicurean."

Declan frowned. "And the son, Viktor, is in the same mould?"

"Worse in every regard, including the violence. Found his mother's body when he was 11 after she committed suicide. Bright but manipulative. I'm torn between calling him a sociopath versus a psychopath, although my profiler says he scores high enough on the Hare scale—a psychological assessment tool—to warrant the latter, with poor impulse control, and sexual promiscuity." She read off her notes. "He exhibits the psychopath's superficial but glib charm, grandiose self-perception, constant need for stimulation, all coupled with pathological lying. There's also an absence of any guilt or remorse, a key factor. Excellent education in Europe, then returned to Russia, but didn't follow his father into his business."

A shiver took hold of Nora at the thought this madman might be the one who had Sean in his grasp. "That's unusual, isn't it? Not to have taken over his father's business?"

"Yes," Chen admitted. "But if he's really as mentally off as we think, he wouldn't have put himself into direct competition with his father as a youth. Better he excelled in a different field entirely."

"I don't think we're going to like this," Declan said. "What's his field?"

Nora expected Chen to say "biology" or "chemistry."

"He holds a Masters in International Security Studies from Charles University in Prague, with a minor in Art History. For 10 years he was head of Security for Russia's Pushkin Museum, where he probably hatched his scheme and made contacts he kept up. In the past two years, he spent time in—Paul's country, setting up the security for his protected lab. That's where their paths crossed."

Nora corrected her. "That's where he knew he could find the man he needed to make his plan work."

Declan drew in a breath. "He certainly fits the profile, then— a maniac with ties to the Pushkin that gave him exposure to the paintings, with a knowledge of the workings of the museum transfers. Plus, he has the finances to support hiring henchmen, like that dead scientist, to do his bidding. Where is he now?"

"We're still figuring that out. We're examining CCTV from Oxford and Bath, but as you can imagine, it's a long process. I've already sent agents to check the hotels in both locations."

"It's been hours. Shouldn't we have heard from Viktor to see if Paul is here?" Fear etched deep worry lines on Nora's face. She became aware that Paul had opened the interview room door and joined them.

"I know what he wants. He hated England and everything British," Paul said. "I remember that about him. He was fascinated by my work, and said it was a good thing I'd left England.

When I pressed him, he shut up. He knows I could make his mutation work."

Chen put her hand up. "Enough. We need to find this creep and soon."

Declan put his arm around Nora. "It's only been five hours, Nora. I know that's an eternity to you, but he has his own time-line and we probably won't hear from him again for another few hours."

"He's right, Nora," Chen agreed. "I suggest even if you don't feel hungry, you two get something to eat while you can. I can have the station order a takeaway. It's going to be a long night."

"You should eat, Nora," Paul said. "You need the energy. Vik-tor will call for me to meet him on his own timeline. We've worked out what to say and do, but you should be in good form."

"I don't know about eating, but I'd like to check on Helen." Nora's lips were set in a firm line.

Chen motioned Thalmann over, and they spoke briefly. "All right. Royal United isn't that far, and your phone is cloned to us. I should send you with a police escort but everyone here is better off working on leads. We'll let Declan stand in. Head there for a short while, and then right back here." Chen looked at Paul. "We'll take care of Mr. P. His handler is due here shortly."

"Come on, Nora. Let's go to the hospital while we have this window of time." Declan thought the change of scene would be good for Nora, and pulled her gently away, while catching Chen's eye. *I'll take care of her*, he telegraphed.

The agent gave him a curt nod, and moved back to her colleague. With one hand on the small of her back, Declan guided Nora through the maze of corridors with the smell of stale coffee and wet clothing, and thought he could feel Paul Pembroke's eyes boring into him. He found the door nearest the car park. He used his fob to pick out his car. The rain had slowed to a scant drizzle.

"Wait here and I'll bring the car around to you."

"It's only a few drops. Let's make a run for it. The fresh air feels good." Nora gave him a weak smile.

Declan grabbed her hand. The two hopscotched between puddles and cars to his, sliding inside, shaking off the droplets that clung to them. He programmed the address for the hospital into his GPS and they set off.

"Do you want to stop for food?" Declan glanced at Nora as he stopped for a light on Upper Bristol Road. They were headed northwest, out of the town center to the suburb of Weston.

Her eyes were glued to the right as they passed Victoria Park. Bright arc lights lit up several sections of the park, and there were clusters of squad cars at entrances. "They're still searching," she whispered.

"They're doing all they can. If this man truly has Sean, he's long gone from the park. They're just making sure." He wouldn't say out loud what the policeman part of his mind told him: It would be far easier to take the child and dispose of him immediately than try to hide a toddler or travel with one everyone was on the lookout for. These searchers were looking for a body in case Sean never made it out of the park.

"I'm sorry I couldn't tell you about Paul right away. It must have been such a shock." Declan felt selfish bringing this up when Nora's mind was focused on Sean, but he had to know if Paul's return had jeopardized their relationship.

"I still can't believe he's alive. It's surreal."

Tread carefully, Dec. "It must stir up all kinds of feelings toward him." He kept his eyes on the road, but Nora was sharp, and he felt her eyes on him.

"He *is* Sean's father, in the biological sense. You think if you've slept with someone, you know them. I mean, what makes relationships differ is the level of intimacy, right? Once you've been intimate with someone, you've been with them in a way you haven't with a casual friend or relation of the other sex. You've shared something special. You don't look at them the same way ever again."

Here it comes. Despite how she's been acting toward Paul, this is where she tells me her feelings have come rushing back for him. Declan held his breath as he downshifted.

"Seeing Paul, listening to him talk, I realized he needs to see himself like a warrior in his lab. It's important work he's doing."

Oh, God, she thinks he's a hero. He felt his heart race.

"He just doesn't need people the way I do. That's why we both ultimately realized it could never work between us."

Declan blew out his breath as his pulse slowed.

Nora held out her right hand. Declan took his left off the gear shift and held hers, threading their fingers together. "I love you, Declan."

"I love you, Nora. And I promise, when we get Sean back, we'll be our own little family."

Chapter Twenty-Three

The rain stopped completely by the time Nora rushed inside the Royal United Hospital, Declan on her heels.

"Visiting hours end soon." Nora pointed to the sign at the entrance desk. "I hope they'll let us up." She had to see Helen. Maybe she'd remembered some small detail that would be of help.

"We've got that covered." Declan flashed his warrant card and a bright smile to the young woman manning the desk. "DI Barnes, here to question Mrs. Helen Sackville."

The receptionist consulted a computer screen. "She's in the Medical Assessment Unit." She whipped out a pad of maps of the complicated floor plan for the large medical facility and tore one off, then circled a ward next to the Emergency Department. She pointed to the pertinent areas. "Two lefts to Zone C. She's in Area A, 10 beds, and she's in bed 2. It says there's a police guard outside the ward door checking all visitors to that area." She handed him the map.

"As he should be." Declan snapped a nod as he took the map. He guided Nora down the hall as directed.

"Thank you," Nora added. She waited until they were out of the receptionist's hearing before she added: "Seconded to Avon and Somerset Constabulary now, Declan?"

"In a manner of speaking. Got you in here, didn't it?"

Nora came to a halt in the middle of the corridor. A junior doctor, head down and intent on his text, zoomed around them. "Declan, what do I say to Helen? She's hurt because she was watching Sean for me."

"She's probably just as worried that Sean was in her care when he was taken, and will need your reassurance. Be her friend so she can continue to be yours."

Nora thanked him for the good advice. She was filled with a wave of love for this strong, determined man. His presence calmed her. "Declan? No matter what happens, just know how much I love you right this minute. Thank you for going through this with me."

"Love you, too. Come on before they find me out and make us leave."

They found Zone C, and Area A was clearly marked. Declan showed his warrant card to the uniformed constable on duty, who dutifully wrote both their names on a log. "Daughter left a few minutes ago with a friend. Her husband is with her now. No one else has tried to get in."

Declan thanked him. They found Helen sitting up in bed, her head wound dressed with a large bulky dressing. A slender man with fair hair Nora recognized as Matthew sat next to her, holding Helen's hand.

Both women spoke at once.

"Nora!"

"Helen—" Nora rushed to her friend's bedside and hugged her. "I'm so sorry you were hurt."

Helen fought back tears. "I'll be fine. A concussion but they'll let me out tomorrow with luck, although I'm holding Matthew to a promise of a huge bouquet from The Fresh Flower Company. I'm the one who's so sorry—any news of Sean?"

"Not yet, but we think we know who took him. This is Declan Barnes, Matthew."

The two men shook hands and introduced themselves better. "Helen, you look ravishing in that turban." Declan's easy manner put everyone at ease.

"It's my new look. Tell me what you've learned."

Nora glanced at Declan. How to tell Helen and Matthew what had happened in the intervening hours without giving away what they weren't able to say?

Declan answered Helen. "This has a crossover to a case I'm investigating in Oxford, the death of a young art conservator from a mutated smallpox virus. MI-5 is involved and think they have a likely suspect."

"Yes, but why kidnap Sean?" Helen's quizzical look said she couldn't see the connection.

"There's a lot we don't know. It could be the kidnapper thinks he'll gain some advantage to have a child to ransom that will distract me from hunting him down for the murder." Declan's persona was reassuring and confident.

"How will a ransom work?" Matthew asked.

An aide bustled in to check Helen's vital signs. They waited silently while she took Helen's blood pressure, then shined a light in her eyes.

The interruption gave Nora time to mull over things in her mind. With her only aim to have Sean back, she hadn't thought through the mechanics of how retrieving Sean would be accomplished in reality. Would Paul actually think of a way to make this evil man think he was cooperating? He and the agents must have concocted some approach in the time they'd spent in isolation earlier.

She hated not being more honest with her friends, but she knew this line was one she couldn't cross, one she would be tested on again and again. It would be a heavy burden to carry. She was just realizing that it meant lying to her friends for the rest of her life. She hated the position Paul had put her in. Better that they had broken up and he'd stayed alive.

At least she had Declan in her confidence. She didn't think she could live with lying to him, too. It would be bad enough being deceitful to her mother, and Val, and especially to the Pembrokes when she saw them again, and she knew the son they grieved for was alive and well.

"I expect MI-5 will handle the negotiations," Declan said when the aide moved on to the next trolley. "We're out of the loop on that one."

Helen grasped Nora's hand. "You must be going mad with worry."

"Hate to think of the little lad being a bargaining chip." Matthew shook his head.

Nora had a sudden image of Sean lying in a dark room, frightened and hungry, cold and wet, not understanding why his mother didn't come to help him. The room got dark around the edges. She reached out to grab the rail of Helen's trolley.

Matthew slid his chair under her as Declan grabbed her arm. "You're white as a ghost, Nora."

"Sorry, just a bad turn there for a moment, letting my imagination wander. We haven't eaten, and I think my blood sugar took a dip." She took a few breaths to dispel the image.

"Have one of these chocolates Matthew brought me." Helen handed over a fancy blue and white box of Rococo chocolate truffles.

Nora gulped one down. The smooth sweetness steadied her. As the others talked around her she felt her strength return. She stood up. "Is there a cafeteria? How about I get us all something to eat before they throw us out?"

"There's a café right behind the main entrance. Go with her, Matthew," Helen insisted.

"Of course. Tea all around?"

"And a nice cookie or Danish if they have it," Helen said.

"I'll stay and chat with Helen." Declan took the visitor's chair and settled in.

Nora gave him a dim smile. Who was he kidding? Declan wanted to see if he could pick Helen's brain for any details she might have remembered.

Not that it really mattered. If Chen was right and this Viktor Garanin was the man behind the kidnapping, they had to find him, and soon. Nora trailed behind Matthew, who waited for her to catch up.

"All right, Nora?" Concern was written on Matthew's face.

Poor man. His wife in hospital with a wound and a concussion, and saddled with another woman on the verge of fainting. "Absolutely." She picked up her pace and they entered the café and stood in line together.

Nora turned to watch the trickle of people coming into the main entrance. She couldn't believe her eyes when she saw a familiar man enter. "Matthew, milk and two sugars for me and Declan. I need to use the ladies."

"Of course." Matthew stepped up to order.

Nora walked out of the café and into the main hall to follow the person she'd glimpsed. What was Paul doing here?

8:38 PM

Viktor Garanin finished dressing. His sleek black leather jacket had deep pockets, and worn with the high-collared black Cossack shirt and trousers, he looked like a Russian diplomat on his way out for the evening. Once he pulled on the balaclava tucked into his jacket pocket, he'd be almost invisible in the darkness.

He'd packed his toiletries and stowed his kit in his prepared suitcase. Now he hesitated over the painting. Should he take it out of hiding, or leave it for his return? He had this wretched room until checkout tomorrow, although he didn't intend to sleep here tonight. Once he had Pembroke's formula, he would have a quick trip back to retrieve his suitcase and the painting. Then he could leave this nightmare of a room and Bath behind him.

Dinner had been quick but palatable, the sea bass perfectly cooked, the buttery fish reminding him of his grandmother. Dessert in his room proved even better. The woman had been lush in her breasts and hips, as promised, and if the orbs were less than natural, he didn't care. Those hips gave him something to hold onto as he pounded into her from behind, and while he couldn't remember her face 10 minutes after she left, it didn't matter. She'd taken all he had to give without complaint, and left 50 minutes after she arrived with his handprints on her buttocks and his cash in her purse.

Yesterday morning when he'd gone on his scouting trip for the perfect venue to meet Pembroke, he'd chosen carefully. Somewhere out of Bath proper, but not too far. Somewhere that could be found easily, yet would be deserted at night. He'd found the site originally in the guidebook, and visited it as just another tourist, but known once inside he'd found the ideal area for his assignation. There was a kind of irony to the setting. Holier than thou for an unholy alliance. Perfect.

All he had to do was make the call to Nora Tierney that would set his plan into motion, and before dawn broke, he would be on his way, the formula he needed in his hand, and Paul Pembroke would be dead—for good, this time.

8:39 PM

Declan could see why Nora enjoyed Helen Sackville's company.

Despite her head injury, the woman answered Declan's questions intelligently.

"So you can't think of anything else that would be helpful about the man in the gallery?"

"We told Detective Thalmann everything we recalled. But there is one thing. For a gruff man, he looked fondly at Sean."

Declan made a note. "That's interesting."

"He's a special child, Declan. I'm so worried about him and about Nora."

"We have to have faith, Helen, that this will turn out well. The Bath police and MI-5 have pulled out all the stops to get him back."

Matthew appeared at the door with a cardboard tray of four teas. "Pretty well out of goodies at this hour, I'm afraid, but the tea is fresh."

"Where's Nora?" Declan's mobile rang. Chen. "Excuse me—"

He stepped outside the ward as he answered. The constable was still on guard. "Chen?"

"We have a problem. Pembroke has disappeared."

"What? How did that happen?"

"I went to the front desk to bring his handler back. Burke was in the cafeteria and the others were all involved and engaged. He just—left."

"He walked out and no one noticed?" Declan knew he did a poor job of keeping the incredulity out of his voice. Everyone had been busy, absorbed in their own tasks. He heard Chen's sigh down the line and didn't wait for an answer. "I'll get Nora and head back immediately." He clicked off and pocketed his mobile, then nodded to the constable and walked back to Helen and Matthew.

Still no Nora. "Where's Nora?" he asked Matthew again.

"She was on her way to the loo, stopped to talk to a man in the lobby."

Declan had a sinking feeling. "What did the man look like?" He had to rein in his anxiety. This was not Matthew's fault.

"Average height, fair hair, slender."

Bloody Paul! "Sorry, I must leave. Helen, feel better really soon." He thanked Matthew for the tea and took his leave, stopping to talk to the constable. "If Nora Tierney, the woman accompanying me, returns, get her to call me immediately. If anyone else tries to get in, hold them and call Security straight away to assist you. Then call Bath station to notify Detective Chen for further instructions."

He left the constable writing down his instructions and sprinted down the hall back to the lobby, dialing Nora's mobile. It went straight to voicemail. Was that because of the poor signal indoors, or had Paul convinced Nora to turn it off? At the ladies room he pushed open the door and yelled in: "Nora Tierney!"

The harsh noise of a hand dryer shut off. *Let her be here*, he prayed.

A stout woman walked out. "No one else in there."

Declan thanked her and rushed to his car, blood pumping through his body. Had Nora willingly gone with Paul? Where were they headed?

His mobile rang and he had his answer.

Chen was terse, and he remembered her mobile was cloned. "Nora just texted us. She met up with Paul at the hospital. They're already on their way. Head straight for—" She gave him a most unlikely destination, just as Nora sent him a text with the same information. Viktor Garanin was sending them to St. Andrews, in Castle Combe.

8:54 PM

When she'd first seen Paul in the lobby, Nora knew right away he could only be there to look for her.

"What are you doing here?" she demanded the minute she saw him.

"Couldn't stand waiting. Once my handler gets here I'll be bundled away until this whole thing is over. This crazy guy, Viktor—he won't leave it much longer. You'll get a call to tell me to meet him and I'll have to go, right then, or he won't hesitate to kill the child."

"You *do* care!"

"Enough that I couldn't enjoy my lab and new life if something happened to the boy."

Nora bristled. "He's not a boy; he's your son."

"For God's sake, don't make this more difficult, Nora."

Her phone rang and she looked at the number. Blocked. The kidnapper? She answered, knowing Chen and Burke had access to the line. Paul leaned in to hear.

Heart pumping hard, she answered. "Nora Tierney."

"Miss Tierney, good evening. I hope you're enjoying yourself."

Bile rose in her throat. "I'd enjoy myself a whole lot more if I had my son."

"That's entirely up to you and Dr. Pembroke. Not an easy man to deal with. These science types have no sense of proportion or humor."

"How can I get my child back?" Nora tried not to plead. That would feed right into this maniac's ego and give him control. Then she realized he held all the cards, and thought maybe she *should* feed his ego. She wished at that moment Chen had schooled her in how to talk to Viktor. Maybe if she hadn't gone to the hospital, Chen or Burke might have done just that.

"I'm assuming Pembroke has made contact and you can get in touch with him."

"What if I said I couldn't? You apparently know his situation."

Garanin's voice became stiff with anger. "Don't play games with me, Nora Tierney. I want Paul's formula carried in person to me. Tell him to come to Castle Combe, St. Andrews Church, and leave it in the tomb of the Norman Knight. Let him know he's getting away easy. I wanted him to come with me, but the maneuverings are too difficult. I'll settle for his formula."

"What about my baby?" Nora hated the quaver in her voice.

"When I'm satisfied Pembroke has delivered, I'll hand over the boy."

"How do I know if you're telling the truth?"

"You don't. Tell Pembroke he has half an hour or the child dies." The line went dead.

Paul started to move away. "Let's go."

"Go where? I have to get Declan—" Nora turned to walk back, only to have Paul grab her arm.

"You heard the man. We have half an hour. Do you know where this place is?'

"Helen took me there once." She cast her mind for details of the 13th century church and its location. "The village is used in period films, with the church in the center of it—"

"I don't need the bloody guidebook! Just get us there, or I'll leave you behind. We need to go now if you have any chance of getting Sean back alive." Paul's sense of urgency got through to Nora. She followed him outside where a string of taxis waited for visiting hours to end. He jerked open the door of the first one and shouted to the driver: "An extra 20 quid if you get us to St. Andrews in Castle Combe in 20 minutes."

They jumped in the back and the taxi roared off.

Nora pulled up the directions on her mobile. Her heart raced when she saw it was 12 miles from Bath.

Paul reached into his jacket pocket. Nora worried he might have a gun. If he killed this freak, all hope of seeing Sean was lost.

Instead, Paul brought out a small plastic bag holding a thumb drive and several discs.

"Is that what you're going to give him?"

Paul nodded. "Chen and I came up with this."

"Is that *the* formula?" Nora was reluctant to talk about details in case the driver listened in.

Paul lowered his voice. "This is actually the way to stop the mutation if it's followed to the end. If Garanin has any biochemical knowledge, it will pass muster as they start out the same. The discs have the same corrupted formula written down and given different dates, so it seems to be what I've been working on over a period of time. It's what we worked on this afternoon after they helicoptered me in. We hope that by handing this over, he'll give us Sean's location, and we'll all get away alive."

Nora's feelings ran the gamut from fear to excitement at the thought of holding Sean very shortly. "How will he be convinced these are real? What if he has a weapon?"

"Hopefully he's crazy enough to think we'll cooperate to get the boy back. Chen and company had your phone cloned, remember? She told me by the time Viktor called, they would have an Armed Response Unit standing by to get wherever he said, Kevlar vests, the whole caboodle. Viktor would have a tough time getting any kind of gun through customs, no matter what passport he was on."

The driver's radio crackled with a new call. "Already out on one, guv. Headed to Castle Combe."

Worry for Sean kept Nora silent. She was tired of pointing out that Paul kept calling his son "the boy," as though he had no attachment to him. Yet the determination with which he'd sought her out at the hospital didn't fit.

Maybe that was Paul's coping mechanism. Knowing he was going back to Belgium or Switzerland or wherever he lived now when this was over, and would never be an active part of his son's life, would make him keep his distance, and not wish to form any attachments. Nora could see the sense in that, but she also knew it was something she could never accept.

She touched Paul gently on his arm and leaned over to whisper. "Sorry I've given you a hard time. It's rough with Sean missing, and the shock of seeing you."

"I understand. You do have a healthy left hook, you know."

"I've never lost control like that before."

"Good thing, or we would have broken up even sooner."

"I'll resist the urge to punch you."

"Declan seems a decent bloke. Loves you."

"I know. I'm lucky." Nora smiled in the dark of the car. This might be the last time they would ever be alone. "Do you mind terribly, not being a part of Sean's life?"

Paul shrugged. "It was a shock when I read in the papers last spring after your exploits that you'd had a child, but I thought perhaps it wasn't mine. Then my handler gave me an update from the fellow assigned to you, and told me you'd met with my parents. I knew then he was mine."

Finally, an acknowledgment. "Isn't there a way I could send you updates and photos as he grows?"

Paul barked a brittle laugh. "That is so like you, Nora. You are so bloody stubborn, you think everyone thinks like you do. I don't. I admit science is my first love. I didn't plan to have children. You've given my parents that, I suppose. I am sorry I hurt you—it was never my intention. I can't form any attachments now. It would be too painful and I've made my choice."

That put her in her place. Nora's eyes filled with tears. Paul could be so awful at times. Memories of their arguments flooded back. He seemed without emotions, but she knew there was a softer side he rarely showed, or she wouldn't have been attracted to him. But she recalled, too, talking it out with Val right after the supposed plane crash, her emotions turbulent, when she'd realized Paul was the person she happened to be with when she felt ready to marry. That often happened, she'd been led to see. Timing in life was everything, her father had told her. She believed it.

So why was she trying to recast Paul in the light of someone he plainly wasn't? She should be thankful he was willing to help her get Sean back and leave it there.

CHAPTER TWENTY-FOUR

Castle Combe

9:13 PM

Declan took the A46 north out of Bath and turned east onto the A420. He calculated he was five or six minutes behind Nora and Paul. Chen called and confirmed she and Burke, with Thalmann, were enroute to the area, followed by a van from SCO19 with an Armed Response Vehicle teeming with a Tactical Support Team as well as a Specialist Rifle Officer trained as a marksman.

The presence of firearms simultaneously reassured and worried Declan, although he saw the need for them. He could understand Nora's impulsiveness, too, but wished she'd waited a few minutes for him to meet up with them. What kind of weapons would Garanin have? Nora would put her own safety aside to save Sean. Worry gripped him as he slapped his magnetic light on the hood and pushed harder on the accelerator, his blue lights and two-tone siren pushing other drivers out of the way as he sped along. He would shut them off as he neared his destination, but right now he needed to clear the roads.

He'd heard Chen's annoyance when she'd said Pembroke simply walked out of the station's back door when they were all busy at other tasks. She wasn't used to people not obeying her orders. She rang his mobile just then, and he hit the answer button on his Bluetooth. Her voice echoed through his small car. "We're nine minutes out on my GPS."

Declan glanced at his. "I'll get there in six, according to mine."

"Rendezvous at Market Cross on Water Street by St. Andrews."

"If Nora's in danger I may have to go in sooner."

"Remember you are seconded to this unit only, Barnes. Approach with caution, and only as necessary."

"Understood." What he comprehended was that once the Armed Response Unit was called out, all of Chen's communications would be recorded until they stood down. The clear message was: *If you get into trouble, it's on your head, not mine.*

His mobile chimed with an incoming text he didn't stop to read. If it was Nora, she would have called. She knew he had Bluetooth in his car. His instincts told him Viktor Garanin had carefully chosen this spot for some reason Declan didn't understand. He raced past a row of benches glowing in the moonlight, set into the walkway facing the narrow River Bybrook he recognized from a Spielberg movie. The charm of the connected golden Cotswold stone houses, with their leaded windows and natural stone tiled roofs that stretched the gentle curve of the opposite bank, was lost to Declan with his increasing fear that Paul and Nora were walking into an assignation with a clear madman.

9:14 PM

Paul paid the taxi outside St. Andrews. Nora tumbled out of the cab, checking her watch as the car took off to its next engagement. Within their time limit. Her heart raced; her hands were slick and clammy.

Could Sean be inside right now? Would she soon be reunited with him? *Please let my baby be all right,* she prayed, lifting her eyes to follow the tall spire that rose behind the church, its crenellated tower reaching into the night sky. When she looked at Paul, he finished a text, then shoved his mobile in his pocket.

"Stay here." Paul checked his pocket for the bag he needed.

His terse whisper annoyed Nora. "Not going to happen," she whispered back.

Paul sighed his annoyance. "Then stay behind me and let me deal with Garanin."

Because you've done such a bang up job of things so far, Nora thought, but didn't say aloud. Garanin had heard Paul arguing with his handler about following Nora. That shouldn't have happened. Then he kept knowledge of that information for when he needed it, and set this entire thing in motion months later.

They walked through an open iron gate and picked their way on the uneven paving stones lit by moonlight to the porch entrance. Paul pushed open the low, ancient wooden door to the entryway, and they stepped inside the darkened church.

Paul gestured for her to wait. Their eyes grew accustomed to the gloom, and Nora turned on the flashlight app on her phone. An eternity light near the altar picked out restored frescoes of saints that adorned a tall gothic arch around the altar and its cross. Four panels of stained glass reached toward the high ceiling, sparkling like red and purple jewels in the muted light.

Nora's skin prickled, the hairs rising on her arms. There were gothic arches everywhere she looked, soaring to the vaulted ceiling, casting eerie shadows around. The bell tower made her think of the movie *Vertigo*, and she imagined her satisfaction at pushing Viktor Garanin off it after she'd safely retrieved Sean. She was going mad.

Somewhere deeper into the church she could see the glow of another light.

Paul leaned toward her and whispered into her ear: "Stay behind me." His breath felt warm; this close, she caught the remnants of his aftershave.

"I think the knight is in the side chapel," she whispered back, inhaling the familiar scent of his skin. With a rush she remembered when she loved this man.

She pointed toward the light, and they moved slowly forward

into the main nave, with Nora shining her flashlight at their feet.

Nora listened carefully for sounds of someone else in the church as they walked over black and gold tiles down the main aisle. Clerestory windows let in streaks of moonlight from their soaring height. An owl hooted nearby. It startled her, and she stumbled into Paul's back.

"Over there." She pointed to the northeast chapel off the main altar. "The knight's tomb is lit." They reached the transept, the corridor that ran east and west before the altar, and turned to the right.

An open-sided tomb rose before them, lit from inside the sarcophagus' chamber. "𝔚𝔞𝔩𝔱𝔢𝔯𝔲𝔰 𝔡𝔢 𝔇𝔲𝔫𝔰𝔱𝔞𝔫𝔳𝔦𝔩𝔩𝔢 * 𝔅𝔞𝔯𝔬𝔫 𝔬𝔣 𝔠𝔞𝔰𝔱𝔩𝔢𝔠𝔬𝔪𝔟𝔢 1270" was printed across the upper edge. The carved stone life-sized image of Sir Walter wore full Crusade regalia, down to chainmail. The side of the tomb had six figures carved into it, but Nora couldn't remember what they represented. In her nervousness, she thought of trivial details.

"His crossed arms show piety; his crossed legs indicated he'd been in two Crusades." Nora wondered why they whispered, even as she spoke quietly into Paul's ear.

"We're not on a bloody tour." Paul shook his head in the dim light. "Focus." He pointed to the knight's stomach, where a laptop stood open and charged up, waiting for them.

"I'm putting a thumb drive into this laptop." Paul's voice burst into the quietness, reverberating through the chapel as his actions matched his words. A series of clicks and whirs indicated the drive was loading. "I have copies of all the various stages of my research on discs I'm leaving next to it. This is all you need."

His boldness allowed Nora to speak up. "Where is my son?" To her ears, her voice sounded weak. She cleared her throat. "I want Sean, now!"

The sound of clapping hands reached them. Viktor Garanin,

dressed in black, stepped into the gloom from behind a stone pillar. Only his face glowed white in the shadows. This was the man who'd taken her son, the same man from that day in the gallery. She wished she had a weapon, to hurt him as he'd hurt Helen. She listened for any signs of Sean, any cries or whimpers. All she cared about was getting him back.

"Very good—very good attempt, Dr. Pembroke. But why did you bring her? That wasn't part of our deal."

"She wants the boy back."

Nora's heart pounded. Could her presence have ruined her chance of getting Sean back?

Garanin stepped closer. His bulk towered over them as he glanced at the computer screen where the cursor blinked, waiting for a command. "Open it."

Paul clicked a few keys and the screen filled with a complicated series of chemical equations. "This," he said, pointing to the opening sequence, "is what you need to start the mutation." He moved the cursor down into a second page. "This is the formula for enhancing the mutation. It accelerates the biosynthesis."

Paul stood by the computer, waiting for instructions. Nora stayed behind him.

Suddenly the sound of Viktor's deep laugher filled the chapel, and echoed in the church.

There was a flash of silver. Garanin reached out one long arm, and Nora felt herself snatched by Viktor. He pulled her roughly to his chest, pinned her there with his left arm locked around her neck. She dropped her mobile. The flashlight pointed to the tomb, bringing Sir Walter and Paul into sharp relief.

"Stop!" Paul shouted. "I've done what you asked. There wasn't supposed to be any violence."

Nora struggled against Viktor's bulk and strength. She lifted one leg and kicked back. Viktor anticipated her action and side-stepped the kick. "Tell your girlfriend to behave if she wants her kid alive."

"Nora, stop struggling." Paul's voice was strained. "We did as you asked. Let her go. Give us the boy. Take these and leave. No one gets hurt."

The knife glittered in front of Nora's eyes. She stopped moving, breathing hard, her pulse pounding in her ears.

"What would be the fun in that?" Viktor sneered. "I want you, science brain. I need you to come with me and make this mutation virulent enough to kill everyone in England. Do you think I would really settle for a few equations on a thumb drive? How do I know you're not tricking me? But now I have not only your son but your girlfriend, too, to make sure you'll do what I want."

"Let her go. I gave you what you need. You have my word."

In that instant, Nora could see Paul's resemblance to Harvey: the raised chin and firm voice, the determination in his eyes. She felt a pang of sadness for what might have been.

"Because the word of a bloody Englishman is always to be trusted, yes?" Viktor's voice dripped with loathing.

Nora's breath was being choked off with Viktor's arm held tightly around her neck. She tried to pry her fingers between his arm and her neck to give her air. The beast's height made it easy for him to subdue her, and she felt her efforts were fruitless.

"Because the child is my son and she needs to have him back." Paul's statement hung in the air between them all. There was a moment of absolute silence.

Then Paul hurled himself at Viktor and Nora screamed. With a vicious movement, Viktor lunged forward, thrusting his knife to stab Paul.

Paul staggered backward, clutching his side where the knife entered. He fell against the tomb. His head hit the stone with a sickening *thunk*, and he slid to the floor.

"Paul!" Nora shrieked with the little air she had, straining against Viktor's arm.

There were running footsteps; then out of the darkness, Declan's voice startled Nora. "Drop the knife, Viktor. You can't get away. There's an experienced sniper with his sight trained on you. Let her go, and we can all go home today."

"Where's my baby?" Despite the nearness of the knife Nora thrashed against Viktor's arm, her thoughts wild. If she bit him would her teeth go through his clothing, or cause her death?

Viktor uttered a stream of Russian words that could only be profanity, and clutched Nora tighter.

Declan shouted: "Nora—RUN AWAY!"

"Declan, no!" If Viktor was killed, she would have no way to find Sean. But what choice did she have with a sniper trained on them both? Nora blinked as her mind raced and she remembered Declan's anecdote in Brighton about Monty Python. Viktor tightened his grip.

She let herself go limp, made herself as small as possible, tucking her head down. Nora sucked in a breath, waiting for the pain of the knife, and heard instead a wet *splat*, followed by a bang that deafened her, as she felt a shower of warmth sprinkle over her.

Viktor's arm relaxed and Nora crumpled to the ground.

Behind her, Viktor Garanin slammed into the stone floor of the ancient church.

9:27 PM

Declan rushed to Nora, who cowered on the floor. He caught her head to stop her from turning to look behind her, and gathered her in his arms as the church burst into life, lights streaming down on them. Helmeted men in tactical gear swarmed into St. Andrews and ran down the aisles as members of the Tactical Support Team filled the church. The one who reached them first spoke into his mouthpiece: "Suspect down. Repeat, suspect down. All clear. Need medics."

"Declan, let me up." Nora struggled against his efforts to get her to stay put. He finally helped her stand, and she ran to Paul. Blood pooled beneath his head and from his side. "Paul!" Nora knelt beside him, her teeth chattering in shock. "Paul," she wailed, crying as Declan gently pulled her up

Two medics arrived and pushed them back, surrounding Paul with their equipment.

"Let them try to help him, sweetheart." Declan held her tightly.

Chen and Burke, followed by Thalmann, hurried down the aisle.

Nora blubbered. "He tried to help me get Sean."

"Shh, I know darling, I heard him." Declan took a handkerchief to clean Garanin's blood off her hair before she felt it.

"Thanks for helping the sniper, Declan." Chen patted him on the arm and then saw the medics working on Paul. "Sorry, I didn't realize—"

"NOOO ... " Nora's wail cut through the babble of crime officers standing over two different men. She pointed at Viktor Garanin's body. "He didn't tell us where Sean is!"

Chen motioned to Burke. "Get the team to search the church for the boy."

He nodded and spoke to the team leader, who dispersed his men around the church. Declan guided Nora to a pew away from the scene. He sat with her, using his handkerchief again, letting her cry until she wore herself out. For the next 10 minutes, the team searched all of the nooks and crannies they found at St. Andrews, reporting back to Chen. She sat in the pew in front of Nora and Declan, texting on her mobile.

"Suspect's rental vehicle empty; boot clear."

"Grounds clear."

"Lower level clear."

It soon became evident that Sean Tierney wasn't on the premises.

"I'm sorry, Nora." Chen sighed. "We'll pull out all the stops to find Sean."

Declan's heart broke when he watched Nora raise her tear-stained face at Chen's statement. "That's what you told me earlier today, and now Paul is dying. The man responsible for taking Sean is dead, and we have no idea where he hid him!"

Nora buried her head in Declan's shoulder. He didn't blame her anger and frustration. They may have stopped a fanatic's scheme, but after what she'd just been through, to not have Sean back seemed a cruel punishment.

It was time to call in reinforcements for Nora. He pulled out his mobile to call Val Rogan. That's when he saw the text he'd neglected earlier, from Paul Pembroke:

I'm trusting you to take care of Nora and Sean.

Bath

10:12 PM

Betty Kaplan paced the floor in her cozy sitting room, holding the little boy left in her care over her shoulder. She hummed lightly, trying to soothe him. Sean MacBride certainly had a bad dose of separation anxiety, missing his mum. After being in an accident and having his mother spirited away in an ambulance, no wonder the babe was distraught.

Wearing footie pajamas, long in the leg but serviceable, he muttered "Mum-mum-mum" in a litany. She'd checked his gums, and while he had two very new teeth on the bottom, she didn't think his distress stemmed from teething.

He hadn't fought her at all when she changed him, and while his appetite lagged, he tasted everything she offered. Betty decided he was usually an easy-going baby. She put his anguish down to being wrenched from his mother under disturbing circumstances.

She'd managed to calm him at times during the evening by distraction with books, and even a bath. Each time he got drowsy and she thought he would doze off, he'd start his chanting again, poor little chap.

Betty rummaged through the nappy bag that nice Pavel Perminov had left. In a side compartment she found a small photo book. She sat near the cot with Sean on her lap and showed him the album.

"Look what I've found, Sean." She showed him the cover photo of Sean with a dark-haired man and an auburn-haired woman he resembled.

His hands reached out toward the book. "Mum! Mum-mum-mum!" he squealed. Then his lips pouted. "Mummmm … "

"Mummy, that's right. And who's this?" She pointed to the man.

"Deca."

"Daddy? Can you say Daddy?"

"Da-da."

She hugged the little boy. "Very good. Mummy and Daddy." She flipped the page. "Now who's this?" A woman with odd golden eyes and a short cap of curls held Sean in an embrace.

"Teeva."

There were photos of two older couples Betty decided were grandparents.

She talked in a soothing voice, going back to the beginning, letting him hold the album himself while she turned the pages. There were photos of cats, horses, and puppies he all called Typo. There were some of different colored blocks, and Betty guessed Mrs. MacBride carried this as a sort of speech primer for her son for names, shapes, and colors.

Finally his eyes were heavy-lidded. She closed the book and rocked him, murmuring, "Mummy and Daddy love Sean" until they closed in exhaustion. She kept rocking a few more minutes until the baby was deeply asleep, then gently laid him in the cot.

Betty stood watching the sleeping child for a minute and made up her mind. She usually slept with a baby monitor on her dresser when she had visitors, but tonight she went to her linen press and made up the bed she used for the older children.

This little one might wake in the middle of the night. Waking in an unfamiliar place with a new person could start the whole cycle over again.

After getting ready for bed, Betty took her copy of the newest Elly Griffiths mystery and settled down in her robe and slippers with a cup of cocoa. As she opened the bookmarked page to follow Ruth Galloway's latest adventure, the pretty auburn-haired mother of Sean MacBride entered her thoughts. She hoped the woman's surgery had gone well, and the young mother wasn't in pain tonight.

CHAPTER TWENTY-FIVE

Bath
Wednesday, 13th October
6:49 AM

Nora's eyes were two points of hot, gritty pain in her face as she sat in the Bath interview room again. She'd thought she was finished with the small den with its scarred table. She propped the door open with a chair for air, but it was clear her presence in the outer room wasn't needed. Some of the faces had changed, but the noise hadn't, with the constant ringing of phones and urgent voices that often seemed to hold promise that hadn't been fulfilled as the hours passed.

She wanted to lie down and sleep with her son clasped tightly in the crook of her arm, her nose buried in the back of his neck, inhaling his sweet scent. It was her favorite place on him. His soft hair would tickle her nose, his milky powdery baby scent like a drug.

Nora took a seat and held her head in her hands to prop it up, her neck sore from Viktor's strong arm around it, her head heavy from grief and lack of sleep. Flashbacks from the evening in no particular order flicked through her memory when she closed her eyes: struggling for breath with Viktor's arm locked tightly around her throat; the metallic scent of blood from Paul's broken body lying against Sir Walter's tomb; the sickening noise of Viktor Garanin's head exploding; feeling his blood rain down on her. She knew these images, sounds, and scents would haunt her dreams—if she ever slept again.

The knowledge of Sean's location died with Viktor Garanin. Nora appreciated the position the marksman had been in. With a knife held to her, and Paul already stabbed, Viktor had shown he wouldn't hesitate to kill. The sniper had taken his shot.

But where did that leave her and her son? Alex Thalmann's team was working the local angle. Viktor had stayed somewhere in or near Bath. Even if Sean wasn't in it, there might be clues in his room once they found it. That was what they were banking on now. Chen and Burke were backtracking Garanin's movements, creating a timeline since his arrival in Bath, in the hope that would lead them to Sean.

These last hours since the incident at St. Andrews had been filled with procedure. First at the church itself with the forensic team swarming over the body. Paul had been taken away in an ambulance and no one would tell her if he survived his injuries or died. After they'd been bundled back to the station, she had to give her formal statement to Chen and Thalmann, sitting with an ice pack around her throat once she'd been cleared by a medic. She recounted Paul's actions from the time Nora met him in the hospital lobby and they left the hospital together after receiving Viktor's call. Neither had berated her for leaving with Paul, and gratefully, Declan hadn't, either. She had a passing thought Declan might think her actions meant she'd chosen Paul over him, but she couldn't let those kinds of worries distract her. He should know Sean had been her focus.

"A burner mobile found on Garanin shows the call to your phone at the time you state, and we've correlated that here on our tape." Chen explained Nora's formal statement was standard procedure for her and for Thalmann's files. No one was assessing blame. It had been Chen's call to have the Tactical Support Team respond and to use the sniper.

It still rankled Nora that she had to justify her movements when they'd heard the call come in themselves. She was tired of all of this cloak and dagger stuff of the movies.

Once her statement had been signed, that left only waiting, and the hours dragged on for Nora.

She rose and paced the room. She ventured into the large room to drink water from the fountain, letting cool water flow over her lips. She wiped them with the back of one hand and dried it on jeans that had seemed crisp and neat 18 hours ago, and now felt baggy and grime ridden. She shuddered when she thought what some of the stains might be. She'd been given a clean scrub top by a medic and her white blouse taken away. That was one item of clothing she never wanted to see again.

She sat down again. The scent of burned coffee permeated the interview room. She wasn't a prisoner, but she had nowhere else to go. She stood again and leaned against the doorframe, part of her still in shock, part of her in a stupefying dream, where she didn't know where her son was or who had him.

Declan stood behind Burke, looking over his shoulder at the computer screen. Burke pecked away at the keyboard and waited for results to appear. If they found anything important, she'd know from Declan's face. He looked up and met her eyes. His face was pale and had a grim look. She retreated into the room to circuit to the window. She'd refused a tranquilizer, wanting to remain alert, but craved sleep. But how could she sleep when she was in a waking nightmare?

The sky had a bruised look to it, faint purple fingers breaking the darkness, heralding approaching dawn, sprinkled with rosy pinks, before the bright sun would show itself in slivers as it rose. She didn't see how her battered mind and body would handle a fresh day that didn't contain Sean. And what about Paul? Her feelings for him were more confused than ever. Had he died the hero he wanted to be, trying to keep his formula out of the hands of a madman? Or was he even at this moment being helicoptered back to whatever tiny country he lived in to recuperate at a hospital there?

The smokers had been banned to the outdoors. A clutch of them stood huddled together, sharing shelter against the occasional light drizzle. Smoke curled out from under the edges of their umbrellas.

It struck Nora that umbrellas were like the shields knights once carried. The thought of knights brought her back to Sir Walter, to Paul collapsing against the stone tomb, to the noise his head made as it connected with the stone as he fell.

She would not go there again. This relentless cycle had to stop. Nora considered herself a person of action, and this did nothing to bring her closer to her son. In the other cases in which she'd been involved, she'd always had an active role. She'd physically investigated a case, using her journalism background to question suspects and gather information. She recalled how many times she had frustrated Declan and Simon by her actions.

Simon. He and Kate would be heartbroken if something happened to Sean. They'd watched over her pregnancy, helped her adjust to motherhood. Simon was Sean's godfather.

She needed to call Simon at a reasonable hour tomorrow—today—and tell them what had happened with Sean and Helen. And Val. Nora missed Val, her touchstone, her best friend who knew her inside out. She couldn't tell them, any of them, about Paul. She felt the constrictions of that paper she'd signed. She could only hope this news didn't reach across the Atlantic to her mother and stepfather in Connecticut before there was resolution, and she knew what line she had to take. What if Sean was never found? How would they all handle that? How would she and Declan handle the loss?

Nora looked at her watch. 7:12 AM. How many hours had it been since she'd seen Sean? 15? No, closer to 17 since Helen left her at Victoria Park with Sean in his buggy, all set for an adventure. Is this how her life would be measured from now on, by the hours since she'd kissed him goodbye, her hand holding his pudgy chin so her lips could brush his soft fringe, each eye, his nose, and his chin in the game they always played when she left him?

Nora turned from the window and slumped in the hard chair. How confused must Sean be? First a stranger took him from Helen, and Nora could only hope he didn't see that bastard hurt Helen. Then he took Sean somewhere and dumped her baby with more strangers, if he was lucky, or abandoned him, or—NO! Nora couldn't believe she wouldn't know if Sean had been killed. She had to stop her mind straying there. It felt like a betrayal to her child. She felt his presence, felt that he lived. She had to believe she would see him and hold him again.

But had he been changed or fed? Was he warm and dry or left alone in the dark, hungry and cold, wondering why his mother had deserted him? She shook her head and her thoughts circled back to the role she found herself cast in: impatient observer. She'd had to sign the bloody Secrets Act, for God's sake. Sitting around, waiting for answers when her son's life hung in the balance gave new meaning to the word "frustration."

Even as the thoughts flitted across Nora's mind, she acknowledged that Chen's international machine was better equipped to ferret out the reasoning and motives of Viktor Garanin. His mumbled statements of hating England went beyond her grasp of the situation. She couldn't think of all the agencies that must be involved in this case, from health departments to the museums here and in Russia; from Chen and MI-5 to Interpol and Declan's Oxford station where that young woman had died.

Nora sat up straighter at the thought of the art conservator. Declan had said Emma Jevons had left behind a father living near Janet Wallace. That poor man had been dealt a weighty blow, losing his only child to a maniac like Viktor Garanin. *Please God, don't let me know the horror he's living with today.*

She looked up as Chen and Declan entered the room. Nora stood up, her fear clenching her sore stomach. She saw Burke hurry out of the office as the two met her.

Chen spoke without preamble. "My unit has been researching Viktor Garanin. We've learned Garanin had a younger brother named Ivan, who now calls himself John Garanin."

Nora's heart sped up with new hope. "Could this brother be holding Sean?"

Declan came to her side and took her hand. He shook his head. "Sorry, no. John broke with the family at 16 when visiting his mother's family. He refused to return to Russia and his father, and lived with his maternal grandparents. He finished his education here in the UK."

Chen broke in. "But we've found him, and Burke's just been talking with him. He lives in Bristol, became a psychologist. We woke him up, and Burke's on his way to bring him in to formally identify his brother, but also for us to question him in more depth as to Viktor's habits, likes, and dislikes. He's being very cooperative. He said he always knew his brother would come to a bad end as he was too much like their father."

Nora's temper blazed. "How does knowing if Viktor liked vanilla over chocolate get us close to finding Sean?"

Chen smiled. "Sometimes the simplest piece of information on someone's habits gives us the biggest break."

"Sorry. I don't mean to appear ungrateful." Nora exhaled. "I do appreciate all you're doing for me—for us—to find Sean. I'm just so frustrated."

Chen gave a brisk nod. "I'm sure you are. Would you consider going to your friend's house for a little sleep, or at least to take a shower? These things take time, and I promise to call you right away if there's any development."

"Why don't you go, Nora?" I'll stay here—" Declan broke off.

"And here's someone to drive you to Helen's."

Val Rogan stood framed in the doorway. "Yankee," she said, and held out her arms.

Chapter Twenty-Six

When Declan offered Nora the keys to his pride and joy, she briefly felt a milestone had been reached in their relationship. His precious car took second place to Sean. It felt good to have that confirmed. The friends' reunion had been a teary one, with Declan offering around a box of tissues before he insisted Val take Nora to Helen's for a shower and a lie-down.

"Make her eat something, too, even if it's tea and toast." He kissed Nora and headed back inside the station.

Val insisted on driving and slid into the driver's seat before Nora could protest. Once in the MGB, Nora programmed the GPS to Helen's address.

"I grabbed a few hours' sleep before I took the first train from Oxford." Val fastened her seat belt. "You haven't slept at all. Buckle up. I haven't driven this fancy car before and we don't need a fender bender."

"It's wonderful you're here." Nora touched Val's arm. She thought about what she could tell Val and what she couldn't. "What did Declan say when he called?" She'd take her cue from him.

Val signaled and headed toward the Somerset hills. "He told me it seemed your stalker kidnapped Sean, and it was somehow tied up with his case with that young woman from the Ashmolean who died. You could have knocked me over with a feather. Why didn't you call me the minute it happened?"

Nora blushed while she silently thanked Declan for coming up with a plausible tale that covered all the bases. "I started to; then I had to go to the police station and I was afraid they wouldn't let you in to see me, and then I went to check on Helen—she's in hospital, you know—and then it was late and I thought I should wait until maybe I had better news today."

"All right, I get that, but let me say Declan just went up a whole lot in my estimation by calling me."

"Then I'm glad. He's been wonderful. He's become—" Nora started to say "become involved with MI-5," but wasn't certain that was part of the need-to-know stuff for public knowledge.

"Become what?"

"Become very protective about Sean." As she said the words, Nora realized they were true. Declan had not only been supportive of her, but she'd seen firsthand his own anxiety to help find Sean.

"Of course he has. You're a family now." Val reached for Nora's hand and gave it a squeeze. "They'll find him. They all looked very competent, and Declan will stay on them. When is Helen coming home?"

"Today, after she's been cleared by the neurologist. Phillipa and the friend she had sleep over may be at the house, unless they've gone to school. Matthew stayed with Helen at the hospital last night."

"Left turn half mile ahead," warned the GPS voice.

Val drove competently and sedately. Nora sensed she resisted the urge to let the car have its head. The rocking made Nora's eyes drowsy. The sun had risen, bringing tendrils of soft early morning light into the car.

Nora looked down, surprised to find herself dressed in a black suit. A long line of people stood waiting for her attention, reaching back up a hill, and as the first stepped forward, Nora reached out to shake her hand. The woman's features were hazy.

"I'm so sorry for your loss." She moved on to be replaced by an equally featureless man. "So sorry for your loss."

Nora knew if she looked over her shoulder she would see a white casket. She refused to confirm her fear as another woman stepped in front of her. "Sorry for your loss."

Her composure slipped. "My son is not a damn worn slipper I've misplaced under the bed!"

"You have reached your destination."

Nora opened her eyes. Val parked next to Nora's vehicle at Hill House. The pale sunlight made dewdrops sparkle on the grass surrounding the copse of trees where parking had been carved out.

"What was that about slippers?" Val reached for their bags and struggled to get out of the low car. "There's a way to do this gracefully, but for the life of me, I can't remember what that is."

Nora decided not to share her brief dream. "You turn sideways on the seat, put your feet on the ground, and just stand up." Nora illustrated, thumping her head on the doorframe as she stood. "Ouch!"

Both women giggled. Nora swiftly felt ashamed. How could she be laughing with her baby gone? She sobered immediately, but as usual, Val read her expression and came around to her side of the car and slid her arm into Nora's.

"Come on, Yankee. Sean doesn't like his mummy all sad and grumpy. He wants Happy Mummy. Let's get you into that shower."

They walked toward the Sackvilles' stone house. Val stopped to admire the expansive view over the rolling hills. "I love this view." She pointed to the art studio. "I want a tour before we go home."

"I'm sure Helen will be delighted to show off her collections." Could she really be talking about normal things?

Val had said "home" as if Oxford were home to them all. But with Sean missing, where was home now? Would there ever be a home for her and Declan if Sean wasn't in it?

Two hens strolled across the yard, pecking at the ground. "They still have the chickens, I see." Val released Nora's arm. "How about I rustle up scrambled eggs after you shower?"

They crossed through the stable forecourt toward the kitchen. Nora's mobile rang. She snatched it from her pocket. Declan.

"More good news. Interpol tracked down the passport Garanin used. Alex's team has a name to go with the photo, when we only had the country before. He traveled into the country as a Polish citizen, Jacek Kokut. It shouldn't be long before we find the room he's been using."

Nora's spirits rose. "Do you think there's any chance Sean could be in his hotel room?" She heard Hester bark at Val in the kitchen.

"Honestly, I don't believe so. Sean would have made some kind of noise, especially if left alone, and a chambermaid would have found him by now." Declan rushed on. "But we're hoping to find clues there to find where he's hidden Sean."

Nora's tendency to investigate hadn't deserted her. "I should be with you, looking for him." Her mind whirled with images of Viktor at the gallery, wrapping her painting, taking her check. Something stuck in her mind.

"Sweetheart, you need to rest and be in a place where I can find you quickly."

"Only the best! Declan, that's it. Viktor Garanin would only stay in one of the top hotels. He wore a bespoke tailored suit, pricey cufflinks, handmade leather shoes. He wouldn't stop at any place he felt was beneath him."

"Brilliant, Nora! I'll let Alex know and we can cut down our search lists." His voice took on a softer tone. "Don't lose heart, Nora. We're so close to finding him."

"I won't. I'm going to shower, and Val's going to make us eggs so I'm ready to go when you need me. And Declan? Thanks for not lying to me. I need you to remain honest in all of this—it's hard on so many levels." Nora hoped he understood her reference to things being left unsaid.

"I know you hate keeping things from Val, but we have no choice. Look, let me go. Alex is letting me scour these hotels with him and I'll tell him we need to concentrate on the poshest. Love you, Nora."

"Love you, too."

When Nora entered the large, welcoming kitchen, she found Val admiring Helen's collection of hearts on one wall as she petted Hester. She needed to find a way to help search for Sean that Val would accept.

"I think she remembers me. She only barked a bit but let me pick her up." Val pointed to a note on the table. "Philly's gone to school. Her friend's mother took them, so we don't have to be quiet."

"What Hester remembers is your scent. Violet is probably asleep on Helen's bed." She told Val about Declan's search. "He's out with one of the detectives searching the better hotels. I wish I were there to help them."

"You need to be on the spot when they find Sean, and easily found yourself, to get to him quickly. Upstairs and shower. Fresh clothes. Washed hair. Go!" Val pointed toward the stairs.

"Aye, aye, captain." Nora took the stairs two at a time to the guest room. Finally, there was movement, and a real promise of clues that might lead them to Sean. She would shower, and then she would find out where Declan was headed and meet him there. Nora opened the door and stopped short on the threshold.

The travel cot stood empty, mocking her. Sean's sailor outfit from his Nain and his used pajamas lay crumpled on a corner of the bureau she'd used as a changing table. Nora's wind knocked out of her. She couldn't breathe.

Then she launched herself to the cot and picked up Sean's yellow blanket, the one with Beatrix Potter characters on the satin ribbon edging that he chewed on. She buried her face in it, inhaling his powdery scent, and started to weep.

9:43 AM

Declan's feet hurt and his lack of sleep caught up with him when he tripped over the pavement. He managed to catch himself before falling flat on his face. Alex had taken the top four luxury accommodations in Bath from his team's listing, and they were heading to enter the last.

He'd accompanied Alex Thalmann to the Bath Priory Hotel and Spa, where its ivy-covered façade reminded him of Oxford's Old Parsonage. They'd tried The Ayrlington, a tall, Georgian stone house, because they thought its proximity to The Holburne Museum might be a factor. They'd gone to the Halcyon Apartments, a Grade-1-listed Georgian townhouse. No one recognized Garanin's photo; no guest had registered under the passport he'd used to travel into the UK as Polish citizen Jacek Kokut.

That left The Royal Crescent Hotel, part of the magnificent 18th-century Royal Crescent in the heart of Bath, a world-renowned architectural marvel.

"Probably the priciest place," Alex commented as they were greeted by a concierge and entered the glossy white entrance door, with stone columns on the first storey above them. An autographed photograph on the wall indicated actor David Suchet, known for playing Hercule Poirot, frequented the place.

Declan's pulse raced in his neck. This was it. He felt certain the man John Garanin and then Nora had described to them would choose a place like this. Thick crown moldings and ornate cornices spoke of an earlier era when heavy decoration equated wealth and social standing.

Alex flashed his warrant card and explained their mission to the young woman at the reception desk, then showed her a photo of Garanin.

Declan saw a shadow cross her face.

"Yes, he's here in one of our deluxe rooms. Let me get the manager. You're the second person asking for him today." She lifted the receiver and pressed an intercom button. "Of course we will cooperate. I was just about to program a key."

A second person? "Can I ask you about this man?" Declan kept his tone neutral. "I couldn't help but notice you seemed to have a strong opinion."

The woman shrugged. "It's not often we have guests who escort different women to their rooms. It's frowned upon."

Alex reassured her. "I don't think you'll have to worry about that any longer."

She spoke into the phone, and Declan whispered to Alex. "Did we get our wires crossed? Is it Chen?"

"No, she's back at the station house. I have no idea—" he stopped short as the manager's office door opened and a man in a neatly tailored dove grey suit came out chatting amiably with Nora.

"These are the colleagues I told you about," Nora assured the manager.

"Gentlemen, always happy to assist the police. I was just chatting with your assistant." The manager showed them to the elevator. As the door closed he said, "Am I correct in assuming Mr. Kokut will no longer be staying with us? I believe he booked only until today."

Declan let Alex answer.

"That would be accurate. Once we're through with the room, his effects will be collected and the room returned to you, but that won't be today."

"I see. I do hope there won't be multitudes of crime scene people coming and going. Once she ascertained that Mr. Kokut was registered here, Miss Tierney called your station and your Forensics team is on its way."

Alex snorted and threw Nora a look, which she returned with a wide grin. "We'll keep our presence to a minimum once we've established the situation. I expect there's a service elevator we could use from now on?"

"Yes, that would be best. Thank you for understanding."

Nora avoided them and stood at the front of the elevator with the manager, asking about the history of the hotel. The ride was so smooth Declan didn't realize they'd moved until the doors slid open and he saw they were on another floor. He wondered how Alex would handle Nora's interfering.

"This way, please." The manager led the way down the lushly carpeted hall and used the key to open the door. He pushed it open, then stood aside to allow the three to enter. The manager poked his head inside. Once assured there wasn't a body to contend with, he left them to their devices. Alex promised to stop on their way out and inform him of their next steps, but it was obvious that Sean wasn't there.

Declan closed the door. Nora stood waiting for her dressing down.

"I think I'll let you handle this, Dec." Alex politely retreated to the other side of the room, pulling on gloves and shoe protectors, and after a moment's hesitation, handed a set to Declan and Nora, who duly donned them all.

"Before you yell, let me explain." Nora stood as tall her petite frame allowed.

Declan stifled a smile. He should have known when they got this close to finding Sean that Nora wouldn't be left out. But she had no official standing and he was unsure how to proceed.

"I'd love to hear your explanation."

Nora explained she'd called a cab from her room after her shower, once her tears dried and she composed herself. "I was tired of cooperating and following the rules. Sorry but it's true." She shrugged.

Declan didn't think she was a bit sorry. "Did you at least eat something?"

"I almost gagged on the eggs Val had made for me, but I forced down a few forkfuls and a slice of toast. I knew today would be a long day and I needed the fuel. But Declan—" Her green eyes met his, pleading with him to understand. "Today's the day I'm reunited with my son."

Declan knew Nora needed to believe that. *He* needed to believe that.

"And Val just let you saunter out?"

Nora grinned. "Helen and Matthew were upstairs napping, and I was trying to think of a way to tell her I was going without an argument. Then the van from The Fresh Flower Company pulled into the yard with a huge bouquet for Helen from Matthew, and right behind it was my taxi. I threw my bag over my shoulder and walked out to greet the florist. He had this huge bouquet of showy ruby red and soft pink roses, surrounded by anemones and slivers of green foliage, all tied with a pale blue ribbon."

Nora actually had a hint of a smile at the memory. "'What should I arrange them in?' Val asked. And then she noticed the taxi and my bag."

"I expect she wasn't best pleased." Somehow Nora had found a way to insert herself. Declan wanted to clasp Nora to his chest but it would be inappropriate at this moment. He should have known she would prevail.

"I jumped into the cab and told her to find a vase for the flowers or Matthew would have her head."

Now that she was here, Declan felt a new sense of purpose. Nora must have felt it, too.

"When Helen came home with Matthew—she's feeling better, just tired—I asked her where, if money were no object, would someone stay in Bath? So I came here and waited for you. I knew you'd eventually get here. Um, that's it."

Her hair was damp. At least she'd had that shower, which was more than he'd had. "So now we're supposed to allow you to investigate this room without a badge? Highly unlikely."

To his surprise, Alex turned from the dresser, where he'd opened each drawer. "Let her stay, Declan. At least we'll know where she's at."

It might be a mistake to allow Nora to stay, but Declan knew she was stubborn and determined once she had an idea in her head. He hid his disappointment at the empty room and kept on his professional face. He hadn't really expected Sean to be hidden here, and doubted Nora had, either, by her stoic expression. He stood at the foot of the bed and took in the room's subtle hunting scene wallpaper and its ornate, padded tartan headboard. It wasn't the largest room, but the en-suite bath was elegant and ornate. He brushed aside a curtain. "The view from the window is spectacular, even in the autumn. Pretty gardens."

Alex rose from checking under the bed. "Nothing here." He spoke to Nora. "Sorry there's no sign of the boy." He picked up Garanin's suitcase and laid it on the bed.

Since Viktor hadn't checked out, the maid hadn't been in, but it was clear he'd been planning a hasty retreat. His packed luggage had been standing near the door. Declan checked the bathroom while Alex made a cursory check of the built-in wardrobe.

"All of his toiletries are packed."

"Empty here, too." Alex motioned to Nora. "Come on, assistant. You can do the dusty work."

She took a chair he pointed to, and stepped up to the wardrobe to run a hand over the top. "There's something here," she said, her excitement evident. "I'm too short to see but I can feel—this." She pulled until the edge of a plastic garbage bag hung over the top ledge. Declan and Alex came over.

"Let me get up there." Declan traded places with Nora and quickly retrieved the bag. He laid it on the desk and felt four thick pieces of carved wood inside, but didn't open it.

"These must be the frame pieces from the Chagall."

"Don't open the bag," Alex warned. "Just a precaution. Leave it for the techs."

He moved it carefully to a side table while Declan had Nora kneel down and look under the bed.

Alex opened Viktor's suitcase. "Unlocked." He took out all the clothing to check the pockets and linings of the folded piles inside.

"He must have intended to come back and lock up." Declan pointed to a combination luggage lock that lay on top of the dresser, open and waiting to be used.

"Let's keep searching." Declan knew Nora thought that finding Garanin's room would give them clues in their hunt for Sean.

"Be my guest." Alex examined the inside of the suitcase first, feeling along the lining, while Declan stood in the center of the room and looked around him.

There didn't seem to be any obvious hiding place in the bedroom. He went into the bathroom and checked the medicine cabinet and the toilet's water tank. Nothing. He closed the toilet lid and sat on it, and looked around the room.

Nora followed him and stood in the doorway. He could hear Alex rummaging in the closet, knocking on its walls, looking for a false panel. That gave him an idea.

The jetted tub had large panels around its skirting to provide access to its mechanicals. He knelt down, his right knee creaking from his rugby days, and started tapping on the panels. The end one nearest the wall sounded muffled.

"Alex, do you carry a penknife?"

Alex came in, holding out a Swiss Army knife. "This do?"

Declan took the proffered knife and pulled out a flat blade. Nora leaned over and watched him intently. This close he could smell her new perfume, and remembered when he'd first noticed the change. Was that really only a few days ago? It felt like so much had happened between then and now.

He inserted the blade between the wall and the panel, and pushed hard. The panel slid forward an inch.

"Keep going." Nora knelt down next to Declan and as the space Declan made widened, she inserted a gloved finger at the bottom of the opening and helped shove the panel. The edge of a mailing tube came into view.

"Stop!" Declan pushed Nora's hand away. "We need to leave this for the Forensic guys and the Detox team."

"You're right. Viktor meant to come back here for the painting and his luggage."

Declan experienced a burst of elation that quickly soured. It seemed likely they'd found the missing painting. That was good news. A health crisis of astronomical proportions had been averted. But where was Sean? Save the country and lose the child? Not this child.

He helped Nora to her feet, and dropped a kiss on her head. "One step closer."

10:33 AM

Nora tried to hide her frustration. They had the painting, but no Sean.

"Declan, there must be a clue here about Sean. What could Viktor have done with him?"

The horror of unspoken images hung between them.

"I think there are no more secrets to be had in this bathroom."

They returned to the bedroom and inspected the room again. Two green suede chairs with a table between them were placed at the foot of the bed. The table held a selection of magazines and the Bath phone book. They each took a chair, Nora flopping into hers.

Nora watched Declan use a pen to flip the pages of the phone book. Viktor, or someone before him, had left a business card buried in the business section. She leaned in to inspect the stiff white card with an embossed gold edge and a local number entwined in the embossing.

Elegant Escorts
Discreet - Refined

"One of Viktor's playmates that hadn't gone unnoticed." Declan laid the card aside to show Alex, now back on the phone with Chen, explaining their finds.

"But was that a random shove into the pages from Viktor, or could there be more meaning to this particular page in the phone book?"

Declan laid the open book on the table between them and they each scrutinized their side of the page. Nora had the page of "N" entries that went to "O" on the bottom of the right hand page: Nail Salons, Night Clubs, Nurseries, Office Equipment …

No entry had a mark next to it. There were no notations in the margins. She started at the top again. Which of these things would Viktor Garanin have need of?

Nurseries caught her attention. Several garden centers were listed, then home health agencies, plus a small, simple ad for "Caring Angels for Children, A Royal United Hospital volunteer wing." Did that entry have a faint dot next to it, or was that her imagination working overtime?

With shaking hands, Nora pointed to the entry. Declan dialed the number.

CHAPTER TWENTY-SEVEN

Declan pulled Nora through the hotel lobby, Alex on their heels. The constable driving had stayed with the car on the road, and turned on the ignition as Alex rushed inside and barked an address, taking the front passenger seat. Declan pushed Nora into the back seat and climbed in beside her.

"Go!" he told the driver, and helped Nora fasten her seat belt. The car took off, siren blasting. Nora's face turned paler, if that were possible. Alex called Chen and on Bluetooth described Declan's call to the Royal United Hospital and their Caring Angels office.

"Their department head wanted to cooperate, but she can't just hand out people's information to any caller," Declan explained. "She did immediately confirm that they hadn't sent any children out recently."

"That's when my phone rang," Alex threw in. "She had her secretary confirm Declan's identity while she spoke to him."

He described how there were currently three volunteers, and how the program functioned. "They knew one of the volunteers was out of town. I reached the second, and she didn't have Sean. That leaves this third. Her line was busy. That's where we're headed now."

"Keep me posted," Chen said, adding, "Good luck" before breaking the connection.

"So you don't know for certain this woman has Sean?" Nora's eyes were huge. "This is all based on your instinct?" Her eyebrows rose into her hairline.

Alex turned around. His voice was firm. "Never mess with a detective's hunch."

11:16 AM

Betty Kaplan wasn't often baffled. A person of action and competence, she decided when no one showed up with Sean Mac-Bride's papers that she'd waited long enough. She called into the office at the hospital.

This was unconscionable. She needed to know more than just the child's age. There was his medical history, any allergies, and most importantly, an estimate on how long he would need to be with her. If it would be a prolonged visit, she would need to get groceries in, or perhaps even arrange a visit for the little one at the hospital with his mother. She was certainly more than disconcerted when she spoke to their receptionist, Carolyn, who told Betty she'd just arrived for the afternoon shift.

"The head's in a meeting, but from what I can see, we don't have any patients by the name of MacBride in the hospital. We don't show any children currently in care, either." She put Betty on hold and checked with the hospital registrar, then came back on the line to confirm there were no MacBrides admitted to any ward at the current time.

"Betty, I know for certain we don't have a new contact in the department named Pavel Perminov. I would know about that. We haven't had the budget to hire anyone new."

"Tall, brawny chap, spoke with an accent? Susan, I just don't understand this." Betty heard police sirens in her neighborhood. She jiggled Sean on her hip. The child had woken early, seemed listless, and had little appetite for breakfast.

"Wait a minute. Betty, by any chance does this little boy have red hair? Don't you watch the news?"

"See, Susan, you do know who I'm talking about. Never

turned on the telly last night—" Betty heard the sirens outside her house. "Have to go. There are police here, of all things. I'll call you back."

She jammed down the phone and strode to her front door, bouncing Sean on her hip. He buried his head in her neck as she opened the door to see a group of people rush up her path: a uniformed policeman, another man in a dark suit holding up his warrant card, then the couple from Sean's photo book. But how did his father get off his submarine? And where was his mother's cast?

The couple stopped in front of Betty as these thoughts flew through her mind. Sean turned his head and took in the people staring at him.

"Mummy!" He held out his arms and the auburn-haired woman gently took him from Betty, clasped him to her chest, and started to sob. The father drew the two of them into an embrace; quiet tears ran down his face when Sean lifted his head. "Daddy!"

11:17 AM

Nora's heart felt like it would erupt out of her chest with pure joy. The leaden cement block she'd been carrying around dropped away the second she saw Sean in Betty Kaplan's arms.

Her son held out his arms and she'd never known a sweeter moment than when she held her baby against her and breathed in his scent. Declan encircled them and when Sean called him "Daddy," he started to cry, too.

The three of them stood there on Betty's doorstep as Alex Thalmann explained to her that she'd been caring for a kidnapped child.

"Kidnapped! Oh, you poor dears. You'd better come inside and tell me all about it."

And so they did.

Declan helped Nora, who refused to put Sean down, navigate the stairs into the Bath station. They followed Alex Thalmann past the desk sergeant, who saluted them, into the main room. A round of applause broke out as they entered, causing Sean to hide his face in Nora's neck.

The clapping advanced to whistles and Alex quieted them down. "Simmer down, you lot. This is the lad you've been working so hard to find. Nora's brainstorm on posh hotels did the trick."

Another round of clapping and whistles, some catcalls and stomping of feet, too. Declan thought the noise might over-whelm Sean. But when he glanced at Nora, her beaming smile was matched by Sean's, who turned to face the crowd to see what all the noise was about. Nora whispered to him. Sean raised his chubby hand and waved at the men and women who had worked through the night to find him. Another cheer went up, and this time Declan motioned to calm them all down.

When he finally had their attention, he stepped forward and spoke.

"Nora and I wanted to stop by and show you who you worked so hard to find. We all know cases involving children sometimes don't end as well as this one did. We both want to thank you from the bottom of our hearts for helping us restore our family. Each one of you contributed in some way, and we'll never forget your efforts on our behalf."

Before he could continue, Constable Morrow stepped forward. She held a brown shopping bag. "When we heard the boy had been found, we took a whip around." She withdrew a toy train and a book, handed the book to Nora and the train directly to Sean. Sean immediately put the caboose in his mouth.

Chen tapped Declan's arm. "I need to see you and Nora before you head to the hospital to have him checked out."

"Of course." He and Nora first made the rounds of the room, stopping to shake hands and be introduced to everyone gathered. Finally, Alex banged on a desk to get their attention.

"Settle down. Those who worked overnight, head home for a kip. Those of you on days, we have other cases, so get cracking. This result has been a shining star for us, but there are others that need our attention, so back to work, team, and well done all. Oh—drinks on me at The Ram at 6 tonight!"

After a last round of applause at this news, everyone drifted back to work. Declan guided Nora and Sean, still chewing his caboose, over to Chen and Burke, who waited in a corner of the room.

"Step in here, please." She ushered them into the same interview room that had been their home for much of the night. "Several things before we head back to London. Declan, I'm sure we'll be in touch, wrapping up reports in the next week or so."

"I'll head back to Oxford tomorrow." He pointed to Nora and Sean. "The rest of today's for them."

"Understood." She included them both in her glance. "I thought you'd want to know Mr. P. didn't survive his injuries." She poked her chin at Sean, explaining her choice of names. "The medical examiner has determined that the cause of death is down to a skull fracture from his fall. The side wound alone, as it were, would probably not have been fatal."

Declan watched Nora's face absorb this news. If Paul hadn't fallen against that stone statue, he'd have survived the stabbing. That would have affected their future together. With Paul in the picture, it would be a vastly different situation, even if he stayed in his lab, wherever that happened to be.

But wait. How would he or Nora ever know that this was the truth with this outfit? This could be yet another cover story to put Paul out of his and Nora's minds. Declan kept his thoughts to himself. Better Nora believe Paul was truly dead. He would keep his assumptions to himself.

"Full circle." Nora nodded. "It means he really did die in an accident. At least part of my story will be based on truth. I won't have to feel guilty lying to his parents after all."

"I can see that," Chen agreed. "But I have to caution you both to remember that paper you signed. Nothing has changed. The official story that will be given to the press today, and I urge you to follow under penalty of prosecution, will be as follows." She read from a prepared press release.

"Bath and Oxford police today can reassure the public that a bioterrorist has been apprehended before he could launch his plot to set a mutated smallpox virus outbreak throughout England. The dead perpetrator, whose identity has not been released, kidnapped a child for leverage. The child has been recovered unharmed. The only death attributable to this terrorist is that of Miss Emma Jevons, an art conservationist from the Ashmolean Museum. The missing virus has been recovered and is in the process of being removed from the two paintings that were used to carry it into the UK for eventual dissemination. Officials with Public Health England applaud the various departments who worked together to bring this case to a successful and speedy conclusion."

Chen looked up and included Declan and Nora and narrowed her eyes. "Do you understand this is how it will be?"

She waited for them both to nod. So this was Chen in her officious mode, Declan thought. So be it.

"You'll note no names, other than Emma Jevons, are being released. That should help with those closest to you remaining in the dark. Right now only this team, the Sackvilles, and your friend Miss Rogan are aware that your child is the one in question. You should caution them in the interests of national security and the child's future privacy to keep it that way. His name was not given out during the search or to the news reporting on the park search for a missing child." She handed them each a copy of the statement. "Your Oxford team and the museum have been brought up to date as far as the perpetrator of the smallpox being caught."

Nora spoke up. "So Garanin was my stalker in this version of events?"

"Don't rock the boat, Nora. This is the simplest way to cover all the bases. If anyone needs to know, Garanin stalked you to find out if your dead fiancé had left you any notes or files." Chen turned to include Declan. "As a police officer, I expect you to rein in any tendencies your partner may have to veer from this."

Declan gave a sharp nod of his head. "Understood."

Nora asked another question. "Does this mean, though, that we have to worry that we'll be watched now by members of your group? Eavesdropping on our private lives?"

It was a good question, Declan thought, and while he wouldn't have asked it, he was happy Nora did.

"Absolutely not." Burke's statement was definitive. "We're already running into our next case. We don't have the time or resources to bother once a case becomes inactive. That doesn't mean if something off the range of our agreement reaches our hearing we wouldn't revisit that situation."

Declan set his lips. "So toe the line and we'll be left alone."

Burke broke out a warm grin. "That's about it, mate. Once we leave here, this subject will cease to be addressed or acknowledged by our team."

"So how would we contact you, if any questions come up?" Declan asked.

"You don't." Burke's cheerful tone became steely again.

Nora wasn't quite done. "What will happen to Mr. P's lab, wherever it is?"

"What lab?" Burke raised his eyebrows. *It never existed.*

Chen sighed and begrudgingly admitted that "Mr. P's" work would continue with a new department head. "All work product will be preserved uninterrupted. There are meticulous notes, backups, other researchers familiar with it. That's all I'm prepared to say. And that's us done, I think."

"One more thing," Nora said. "Tell your undercover agent it's not a good idea to use fictional detectives' names—or to cover a bald spot he doesn't have with a succession of baseball caps."

Chen raised an eyebrow. "I'll take that on board." She turned to Declan. "Barnes, I can't say it's been great fun, but it had a good outcome. I enjoyed working with you." Then to Nora. "I'm very pleased you have your son back. He's a sweet boy. Good luck to all of you."

Chen excited the room, Burke in her wake.

Declan put his arm around Nora. "I think a nap at Helen's, and a little discussion with Val and the Sackvilles is in order." He guided Nora out of the room, making a mental note to call Watkins and fashion a story that would fly. He stopped at the door and turned to face Nora. "Sweetheart, I don't think we can bring Simon or Kate into this now."

Nora's frown let him know she wasn't happy with him. "But what about my stalker at Ramsey Lodge? There's the little thing with those bugs I found that Helen and Val know about. That can't be put down to my overactive imagination."

"We blame everything on Viktor, as Chen suggested. That's where it all lies, anyway."

They waved to the roomful of staff, phones to ears, computers clacking away, already back to work.

"We'll figure it out," he promised. "I propose a relaxing afternoon and evening at Helen's and tomorrow, life for us in Oxford starts over."

2:59 PM

As Declan showered, Nora placed Sean on the big guest bed at Hill House and prepared to nap. She traced her fingers over his face, telling him the names of all of his features, reveling in the feel of his soft skin under her hand. Pure bliss.

"Here we go, lovey. Mouth ... nose ... eyes ..." she used the opportunity to close his lids with each pass until he dozed off.

Nora laid her head against Sean's tiny chest, listening to his heartbeat. The agony of the past hours might be over, but it wasn't finished by a long shot in her mind. She knew just how close she'd come to losing her child forever.

She fell back against the pillows and considered her future options as she recalled coming back to Hill House with Sean.

It had been a sweet reunion with Helen, Matthew, and Auntie Val. Sean's good humor returned once he was surrounded by familiar faces and the Sackville dogs. Everyone saw the sense in leaving Sean's kidnapping in the past. Nora was determined Sean would only have good memories of his trip to Bath. While he might never remember what actually happened as he matured, she persuaded Val, Helen and Matthew to agree to never mention it again. Everyone also agreed naps were in order, and a quiet night at home.

"I'll make my special Pasta Rogan tonight," Val offered.

"I'll run you to the shops later," Matthew agreed. "Maybe some crusty bread to go with that?"

"And a salad with olives," Helen called out as she climbed the stairs to their bedroom.

Sean fell asleep and for a moment Nora just watched him breathe. His lashes splayed out against his cheeks. His eyebrows were a replica of Paul's. His mouth bore her own bow shape. She leaned over closely to feel his breath on her face. A small voice rankled at the back of her mind. Was Paul really gone this time, or was this another MI-5 story? Nora decided since she would never really know, there was no need to share her suspicions with Declan.

Declan came out of the bathroom wearing gym shorts. He ran a towel over his hair, finger-combed it into place, and slid onto the bed on the other side of Sean.

"Asleep? Think it's our turn." He reached across the sleeping boy and kissed Nora lightly. "I know how tired I am. You must be exhausted." He turned on his side, closed his eyes, and held her hand across the warm little body between them.

"Declan, I did some thinking while you were in the shower."

"I'm listening ..."

"When we get back to Oxford tomorrow, I'm going to call the estate agent. Instead of renting Haven Cottage, I want to buy it and make it ours. Then I'm going to call Neil and Sally Welch, and ask them to keep fostering Typo until we get back from the States, when we'll take him."

He opened one eye. "New house and new puppy all at once? Sure you want to do that?"

"Absolutely." Nora's strength and determination were back in full force with her family restored. "You'll sublet your place and move in with us, despite the chaos?"

Declan's chest rose and fell. Nora thought he'd dropped off to sleep. She squeezed his hand and was just about to let go when he squeezed back and said, "I love you."

CHAPTER TWENTY-EIGHT

Ridgefield, Connecticut
Saturday, 29th October
1:27 PM

Declan sat on the wide porch of Nora's childhood home in Connecticut. The white two-storey Colonial boasted deep green shutters; its front door held an oval of stained glass depicting a flower basket in bright jeweled shades of red, pinks, and blues. On the tree-lined street, autumn color waned in leggy elms and oaks, almost bare of their crispy leaves of gold and red.

He sprawled on a wicker lounger, nursing the glass of lemonade he drank to wash down several of Amelia Tierney Scott's ginger cookies. He'd make certain Nora brought home the recipe. The pungent scent of cinnamon, ginger, and molasses made the cookies a chewy treat.

The trip across the pond had given him his first glimpse of the United States. Despite Nora going over a map with him before they arrived of where her home was located in the southwest corner of the state, the vastness of the country boggled his mind. In England, you could visit virtually any corner of the country with a long hard day's drive. Here it would take about an entire week to drive cross-country, and that would be without stopping often.

Over the past few days he'd been shown off at Amelia's book club, where the ladies fussed over him and plied him with baked treats. At Roger's golf club, Nora's stepfather wanted everyone to meet "Nora's Brit detective," and they all wanted to buy him drinks. Jet lag plus gin and tonics had made for a pleasant buzz.

Tonight friends were coming in for Sean's birthday dinner.

Monday was Halloween, and Amelia had sewn Sean a costume he would adore: a speckled puppy with long floppy ears that looked suspiciously like a beagle. Every time Sean saw it hanging on the back of a closet door, he would point to it and say, "Typo." Declan had to admit he was looking forward to seeing Sean's reaction to being dressed up as the dog.

Amelia didn't blink an eye when they arrived two days ago and she proudly showed them to Nora's old bedroom, redecorated with a new queen brass bed, covered in her grandmother's hand-stitched quilt. The pale blue walls sported an ivy vine stenciled near the ceiling. The woodwork gleamed in shiny white enamel. "We needed a guest room, and I had fun decorating it," Amelia said when she'd showed them to the room. She'd borrowed a porta-crib for Sean, and had stowed it and a changing pad on top of the dresser in the small room she and Roger used as an office right next door.

He'd worried Nora's mother might insist on separate bedrooms while under her roof—who knew with those Yankee sensibilities Val Rogan was always going on about? But with a grandchild already on board, Amelia considered them a couple, and introduced Declan as "Nora's partner." Everyone they met assumed he was Sean's father and he never corrected them.

"Your childhood things are in a few cartons in the attic, Nora," Amelia told them. "I put your early books for Sean on the bookshelf, and left up that photo collage you put together."

Declan had looked at it with interest. Nora's college graduation photo was in the center, the anchor to a host of others: Nora in white face, costumed in something that resembled a curtain, playing the ghostly Elvira in *Blithe Spirit*; a teenaged Nora, wearing a red-and-white cheerleader outfit, hugging a collie; Nora outside the Radcliffe Camera, surrounded by a group of other students mugging for the camera, her hair cut to her chin and falling in tousled curls around her face; Nora, a young girl with long strawberry blonde hair in braids, arms wrapped around the legs of a lanky man who bore a striking resemblance to a fairer Cary Grant.

"You never told me your father resembled Cary Grant," he'd said, peering at the collage.

Nora had stopped unpacking to come over and inspect the photo. "I never thought of him as Cary Grant. He was just Dad." She pointed to different photos. "That's my first dog, Princess— oh, here I am as Elvira!"

"I noticed that one. I was around for your reincarnation in that role, remember, when you narrowly missed a falling chandelier."

She'd broken into giggles.

He smiled and sipped his lemonade, remembering her face as she'd laughed. It was good to hear her laugh again, even if it didn't happen often enough yet. Their trauma had taken its toll and would take time to get over.

He broke from his reverie and observed Nora. She leaned against the porch banister. Muted sunlight highlighted the gold in her hair. She'd lost weight, her small frame looking trim and slight in her jeans and denim shirt. She stood craning her neck out over the railing, and looked down the broad road toward the historic Main Street.

On walks with Sean he learned the 1709 town had evolved into a pastiche of late Victorian and Colonial Revival homes, with several of the largest turned into bed and breakfasts or inns. There was a renowned playhouse and an equally famous contemporary art museum. There were spired churches and a new library tucked down a side street, with landmarked buildings sandwiched between modern day improvements. The entire area retained the feel of New England small town charm. It reminded him of some English towns, and he felt right at home.

"Come and sit." He patted the cushion next to him and moved over.

He'd been waiting for this opportunity, and this morning when Nora had gone up after breakfast to dress herself and Sean, he'd corralled Amelia and Roger, and explained what he needed—an hour alone, Sean wholly occupied. Amelia had whooped with delight and promised to make it happen that very day.

"I'm just looking out for Sean." Nora stayed at the railing.

"Your mum and Roger said they'd be at the shops for a while. I'm pretty certain two adults can handle one toddler."

"I suppose. I can't believe she forgot birthday candles for her only grandchild's first birthday cake. She's usually so organized."

All right, so he'd have to move from his comfy seat. She wasn't going to make this easy.

Declan stood and stretched, then sauntered over to the railing next to Nora. He leaned on it and followed her line of sight, past the Little Red Schoolhouse.

"They probably ran into some of the celebrities who live in town and are bending ears with Sean stories."

"Right—as if Judy Collins or Harvey Fierstein care, much less know my mother." Nora shook her head. "I'll say it before you do. Stop hovering."

"I wasn't going to say that."

Nora swatted at him playfully and turned back to the railing. "No, you were just thinking it. I'm trying. It's hard at times to remember what we all went through just a few weeks ago, and now we're expected to carry on and not talk to anyone about it. No one here knows any of it."

"I know, sweetheart. British reserve in all its ugliness to a heavy extreme. But we'll cope."

Ever since reading Paul Pembroke's text, Declan had felt the man's presence, pushing him hard to find Sean. Whether Paul had a presentiment he would die, or if he were recovering in his lab, that text had given Declan the permission he desired to show Nora he could protect her and Sean.

He needed to solidify their family. It was what fathers did—they protected their family.

Nora tried to relax. She wasn't really worried about her mother and Roger taking care of Sean. It was more that she didn't want to let him out of her sight after what had happened. Yet she knew she had to let go of that tendency before it became stifling to Sean.

She would work harder on it.

Nora had swung into action once they returned to Oxford. She made her promised call to the agent, and her offer on Haven Cottage was accepted, pending the survey report.

She and Val traveled to Ramsey Lodge, where she'd spent two emotional days packing up her things from the suite where she'd been living. Simon and his girlfriend, Maeve Addams, had helped, as had Kate, who had been full of plans for renovating the area.

Agnes, the Scottish cook at the lodge, had taken her fill of Sean, keeping him occupied as they packed up the station wagon and the small rental trailer they towed for the few pieces of furniture that were Nora's.

She had called Harvey and Muriel and fixed a date for when they returned from the States to have their help emptying her storage unit the week after Sean's party, when Declan and Val would get their first glimpse of Port Enys.

It had been hard to leave the people who had watched over her during her pregnancy and most of Sean's first year. When she first arrived back in Cumbria, she thought she noted a glow about Kate, who confided that first night that she and Ian were expecting. "But it's early days and we're not announcing it yet, so keep it under your hat. Only Simon knows so far."

It seemed everyone wanted her to keep their secrets.

They decamped to Declan's flat until the house purchase went through when they returned. Then she would have the rooms painted at Haven Cottage before moving in. She had brought along her paint sample book to finalize her color decisions and poured over them with Amelia.

"Real estate will only escalate in the heart of Oxford," said her financial advisor, a little man who favored tweed jackets and had white hairs growing out of his eyebrows. He'd approved of the purchase.

She'd had a brief phone conversation with Mrs. Charles Wright, who had found Nora's check for the Chase study tucked in a drawer at her husband's shop.

At first Nora had been afraid the painting would remind her of the man who'd stolen her son, and of the deaths by the ancient tomb. But when she examined it, all she felt was the moment she'd seen it, and known it was right to want to live at Haven Cottage. She'd told the woman to cash the check, and kept the painting. It would hang over the fireplace.

The Welches had agreed to take care of Typo for a few more weeks. After that, puppy classes would be in order.

She and Declan and Sean had been given a new chapter in their lives to start together. Nora wanted to take advantage of that and provide a stable home for Sean. Once Declan had shown her Paul's text, she felt they had his blessing. Everything was falling into place, but one thing remained to be sorted.

Nora leaned against the railing, inhaling Declan's woody scent with its hint of peppery honey. Her heart sped up.

"Declan, I've been thinking—"

"Yes, I do like periwinkle blue for our bedroom."

"I'm glad you've been listening." She smiled and turned to see his grey eyes crinkle up in good humor.

The light gave them an aqua glow against his olive skin and square jaw that she found incredibly sexy. His dark wavy hair, perpetually in need of a trim, was starting to curl over the collar of his oxford shirt. With a start, she remembered her father used to roll his shirtsleeves just like Declan did when he was home from work. Her throat clogged with emotion. She could feel his presence at this moment.

She turned back to the railing to gather her thoughts before Declan's nearness overwhelmed her and her nerve failed. She looked out at the street she'd grown up on, the sidewalk where she'd drawn chalk figures, the jack-o-lanterns on the steps of the neighbors, waiting to be lit. This was the moment she'd been waiting for.

Nora steadied herself even as she felt Declan moving beside her. "But what I was going to say was—I'd like us to think about eventually giving Sean a sibling. I never had one. And I don't want to be an unwed mother forever. I love you—will you marry me?" She sucked in her breath. There. It was out.

She turned back to gauge his reaction, only to see him down on one knee, holding out a small, blue octagonal box, leather stamped with gold leaves around its lid. "You really know how to steal a guy's thunder, Nora."

He opened the box and Nora gasped. It held the ring they'd seen in Brighton. The sapphires and side emeralds glowed against the white satin lining, highlighting the shining oval diamond in its center.

"It's the ring!" Nora's heart thudded with unbounded joy.

"I think you're supposed to put it on your finger, Baroness. For an old rugby player like me, it's tough kneeling this long." He stood to slip the ring from the box. "I love you, too. Since we asked each other, I'll take that as a yes." He slid the ring onto her finger.

"Yes," Nora confirmed as she looked at the ring sparkling on her finger. It was a perfect fit.

Acknowledgments

The Nora Tierney novels are set in real places in the United Kingdom. For anyone wishing to visit the towns Nora does, all of the streets, villages, cities and roads can be found, even St. Andrews in enchanting Castle Combe. Nora's Haven Cottage, although charming, is not real, and sits on what is actually the back garden of The Old Parsonage, my favorite place to have afternoon tea when in Oxford. And while St. Giles Church has that same graveyard, there is no rectory attached, nor a family living there. Similarly, Port Enys is physically based on the Cornwall estate of Port Eliot, with many of its attributes as described. But while visitors to it and the church during its open season may see some of the features noted, they will not find the copse with Paul Pembroke's memorial.

Talented authors Ausma Zehanat Khan, Sarah Ward and Elly Griffiths have my deep appreciation for their cover blurbs. Special thanks to Elly for appearing as a character to assist Declan in his hunt for the perfect engagement ring.

Giordana Segneri is responsible for the grand cover and layout design; Becky Brown ensured the copyediting. Thanks to both women for helping me to create a lovely book.

Writing a series set across an ocean requires the assistance of many people, despite my travels and photos to refresh my memory. My sincere thanks to so many willing to share their expertise or give their time to read and comment on this dark and different book in the series.

In the United Kingdom: Averil Freeth, Joyce McLennan and Helen Hood gave the manuscript a close reading, and all helped me correct my "Britspeak," in addition to their cogent comments on the storyline which only strengthened it. Helen also allowed her family and home to be the models for Nora's Bath visit to Helen Sackville. My stay with the Hood family while researching the area led to meeting Nic Bottomley and his charming shop. Do stop in for a visit at Mr B's if you find yourself in Bath. When I hastened to point out that no one would be murdered on the premises, I'll never forget Nic's disappointed face and typically British answer: "Could do!" Thanks to Nic for allowing Nora to read there.

Helen hastens to point out that in reality the process for inter-museum loans, often organized years in advance, would be vastly different and totally more secure than I've described. Loans involve a specialist art handling company, CCTV, and other safety regulations far and above what I've written to accommodate my plot. In reality, it is highly unlikely a piece would ever leave the loan institution, but the Chagall does in Nora's fictional world.

Jevon Thistlewood, Paintings Conservator at the Ashmolean Museum, Oxford, offered a wealth of information on Emma Jevons' work, and kindly lent his name to her.

Also for information and corroboration, thanks to Richard Pinder, Managing Partner, Cotswold Information; and Louie Allen of the Oxford Pruning Company.

In the United States: Vicki Morris, MD, FACP, lent her expertise to the question of the smallpox virus and fomites. Of great help was *Pox Americana* by Elizabeth A. Fenn, as was Lisa B. Hines of the CDC in Atlanta.

Sally Heiney, horticulturist for North Carolina's Botanical Garden, put me in contact with Nina Ellis, a volunteer who once lived in Moscow. Nina filled me in on what would be blooming outside Moscow in the early fall.

Any errors or mistakes are entirely my own.

My writing colleagues helped shape drafts during our yearly

workshops and are always on hand to lend their expertise and advice. Thanks to Mariana Damon, Lauren Small, Nina Romano, and Melissa Westemeier. I value their input and critiques over the past 14 years, and appreciate Lauren for Bridle Path Press.

My family and my mother are a source of constant support for my writing, but my husband, Arthur L. Graff, deserves a special nod of recognition for always encouraging me, discussing endless plot points, and giving his honest opinion when asked. He tolerates living with a distracted writer—I *do* know how lucky I am.

This is the first book that contains two characters named for real people. Betty Kaplan was one of the first pediatric nurse practitioners in California; her daughter, Lisa, won naming rights for a character of mine in an auction for the Triangle Literacy Society at Bouchercon Raleigh. Betty's role was originally to be that of a minor maid, but her real life proved perfectly suited to be the Caring Angel for Sean, a fictional program also only in Nora's world. Lisa describes Betty as "a bit of Debbie Reynolds" physically, and notes that she is so amazing with machines, the Sears Parts Department would sell her replacement parts they would normally only sell to licensed repairmen. Happy 80th birthday, Betty!

Alex Thalmann was a young Marine veteran and dedicated police officer in the North Carolina community of New Bern. His character is named in honor of Alex and of all the dedicated men and women who serve to protect us in any capacity. I'll let Sean Burk describe why he asked me to name a character for Alex:

"I met Alex Thalmann in the police academy in 2013; he was a Marine and I was a paramedic changing careers. Alex sat next to me and always had a story about playing with his dog, or about his amazing mother, Stacey. We helped each other with classroom work and testing. Alex became the motivator for myself and others, especially during Physical Training. He would be at the lead, but had no problem running back to the slower guys who were struggling, encouraging them, telling them over and over, 'You've got this.' I feel I am a police officer now because Alex was there then. We kept in touch after graduation that first year, but in 2014, Alex was tragically killed while on duty for the New Bern Police Department. Alex loved life, he loved his job, and he loved his family. Alex, you will never be forgotten and now you are in England solving crimes! Rest well, brother. You will always be on duty with me. Thanks to M. K. Graff for allowing Alex to be known to others and for allowing me to tell you of his sacrifice."

This book is dedicated to the woman I met the first day of kindergarten. Barbara Bohner and I were drawn to each other from the start, as we were the only two in the class who could already read when we met in Miss Schaeffer's room at Floral Park-Bellerose School. Our friendship has always given me great joy, and continues to do so all these years later. Edith Wharton said: "There is one friend in the life of each of us who seems not a separate person, however dear and beloved, but an expansion, an interpretation, of one's self, the very meaning of one's soul." This book, with its theme of making our own family, is dedicated to Barb, sister of my heart.

ABOUT THE AUTHOR

M. K. Graff is the award-winning author of *The Nora Tierney English Mysteries* and *The Trudy Genova Manhattan Mysteries*. She is Managing Editor of Bridle Path Press, and writes crime book reviews at www.auntiemwrites.com. A member of Sisters in Crime, Graff is also published in poetry and non-fiction, teaches writing workshops, and mentors the Writers Read program in Belhaven, North Carolina.

Lightning Source UK Ltd.
Milton Keynes UK
UKOW04f2345081117
312395UK00001B/53/P